Driven By
CHANCE

Driven by Chance Copyright © 2024 by Kaliope
All rights reserved.

This book or any portion thereof may not be reproduced or used in any manner whatsoever without the express written permission of the publisher except for the use of brief quotations in a book review.

Printed in the United States of America

This is a work of fiction. Names, characters, places and incidents either are products of the author's imagination or are used fictitiously. Any resemblance to actual events or locales or persons, living or dead, is entirely coincidental.

Cover Design by WriterSpark Book Covers
First Edition: November 2024

Driven By CHANCE

KALIOPE

CHAPTER

I drive fast.

That's likely the reason I earn a decent income from my jobs. I navigate the roads as an ExpressWay driver—a modern version of a taxi service. I also fulfill deliveries for the same company. The app lets me log in and choose between driving people or delivering food. My choice is simple—I work when I want to.

I refuse to be dictated by a set schedule, spending eight hours held hostage at a job that offers me meager pay. Compensation for my current job may not be ideal, but at least I have the freedom to decide when I want to put in the effort. It's always been difficult for me to hold down a stable job; boredom sets in quickly, prompting me to quit rather than be miserable. Living life on my terms is what brings me happiness.

I open the ExpressWay app and accept a ride that's about ten minutes away. I prefer driving in the evenings—it's usually busier, and the tips tend to be better. Normally, when I arrive, the passenger is already waiting outside. But this time, when I pull up to the address, I send them a quick message to let them know I'm here, and he replies, "One minute."

So, I patiently wait... for ten minutes. Finally, I give a quick honk, and he opens the front door.

"I'm coming, chill," he shouts, slamming the door shut once again.

Five minutes later, he storms out of the house, yelling at someone inside as the door crashes shut behind him, making the windows rattle like they might shatter. He marches down the snow-covered sidewalk, his shirt half-unbuttoned and half-tucked in. Given the situation, it seems this probably isn't even his house; he was likely tending to another man's wife. But it's not my place to judge this idiot.

He yanks open the back door, tossing a bag across the seat as he slides in, slamming it shut behind him. He smells like BO and sex, and his armpits are stained with sweat. "This is a neighborhood; quit laying on the horn like that," he snarls angrily. "I don't want the whole block knowing my business."

"I'm only required to wait for five minutes before I can cancel your ride. You should be grateful I didn't leave."

He scoffs. "Grateful? You're not even driving. You only get paid if the car's moving."

"I'm not moving until you put on your seatbelt." I stare at him through the rearview mirror.

"Mind your own business," he mutters, pulling his phone from his pocket and dismissing me.

"Put on your seatbelt or get out," I insist.

He glances up from his phone, a fiery rage burning in his eyes. "I said fucking drive."

Without hesitation, I step on the accelerator, sending the car lurching forward. Then, just as quickly, I stomp on the brakes, watching his face smash off the back of my passenger seat.

"Fucking bitch," he shouts, retrieving his phone from the floor, then settling back into his seat, angrily grabbing the seatbelt and finally fastening it.

Now that we've established whose vehicle this is, maybe he'll sit quietly until we get to wherever he's having me dump his douchey ass off. I've never been ashamed that I have a lead foot on the gas pedal, especially in situations like this. I just want to get this asshole out of my car as soon as possible. Maybe this is why the five-minute policy exists—anyone who makes you wait longer than that, knowing exactly when their ride would arrive, is clearly self-serving and a nightmare to have as a passenger.

"Whoa, slow down. You're fucking insane," he comments as I maneuver through traffic.

I have twenty minutes to get him to his destination. Challenge accepted—I'll get him there in fourteen. I'll need to shampoo the seat after his stinky ass gets out and then find the nearest store for an air freshener. I'm sure any passenger who gets in after him will think I'm the stinky bitch that didn't shower today.

We're stuck at a red light, and I tap impatiently on the steering wheel, my fingers drumming out a rapid, frustrated rhythm.

"Change the music," he says, still scrolling on his phone.

I choose to ignore him because my music is the only thing keeping me sane right now.

"Hey, bitch, are you fucking deaf? Change the music," he demands, leaning forward as if getting closer will make me comply with his demands faster.

I glance over at the SUV next to me, sizing up the driver to gauge whether he's going to be fast or slow when the light changes. He's not old by any means, but he's dressed sharply in a suit and tie. Definitely a rule follower. Sorry, sir, but when that light switches, I'm cutting you the fuck off.

When the light turns green, I go the instant the car in front of me does.

Suddenly, the piercing screech of tires fills the air, followed by the sickening crunch of metal colliding. The SUV to our right is struck hard on the front side by a vehicle that barrels through the red light. The force of the impact causes their hood to crumple like paper, and a shower of broken glass scatters across the asphalt. The sound is harsh, like aluminum being torn apart, and for a second, everything feels like it's moving in slow motion. I observe the driver's shocked expression as the airbags deploy, the impact jarring but not catastrophic. Still, my heart races as I glance at the wreckage and silently thank the road gods it wasn't me tangled in that mess.

Once I clear the intersection and switch to the right lane, which is now sure to be backed up for a while due to the accident, I pull over to the side of the road. I've had enough of this guy. At least now he will have something to entertain him while he waits for someone else to pick him up.

"Get out," I tell him firmly.

"This isn't the address I gave you, moron."

"Well, your ride ends here, moron," I retort, ending the ride on the app.

I can't stand entitled jerks. He thinks he can treat people however he pleases and get away with it. He got in the wrong car for that—I'm not the one. He can enjoy standing in the snow while he waits for another ride.

"I'm not getting out. It's winter. I don't even have a coat. You're getting paid to take me home," he snarls, his face growing even more red.

"My vehicle, my choice. Get out," I turn to look at him to make sure he knows I'm not intimidated. As I do, I reach into my door and grip the taser tucked away there. I kind of hope I get to use it on him.

"Just take me home," he settles back in his seat, dismissing me.

"I don't get paid enough to deal with assholes like you. Get out of my car, or I'll make it my personal mission to find your wife and give her the address I just picked you up from. I'm sure she thinks you've been at work this entire time." I continue to stare him down.

He narrows his eyes at me, as if contemplating whether I'm serious. He clenches his jaw, weighing out his next move. He half looks like he's trying to decide if I would actually follow through on my threat and if he would be fast enough to attack me. Either way I look at it, cops are on their way for the accident right behind us, so he's fucked from every direction at this point.

"By the way, these drives are recorded," I point to the camera above my rearview mirror, "in case you think she would want video proof," I add, starting to believe the direction he's set on is strangling my ass.

He shoots a look at the mirror and then back to me. "I'm not paying you, bitch," he says, climbing out and leaving the door wide open behind him.

What a tool.

I lean forward and switch off my ExpressWay light on my windshield. One and done—that's enough stupidity for today. I'd rather be at home watching TV than dealing with that. At least my suspicions were confirmed: he was, in fact, not at a house he should have been at. Though I assumed it was the woman who was married, perhaps they both are.

He's about to see a raging bitch when my car jostles and the door shuts. Glancing back, I fully expect to see Stinky McGee waddling back, prepared to muster whatever semblance of decency he can scrape together—though I know that will be quite a stretch for him. Instead, my eyes land on someone entirely different. A man in a suit, settling in like he owns the damn car, reaching across his shoulder for the seatbelt. He's calm and composed, a stark contrast to the previous passenger. Props to this gentleman for having the utmost audacity *and* putting on his seatbelt.

"I beg your finest pardon," I turn and gape at him.

"I need to get to this address," he leans forward, handing me a gold hotel card with the name and address on it.

My mouth hangs wide open. "Excuse you. I just turned off my light. I'm not taking any more rides today."

He impatiently stares back at me. "I'll tip you $100 if you can get me there in fifteen minutes."

Contemplating for only a brief second, I extend my hand. He looks down at it and then back at me, confused.

"Pay me before I drive. I won't move an inch until I get the money," I say firmly. He could easily get a ride and bail without paying. Even though he looks like he has plenty of money, I'm sick of douchebags today. Plus, it's always the rich assholes that tend to be little penny pinchers—probably how they manage to keep their wealth.

Annoyed, he lets out a sigh and reaches into his coat pocket, removing a clip of money. He pulls out a hundred and thrusts it into my palm then puts the clip back.

Smiling, I turn back around and swerve into traffic. If he wants to reach his destination in fifteen minutes, I'll make sure he gets there in fifteen minutes. I press on the gas, inwardly finding it amusing as he grabs the seat next to him and the headrest in front.

Out of my peripheral in the rearview mirror, I can see that my driving has caught him off guard. I skillfully maneuver through traffic, running a couple "yellow" lights as he mutters in the backseat, "Christ." Had he used the app like he should have, he would see that my reviews have mentioned a time or two that I drive slightly fast.

"I should have waited to pay you until I knew I'd survive this ride," he mutters, glancing out the windows and looking behind us as if checking to make sure there isn't a high-speed pursuit with a string of police cars tailing us.

"You'll arrive in one piece," I scoff.

A single glance and it's obvious: this guy is filthy rich. His suit screams high-end. It's perfectly pressed, and he literally smells rich—is that even a thing? He smells better than anything I have ever smelled in my life. But the entitlement is just as obvious. He slides into my car like he owns it, not bothering to ask if I'd be willing to give him a ride, then starts bossing me around like I'm his chauffeur.

New ick unlocked.

We arrive at the hotel, and I jokingly remark, "Looks like you made it in one piece." I turn to him with a proud smile, knowing that he was unnecessarily worried about my driving. Or maybe he had every right to be worried, but not a strand of his perfect hair is out of place. He might have blisters on his palms from how hard he was gripping the 'oh shit' handle, but that's on him, not me. He's here and can go on his merry little way.

I'm also relieved that I earned enough money from him to call it a day. I had assumed my day was soured from the first bad apple I picked up, but now I feel like my day wasn't a total waste.

As he unbuckles his seatbelt, he announces, "I have a meeting. It'll be done in an hour. Wait here," he instructs, already opening his door to leave.

"Um, no. I already told you, I'm done giving rides for tonight. Have a great meeting. See you never."

I watch as he rolls his eyes in exasperation, finally closing the door behind him. Despite him being an unwelcome passenger, I'm certainly enjoying the lingering scent of him in my car. He practically saved me a trip to the store for an air freshener because all I can smell now is him. Just as I press the brake and shift the car into drive, the passenger door suddenly swings open. I barely have time to react as he leans in, shoves the gearshift into park, then reaches over to shut off the engine. He plucks the keys from the ignition and tucks them into his coat pocket. "I'll be back in an hour," he says, his face inches away from mine. Then he stands, shuts the door, and walks into the hotel.

I sit here, completely stunned, my eyes locked on his retreating figure as he nonchalantly strolls through the hotel. He pauses at the front desk, exchanging a few words with the receptionist, and then disappears down the hallway. My mind is racing, trying to catch up.

What the fuck just happened?

Did I just black out?

I'm sure as shit not sitting here for an hour. What an idiotic thing to expect from a random stranger.

Where did I put my spare key? Crap! Chloe has it, and she's out of town for another four days. "Damn it!" I mutter, slamming my hands on the steering wheel in frustration. Who does this guy think he is? You can't just take someone's car keys like that.

Panic sets in as I realize I'm parked in the drop-off lane directly in front of the hotel entrance. It's already 8:00 PM, so I highly doubt anyone will be arriving. Still, the glaring sign clearly prohibits parking where I am.

I shift restlessly in my seat, glancing at the clock and wiping my clammy palms on my black yoga pants in a futile attempt to dry them. Every minute feels like an eternity as I anxiously check my mirrors, hoping no one will show up and make my predicament worse.

Just when I think my nerves can't take any more, it's as if I've conjured up the van that pulls up behind me. They don't get out or put their vehicle in park; they just idle directly behind me, as if they're waiting for me to move. Through the rearview mirror, I can see the couple inside exchanging irritated looks and murmuring to each other, likely about the idiot who parked in the no-parking zone.

My heart sinks as I see an employee coming out, fearing that I'm about to get in trouble. How am I even going to explain what happened? It's going to sound like I'm making it up. I don't even know who the man is; I have no clue what his name is or why he stole my car keys. Quickly coming up with the plan that I will say I was carjacked, I wait for them to approach. But they don't. The employee walks over to the van and starts talking to them, pointing towards another area. I see the driver nodding and then backing up, driving around the drop-off zone.

I'm torn between heading inside to search for the car key thief or just waiting in my car. He's dressed in an expensive suit, while I'm in yoga pants, a sweatshirt with a hole in the front and sleeve, and snow boots. Even though most of the snow has melted, more is expected in the coming days, which made my outfit seem suitable when I put it on. Even with the proper attire, the freezing temperatures don't help—the heat that lingered in the car before my keys were stolen is long gone. My breath fogs up the windshield as I shiver, and I quickly recognize that sitting here, freezing in my seat, will probably feel just as miserable as going inside to face this stupid situation. Though inside, there's warmth—my car is death by way of frostbite.

Deciding I need to get my keys, I step out of my car and lock it behind me. I know that by the time I come back out, I'll have my keys in hand, so locking myself out now won't be a big deal.

As I walk into the upscale hotel, I stick out like a sore thumb. The staff is dressed impeccably, the lobby is decorated in high-end furnishings, and the floor looks freshly polished. I couldn't even afford to sit on their couch. I doubt I can even afford to breathe the same air as them. The only thing I probably can afford to do is get the fuck up out of these people's faces.

"Hi, I'm an ExpressWay driver," I begin, forcing a smile that feels as awkward as I sound. "A gentleman came in here earlier and, um, accidentally took my keys with him."

It sounds even dumber when I say it out loud. I imagine the receptionist's thoughts: How did a random stranger get your car keys? Oh, you know—because he ripped them from the ignition and stalked off with them in his coat pocket.

I tug at the sleeves of my oversized sweater, using the fabric to cover my hands as I nervously grip the cuffs.

"Just follow the long hall straight back; the meeting is in the Stafford conference room." She gestures toward the large hallway straight ahead.

Not sure how that's going to be helpful, I assumed she would go back and get my keys for me. What if I just lied about who I was and planned on going into the conference room wielding a weapon? Oh, my handsome passenger would kick the ever-loving shit out of me, up one way and down the other, before I even tried brandishing it. But whatever—I'll get them myself.

As I stroll down the long corridor, I pass three elevators on either side, each flanked by mirrors. Glancing at my reflection, I take in my appearance and want to laugh—then immediately want to cry when I see the gaping hole in the back of my leggings, right on my butt cheek. It wouldn't have even been that bad if I didn't need to do laundry and wasn't currently going commando.

"For the love of Pete, seriously?!" I mutter, stepping closer and twisting to get a better view. Yep, white butt cheek, exposed for all to see. I reach my hand down my pants and poke my finger through the tear, somehow believing my eyes are deceiving me, but my finger is fully through the fabric.

Fucking brilliant.

I have all of a single second to consider going back and sitting in my car, but I had the foresight to lock it, confident I'd be back with my keys. Adjusting my sweater higher on my neck so I can pull it lower in the back, I turn to check if the hole is covered. It is… ish.

Continuing forward, I reach the first set of double doors, which lead to a spacious, vacant banquet room. From here, my only options are to either go left or right. Opting to go right, I proceed past several rooms until I reach the end of the hall. There, I notice a plaque on the door that reads "Stafford."

With caution, I quietly open the door and peek inside. The room is dimly lit, with the only source of light coming from a large projector. Carefully, I widen the door just enough to slip through, making sure not to make any noise that might attract attention. I hold the door behind me as I try to silently guide it shut. The room is large, with a conference table seating about twenty people, all facing forward and attentively listening to the tall man who possesses my keys.

I hadn't expected him to be the one leading the meeting. As he continues speaking, clicking through slides on the projector, he barely acknowledges my entrance, just a quick glance before returning to his presentation. It seems as though he doesn't even recognize me. Bet it's quite a shock to see a homeless girl walking in your fancy meeting looking for her keys.

I awkwardly wave at him and then scan the room. My gaze lands on his coat—the same one in which I witnessed him place my keys. It hangs on the back of the only unoccupied chair at the head of the table.

Right. Next. To. Him.

Even better, I grumble to myself as I attempt to sneak toward the front without interrupting his speech. As I carefully make my way around the space, I notice the people seated along the visible side starting to stare in my direction. I offer them a mouthed apology, feeling the heat rise in my cheeks as I try to stay as inconspicuous as possible. With each step, I crouch lower, hoping to blend into the background as I near the front.

Realizing that I have to walk in front of the projector, I resort to the only plan that comes to mind. I drop to my hands and knees, silently crawling toward the chair and reaching my hand into his coat pocket, somehow believing I'm going undetected. When I feel my keys, I get excited, inwardly celebrating—prematurely—when I feel his hand wrap around my arm and pull me up, forcing me into the chair next to him—his chair. He uses his foot to push the chair away, then locks it in place with his shoe on the wheel, all while continuing to talk as if nothing happened.

Thankfully, the room is dark, which helps conceal my embarrassment. Not only was I caught crawling on the floor and rummaging through his jacket, but now I'm forced to sit in front of everyone. Surprisingly, no one reacts as if they saw anything.

Did they really not notice? Their secondhand embarrassment is probably so severe they're going to ignore my existence so they don't have to continue living with that feeling. Welcome to my life 24/7. Maybe this meeting is so interesting that they didn't pay attention to him pulling a woman up off the floor.

There's no way I'm that lucky...

It feels as if I was just silently reprimanded by an authoritative figure. I can't even muster enough courage to look around to see if anyone is staring at me—though it feels like everyone is. But as I catch a glimpse of this man, I realize there is no way in hell anyone would be looking at me when he's the focal point.

I become even more aware of him as I realize my thighs are wrapped around his leg, clamping him between mine. Horrified by this, I loosen my hold on him, but he still shows no reaction. I casually peek down between my legs to make sure I don't have a huge thigh hole or crotch hole, because that would be even worse than my back hole, as my fur burger would be on complete display.

There's no extra surprise tear in my leggings—a small blessing—but I do have a glaring white mayonnaise stain on one thigh, along with something crusted on the other. I absentmindedly scratch at it, trying to recall what I ate that could have left such a mark. There's a buffet of possibilities. As I flick the flakes off, I watch in horror as they land on his pants.

Shit.

Panicking, I try to delicately pinch the fabric of his pants to flick the crumbs off without him picking up on it, but just as I'm about to, he abruptly pushes the chair back, and the lights flicker on. I must've gone into shock or suffered from sheer mortification because, as the meeting wraps up, everyone starts rising, exchanging handshakes, engaging in friendly chatter, and I hadn't even realized the meeting was over.

Nonchalantly, I reach into his coat pocket to retrieve my keys, only to find it empty. Maybe they're in the other one. I'm probably just disoriented. Leaning to the other side, I dig around. I feel his wallet and money clip, but not my keys. Turning to look in his direction, his lips curve up into a smirk as he continues talking with an older gentleman. So he finds this amusing.

What a loser.

I sit here feeling incredibly awkward while he finishes his conversation with the other meeting attendees. I'm not entirely sure how I plan on walking out of here when everyone is just lingering around. I assumed they would rush out of here after the meeting, as it's late and probably well after all their bedtimes, but nobody seems in a hurry. The pit of my stomach about gives out when he turns his attention in my direction, shakes hands with the gentleman he's speaking with, then strides over to me. Casually retrieving his coat from the back of the chair, he puts it on and says, "Let's go," waiting for me to stand up.

"I'm comfortable," I say, wishing everyone would hurry and leave already.

He stares down at me, waiting for me to get up, but I remain in the chair. Funny how he seems impatient when he just made me wait an hour for him, and I got to embarrass myself ten ways to Sunday. "Come on," he repeats, reaching for my arm and attempting to pull me up.

"I said I'm comfortable." I jerk my arm from his grip.

With a heavy sigh, he reaches for my arm once more, effortlessly lifting me from the chair. My hands hurry to cover the hole in my pants, a desperate attempt to hide that monstrosity. He looks at me, confused, then looks behind me.

"I need to do laundry," I admit. "I don't need everyone in here seeing my butt."

He pries my hands away and looks at the hole, letting out a frustrated exhale. With a swift motion, he shakes his coat back off and holds it open for me. My arms are in it so fast, I don't want him to change his mind. As I settle into the warmth of the fabric, I feel his hand rest on my lower back as he pushes me toward the door.

"That peep show wasn't free," I whisper as we step past a group of remaining meeting attendees.

Exiting the room, I feel a gust of fresh air sweep over me. I fill my lungs until I can't possibly take in any more oxygen. I could kiss the floor I'm so thankful to be out of that room.

CHAPTER
Two

As we step outside, he unlocks my car and goes around to the driver's side, opening the door. I didn't expect him to get the door for me, but I'm even more surprised when he pushes the seat all the way back, climbs into the driver's seat, and starts the car as if it's completely normal.

After he shuts the driver's door, I pull it open again, planting myself there and leveling a stare at him. My brows shoot up in silent question, expecting some sort of explanation for what he's doing. But as he fiddles with the mirrors, completely absorbed in his own world, it becomes clear he has no intention of getting out or even acknowledging me.

"What are you doing? This is *my* car. *I'M* going to drive." I plant my fist firmly on my hip, popping it out in an exaggerated gesture, trying to assert myself in this bizarre situation.

"Your driving is reckless. I'll drive," he says pointedly, staring back at me.

Ignoring his words, I reach across him and unbuckle the seatbelt, forcefully removing it and instructing him, "Get to steppin'." He stares straight ahead, his nostrils flaring, like my insistence is annoying him, before reluctantly getting out of the car. He grabs my arm and pushes on my back as he guides me around toward the passenger side, opening the door for me and then nudging me toward the seat.

"No." I jerk my arm away from his grasp and turn to face him.

I take him in; he's bigger than me, at least an entire head length. I certainly can't overpower him. I wonder if I can climb in, lock the doors, and crawl to the driver's seat fast enough to keep him out. Then I can speed away, leaving him behind.

He must detect my contemplation because, from the silence, he barks out, "Get in now!" And I immediately comply.

As soon as I'm seated, he leans in, grabs the seatbelt, and secures it across me, his glare never leaving my face. Then he stands, grabs the strap, and tugs on it so it's cinched tight. Satisfied, he shuts the door, leaving no room for further discussion.

"That was really rude," I snap at him once he climbs back in the driver's seat. "You don't slam other people's car doors," I continue, knowing it didn't do any damage, but it still felt disrespectful.

Honestly, everything he's done so far has been disrespectful. Who in their right mind forces an ExpressWay driver to wait for an entire hour while they conduct a meeting?

"You're going to pay me for the drive to your house *and* for the hour of my time you wasted back there." I stare at him.

In response, he lets out a soft chuckle.

"Laugh all you want, but you're paying me." I cross my arms over my chest.

He turns to look at me. "Fine." Then shifts his attention back to the road. "Is this how you always treat your passengers? You're this rude?"

Flabbergasted, I let out an astonished snort. "Me? You have been rude this entire time. You didn't even ask if I would give you a ride. You just got in and expected it," I bite back. "You didn't even know whose car you were getting in. What if I was a murderer?" Reflecting on it now, the only reason I caved was because he had an unwavering confidence that caught me off guard. But looking back, it's frustrating that he made me feel any kind of way.

"You don't look like a murderer."

"You wouldn't have known that when you got in my car," I retort.

"I saw you at the light. You didn't strike me as a murderer," is all he says.

"You saw me at what light?"

"I got T-boned and needed to get to my meeting," he says matter-of-factly.

"Excuse me? That was you who got in an accident?!" I exclaim in disbelief, feeling like I'm somehow an accomplice to something illegal just by being in the same car as him.

"My driver stayed behind."

"And that makes it okay that you left the scene of an accident? We're going to get arrested!"

"For someone who drives so careless, you're sure being a baby about something else that's illegal," he glances over at me, then looks back at the road.

I sit there thinking about his words. He's right. I speed and run red lights quite often; I cut people off and swerve in and out of traffic, which is half illegal. So what's different about what I do verses what he did?

"I'd rather be a criminal alone," I remark.

"Not me. I'd much rather go down with an accomplice."

I turn and look at him to see if he's messing with me, but his eyes remain on the road. "How much longer until we're at your place?" I want him out of my car as soon as possible.

He doesn't say anything; he just continues driving with one hand rested on the steering wheel, leaning the other arm on the center console, tapping his thumb on the gearshift.

I feel conflicted about this man—he irritates me, but not to the extent that I want to throw him out like I did with the previous guy. The two of them are worlds apart in every way imaginable. While this situation has been strange, he has consistently shown a level of respect that the earlier passenger completely lacked. There's something almost ethereal about his scent, as if he were crafted by the hands of the heavens. His appearance even suggests they invested significantly more time and effort into his looks than the average person. And I kind of don't want to get out of his coat.

My confusion peaks when I see him pulling into the McDonald's drive-thru. "What are you doing?"

"I'm hungry," he replies as he pulls up to the speaker. Rolling down the window, he scans the menu then proceeds to order.

"Give me two Big Macs, a large fry, and a large Coke," he says confidently. This man looks like he's never eaten at a McDonald's in his life. Yet here he is, ordering it like he's a frequent customer.

"You need to use manners," I chastise him. "Say please next time. And when they hand you your food, say thank you."

When we pull up to the window to pay, he leans over me, popping open the top two buttons on his coat and reaching inside, pulling open his coat pocket and grabbing his wallet.

As he's handed his food out the window, he makes no attempt to say thank you. Frustrated, I lightly hit his arm with the back of my hand.

Finally, he says, "Thank you," to the teenager.

"Have a good night," the teen responds back as we drive away.

He pulls around to the parking lot and parks in an empty spot, then digs into the bag and holds one of the Big Macs out to me. I just stare at him until it becomes clear that I have no intention of taking it. He sets the box on my lap and digs into the bag again, pulling out the fries and placing it in the other cup holder.

"This is bizarre," I comment, observing him settle into a more comfortable position in my car. He's sure making himself right at home.

"I'm hungry. Anywhere I would have chosen, you can't go in dressed like that." He scans my outfit up and down. "So, food fitting for your attire," he adds with an air of arrogance, turning back to his meal and taking a big bite of his hamburger.

"I'll have you know, I'm wearing a really expensive coat. And I could have robbed you since you carelessly left your wallet unattended with me."

He leans over, putting his wallet back in the same pocket of his coat he retrieved it from, then sits back in the seat and takes another bite of his hamburger.

"Whatever. Enjoy your food. I'm used to this trash. You're going to be shitting your brains out later tonight, so I will get the last laugh," I remark as I open my hamburger box. Upon discovering there are pickles on my burger, I close the lid.

"What's wrong with your hamburger?" he questions, giving me a skeptical look as he wipes his mouth with a napkin.

"I don't like pickles."

He sets his hamburger back in the box and leans over to open mine. He lifts the bun, plucks off the three pickles, pops them into his mouth, then puts the bun back and gives it a little pat. "Better," he says. I sit there, dumbfounded, staring back and forth between him and the burger.

I'd be lying if I said I didn't eat McDonald's at least once a week. My roommate Chloe and I indulge more often than we care to admit. With her hectic work schedule as a flight attendant, we rarely have time to cook, so we end up grabbing takeout a lot. Sometimes, we'll make a quick drive-thru stop at McDonald's, always getting Big Mac meals without pickles.

Strangely enough, even though this one had pickles, I assumed the pickle juice would completely taint the taste. But when I take a bite, I'm surprised—it's really good, even better than usual. Maybe I somehow like pickles all of a sudden? Don't your taste buds change every seven years?

As we sit quietly eating, he starts clicking on my phone screen, scrolling through the music. He eventually settles on a song and leans back in his seat.

"You must have forgot your manners at home when you left this morning," I sarcastically remark, annoyed by his invasion of my personal phone and his audacity to not only touch it without permission but also change the song that was playing.

Ignoring my comment, he takes a sip of his drink and extends it toward me. I stare at it, confused as to why he's offering it to me, and wonder if he's just now realizing he didn't get me one. Or maybe he meant to only get one for us to share. Internally musing over it, I dismiss that idea.

Hasn't he ever heard of oral herpes or some other kind of mouth STD? He has no clue where my lips have been, and frankly, I don't know anything about where his have traveled either. His mouth is so strikingly beautiful; it seems likely they have graced the lips and bodies of countless women throughout the city.

One final look at his mouth has me grabbing the drink from his hand, taking a sip, and placing it back in the cup holder. "Thank you," I mutter, feeling a bit awkward, then remember that we were talking about his manners and how he needs to stop touching my things.

"Would you like to know something really neat?" I ask, raising my brows as I look at him.

He peers out of the driver's side window and then turns his head to face me. "What's that?" he asks, sounding completely uninterested.

I whimsically move my hands in the air. "This is *my* car. And this—this is *my* phone. These are *my* hands, and only *my* hands touch *my* phone," I say, holding my fingers up and wiggling them. Then I reach over and pat both of his pants pockets, followed by his suit jacket pockets, until I find what I'm looking for. He just observes as I retrieve his phone. "This. This is *your* phone. *You* touch your phone, and *I* touch my phone. Capeesh?" I say mockingly.

He stares in my eyes, then shifts his gaze down at my lips, then leans closer to my face. The joking tone in me dissipates, and I find myself staring at him as he inches closer. Would I stop him if he were to actually kiss me right now? My reaction in this moment is no; no I would not stop him. I would stupidly accept his kiss.

He brings his thumb to my lip and roughly wipes the side, making me instantly self-conscious that I was scolding him with sauce or something on my mouth. He grabs the empty box from my lap, opens the driver's door, and walks over to a nearby trash can to toss our garbage. I watch, all but drooling at his backside, then turn away as he walks back to the car.

I take advantage of this time to step outside and brush off the food crumbs on my clothes. Well, more his coat, but at least I'm trying to clean it off. I also need some fresh air to shake off the embarrassment of assuming he would attempt to kiss me. Why would he even do that? What kind of delusional thinking was that.

I rest my back against my car and release a deep breath, letting my head drop back to take in the sky. I feel his presence next to me and then the subtle shift of my car from his weight as he leans against it. I turn to look at him. He's propped against the car with his hands in his pockets and feet casually crossed in front of him.

"Your belly upset yet?" I grin at him.

"Nope," he says, glancing down at me. "Yours?"

"Nope. I'm sure you won't believe this, but I eat this food a couple times a week."

"You know how bad it is for—"

I interrupt him before he can finish his sentence. "You know, when I said that, what I was really hoping for was for you to lecture me on how bad it is for me."

"It's incredibly—"

"Don't wanna hear it," I interrupt him again, putting my hand up to silence him. "You could tell me it will make all my hair fall out and the workers put eye boogers in the meat, and I'd still eat it."

"Because you enjoy the taste?" he questions.

"Obviously not. Because it's cheap." I doubt he's ever had to think twice about money, never had that sinking feeling of wondering if he could stretch a dollar far enough to make it to his next meal. Trying to explain something so basic to someone like him feels like a waste of breath. "Let's get you home," I suggest, attempting to walk around him.

He quickly grabs my arm, steering me back toward the open passenger door.

"Let's," he replies, gently guiding me into the seat and closing the door behind me.

I watch as he walks around the car, climbing in and fastening his seatbelt.

Whether he thinks I'm a bad driver or not, he chose to get in my car. He should accept my driving for what it is. Him driving makes me feel like I can't even demand payment from him since he's doing the work. On second thought, he's got my brain working overtime, so I should definitely demand payment.

Ten minutes later we pull up to a 21-floor high-rise building. He pulls to the front, where a grand entrance unfolds. A sleek awning extends over the entrance, and a doorman dressed in a sharp uniform stands at the ready.

I stare with my mouth hanging open as I look up at the incredible building, momentarily forgetting that he's still here. As he puts the car in park by the front doors, I snap back to reality and suddenly become aware of just how out of place I am.

"Thanks for the ride," he says, looking at me.

I glance over at him, and our eyes meet, sending a rush of unwanted butterflies through me. I hate that—I don't want to feel anything for him. Without wasting another second, I slide out of the car and march to the driver's side. Yanking the door open, I step aside, giving him space to get out while I make quick work of unbuttoning his coat, eager to shake off whatever it is he's making me feel.

"I said thank you," he repeats, climbing out standing toe-to-toe with me.

"I heard you."

"You lectured me on manners, and now you're refusing to use them. I have a good book you should read; it's an entire lesson on manners," he grins.

Scoffing, I reply, "You're one to talk. Maybe next time we can read it together," saying it sarcastically and immediately hating how that actually didn't sound like as much of an insult as I intended. "Better hurry inside; you're gonna need to get to your porcelain throne soon."

As I go to remove his coat, he reaches his hand inside, retrieves his wallet, and shoves it in his back pocket. Then stalks off toward the door.

"Your coat," I call after him.

He's nearly at the door where the doorman waits, holding it open, but he turns and strides back, closing the distance between us until he's intimately close. He reaches for the coat buttons and starts fastening them one by one. "Your entire ass cheek is showing. Get in your car, go home, and throw those leggings in the trash." His tone is clipped, but it sounds like he's mad… at my leggings.

Rolling my eyes, I bite back a retort, as he finishes with the last button. Without wasting another second, I move around him and slide into the driver's seat, immediately adjusting it back to where I can reach the pedals. I tug on the door, wanting to get far away from him, this building, and the way he's making me… feel.

He grabs the door frame, holding it open, resting his arm on the top of the door and my car, leaning his head down. "Thank you."

"Yeah, yeah, yeah, you're welcome. Now go." I reach around him and grab my handle again; this time, he moves and lets me shut it.

When I arrive back to my apartment, I notice he slipped another $100 in the opening below the radio. With a smile on my face, I swiftly grab it and decide to tuck it away in my purse. Feeling it's more than one, I slide the bills apart and stare down at them. It's not just one $100 bill, but five of them! He has given me a total of $600 tonight. I stare in disbelief, almost feeling a twinge of guilt, but then I quickly remind myself that I deserve this after enduring everything he put me through all night.

CHAPTER
Three

I decide to take a break from work for the next three days since I earned enough money to cover my expenses for a week. It's a nice opportunity to catch up on some household chores, especially laundry. After spending a couple days getting my home in order, I finally feel ready to venture out again. As I prepare to leave, I remember his comment about how unprofessional I looked in my yoga pants. Well, his exact words were something about me being dressed for dinner at McDonald's. That comment still packs quite a solid punch. So, this time, I opt for jeans, snow boots, a sweatshirt, a winter coat, and a scarf, especially because there's snow on the ground today. And my only good pair of leggings did, in fact, go in the trash. I don't even know how I managed to get a hole in the butt of them.

It snowed steadily throughout the morning and into the early afternoon, blanketing the streets and rooftops in a thick layer of white. I keep an eye on the weather reports to see when the snow stops so I can head out to work.

The weather app says we got five inches since last night, but that snow plows were on the road all morning. I pull on my snow boots, step outside, and huff. The apartment complex believes in doing a janky shovel when it first starts snowing, and then the snow just re-covers what they shoveled away. Because my designated parking spot is at the end under an awning, right next to the uncovered spots for visitors or extra cars in the unit, snow often drifts up along my car and piles up on the passenger side. I sigh, realizing I'll have to clear it if I want to get going.

I make my way over to the snowbank, and without much thought, I start trying to kick the snow away from my car. Snow flies in every direction, but more of it ends up in my boots than in the empty parking spot I was aiming for. Quickly figuring out this isn't going to work, I bend over, spreading my legs wide, and start scooping the snow between them, one hand at a time, like a dog digging a hole. It's not exactly a graceful move, but it's effective, and the pile begins to shrink. Yes, all the snow is going in the free parking space behind me, but that sounds like a them problem, not a me problem.

As I stand up, I feel a small smile creeping across my face, satisfied with my work. When I turn around, I see my upstairs neighbor leaning against the apartment by the stairs, in pajamas and a robe, cigarette in hand, watching me with a look that's somewhere between disgust and confusion. "Weird ass," she mutters taking a drag and heading back toward her apartment.

"You too, Nancy," I call after her, and wave.

As I open the ExpressWay app, multiple notifications for delivery orders pop up, and I accept the first food order. I spend the first couple of hours delivering food to people with regular jobs. While I usually make the most money at night by driving drunk people around, food delivery brings in decent earnings too, likely because I ensure the food arrives hot.

I accept another order and always find it amusing when people spend hundreds on extravagant lunches. The current order I'm waiting to pick up is over $500, and according to the app, it's only two big bags. That's a clear sign this food is ridiculously expensive. And it always seems like the big orders like this tip like crap—probably how they afford their expensive food, by not tipping the person actually delivering it.

While I wait for the order to be brought out, I study the menu, and my jaw drops at the sight of the prices. There isn't a single lunch item under $80. That amount could feed me at McDonald's for an entire week! And the dinner prices aren't even listed.

I ponder how these people make so much money that they can afford to eat like this. It feels like they're just throwing their money down the drain—or should I say, flushing it down the toilet, since that's where this expensive food is headed by the end of the day. None of the items on the menu even seem worth the price tag.

The hostess approaches with my order, likely having noticed the critical expression on my face as I scanned the exorbitant menu. She shoots me a curt look, handing over the bags. I offer her a polite smile, set the menu aside, thank her, then head out.

"Hey!" someone calls out. I turn to see a man quickly approaching me. "Are you going to Shaw Industries?" he asks as he gets closer

"Did you hear me say I was picking up an order for Shaw Industries?" I respond, continuing to walk.

He follows after me. "I did."

"Then why are you asking if that's where I'm going?" I open the passenger door and place the food on the seat.

"Can I get a ride?" he asks. "That's where I'm heading."

"Sure, but you're paying for the ride," I reply as I make my way around to the driver's side.

"But you're already going there?" he protests.

"Bye," I say, getting in.

He opens the back door, climbs in, and places a twenty in my cupholder. "I appreciate the ride," he says, buckling up.

As I drive up to the massive building, I double-check the receipt to see where I need to deliver the order. Of course, my worst fear is confirmed—I have to go all the way up to the 14th floor.

Gag.

"They won't let you park here," he says as I get out and start walking around the car.

"Then take the order up for me," I suggest, hoping he will.

"Give me my twenty back and I will," he grins.

"As if," I roll my eyes, grabbing the bags and following him toward the entrance.

"Miss, you can't park there," the doorman calls out as I approach him.

"I'm just dropping off food for a Mr. Shaw." I hold up the bags. "Can I leave them here and have someone deliver them to him?" I ask. Before he can respond, I quickly add, "That way, I can get my car out of the way."

He pulls the door open for me and says, "Go on in, head to the elevators, and go to the top floor," gesturing toward the elevators on the far left wall.

Well, that didn't go quite as I imagined. Why did I think anyone would willingly trek all the way up to the top floor to deliver food? It's wishful thinking. At least the elevators look new and well-maintained. I don't anticipate any issues going up or down.

A woman standing near the buttons, every inch the picture of success in her tailored pantsuit, asks for each passenger's floor. When it's my turn, I mention the 14th floor, but I see she's already pressed the button. She must either work there or have some business of her own to attend. Her attention flickers over me briefly—a polished look of judgment. The subtle upturn of her brow says more than any words could—like I've been weighed, measured, and found lacking.

As the elevator ascends, we're the only two left, and an uncomfortable silence settles between us. When the elevator finally reaches the top floor, the doors open with a soft chime. The woman strides past me with purposeful steps, casting a disdainful glare in my direction before striding out and disappearing down the hallway.

I step out and head towards the reception area. The receptionist is deeply absorbed in her computer screen, so I wait for her to finish whatever she's doing. She sits behind a large, semi-circular desk, with a glass partition attached to a half wall behind her. The partition's purpose eludes me, but I can see through it to offices beyond—rooms with glass walls and doors, offering a curious blend of transparency and privacy.

She doesn't bother to look up, so I place the bags on the counter with a loud thud. "These are for a Mr. Shaw," I announce, my irritation seeping into my voice, feeling annoyed that she's wasting my time.

She finally looks up, her eyes flickering between the bags and me. "You can leave them there," she says curtly. Without missing a beat, she answers the ringing phone, her surprise at the interruption barely masking her disinterest for me. The brief moment of attention quickly fades as she turns her focus fully to her call, dismissing me with the efficiency of someone who has long grown accustomed to such disruptions.

I turn and eagerly head back toward the elevators. For orders of this size, ExpressWay usually requires a signature—part of their strategy to coax a tip from the customer. But given the price tag on this one, I won't even waste my time or allow them the opportunity to insult me when they write a zero crossed out on the tip line.

As I wait for the elevator, I glance around, thinking I don't remember them being this slow on the ride up. I notice she's now staring at me, and I silently urge the elevator to hurry the fuck up. Once her call ends, she rises from her desk and practically rolls her eyes at me. "Mr. Shaw will take the bags in his office." She motions for me to follow her, and I debate whether I should ignore her just to see if she will take the bags herself, but her beady little eyeballs are glued to me.

The elevator doors open, and I shift my attention between them and her. "Do you mind taking them? I have other orders."

"This is part of your job. My job is doing as Mr. Shaw says. Please take the bags and follow me," she replies with a sense of finality.

Sighing, I grab the bags and stare longingly as the elevator doors shut again without me inside.

She guides me to a set of double doors and gently knocks. I doubt anybody even heard that; she could have blown on the door, and it would have made more noise than that tap. Stepping around her, I rap on the door way louder to ensure the knock is heard. Her mouth falls open as she gapes at me, and then the door swings open, revealing two men, one of whom remains in the doorway.

My heart plummets. This is just perfect. I'm standing face to face with Mr. Disrespectful.

"Thank you, Savannah, that will be all," he dismisses the receptionist.

She offers him a polite smile and a nod, but then her expression shifts as she narrows her eyes at me. Without another word, she strides past, returning the way she came and leading the gentleman out of his office with her.

I stand there, frozen, unable to look away from him. It's almost amusing that this is the second time I've encountered him, and the second time he has no recollection of me. The first was when I walked into his meeting at the hotel; he barely glanced up before continuing his slideshow presentation. And now, here he is again, showing no sign of recognizing me.

"You can set the food over there," he directs, heading toward the large desk at the center of his office. I step inside looking to where he's gesturing: a small conference-style table to the right side of the room, surrounded by six chairs. I quickly place the bags down then turn to leave.

His voice cuts in as I make it to the doors. "Do I not need to sign anything?"

I hesitate, then reply, "Nope. Bye," eager to get out of this room.

"Come back," he orders.

"Fuck," I mutter as I make my way toward his desk.

"So, you drive for ExpressWay at night and deliver food during the day. What else do you do?" he inquires.

"Sign, please." I hand him my phone, trying to wrap things up and leave. I hold onto the receipt, patiently waiting for his signature.

"In a hurry?" he asks, a mix of arrogance, annoyance, and amusement in his tone, but he doesn't bother to sign.

"Yes," I respond flatly, maintaining eye contact with him.

He reaches over, jerking the receipt out of my hand and examines it.

"Hey!" I hiss. "You just gave me a paper cut!"

He reaches out, grabs my hand to inspect it, then smirks and releases it. "Where?"

"Well, you could have if you do stuff like that! You're so rude," I snap at him. "Hurry up and sign." I hold out my open hand toward him to return my phone.

He does as I ask, scribbling his signature on the screen before extending my phone toward me. But just as my fingers brush the edge of it, he pulls it back, a hint of amusement lighting up his features.

"My car is still being repaired. Be back here at 7:00. I've got a dinner to attend," he says smoothly, placing the phone in my hand and returning to his desk, sinking back into his chair. The folder in front of him is already open as he casually flicks through the pages, reading the contents inside.

"I'm busy tonight. Download the ExpressWay app and request a ride. Someone will pick you up. Plus, seafood smells like dirty pussy, so my car is already reeking from your order. I don't need to smell it on your breath." Turning around, I confidently walk across his office. I swing the door wide open and stroll out.

"See you at 7:00," he calls out.

When I reach my car, the smell of seafood wafts out as I open the door. Fucking barf. And seriously, who orders $500 worth of lunch just for themselves? That's absolutely insane. Well, it's pretty obvious that it wasn't just for him. I wonder who he ordered such fancy food to have lunch with. Maybe it's the woman I rode the elevator with?

None of your business. I remind myself.

I open my app to check for any new orders. I peer up from my phone and do a double take at the building. Shaw Industries. This is *his* building. No wonder he's so arrogant.

As my app dings with the completed order, I quickly open it to see how he signed his name. Maybe I misread the receipt or something. But nope, it's Beckett Shaw.

My eyes widen in disbelief when I see that he left me a $100 tip—even after I just insulted his raunchy squid pussy-smelling food.

Who exactly are you, Mr. Disrespectful?

After a quick Google search, I discover that he's ridiculously wealthy, ridiculously good-looking, ridiculously arrogant, and ridiculously smart. And I'd be stupid not to come back at 7:00. After all, I don't have anything exciting in my life; why not spice it up with more embarrassment? I seem to have a never-ending supply of that up my sleeve.

It's only the third day of the month, and I will have all my bills covered for the month if he keeps tipping me like this. One more drive will be fine. Plus, I need to give him back his coat. Which I happened to Google how much that coat cost when he let a stranger take it with them, thinking maybe he would be out a couple hundred dollars. No. This man let me take his black cashmere peacoat that cost eight thousand dollars. And I had dropped McDonald's hamburger bun crumbs on it.

I head back to my apartment, hoping to catch a quick nap. But instead, I toss and turn in bed, anxiously waiting for the time to pass. I glance over at his coat, which I've been sleeping with—because it smells so good. *Only* because it smells good. Not because I want to smell *him* on me... in my bed. Grabbing it one last time, I hug it to me and inhale. Why does he smell so good?

With his coat in hand, I wander to the living room, setting it down on the couch next to my purse so I don't forget it. Then I proceed to aimlessly walk around my apartment, peeking out of different windows. I don't know why I feel so nervous about leaving. I've been pacing back and forth in my living room for the last twenty minutes, checking the clock every time I walk past the fireplace mantel.

I even wait an extra five minutes before leaving, just in case he found another ride. I could pretend I wasn't back for him and keep on driving. Or maybe he never expected me to come back in the first place—maybe he was just messing with me. Or maybe he downloaded the app like I suggested and found himself a ride. Surely he wasn't just going to bank on me coming back? Besides, do I really want him back in my car after he ate all that stinky food?

Regardless, I still leave to go pick him up.

Despite leaving later than I should have, I manage to arrive a few minutes early. The snow is falling steadily, and the roads are already turning white. According to the weather report, it will continue all night.

Right on time, at 7:00, I see him emerging from the building, accompanied by a man who's holding an umbrella over his head. The other gentleman opens the backseat door, and they exchange a few words before he shuts the door and opens the front passenger door. Beckett gets in, continuing his conversation, and retrieves a neatly wrapped stack of folders the gentleman holds out to him, as well as a folded-up umbrella. Then the door shuts.

Alone again.

He leans over, plucking my phone from the holder on the dashboard and starts entering some information.

"Excuse you, Beckett," I emphasize his name. "Stop being so rude," I snap as I try to grab my phone.

He pushes my hand down and places my phone back in the holder. He has entered a restaurant address into the GPS. Sitting back in his seat, he reaches for the seatbelt and secures it in place. "I'm your designated driver. Don't you want to sit in the back seat like a typical passenger?" I say, starting the mileage tracker on my app.

"No."

"Why?" I glance at him, genuinely confused.

"Am I your typical passenger?" He meets my gaze.

"Not even close. I'd tase someone who tried touching my phone, or driving my car, or getting in without my permission," I say transparently, then begin driving. "I can also tell you brushed your teeth since I smell mint and not putrid squid."

He turns to me with a blank expression. "Do you not brush your teeth after you eat?"

"I brush my teeth once a month."

He stares at me, utterly unimpressed. I flash him a wide smile, showing him my clean, white teeth. "I brush when I wake up and before bed."

"And you want to call the food I eat disgusting?" He raises his brow.

"Do my teeth look bad?" I ask mockingly.

"For someone who brushes twice a day—they look decent."

"I can't judge yours because they are hidden under ten feet of grumpy scowl." He doesn't even crack a smile.

"Did you call for any other ride?" I switch the topic.

"No."

"What if I didn't come back?" I stare pointedly at him and then back at the road.

"Looks like I didn't need to question it," he says casually.

That's quite a bold move on his part. Still, he has a point—he practically had me eating out of the palm of his hand.

It's a one-hour drive, but I don't mind because I'll be getting paid for it. However, it dawns on me that I won't be paid for the return trip once I drop him off.

I really hope he needs a ride back, not just for the money. The weather forecast says it's going to snow all night, and I'd rather have the potential of getting stuck with someone else than find myself stuck in the snow alone in this weather.

He's busy going through file after file. I notice it's difficult for him to see in the darkened car on the back roads, so I click on the dome light to help him. He immediately reaches up and shuts it back off.

"I was just trying to be helpful," I say, feeling a bit offended that he shut it off.

"It could hinder your ability to see clearly in this weather," he responds, not even looking up from the files.

"I'm surprised you don't want to be a passenger seat driver. You must somewhat trust my driving."

"I don't at all," is all he says.

"Oh yeah? Well, I hope reading in the car gives you a headache," I retort. He shows no reaction to my words. He probably doesn't even pay attention when I speak; I inwardly laugh at the truth in that thought. "I brought your $8,000 cashmere coat back." I stare directly at him.

"Thanks," he says, unfazed.

"I actually think I'm going to keep it."

"Then why'd you bring it with you?" he turns to the next page he's reading through.

"Because it's an $8,000 coat. Why would you buy such an expensive coat?"

"I didn't buy it," he says, skimming the papers in his hand.

"Ew, was I wearing someone else's coat?" The idea that I've been snuggling up with someone else's coat instantly irritates me.

"It's mine. I said *I* didn't buy it."

"Someone gave you a coat that expensive?" My mouth hangs open at the thought of this.

"Yes."

"What about your fancy watch," I nod to his wrist.

"I bought it," he says, not even taking his eyes off the papers.

"Can I have it?" I ask, just to try and get a reaction out of him.

He smirks. "You're freaking out about my coat, but not the price of my watch?"

"Nobody even wears a watch anymore except for old baby boomers who don't track their steps."

He looks at me and quirks a brow.

"It's true," I shrug, then allow us to fall into silence for the rest of the drive as I quietly sing along to the music from my playlist.

CHAPTER Four

We finally arrive at our destination, and I ease the car to a stop at the entrance, shifting into park and reaching for my phone to complete the ride. He doesn't spare me a glance or a word of thanks. He steps out, smoothly unfurling his umbrella like he's done this a thousand times. Before I leave, out of sheer curiosity, I pull up Google and type in the name of the watch he's wearing. I'm stunned by the results, and I actually gulp when they populate.

I jump when my car door swings open, cold air rushing in. He leans across me, unbuckles my seatbelt, and grabs my elbow, pulling me out of the car.

"Hey! What are you doing?" I protest, yanking my arm back, but his grip is firm. The umbrella is held over the door protectively, shielding us both from the falling snow, but he doesn't ease up as he pulls me from my car.

"These meetings are tedious, and it's going to be a couple of hours," he responds, keeping a firm hold on me and wrapping his other arm around my waist. He releases me and retrieves a ticket and the umbrella from the valet man as we walk toward the entrance together.

I was so buried in my phone I didn't realize he had the valet holding the umbrella for him. Without even having seen it, I already know how that went—he shoved the umbrella in the man's hand, giving him no other option but to hold it.

"I'm not going in there, Beckett," I stop mid-walk, but he firmly pushes on my back to keep me moving. "I know you've already noticed I might not be dressed for McDonald's today, but definitely chick-fil-A—certainly not this place," I continue, walking alongside him.

When we reach the hostess, he hands over his umbrella and coat with a casual flick of his wrist. He turns to me, unwrapping my scarf from around my neck and tossing it to the same woman as if she were a coat rack. I watch as she scrambles to catch the various items he's carelessly relinquishing, grateful I'm not on the receiving end of his whims. Before I have a chance to protest, he roughly yanks down the zipper of my coat and removes it, sending it flying toward the same hostess who barely managed to gather my scarf.

"You are too handsy and rough, Beckett," I snap.

He disregards my comment and strides away. I quicken my pace to catch up with him, falling into step beside him. "You paid $100,000 for your watch?!"

"Yes."

"Why?" I press, trying to wrap my head around why someone would pay that kind of money for a watch. He doesn't even deem me worthy of a response, his eyes focused ahead as we're led to a dimly lit private room, where four men in tailored business suits are already seated and talking. The silence gnaws at me, but I push it aside, determined not to let his indifference get under my skin.

I stick out like a sore thumb, instantly feeling self-conscious. I look like some charity case he picked up off the side of the road and brought here to feed me the scraps of the rich.

The men all stand as we enter, greeting Beckett and shaking his hand. It's clear that Beckett is the one in charge in this room. His presence commands attention, which is both impressive and probably intimidating to these men that were waiting for him.

His next actions confuse me. He completely ignores me, and everyone else seems to follow suit. I never expected him to introduce me to the men he's meeting with, but it seems odd nobody is questioning who the woman is he brought with him. Unless he typically brings a plus one to business dinners.

Continuing to act like I don't exist, he nonchalantly pulls out a chair and guides me to it by my waist. Apparently, I'm not completely invisible. I had planned on holding up the wall in the corner and trying to fade into the shadows. Instead, I'm thrust into close proximity to Beckett as he grabs the chair beside mine and sits. Chloe literally won't even believe any of this when I tell her, because this sounds too made-up to even be real.

The waiter promptly arrives to take our drink orders and discuss their best wines. After glancing at the menu and having a heart attack at the prices, I decide to stick with water. Perhaps I'll have some ice cube soup for dinner, as that's all I can afford. Maybe they can go fetch me a pile of snow from outside and put it in a bowl for me. That might be cheaper than their ice cubes, I'm sure.

Beckett orders two cokes and begins talking to the other men once the waiter leaves. Meanwhile, I find myself trapped in an awkward silence, glancing around at the unfamiliar faces, unsure of where to direct my attention. My gaze inadvertently locks onto the bigger man sitting directly across from me. The top button of his shirt is so tight on his neck its dipping into the skin, causing his face to flush a deep crimson. I half want to tell him if he loosened his tie and unbuttoned that restrictive collar, he might actually breathe easier, but I'm assuming he's trying to keep up appearances.

We never even discussed what I'm supposed to be doing here. Am I supposed to be a distraction for him? Am I supposed to remain invisible? Going by the way he's ignoring me; I will go by way of the latter and remain invisible. I shift in my seat, thinking a more comfortable position will help me concentrate better while I try to listen to their conversation, but I don't understand a word of what's being said. I gather it's definitely business-related but other than the flecks of spit that keep flying across the table from the shorter man with glasses, I can't follow along with any of this.

Documents are handed to Beckett, and he carefully examines each one, periodically glancing up and nodding in acknowledgment as each man speaks about the documents.

He was right about one thing: this meeting is boring. So boring that I let out a loud yawn without even realizing I did it until the man who is talking, abruptly stops and all eyes shift in my direction. I can see Beckett's jaw flex, and then he motions for the guy to proceed, in which he immediately starts up again.

I awkwardly run my fingers down my pants in a soothing gesture. When my nails trail back up, I can feel a hangnail that keeps snagging at the fabric of my jeans, so I proceed to pick at it. I want to bite it, but I can only imagine the look Beckett would shoot me with. Reaching in my purse, I find my nail clippers and bend off to the side, glancing around to make sure nobody is paying attention to me.

Looking back down, I begin trying to quietly clip my nail. When Beckett's hand lands on my lap and he squeezes my thigh, I sit up straight, adjusting in my chair. His hand remains in place, so I assume maybe he's wanting me to trim his nails too. Though they're already short and look as if he recently had a manicure, I can see there might be something I can trim. Putting the clipper under his first nail, I go to clip it, and he jerks his hand away and rips the clippers from my grasp, slipping them in his pocket.

I sit quietly for at least two minutes, and I'm about to fall asleep if I don't find a distraction. Subtly pulling my phone from my pocket, I discreetly pull up TikTok to pass the time.

The first video blares so loud I simultaneously hear knees smashing under the table, jostling everything on top, and a gasp from the older gentleman across from me, his eyes widening and mouth dropping open.

Beckett looks down at me, his nostrils flaring, and I pinch my lips between my teeth as I lock my phone and hand it to him. He reaches over, plucking it from my fingers, places it in his pocket with my nail clippers, then resumes talking.

The waiter returns with drinks, and Beckett takes both cokes, placing one in front of me and one in front of himself.

"Thank you," I say, unsure if I'm thanking the waiter, Beckett, or both of them simultaneously.

When it's time to order, the men each go around and order their meal one by one. When it's my turn, the waiter looks at me, but Beckett cuts in before I can even say a word. He starts ordering using words that I don't understand—probably talking about different types of meat and how they're cooked, but I'm completely lost.

I'm so out of my element here.

He finishes ordering, then plucks my menu up and hands it to the waiter, who retrieves both menus from Beckett and promptly leaves.

I'm so embarrassed right now, I'm glad the proper etiquette I obtained from TV is that you don't put your elbows on the dining surface. If my hands were anywhere near it, I would send everyone frantically looking around the room, wondering if we were experiencing a mini earthquake with how much I'd be rattling things. I can only imagine how much more embarrassed I'll be when the food arrives and I'm the only one sitting here not eating.

Why did he even bring me in here? To humiliate me? He didn't even give me a chance to say I wasn't going to eat. He just assumed.

Beckett randomly stands to hand a file back, which seems odd since he can easily hand it back without standing. When he sits down, he accidentally moves his chair closer to mine. I assume this is unintentional until I feel his hand rest on my knee and give a squeeze. Instantly, my legs stop shaking. This gesture doesn't seem to stem from annoyance or anger the way it did moments ago when I was clipping my nails. It feels more like a comforting touch that causes my entire body to relax.

The waiter returns, and Beckett removes his hand, leaving a warm spot where his hand was resting.

The waiter comes back with a bottle of wine, smiling and displaying it in his hands as if he is hoping to impress Beckett. He introduces the wine and with a single nod from Beckett, the waiter swiftly opens the bottle and pours wine for everyone. When he gets to Beckett's glass, he's stopped with a single raise of his hand in a dismissive gesture. The man nods in acknowledgment, places the wine in the bucket of ice, and leaves.

The men all begin talking again, drinking the wine like its water.

"Try the wine; I think you'll like it. It's a lot different than the gas station box wine you probably drink." Beckett reaches over to slide my wine glass closer to me. He then casually rests his arm on the back of my chair, leaning in slightly as he speaks.

"I'm your driver, remember? Do you want to make it home alive tonight, or would you rather see your driver get a DUI?" I whisper back, a little more snappily than I intended.

"You really think I'd let you drive me home in these conditions?" He tilts his chin towards the large windows, where I can see it's dark outside and everything is covered in a thick layer of white snow, with big, golf ball-sized snowflakes still falling.

"Are we just going to walk home then?" I retort, as our only other option would be sleeping in my car. It might not be comfortable, but the thought of him struggling to get sleep in the front seat, using his coat as a makeshift blanket, strangely brings me satisfaction.

"I'm driving," he says bluntly, staring across the table as if he's listening to the men talking.

He reaches over, grabs the glass from the table, and holds it out to me. "Try it," he encourages.

I lazily extend my hand, and he places the glass in my fingers, letting go once I have a firm grip. He watches as I bring it to my lips and take a sip. Well, damn, this is definitely not your average boxed wine. It's incredible. I take a bigger gulp, savoring the taste.

Whispering out the side of my mouth to Beckett as I stare at the men, I say, "Careful, I think you just glitched; it almost looked like you smiled." Taking another sip of wine, I keep my head straight but shift my focus to him.

A full smile spreads across his face. As in, showing his perfectly white, straight teeth.

Damn him. How does he look so good? Why are his teeth so white?

"Are those veneers?" I ask, my expression serious. Then my brain catches up with my words and that might be considered a rude question. "Never mind," I quickly backtrack, trying to correct my rudeness, and take another sip.

"No, these are my real teeth. Good genetics," he says arrogantly.

"You're so full of yourself." I finish my wine and set the empty glass on the table.

He grabs the bottle from the ice bucket and refills it halfway with more. I can't help but smile at the sight of the burgundy liquid swirling inside.

"Thank you," I grin, picking it up again.

When the food arrives, I'm surprised to see a plate set in front of me. Beckett ordered me steak. That was super nice, but now I get to internally panic at the fact I almost cut my finger off the last time I had one. Since then, Chloe always cuts mine for me. I trace my thumb over the scar where I had to get eight stitches to mend the gash.

I chew on the inside of my lip, looking at the sharp knife. Discussions about how delicious the food is have already begun, and Beckett mentions another restaurant, asking if they've tried it. He reaches over, pulls my plate closer to him, and begins cutting my food into thin slices while he continues talking like it's no big deal.

I'm convinced at this point everyone here truly believes I'm a charity case, especially with him treating me like I'm a child. Though I would rather have him treat me like a child than risk cutting my fingers off, because if I did that, I would have to put said finger in my pocket and discreetly leave so nobody knew what happened, all while praying my blood wasn't dripping through my pants and onto the floor, leaving blood drops with each step.

When he returns to his plate, I wait until he cuts a piece of steak from his and takes a bite, wanting to make sure I do it properly. He reaches over, snatches my napkin from the table, and places it on my lap. Then, grabs a fork holding it out to me.

"Nobody cares about your McDonald's manners," he says, waiting for me to take the fork.

Normally, his comment would have probably bothered me, but the wine is already making me feel a bit hazy, causing me to shrug off his words and reach for the fork. However, he grips it tightly, and I can feel the warmth of his hand beneath mine. I must have looked entranced staring at our hands together because he releases the fork and begins eating again.

Let me tell you, this meal is the most delicious food I've ever tasted in my entire life. I could die a happy woman right now. I enjoy my food in peace while the men joke around about lighthearted topics, though I don't find anything they are saying amusing. I notice Beckett never joins in on the laughter either. The bottle of wine is emptied, and the men get louder and more boisterous as they become more intoxicated.

Once dinner is over and the meeting wraps up, handshakes are exchanged. I have no idea what this little gathering was about, but it seems to have gone well since everyone appears satisfied as they linger.

Not wanting to be that person who leaves nail clippings on the floor, I bend down and start picking the little pieces from the carpet when Beckett grabs my arm and pulls me back up, discreetly saying, "Drop them." In which I immediately do.

As one of the hostesses brings me my coat, Beckett takes it from her and holds it open for me. I slip my arms in, and he zips it up. Then, he takes my scarf and wraps it around my neck, tucking the loose ends in.

"Why do you treat me like a child?" I scold, swatting his hand away.

"I have never been around children, so I wouldn't know how to treat someone like a child," he says, slipping on his own coat and grabbing his umbrella.

He heads towards the exit, and I follow closely behind. My car is already parked right in front, and I wonder how they knew when to bring it up.

The door is held open for us by the restaurant's doorman, and I thank him as we pass by. Beckett opens the umbrella as we step out, grabbing my shoulder and pulling me under as he opens the passenger door for me, and I climb in. Then, he hurries around to the driver's side.

My car is already warm, and I melt into the seat with a groan. "This feels amazing," I exclaim, rubbing my hands together and grinning as I place them near the heater.

He watches my movements, staring between me and my hands. "Why do you never wear gloves?" he scolds.

"I don't go hang out in the snow." I position my face near the heater, soaking in as much warmth as possible. "Why are we not driving?" I ask, leaning back and staring at him coming toward me, my heart thrumming as he inches closer. I press deeper into my seat. He reaches around me, grabs my seatbelt, secures it in place, then puts on his own. I stare down at my now-buckled strap, realizing I had completely forgotten I needed to do that. "Can I have my stuff back now?" I extend my hand, waiting for my phone and nail clippers.

He retrieves them and hands them back to me.

"I had a hang nail." I hold up my ring finger so he can see what I was clipping during his meeting.

He looks at it, then takes the clippers from me, gently holding my finger. I watch as he carefully cleans up the nail I hadn't finished trimming. He flicks the nail clippings out the window and places the clippers into my cup holder.

I stare down at my perfectly trimmed nail and smile. "Thank you. Can you do the rest of them? I have a cuticle trimmer too." I grab my bag, rummaging around inside to find it.

"Later," he replies, shifting the car into drive.

As we pull out of the parking lot, I start to relax. I remind myself to put my clippers back in their pouch, but that can wait. I unlock my phone to enter my home address, but it slips from my hand and clatters to the floor. Letting out a giggle, I lean forward to pick it up and give it another try. Beckett takes my phone and places it in the other cup holder.

"You don't even know where you're going," I slur, stumbling over my words, then stop to stare at him and burst into laughter. The way my mouth betrayed me makes it even funnier—I don't feel as drunk as I just sounded. That was ridiculous.

As snow continues to fall in heavy, relentless sheets, Beckett grips the wheel, eyes fixed on the treacherous road ahead. His focus is unshakable, and the silence in the car grows.

In the mere two hours we spent at the restaurant, a fresh blanket of at least three inches has layered itself over the already slick streets, compounding the mess I drove through hours ago.

On the way there, I had focused intently on keeping my tires in the tracks left by earlier drivers, fighting to stay in the grooves without swerving out of control. Now, the tire marks are deeper, carved into the snow like trenches, and my car's undercarriage drags against the heavy powder. I keep expecting us to get stuck, yet Beckett steers us through the mess with great precision. Even the thought of turning on music feels risky, like any disruption could break his concentration.

About twenty minutes into our drive from the restaurant, flashing blue lights pierce through the swirling snowflakes. They flicker ominously in the distance, growing brighter as we approach. I glance over at Beckett, but he remains calm, his eyes narrowing as we near the police car stationed directly in the road.

My car gradually slows to a halt, the tires slightly skidding on the snow-covered road before settling. Beckett rolls down the window, letting in a gust of cold air, as the officer approaches. "There's a wreck a mile or so up the road. It's not lookin' good," the officer informs us. "The snow is piling up quickly, and the snow plows won't be able to clear it."

Beckett rubs his jaw, contemplating our options. "How long do you think the road will be closed?" he asks.

"At least four hours, maybe longer. I suggest turning around and finding a room at the hotel back the way you came," the officer suggests.

Beckett looks ahead, weighing our options. "Thanks," he replies, and the officer nods as Beckett rolls up the window.

"Do you think someone died?" I glance past the lights.

"I don't know," he responds as he slowly starts to turn the car to head back the direction we were just coming from.

Through the silence comes shouting outside the car from the officer. "Slow down! Slow down!" he says, waving his hands in the air.

Turning to look in the same direction as the officer, I look at Beckett's window and shriek, "Beckett!" as blinding headlights careen toward us. The car slams into the back side of mine, sending both vehicles into a tailspin right off the road into the snowbank.

The car has stopped moving, and I sit in stunned silence, my heart racing, as the remnants of the collision fog my mind. The world outside feels unreal, blurred by shock, while I stare down at my lap. My breath comes in shallow gasps, and I barely register the officer's distant voice talking into his walkie-talkie. It sounds muffled, then a sharp knock at my window jolts me from my stupor. I peer up, blinking as a flashlight beam pierces through the darkness, illuminating the interior of the car. The officer's silhouette is framed by the swirling snow, his face obscured, but he tugs at the handle, trying to open the door.

"Are you both okay?" he asks, attempting to open the locked door again.

I stare straight ahead in shock, then shake my head to snap myself out of the daze I'm in. "I'm fine," I call out, my voice sounding foreign to my own ears. I turn to Beckett, his face tense with fury as he rams his shoulder into the door, trying to force it open, but it's jammed against the other car.

"We're fine. Go check on the other driver," I urge the officer. He hesitates, his eyes flicking between us before heading toward the other vehicle.

"Beckett, talk to me," I say softly, reaching for his face and gently turning it toward mine. His gaze softens when our eyes meet, the anger slowly melting away. "Tell me you're okay," I speak softly, needing the confirmation.

After a beat, he lets out a long breath. "I'm okay."

"Good. Because I need to pee really bad," I tell him, hoping he has some sort of convenient solution for me. He scans the surroundings, then stops on the treeline up ahead. I follow his gaze and immediately shake my head. "No. Absolutely not."

"There are no other options that I can see," he says. "Unless you can hold it for a bit longer."

"There are monsters in there," I protest, staring at the dark expanse of woods.

"It's either that, or you'll have to wait," he says with finality.

With a sigh of resignation, I push open my door, grumbling. As I step out into the cold air, two more officers approach.

"You all alright?" one of them calls out.

"We're fine, but she needs to use the bathroom," Beckett says, hopping out of my side of the car and grabbing his umbrella. "I'm going to have to take her out there," he calls to them.

"Are either of you injured? Did you hit your head? Any broken bones or bleeding?" the officer asks.

"We're fine. I really need to pee," I say, doing the pee dance.

When we are far enough away that nobody will see me, I start undoing my pants. "You don't have to stand so close," I mutter, trying to get him to move away.

"I'm not going anywhere. It's dark, and we don't know what's out there," he tips his chin to the woods behind me.

"There are monsters, huh!" I groan.

Beckett stands above me, holding the umbrella like some disgruntled guardian. "It's freezing. Pee already."

"I don't know what's worse—us being stuck out here, my car getting hit, or peeing in front of you," I mumble as I squat.

After I finish, I stay squatting long enough that he comments, "Isn't your butt cold?"

"Yep."

"Then what are you doing?"

"I was trying to figure out what I was going to wipe with, but there isn't anything out here, so I was trying to drip dry."

With an exasperated sigh, he pulls a neatly folded pocket square from his shirt and hands it to me.

"Fuck no," I protest.

"Do you want wet panties?"

"Don't ever use that word around me again." I snatch it from his hand, grumbling under my breath. "Did you sweat on this?" My teeth begin to chatter as I put all of my pride in the metaphorical toilet and flush it.

"Maybe," he shrugs.

I stand, yanking my pants back up, pinching the edge of the now-defiled pocket square between two fingers. "How much did this cost?" I ask, though I'm already planning its burial in the snow.

"Doesn't matter," he replies, taking it back without a second thought and stuffing it into his coat pocket.

"Beckett," I glance at the spot where I'd rather leave it behind. "I'm going to bury it in the snow."

He reaches for me, grabbing my arm and guiding me back toward the car. As we crest the snowbank, I notice the man who hit us, now in handcuffs, being searched by an officer.

The original officer approaches us, shaking his head in disbelief. "He's drunk. Blew three times over the legal limit." He gestures toward the snowmobile parked nearby. "My buddy's here to drive you both back to the hotel. Grab what you need from the car. We'll have to tow it, and I'll contact you with the location."

Beckett pulls out his wallet, retrieving a sleek business card, handing it over to the officer. "Call me, please."

The officer takes the card with a nod of understanding. "Yes, Mr. Shaw. We'll be in touch," he responds, slipping the card into his coat pocket.

I turn back to the car, but there's not much to gather. An empty backpack has been sitting in the backseat for who knows how long—I'm honestly surprised no one's stolen it yet. I grab my purse and Beckett's folder of documents, shove them into the bag, zip it up, and sling it over my shoulder.

He takes his peacoat that I had in the back seat and holds it open, a silent offer I don't even think to refuse. I'm so cold that this extra layer instantly feels slightly better. He takes the backpack from me without a word. Handing my keys to the officer, I give my car a farewell look then head toward the man waiting on the snowmobile.

"Hop on," he calls over the humming engine.

Beckett mounts the snowmobile, slinging my backpack over his shoulder before scooting back to make room for me. As I step forward, he taps my right leg, signaling for me to swing it over first.

"What?" I ask, momentarily confused. The way he's motioning would have me literally sitting backward.

He opens his coat and gestures again, this time more clearly. He wants me to sit with my legs across his lap, cocooned inside his coat. I step over, settling myself on the seat as he pulls my legs up on his lap, pressing me snuggly against his body. The peacoat wraps around us both like a blanket, sealing us together against the wind.

"Y'all ready?" the man calls.

"All good, boss," Beckett answers, his grip firm around me as we take off. The snowmobile lurches forward, and I cling to him, my fingers digging into his sides as I watch the officers lead the drunk driver toward the patrol car. The flashing lights shrink into the distance, eventually swallowed by the falling snow.

The cold is relentless, each gust of wind piercing through all the layers of clothing. I bury my face into Beckett's neck to keep warm as I cling to him. His face presses back into mine, our skin freezing against each other as we ride through the dark.

Minutes drag on, everything around us a blur of snow and ice, until finally, the faint glow of lights catches my attention. I glance over my shoulder and spot the hotel emerging into view. The parking lot is packed, cars filling every available space. I wonder how many people are stranded here, just like us, caught by the road closure with nowhere else to go.

"Oh, thank God," I murmur, my words barely audible through the chattering of my teeth. The sight of steam rising from the hotel sends a wave of relief washing over me that we will be warm soon.

The snowmobile grinds to a halt in front of the hotel, and the driver turns toward us.

"Thank you so much. You're a life saver," I say, climbing off with stiff legs, followed closely by Beckett. The wind is picking up, and the snow falls in thick, relentless flakes.

"Thank you," Beckett says with gratitude as he pulls me toward the glowing entrance of the building.

The moment we step inside, the warmth instantly embraces my freezing body.

"I'm sorry, we're fully booked," the woman behind the front desk says apologetically as we stomp our boots on the rug.

My heart sinks, the flicker of relief I'd just found fading away as fast as it came.

CHAPTER
Five

Beckett brushes off the snow clinging to his coat as he looks up at her, and suddenly, a spark of recognition ignites her expression. She starts typing furiously on her computer. "Actually, it seems like we have one room left," she corrects herself.

He strides confidently through the lobby, extending his hand toward her. She places a room key card in his palm, her face flushed with apology.

Ignoring her, he glances at me, signaling me to follow, and I comply without uttering a word.

We step into the elevator and ascend to the fifth floor. Exiting the elevator, I trail behind him as he leads us to our room. I wonder why hotels do that; they pretend they're fully booked when they still have rooms available. Tonight is kind of an emergency-type situation, and they were literally going to turn us away.

He holds the card against the door lock, and with a satisfying click, the light turns green, indicating it has successfully unlocked. He pulls the handle down, forcefully swinging the door open, and enters first, holding it open behind him for me to follow.

Flicking on a light, he strides into the room, briefly scanning the surroundings, then heads toward the bathroom to repeat the process.

"What are you looking for?" I ask, watching as he peers into the closet next.

"Making sure nobody is in here," he replies, his tone implying that the answer should be obvious.

"Why would somebody be in here? We just got here."

"You're scared of monsters in the woods, but not of someone hiding in a closet of a hotel room out in the country?" He mocks.

He has a point. Deciding to drop it, I walk into the room. My eyes land on the two queen-sized beds, and a wave of relief washes over me. I venture in further, passing him as he removes his coat and casually tosses it onto the bed closest to the door. Taking it as a sign that he's claimed that bed, I make my way to the table by the window. Unzipping my jacket, I drape it over the chair before settling onto my bed and removing my boots.

He walks over to the thermostat positioned beside the window, and I observe him as he adjusts the dial. The heater rumbles to life, and he turns his attention outside, shoving his hands into his pockets as he stares at the snow still falling beyond the glass.

Despite knowing that hotels can be dirty, my feet were sweaty during dinner and now freezing, and damp from the snow. At this point, the questionable cleanliness of the hotel floor doesn't bother me in the slightest.

Climbing onto the bed, I untuck the blankets and snuggle beneath them. There's no way I'm sleeping in my wet pants. Once I'm certain I'm fully covered, I swiftly unbutton my jeans, wiggling and pulling to free myself from the damp fabric.

As I struggle, he turns and watches me, raising a brow in my direction.

"What? I'm not sleeping in wet jeans," I assert defensively, feeling like he somehow thinks I'm being weird. I'm already tipsy, cold, tired, in a hotel with a stranger, and just want to sleep comfortably.

He pulls his hands from his pockets and retrieves the TV remote from the dresser positioned directly in front of my bed. He sits in the same spot I was just in and leans forward to untie his shoes. The screen flickers to life, illuminating the room as he kicks off his damp shoes beside mine. I can only imagine how soaked they are. I was wearing snow boots, yet snow still managed to seep in, and he's dressed in nice pants and polished shoes.

He starts flipping through channels until he settles on a movie I've never seen. I prop myself up on two pillows, trying to piece together what's even happening in the film. My body begins to relax under the bedding, but I don't dare move because I know every spot in this bed, other than where every inch of me sits, will be as cold as ice. My eyes remain locked on the TV until he rises to his feet, and my gaze drifts to him as he removes his tie… then his shirt.

I pretend not to notice, even though I'm desperately in need of water as the room just became as hot as a sauna. He's toned, with a half sleeve of intricate tattoos on one arm, from his elbow up, and an entire sleeve of tattoos on the other. I definitely didn't see that coming. He looks like he would have never stepped foot in a tattoo shop, yet he's clearly spent a lot of time in them. I watch his tattooed back muscles flex as he begins unfastening his belt and then his pants, and I stare, unable to look away as he pulls his pants down over his thick, muscular thighs and drapes them over the chair where his coat and shirt are.

Don't look, don't you dare look. When this man turns, my eyes immediately go to his boxer briefs. *Crap!* I looked. And damn, it's good. I watch *it* all the way around the bed, not even realizing I'm still staring until he's untucking the bedding on the other side of *my* bed.

"What do you think you're doing?" I snap, tugging at the edge of the blanket to cover my lower half, not wanting him to see my underwear. He doesn't even acknowledge my question. He jerks the bedding up from my grasp, revealing my legs, and settles in without sparing me a single glance. Instead, he fluffs the pillows behind him then pulls the blankets up. Apparently, my legs didn't render him with a dry mouth the way his entire body did to me.

Since I planned on being in this bed alone, I didn't think I needed to be on my own side. I made myself comfortable right smack dab in the middle of the mattress and he, too, decided that's where he wanted to be. I narrow my eyes at him, half in disbelief and half in annoyance. "You really are something else, Beckett."

He shifts, muscles rippling under his skin as he leans over to flick off the lamp. The room plunges into a muted darkness, the TV casting soft shadows while snow flurries outside the window. I wait for him to say something, anything, but he doesn't. His silence irritates me. He's always shrugging off everything I say, like my words don't register. This has to be so unbearable for him—being stuck here with me.

He grabs one of the pillows behind him and throws it to the couch across the room, then lies down on his side, facing me. His arm slides beneath the remaining pillow, while his forearm and hand settle on mine. He exhales deeply, closing his eyes as his chest rises and falls in a slow, steady rhythm.

I meant to cast a fleeting look at him in disbelief at how brazen it was of him to get into my bed, but now I can't seem to pull my gaze away. He's incredibly handsome—so handsome my stomach starts to feel funny as I stare at him. Yet, that funny feeling goes right between my legs.

I once read that gray eyes are the rarest, and it makes perfect sense that he would have them. He seems to have everything going for him. Add those exotic eyes to the mix—so striking, they seem almost otherworldly. I can imagine women falling at his feet, drawn in by that hypnotic gaze.

"Do you need something?"

My eyes widen briefly. I didn't realize he could sense me staring at him. "I need you to scoot over," I snap, irritation lacing my voice to mask the embarrassment creeping in.

With his eyes still closed, he scoots *closer* to me.

Turning my face back towards the TV, I ignore him and try to act like I wasn't just practically caught being a creep. I hear him let out a breathy laugh, sending a flush of heat through my cheeks. I don't dare look his way again. He knows—somehow, he knows exactly what I was doing, and the thought makes my skin prickle.

So far, what I've gathered from the movie is that the main girl is hiding from kidnappers, and some guy she doesn't know is trying to protect her. I only seem to pay attention when something startles me, and my brain is back on the movie.

There is no way I'm going to be able to fall asleep tonight, especially with him in my bed. Glancing across him at the nightstand, I see the remote. "Hey, give me the remote." But he doesn't move. "Beckett," I poke his chest—his glorious, firm, soft chest—but he remains still. I really don't want to sit here watching this. Gently peeling the covers off of me, I go to swing my feet out of the bed, and a large, muscular arm wraps across my waist.

"No," he growls.

When I still under his arm, I look over at him, expecting him to be watching me, but his eyes remain shut, serene and unreadable. I let out a frustrated sigh. "Then give me the remote. You put on a scary movie, and it's doing its job because I'm scared."

When he makes no attempt to help, I shove his arm off of me and lean over him to grab the remote. My bare legs pass over his torso, and I almost think I feel his breathing hitch but, he gives no indication this has affected him. I stretch further, fingertips just inches from the remote. Almost there. I'm just about to snatch it, and it scoots away from my grasp.

Cursing under my breath, I lean in harder, my body pressing into his as I try to make it quick. But in my attempts to be fast, I lose balance and go tumbling forward, my body folding over his. Before I can brace for impact, his hand clamps down firmly on my butt and thighs, halting my fall with a solid grip.

I dangle awkwardly over him, my hair brushing the floor as I stare at the carpet inches below, suddenly aware of just how close I came to a broken nose. Heat surges up my neck as I struggle to collect my thoughts. "How about you help me up instead of squeezing my butt cheeks?"

With an effortless move, he shifts, sliding an arm beneath my stomach and barely exerting any energy to lift me back on the bed. Since I don't plan on falling off the bed and he's now lying on his back, staring up at me, I shake my head in disbelief—at my stupidity and his refusal to help me get the remote. I swing my leg over him, balancing on both knees, one hand flattening on his chest as I lean forward to grasp the remote. As I climb off his lap, I glare down at him so he knows I'm not impressed with his antics, but I find myself caught in the intensity of his gaze—deep and smoldering, holding me captive.

I'm off him so fast, grabbing my pillow and moving to my own side of the bed. A rush of heat floods through me, making it feel as if I could go outside and melt every bit of snow. As I start to settle on my new side of the bed, a jump scare on the TV sends me scurrying back to my original spot in the middle, close enough to him our bodies slightly brush against each other. He doesn't move; he doesn't even acknowledge that we barely touch or how electric it feels. He goes right back to pretending he's sleeping.

I put on *The PowerPuff Girls* since I'm scared now from whatever that movie was—in the dark, in a hotel with a stranger that could kill me, and nobody would be the wiser. I didn't even tell Chloe where I was going or with whom. So this is wonderful. At least the cops saw me—and the lady at the front desk. She would know if he checks out and I don't check out with him. Would she even notice? She seemed flustered by him as soon as she saw him. Everyone seems to have that reaction when he's around, which is so odd since he's so arrogant and rude.

I jump when I hear a loud thump against the wall behind us. When it happens again, only louder, I scoot down lower in the bed, pull the covers over my head, and wrap my arms around Beckett. The panic I feel overshadows the incredible softness of this man's skin, so I pay it no mind. "Do you hear that?" I whisper, feeling terrified, then start chanting, "Any demons around me, I rebuke you in the name of Jesus Christ."

It almost feels like he's laughing. Then, another bang on the wall makes me tighten my grip on him. When I look up, I see he *is* laughing.

"This isn't funny, Beckett. Something is happening—"

The knocking becomes more consistent and louder. "Oh yeah, do you like that, daddy?" a woman's voice rings out. The moans grow louder as the thumping quickens.

Pulling the blanket down, I hang my mouth open, and he laughs harder.

"They're doing it," I mouth to him, pointing at the wall.

"I know." He closes his eyes again.

And just as quickly as it started, it goes quiet once more.

"What's happening now?" I ask after the knocking stops. I find myself staring at the wall, as if focusing hard enough will let me hear more clearly or even see through the drywall to whatever's happening on the other side.

"Hopefully, they're going to do what we're doing and go to bed."

I stare at the wall, mentally counting how long that noise lasted. "That wasn't even ten seconds," I whisper as I lay back down.

"Don't judge," he smirks.

"Ohhhh, you're feeling self-conscious," I tease.

"He lasted at least five seconds longer than I would have."

"You're gross," I mumble as I turn over to face the window. Mimicking his earlier move, I take one of my pillows and toss it to the couch.

I watch *The Powerpuff Girls* for a while longer until sleep envelopes me. At some point during the night, I thought I felt his arms wrap around me. But there's no way that would have happened because, in my slumber, I also thought I laced my fingers in his and he squeezed my hand back in an accepting gesture.

When I turn over hours later, needing to adjust my position, he's sleeping on his stomach with his head facing away. I really must have dreamt the entire thing. I discover the covers are off him and I have almost all of them. I know I'm a blanket hog; that's why I never share a bed with anyone. Adjusting the sheets, I pull them back onto him, my touch lightly grazing his back as I bring them to his shoulders. I feel a little guilty when I feel how cold he is, but I corrected my error and covered him back up. He will never even know I almost froze him to death in the night.

I startle awake when a knock sounds at the door. Groggily, I reach across the bed, tapping the other side. "Go get the door," I mutter, expecting him to respond, but my hand hits nothing but a pillow.

Turning to look, the bed is empty, and I can hear the shower running. Another knock on the door sounds, and I scramble out of bed, hurrying to open the door.

A man stands there with a cart. "Your breakfast," he announces, wheeling the cart inside.

"Did Mr. Shaw order it?" I've stayed in countless hotels in my life, but never once have I experienced breakfast being delivered to my room like this.

"Yes, ma'am," the gentleman says, wheeling the cart toward the bed, then turning to leave.

At that moment, Beckett emerges from the bathroom, steam trailing behind him, wearing only a towel slung low around his waist. His hair is damp, beads of water still clinging to his skin. "One second," he says to the man at the door before turning his attention to me. His gaze trails up my legs to my underwear, and then he orders, "Get back in bed."

I do as he says, moving toward the bed, and he follows closely behind, positioning himself like a shield to block the man's view as I slip under the blankets. Once I'm fully covered, he strides across the room, pulls out his wallet, and hands over a tip. "Thank you," he says with a curt nod, and the man quietly exits.

Beckett moves to the cart and begins setting trays neatly on the untouched bed. I head to the bathroom and cringe when I catch sight of my reflection in the mirror. I look like I've just crawled out of a swamp—my hair's a tangled disaster, and the bags under my eyes could rival a raccoon's. I need a shower something fierce. I have no clean clothes and the thought of putting back on the same dirty clothes makes my skin crawl.

"Come eat," he calls.

Giving myself a final parting 'ugly smile,' I head back to the bedroom. Sliding onto the edge of the bed by the wall, I grab a pillow and place it over my bare legs, trying to somewhat cover myself.

There are two trays on the bed, and he's already eating from the one in front of him—an omelet packed with every ingredient in the hotel kitchen, it appears. I watch in confusion as he cuts off a piece, then douses it with hot sauce and takes a bite. I've never seen someone put hot sauce on their breakfast. I hesitate to lift my own tray, in fear something similar waits beneath, but I'm pleasantly pleased when the smell of bacon greets me. Mine is far more appetizing: a classic breakfast of scrambled eggs, crispy bacon, hash browns, and French toast drizzled with syrup and sprinkled with powdered sugar.

We eat in complete silence, and not once does he look in my direction. I know this because I have been absentmindedly staring at him the entire time. It's unintentional—my gaze lingers even as I scold my eyes to look away, but they don't, as if I have no control over them. I drift down the line of his chest, lingering on the intricate tattoos that snake across his right pec, wrapping around his shoulder and disappearing out of sight behind him. I trace the ridges of his toned abdomen, leading down to where the towel rests low on his hips. I know exactly what lies beneath that towel, and the way he's positioned—one leg bent on the bed, the other still on the floor, leaning slightly to the side as he eats and scrolls through his phone—stirs something in me. A quiet, irrational wish crosses my mind that his towel were just a little smaller—so much smaller that it didn't even fully wrap around him. As soon as I catch where my thoughts have wandered, I shake them away.

"When can we leave?" I ask, taking a bite of bacon.

His eyebrows lift as he inhales deeply, then slowly lets it out as he sets his phone down. Well, this doesn't seem like a happy answer. He looks frustrated.

"The roads are bad," he says flatly, picking up his fork and continuing to eat. "They're advising people not to drive. We're staying put for at least another night."

I'm not staying another night here. I need a real shower, fresh clothes, and, more importantly, I need to put some major distance between Beckett and me. "What if we get an ExpressWay driver? I get a discount. I can probably get someone with a truck."

"We're not leaving," he replies firmly, glancing up at me with a steely gaze. "Did you not hear me? It's not safe."

I bristle at his dismissive tone. "I heard you, but people drive in snow all the time. Especially professionals. I'm sure we can find someone from ExpressWay who can handle it."

"There's a robe hanging in the bathroom. Shower and put it on. They'll be back to get our clothes in ten minutes and will bring them back when they're washed." He effectively ends the previous conversation.

"How long will it take to get our clothes back? I don't want to sit in a robe all day... I'll find someone who will drive in the snow," I add as I take the last bite of my eggs.

"You're impatient. The roads aren't safe. You don't know better than the professionals. Drop it. I'm not going to risk my safety because you're in a hurry to get out of here."

"I have plans tonight," I say dryly.

"Date?" he asks, his tone indifferent as he spears another bite of food.

"Yes, actually," I bite back.

I've been casually seeing Elliot for a couple of months now. We're taking things slow, which I appreciate—our fourth date is supposed to be tonight. We never text or talk on the phone unless he's asking me to dinner, which is fine since neither one of us ever seem to know what to say to the other. On our last date he kissed me for the first time. It was so painfully awkward I chalked it up to nerves, but it made me avoid answering his date invite for a week.

"Well, unfortunately, you won't make it," he says, unbothered.

Rolling my eyes, I stand from the bed, tug my sweatshirt off, toss it at his face, and walk to the bathroom, not even caring if that just made him mad.

Just as he said, there's a white robe hanging neatly on a hook beside the shower. I spot the extra bottles of shampoo and conditioner already neatly inside—the ones he clearly requested. The used ones are already discarded in the trash. Hotel shampoos always make my hair feel like brittle straw, and I know even after my shower, I won't feel the least bit refreshed, but I'm thankful to have this shower as an option.

Grabbing a small hand towel, I scrub my body with unnecessary force, venting my pent-up frustration into the act. The door eases open, and I glance over to see Beckett shielding his eyes with one hand, as if he's doing me some grand courtesy. He snatches up my discarded clothes and exits just as quickly, muttering something to someone at the door. It sounds like he's speaking to whoever's come to collect our laundry, but I can't quite make it out over the sound of the water in this tiny shower.

After my shower, I pat myself dry, twisting the towel around my hair and wrapping the soft robe snugly around my body. As I reach for the bathroom door, a wave of discomfort hits me—the awareness that I'm going to be stepping out wearing nothing underneath feels… too intimate. I pause, thinking of the endless possibilities of ways I can embarrass myself in just a robe. Maybe I should forewarn him and tell him from this point on, he should ignore anything I do to prevent us both from dying of embarrassment.

Stepping out of the bathroom, I freeze momentarily. Beckett is lounging on the bed, also dressed in a robe. One of his legs is stretched out lazily across the mattress while the other is planted on the floor off the side as he casually scrolls through TV channels.

The room feels noticeably tidier—the plates and leftovers from breakfast have been cleared away, and I spot a charger plugged into the outlet, that he's clearly borrowed from someone in the hotel. I walk over and tap the screen of his phone, checking how much battery he has. I see 58% blinking back at me. My own phone had died at some point during the night, so I rifle through my purse for it, then unplug his phone and connect mine instead.

This gets his attention.

"My phone wasn't done charging," he says, his voice tinged with mild annoyance.

"Well, mine's dead," I reply, pulling back the covers on the other bed and climbing in. "I have a date tonight, and I need to let him know I'm stuck here."

He continues scrolling through channels until he lands on a history channel. We settle into silence and watch three episodes. I hadn't thought I was tired until I wake up, groggy and disoriented. Glancing down, my robe has completely fallen open, exposing my chest. Relief floods me when I see Beckett isn't in the room.

I quickly pull the robe back around myself as I sit up. My clothes are neatly folded and placed on the dresser in front of this bed. Standing, I let the robe fall to the floor and slip into my underwear just as the door opens and Beckett walks in.

"I'm not dressed," I shout as he looks at me.

"Think I've never seen boobs before?" he quips, strolling across the room.

Scoffing, I hurry to pull on my tank top, then grab my sweatshirt, yanking it over my head. When I pull it down, I look over and see Beckett sitting at the table with his arm resting casually on the surface, his chin propped on a fist, watching me.

"What?" I snap, irritated that he's staring.

"Just waiting for you to get dressed," he replies.

"For what?"

"We don't need to sit in the room all day. There are a couple of shops on the main floor," he says, tapping his thumb rhythmically against his knee.

I tug my pants up and fasten them quickly, then settle onto the edge of the bed to pull on my socks. Beckett strolls over and sits on the opposite bed from me. As I put on my last sock, he reaches over, grabs my foot, and puts my boot on.

"What are you doing?" I ask, wondering why he's putting my boots on.

"You ask rhetorical questions a lot. I'm obviously putting on your boots," he replies, deftly tying the shoelaces.

"Okay, *why* are you putting my boots on?"

He releases my foot and then takes hold of the other one, repeating the action.

"Because you're moving at a snail's pace. You're welcome," he states dryly as he sets my foot down and strides to the door. He swings it open and waits for me. "Let's go."

I make my way to the table, retrieving my purse, then head toward the door where he waits.

"You won't need that," he says, irritation seeping into his tone as he shifts his weight from one foot to the other, as if I'm taking too long.

"I might want to buy something." I hurry toward the door he's holding open for me.

CHAPTER Six

As we make our way down the hall, the soft murmur of voices grows louder, and we approach the elevators where three girls are already waiting. Their eyes land on Beckett, and a silent exchange passes between them—quick glances, followed by smiles that spread across their faces like they're completely enamored by him. I wonder how often he deals with this kind of attention. It must get old fast. Then again, he's either oblivious or simply used to it, because he doesn't even acknowledge them.

When the elevator finally arrives with a soft chime, the doors slide open to reveal two more girls inside. They light up the same way—staring at Beckett, then giving each other subtle looks of awe.

We step into the elevator, and Beckett moves wordlessly to the far right, leaning against the wall. I stand near the doors, acutely aware of the lingering stares from our fellow passengers. The elevator hums as we descend, and just as I think we might get through the ride in relative peace, the doors open again on the third floor. A couple steps inside, breaking the spell of silent admiration.

The man surveys the elevator's occupants, and then lastly, his gaze falls on Beckett. "These all yours?" he jokes with a wink.

Beckett smirks, his hand reaching out to grab the back of my sweatshirt. "Just this one," he says, pulling me back toward him to make room for the couple to step inside.

He nearly pulls me entirely flush against him, his hand still gripping my sweatshirt and resting on my hips. I can feel the tension in the cramped elevator as the five other women inside continue to stare between us.

When the doors open, the couple leaves, and I start to follow, but Beckett grips my sweatshirt more firmly, gesturing for the others to exit before us. Each of the women file out, one by one, offering him flirtatious looks as they go.

"Can we go now, *dad?*" I ask, raising an eyebrow at him as I wait for his permission to leave.

I get my answer when he presses on my back, nudging me forward, signaling for me to start walking. He leads me toward the convenient store on the main floor, his hand falling from my sweatshirt as we step inside.

As we wander through the aisles, I stumble upon two novelty shirts that fill me with instant delight. One reads, "I'm with stupid," while the other says, "I am stupid." Without hesitation, I find a medium in the "I'm with stupid" shirt and an extra-large in the "I am stupid" one, already imagining the two of us lounging in them. I toss them into the basket, smirking at the thought of Beckett wearing his.

In the far corner of the store, I discover a display of trinkets and keepsakes. Each shelf is brimming with random items. My attention is drawn to a large bowl filled with polished rocks in an array of vibrant colors. I pick up a bright green stone, running my fingers over its cool, smooth surface. It's oddly soothing, but I place it back down and turn toward a small rack of handmade jewelry. The pieces—earrings, rings, and a few necklaces—are unique, delicate, and clearly crafted with care.

I spot a rack of keychains and start reading through the various messages on them—some funny, some sentimental, some with your average run-of-the-mill names. Next to the rack is a display of postcards and souvenir spoons. I thumb through a few, thinking how they would make a really neat keepsake of this unexpected stop, but decide against getting one. I make my way toward the counter, gathering my chosen items: the T-shirts, a bottle of water, a bag of chips, and Skittles. The cashier rings everything up then proceeds to place them into a plastic bag. As I set my purse on the counter to grab my wallet, Beckett steps up beside me, casually adding a couple more things, and tells the cashier it's all together.

I fish out my debit card, ready to pay, and stand there expectantly.

"Cash or card?" the cashier ask, glancing between us.

"Card," I respond, holding it up.

"Cash," Beckett corrects, pulling a crisp $100 bill from his wallet and laying it on the counter with a definitive tap.

The cashier takes the money, quickly counts out the change, and hands it to Beckett. I grab the bag of our things, and head toward the exit.

Just outside the entrance, I spot one of those old-fashioned penny-smashing machines—the kind that flattens and imprints a design on your coin for a small price.

"Thank you for paying back there. Can I have fifty-one cents, please?" As I hold out my hand, knowing he has enough change.

He reaches into his pocket then opens his palm, letting me pick out a shiny new penny and two quarters. I feed the coins into the machine, and it whirs to life, rumbling as it presses the penny.

I smile when I pull out my perfectly pressed penny with Santa Clause' face stamped on it, along with "Merry Christmas 2024."

"Want one?" I ask, feeling completely happy with mine.

"You took my last quarters."

I rummage around the clutter at the bottom of my purse, finally finding two quarters covered in crumbs and lint. Brushing them off on my pants, I hand them over to him. "You had another new penny," I say, reaching into his pocket to retrieve the penny. A couple walks by and eyes us warily, like they're convinced I'm giving him a handjob in the hallway. I scoop up the change, pluck the penny out of my hand, drop the rest back in his pocket, and hand it to him. He, too, seems unfazed I was digging around in his pants, and I wonder why that couple just dogged us.

He chooses the Mrs. Clause design that reads "Merry Christmas 2024," and we wait for it to drop. When it finally does, he retrieves it and holds it in his palm.

"Love it," I say peering over his arm, then walk toward the next store.

This shop is a little more family-oriented, filled with books, magazines, board games, and all sorts of things designed to keep people or their kids entertained. As soon as we walk in, I spot the same three girls from the elevator, and they immediately zero in on Beckett. He drifts over to the magazine rack, while I head toward the other side of the store, browsing through the word search books. These were my favorite when I was younger, and I figure it'll keep me entertained later tonight.

I flip through the pages to see how many words are on each page, when a voice breaks through the silence. "Is he your boyfriend?"

I look up to see the three girls standing in front of me, the one closest to me being the one who asked the question.

"Is he your boyfriend?" she repeats, only her voice is more insistent this time.

I stifle a chuckle and shake my head. "No, brother."

"Told you." The girl turns to her friends with a triumphant grin. "I told them there was no possible way he'd be with you… no offense." The three of them giggle, their smugness on full display.

I join in, right along with them. "Same to you. He's gay." I let my face fall flat and walk away. The abrupt silence behind me tells me they've, too, stopped giggling.

I keep perusing, but it seems they either didn't believe me or wanted to confirm for themselves as I see they're now over talking to him. He looks annoyed, glancing over at me then turning back to them as he talks. Then he steps around them and begins walking toward me.

I head to the counter, placing my things down as the cashier begins scanning my items. Beckett walks up behind me, close enough that I can feel his body heat, waiting silently as I pay.

As we step out of the store, the girls are still watching us, they're locked onto him like a hawk. Out of nowhere, Beckett gives me a playful slap on the butt, drapes his arm over my shoulder, and presses a kiss to the top of my head, all while locking eyes with them.

"Gay brother?" he whispers sarcastically in my ear.

I grab his hand and shove it off my shoulder. "You could have told them I was a liar if you were interested in them."

He leans in and says, "I told them I'm definitely not your brother… and your favorite position is anal."

"You did not!" I stop in my tracks, staring at him in disbelief.

"Is that worse than what you told them?"

"Yes!" I shoot back, feeling my face heat.

He shrugs casually, continuing without missing a beat. "Well, I'm not your brother, I'm not gay, and you clearly don't like anal. So, we've just spun a bunch of lies to people we'll never see again," he says as he starts walking again, leaving me a few steps behind.

"Whatever," I mutter, making no effort to catch up.

"You do like it in the butt?" He quits walking and waits for me to catch up.

"No!" I practically shout. "I'm NOT having this conversation with you!" I retort, feeling my face grow even hotter.

He just grins wide as we continue walking. "You're more of a missionary-style-with-the-lights-off kind of girl? Sweatshirt zipped up with your pantaloons still on and pulled to the side?"

"Pantaloons?" I gape at him, unbelieving he went from using the word *panties* to *pantaloons*. "You're like a bend-over-and-take-dicks-in-your-ass kind of guy. With the lights on so they can really see your butthole stretched wide open?" I snap, making sure he knows I'm irritated.

He lets out a laugh. "Why do you get so embarrassed talking about sex?"

"Why are you trying to talk about sex with me?" I fire back.

"Because your cheeks get so pink when I say the word 'sex.'"

I roll my eyes, desperate for a change in topic. "Did that McDonald's ever make you have diarrhea?"

"It didn't. Thank you for being concerned about my bowel movements," he says, completely unfazed. "Did you get diarrhea from yours?"

"Yes," I reply sarcastically. "Would you like me to tell you all about the consistency of it?"

"If you'd like."

I groan in exasperation. "Okay, no more talking." I pick up my pace, trying to get some distance between us, but it doesn't take him long to catch up, matching my stride.

We walk in silence until we come to a set of double doors glowing with neon lights. I stop and peer in—it's an arcade. I head straight for the token machine, pulling out a crumpled $20 bill, smoothing it between my fingers and feeding it into the slot. On top of the machine is a stack of paper cups, and I grab one, watching as the tokens spill out into the metal tray. I drop them into the paper cup, and give it a little shake, enjoying the satisfying rattle of coins.

My gaze sweeps across the room until I spot the skee-ball machine. "Come on, I'm about to kick your ass and send you crying to your mommy," I say as I walk over to the four games lined up. He laughs and follows me, taking the lane next to mine. I put the cup of coins between our games, take out four tokens, hand him two, and put two in mine.

"Ladies first," he gestures for me to go.

I grab the first ball and land it perfectly in the 50-point ring. He raises his eyebrows, appearing impressed. He takes his first ball, sending it straight into the 100-point ring.

My mouth immediately falls open. "The fuck?"

We go back and forth, laughing each time one of us misses the target or scores big. When we run out of balls and the game ends, Beckett glances at the scoreboard, then back at me, grabbing the cup of tokens and walking past me. "I'll pretend I didn't just completely wipe the floor with you."

I catch up to him and impishly shove his shoulder. "Whatever. You were practically dropping the ball directly in the hole."

"Don't be a poor sport."

When we approach a racing game, I sit in the red car while Beckett takes the black one. "Okay, this is a sure win for me," I say confidently.

"I'll bet it is, Lightning McQueen."

As the countdown begins, I lean forward, gripping the steering wheel, revving my engine as I grin at him. The race starts, and we both take off, weaving through the virtual streets. I bite my lip as I easily maneuver the roads and obstacles in the way. The race isn't even close, and I pump my fists in silent victory as I win first place. I swing my legs over the side of the seat toward his car. He's leaned back in his seat, head resting lazily against the headrest, his car idling in dead last. He didn't even try from the looks of it. His gaze is fixed on me, not the game, a slow, amused smile playing on his lips.

"Don't try to play this off like you let me win," I say as I stand and grab the cup.

"I wouldn't dare."

We stop at an air hockey table next, each of us picking up our paddles as he puts the puck down. "I'm going to beat you," he shrugs confidently.

"You can try," I shrug back.

We go back and forth, hitting the puck across the table and blocking each other from scoring. At first, we were both doing really good, blocking every shot, but then, with a snap of his wrist, Beckett pretends to shoot the puck to the left, stops the puck from moving by placing his paddle on top of it, and slaps it right into the goal, scoring the first point.

"Zip it," I say before he has time to gloat.

We go back and forth, with him scoring four times and me only once. "Well, I officially hate this game," I tease as I put the paddle down.

We wander around, looking at the other games, when I spot a claw machine with an Ursula plushie. "I practically *need* her," I point.

"Of course you want the one that's under a pile of other stuffed animals." He feeds a token into the slot, and the claw whirs to life. Positioning the claw over the plushie, I watch him with bated breath, silently willing it to cooperate.

As it descends, grasping at the plushie, Ursula slips out of its grip and drops back into the pile of toys. He tries over and over again, with no luck.

"These things are rigged. It's okay, let's go," I say, grabbing his arm.

"Absolutely not. You want her, we're leaving with her," he insists, placing another token in the machine. Five tokens later, we're both watching as the claw carries Ursula across the large glass case. I gasp when she slips, but the claw hangs on, not letting her fall until she's fully over the chute.

Beckett reaches down, pulls her out, glances at her, then tucks her under his arm as he turns to walk away.

I grab the cup with two tokens left and chase after him. "Hey, she's mine!" I reach out, but he lifts the toy higher, keeping it out of reach. "Give her to me!" I jump as he moves it from one hand to the other, teasing me and preventing me from grabbing it. Finally, he lowers his arm, letting me take her. Once she's in my hands, I give it a big squeeze and smile up at him. "Thank you."

"You're welcome."

We continue walking around the games until he stops at a motorcycle—or rather, a crotch rocket. He dumps the last two tokens in his hand and sits on the bike. Even though this is just a game, he looks sexy.

"Come here." He holds his hand out to me. I'm not sure what he's going to do, but I still step forward. He scoots back on the seat and taps it, signaling for me to get on in front of him.

"So you *do* trust my driving." I swing my leg over the bike and climb on. He scoots into me, our bodies flush against each other, then wraps his arms around my waist, resting his chin on my shoulder.

"Sure—I trust your driving," he teases. "Ready?" His breath fans across my neck.

"Ready," I reply, acutely aware of his arms wrapped around me, sending a warmth directly to my core.

Concentrate. Just concentrate, or you'll end up sliding right off this bike, you slimy snail.

The game starts, and the virtual engines roar to life. I twist the throttle, smiling as the bike lurches forward on the screen. He leans with me as I navigate the winding roads, his arms securely around me, helping guide my movements.

"You're a natural," he compliments, and I grin, weaving in and out of the other bikes. The bike tilts side to side, responding to our every move. As I see the finish line ahead, I don't want it to end.

When I cross the finish line, I turn to look at him and shrug like it's no big deal that I got first place again while driving. He looks amused as he gets off the bike, waiting for me to grab Ursula so we can head out.

"Hungry?" he asks as my eyes adjust to the light in the hall.

"I could eat," I say as we walk past the first restaurant.

"Looks like this place has burgers. This good?"

"Sure," I reply, following him inside.

There's a sign that says, **"Please wait to be seated,"** so we stop there. The hostess hurries over after seating a couple before us. She greets us, then leads us to our booth. As I sit, he slides in beside me on the same side.

"Yuck. I hate when people do this—sit on the same side of the booth and leave the other side empty. Get on your own side," I tell him.

"You took the side I wanted."

"Let me guess, so you can survey the surroundings to make sure there is no danger."

"Maybe," he muses.

"Well, get out, and I will sit on that side." I push his arm.

Before he can respond, the waitress appears beside the table, notepad in hand. "Are you two ready?"

"Yeah," Beckett answers smoothly. "We'll have two number 4's, one without pickles, fries for both, and two cokes."

"Coming right up," she says, jotting it down and disappearing toward the kitchen.

"Move so I can get on that side," I tell him once she's fully out of earshot.

"I can't. Once they take our order, you can't change spots. It confuses them when they bring out the food."

I roll my eyes. "Oh yeah, it will be *so* difficult for her to figure out that one of the two people at the table moved to the other side."

He playfully lifts his hands. "I don't make the rules."

A few moments later, she returns with our drinks, placing them carefully in front of us. As she starts to walk away, I quickly call out, "Oh, sorry—could I get a straw, please?"

"I'll take one too," Beckett chimes in.

She pulls two straws from her apron and sets them on the table. I unwrap mine, take a sip from my coke, and the next thing I know, something light taps the side of my head. I turn, and there's Beckett, straw to his lips, grinning like a kid.

"I didn't think that would work so well!" He looks far too pleased with himself as he picks up the straw wrapper from where it landed on the bench. "I've always wanted to do that."

I narrow my eyes. "You know how in movies, the girl splashes her drink in the guy's face? I've always wanted to try that."

"I'd prefer you not."

"You know what, you don't deserve a straw," I declare with mock seriousness, reaching over and plucking his straw right out of his cup. Before he can react, I dunk it into my drink, sipping from both straws at once and shooting him a smug side-eye.

He reaches over, trying to pull my cup to him, and I laugh as I hang on, keeping my mouth on the straws. "Give me some of that," he says, leaning in to try and take one of the straws from me.

"No, you don't get a straw now," I say, holding onto them with my teeth.

"Hamburger with no pickles," the waitress cuts in, and we both sit up and turn toward her. I awkwardly raise my hand to her so she knows it's mine.

She sets Beckett's food down in front of him, then walks away. We fall into silence as we start to eat, the earlier banter forgotten. He reaches over, pulls my cup between our plates, and takes a sip from one of my straws. As the drink gets lower, he picks up his own and dumps it into my glass.

Both of our attentions are drawn to a table next to ours, where an older gentleman with a large round belly is sitting with a young woman in a tiny dress so snug it looks like it's a second skin. Her high-pitched giggle fills the area, and then she coos, "You're so funny, daddy," batting her lashes in exaggerated flirtation. The man's face twists into a grin so unsettling that I feel my vagina suck up inside itself and seal shut for the end of time.

Beckett's gaze shifts from them to me with instant recognition. My eyes round in shock, realizing these are the same neighbors whose bed was banging against our shared wall last night—for all of two terrible seconds. Beckett's laughter bubbles up quietly as he takes a long sip from his straw, trying not to choke.

"Oh my gosh," I whisper as I lean into him.

The rest of our meal becomes an exercise in restraint as we try, and fail, to tune out the awkward conversation unfolding beside us. Every topic the man brings up seems to fall flat—his attempts at connecting with her are met with forced smiles or hollow laughter. The massive generation gap is painfully obvious, and it's abundantly clear she's a sugar baby of some sort.

By the time we finish eating and pay the bill, we both can't wait to get out of there. Immediately after the restaurant doors shut behind us, we explode into giggles, echoing through the hall as we walk away.

CHAPTER Seven

When we get back to our room, he empties his pockets and places the contents on the dresser. I set my bags down on the bed, then pull out my penny and walk over to his change, flipping over his Mrs. Claus penny and placing mine on top of her.

"What are you doing?" he asks, leaning over my shoulder and looking down.

"Putting them to bed. They're kissing."

He lets out a soft chuckle, shaking his head. "Wow."

"You're just jealous you didn't think of it first," I reply. "I got us shirts for bed." I proudly produce our new shirts from the bag.

I remove the tags and toss him his, then take off mine, turning around as I begin removing my sweatshirt and tank top to put on my new shirt. He starts laughing when he reads them, but surprisingly, he removes his shirt and puts it on. He stands in the mirror, staring at it, so I walk over and stand next to him.

"They're perfect," I smile.

"You no longer get to call me rude," he laughs as he walks to the bed, removing his pants and climbs into the middle where we slept last night.

I return to the bag and pull out my word search book and pen, placing them on the nightstand between the beds before slipping off my pants and draping them over the back of the chair by the window. I move around the room, retrieving my book and pen again, then turn to pull back the blankets of the other bed. Just as I'm about to settle in, I feel a sudden tug on my shirt. His hand grips a fistful of fabric, and he pulls me back onto the bed, rolling me over top of him to the same spot I slept last night, effortlessly trapping me beside him.

"You bent my book," I say with mock indignation as I notice the slightly creased cover of my word search book.

"I'll buy you a new one," he replies casually, tossing the blankets over my lap.

I smooth out the cover, folding it back and forth in a futile attempt to erase the crease, then flip the book open to the middle. Yes, I'm starting in the middle because it will be easier to hold that way. As I settle in, he turns on the TV, the soft glow from the screen illuminating the room while I begin circling words.

"There's 'countryside,'" he says unexpectedly, his finger gliding across the page. I hadn't even realized he was looking over my shoulder. His voice startles me slightly, but I circle the word and keep searching for the elusive "masterminded."

Before I can focus too long, his head rests on my shoulder. He points to another word, then two more in quick succession.

"How are you finding these so fast?" I ask in disbelief. "I still can't find 'masterminded.'"

He doesn't respond with words—just taps the spot where "masterminded" has been hiding all along. It isn't until I'm no longer focusing on the puzzle that I acknowledge he's laying his head on me. There's a quiet intimacy in the way his touch lingers, and my chest constricts, not with anxiety, but with the strange comfort of wanting him closer. I don't want him to move. His warmth, his scent, the light pressure of his body—it all stirs something in me that makes searching for words feel irrelevant.

I inhale softly, catching the familiar scent of him, and it sends a spark of desire through me, so subtle yet undeniable.

When he points to the last word, I silently circle it, my mind no longer on the puzzle. I flip to a new page, not because I want to keep searching, but because I want to prolong us touching.

"Wanna race?" I ask, turning my head slightly, hoping for any excuse to stay like this a little longer.

"Sure," he says, leaning in just a fraction closer.

"K, I'll take the left page." I balance the book between my knees with the pen in my hand. He reaches over and plucks the pen from me, circling four words in quick succession, then hands it back to me. I barely have time to adjust when he takes it again, circling yet another word.

I'm so excited when I finally spot my first word that I practically rip the pen from his hand and circle it. He reclaims the pen, marking three more on his side. We continue, passing the pen back and forth until he's down to just one word left to find.

When he takes the pen again, I assume he's found his last word, but to my surprise he starts circling words on my page. Before I know it, all my words are found, and I've barely had a chance to find any myself.

"Guess we should find your last word." I flip the book so his side rests in the middle of my lap. He points to the word, sliding along the letters he's clearly known were there all along.

Laughing, I close the book and set it on my nightstand.

He takes this time to toss one of the pillows behind him on the couch, just like he did last night. Then he lies back. Copying him, I take my extra pillow and throw it to the couch as well, then switch off the lamp. The room plunges into darkness, the only remaining light coming from the flicker of the TV screen. He even pulled the curtains closed this time, leaving us in shadows.

I stare at the ceiling, thinking about my car, the drunk driver, being here with Beckett… Beckett. Turning my head toward him, I watch him sleep. He must truly be sleeping because he doesn't comment on me staring. Rolling on my side, our faces are inches apart as I memorize every detail of his features. A part of me wants to reach out and trace the shape of his jaw, to feel the softness of him under my fingertips, but I hold back, not wanting to wake him.

Then, reality crashes back. I never texted Elliot. Dread coils in my stomach as I remember I still need to call him. Reluctantly, I slip out of bed, careful not to disturb Beckett, and grab my phone. The screen lights up, revealing two missed calls, one voicemail, and three new texts.

I glance down at the bed and he's completely out, not stirring at all. Slipping quietly into the bathroom, I click on Elliot's contact and press the call button. He answers on the second ring.

"Brynn?" His voice is thick with concern.

"Hey, Elliot. Sorry about tonight—my phone died, and I just turned it back on." I try keeping my voice low.

"Where are you? I drove by your apartment, and no one was there."

"I got caught in this snowstorm," I explain, leaning against the bathroom counter. "I had to stop at a hotel. I'll head home first thing in the morning, assuming the roads clear up."

"Cool. Wanna grab lunch?"

"Sure," I reply, glancing at the clock. "I'll text you when I know what time I'll be home. It depends on the weather."

"Okay. Sounds good. Sleep well, goodnight." Then the call ends.

I tiptoe back into the room, slipping under the covers next to Beckett, who hasn't moved an inch. As I settle in, I let the steady hum of the TV and the quiet rhythm of his breathing lull me back into the moment.

I pull the covers higher, trying to trap whatever heat I can, but it's futile. The only warmth I feel comes from Beckett in soft waves from his body. I inch my feet toward him, just trying to get warmer, and my cold toes brush against his skin.

"Christ, Brynn!" he shouts from shock.

My mouth falls open, and I prop myself up on one elbow. "You actually know my name?!" I blurt out in surprise. It wasn't until right now that it dawns on me: I've never told him my name, and I have no idea how he even figured it out.

He doesn't answer, just shifts a bit, so I mischievously press my icy toes against his leg again. This time, instead of protesting, he sits up, grabs the collar of his shirt from the back, pulls it off in one swift motion, and tosses it onto the other bed. Then, he rolls over and wraps an arm around me, tugging me toward the middle of the bed, cocooning me in his warmth.

I laugh as he pulls me closer. Determined to get warmer, I press my feet against his legs again. He tightens his hold, resting his head on my chest. One of his knees slides between my thighs, and I press both feet flat against the back of his leg. The warmth rushes through me, and I relax into him, finally feeling some relief from the chill.

I even use his back as my personal heater, switching between my palms and backs of my hands, pressing them into his skin. He just lies there, allowing it.

Eventually, my body warms, and the weight of sleep begins to pull at me. I nestle deeper into him, my muscles unwinding with the newfound comfort. "Thank you," I whisper. "I feel much warmer now." He stays silent, and I peer down to see if he's actually asleep but I can't tell.

"Beckett?" I try to get his attention, but nothing. There's no way he's out that fast.

Despite his solid, muscular frame, I try to scoot down a bit, needing to find a better position. It feels like trying to move a mountain, but after a moment, I feel him shift ever so slightly, just enough for me to adjust. Once I'm settled, he shifts back, resting against my chest again, his leg still nestled between mine, and my arms find their way around his neck.

I wake up feeling so well-rested, I don't even know what dimension I'm in. I blink a couple times, my eyes focusing as I peer around the room. The bed is still warm where Beckett was lying, which means I must've stirred when he got up. I glance at the clock—10:12 in the morning. Already? I sit up slowly, my body protesting as I stretch, trying to shake off the lingering grogginess.

He steps out of the bathroom and sits on the edge of the bed. Picking up the phone from the nightstand, he presses a few buttons and waits. I watch as he orders breakfast, then casually asks about the road conditions. The pause that follows makes my chest tighten—I already know the answer before he thanks the person and hangs up.

"How are the roads?" I ask, my voice still thick with sleep.

Taking his silence as confirmation we might not be able to leave, I push the blankets aside and swing my legs over the edge of the bed. "I'm sure I can find us a ride out of here."

"We can't leave. The roads are red, Brynn. It's not good enough to risk it. We have to stay another night."

I roll my eyes, already halfway across the room. "I can find us a ride," I respond confidently.

His tone shifts, sharp and unyielding. "I said no."

I freeze, turning to face him. His stare is steady, his jaw set. "Why do you not want to get out of here? You're adamant on staying when I know I can find us a ride."

His voice snaps like a whip. "No!" The intensity in his words stops me cold.

"Fine. You can have fun staying; I'm finding myself a ride out of here." I grab my phone and pull up the ExpressWay driver chat.

"You're not leaving." He stands abruptly, his voice carrying a sharp edge of finality.

We stand there, staring each other down. I can feel the tension crackling in the air between us. My pulse quickens, but I let out a long, exaggerated groan instead of pushing further. Throwing myself dramatically onto the bed, I bury my face in the comforter, muffling my frustration.

He lets out a heavy sigh and crosses the room, his footsteps quiet as he approaches, standing over me. "I get it," he says softly, climbing on the bed, straddling my legs, and sitting on my thighs as he starts massaging my back. "But we can't go anywhere right now. It's not safe."

I remain face-down, my body relaxing completely into the bed. His hands start at the base of my spine, firm yet gentle, the warmth of his palms radiating through the fabric of my shirt. He applies just enough pressure to make my body respond, coaxing out the tension that has settled in layers beneath my skin.

His fingers move slowly, skillfully, up the length of my back, working along the muscles. Each stroke feels practiced, like he knows exactly where to press, where to knead, where I'm holding onto stress. I relax into it, feeling the knots untangle beneath his touch.

As he works his way higher, toward my shoulders, his thumbs dig in just the right way, and the pressure is so perfect I almost groan. His fingers are magic—skilled and precise, finding every sore, tense spot with ease.

I groan in protest when a knock on the door announces the arrival of our breakfast. I pull my feet toward him, trying to keep him from getting up.

"Don't stop," I mumble into the bedding, and he lets out a soft chuckle as he climbs off the bed and tosses the blanket over my backside.

The hours crawl by as we remain cooped up in the hotel room, the monotonous lull of the TV and the glow of our phones the only distractions from the boredom. By the time the day begins to slip into night, restlessness gnaws at me so fiercely that I feel like I might scream.

He lounges on the opposite bed, engrossed in his phone. Meanwhile, I fidget, my gaze falling on a crumpled receipt on the nightstand. I tear off a corner, rolling it into a tiny ball, and toss it at him. My first attempt misses. I try again—another miss. I continue three more times until it finally lands in his hair.

"I know what you're doing," he comments, not bothering to look my way.

I huff and push myself off the bed, making my way over to where he's stretched out. "I'm booored," I whine, shaking the mattress with my knees in an attempt to get his attention.

"Beckett," I try again, but still no response.

With a resigned sigh, I climb onto the bed and straddle his lap, prying his arms apart to finally force his attention on me. He lifts his gaze from his phone with mild amusement. I press my forehead to his, gritting my teeth as I shake his arms. "I'm sooooo bored."

"Let me finish this email, and we can go out for a bit."

"No, now," I pout, my lips barely inches from his.

He leans forward, wrapping his arms around me, and effortlessly flips me onto my back, settling between my thighs as he goes right back to his phone. I wrap my legs around his waist, playfully locking my feet together as I rock us side to side, trying to get a reaction. He smiles without looking up, still focused on typing. I relax beneath him, enjoying the weight of his body pressing down on me, until I feel a slow warmth building in my core. I slowly unlock my feet, trying to ease some of the closeness without drawing his attention.

As he subtly shifts his position, I feel his unmistakable hardness pressing firmly against me. Though he's coming off as unbothered by our proximity, it's obvious he's just as affected by it as I am. Only, I can hide mine a little better than the massive appendage growing between us—unless my wetness is seeping through my underwear.

Eventually, he climbs off me, delivering a smack to the side of my bottom. "Get up, whiner," he teases, already heading toward his clothes.

Excitedly, I jump from the bed, scrambling to get dressed. "Where are we going?" I ask, pulling on my jeans and searching for my sweatshirt.

"Hurry up and you'll find out," he replies, slipping on his coat and adjusting the collar.

"Is it going to be cold?" I ask, yanking my sweatshirt over my head.

"I don't actually know," he admits.

We head down to the main floor, and he leads me down the hall, past the arcade, and through another seemingly empty corridor until we reach a room with a sign outside featuring a *Titanic* poster and its showtimes.

I gasp, my excitement barely contained. "Shut your filthy mouth! Are we really watching *Titanic*?!"

"We are," he confirms.

We walk down the dimly lit hallway, and a hostess greets us. After taking our names, she leads us into a cozy theater where tables are arranged throughout the room. We're seated at a round booth in the back, offering a perfect view of the screen.

Beckett takes his coat off, places it beside him on the bench, and scoots closer to me. The waitress arrives to take our dinner orders, and Beckett orders for both of us—chicken tenders and fries for me, finger steaks and fries for him.

"I've never had dinner and a movie like this," I glance around the room at all the tables, each with a tealight candle at their center. Though it feels romantic, and I know it's not meant to be that for us, there's nobody else I'd rather share this experience with than Beckett.

As the lights dim and the movie begins, I eagerly grasp Beckett's hand, squeezing it in excitement. When I attempt to pull away, he gently intertwines his fingers with mine, and a flurry of butterflies take flight in my stomach. He glances at me briefly, then turns his attention back to the screen. The room begins to fill with the aroma of dinner orders being served. When our food arrives, my mouth waters at the spread of delicious dishes placed in front of us, and I finally withdraw my hand from his.

Dipping my chicken strip in ketchup, I take a bite. Dipping it again, I offer a bite to Beckett, not expecting him to take it, but I find it utterly sexy when he leans in and does. When he does the same with one of his finger steaks, I lean in and take it, not missing the way his eyes track my mouth as I chew. "Not bad."

We eat our meal, periodically offering each other bites of our food until we're finished, then settle back into the booth. Beckett shifts, resting one leg on the bench and leaning into me. He drapes his arm behind me, and his thumb begins tracing gentle patterns along my shoulder.

As the movie continues, I gradually let my head rest against him. His body responds in kind, leaning back into mine. The subtle closeness feels good, and I shift to settle more comfortably beside him. My arm naturally drapes over his leg, my fingers idly tracing slow, unconscious movements along his thigh.

A couple seated at the table in front of us, to our right, catches my attention. At first, they're simply sitting close, but as the movie progresses, their bodies inch toward each other until they're practically fused together. Before long, they're making out, oblivious to their surroundings. I wonder if Beckett even notices—though it would be hard not to when the guy starts fingering her. At first, I convince myself they wouldn't be bold enough to do anything so inappropriate with several tables behind them, within clear view. But when her hips start moving against his hand, it becomes very obvious what they're doing.

I glance up at Beckett, though his eyes remain fixed on the screen, the corner of his mouth quirks into a grin. "I'm not doing anything like that in here, so don't get any ideas."

I playfully hit his chest and turn back to the screen.

By the time the credits roll, it's dark outside, and we make our way back to our room, still talking about how cool it was to have dinner and a movie at the same time.

Once inside, we waste no time stripping down to our underwear, even though our room feels oddly cold. I remember seeing Beckett fiddle with the thermostat, but I can't imagine why he'd make it this chilly. Maybe I'd just grown accustomed to the warmth of the theater, with all the bodies packed together radiating heat.

Beckett strips down to just his boxers and I gape at him. "It's too cold for that," I say, already feeling like I'm going to start shivering.

He climbs in the bed, sprawls out, and begins moving his hands and feet on the bed as if he were making a snow angel.

"What are you doing?" I laugh.

"Warming up the bed for you," he continues, then scoots over as I get to my side.

The bed looks more inviting than ever after the long day. I climb in, grateful for the slight warmth he's already worked into the blankets. Reaching for the remote, I settle into the softness. "I'm picking the show tonight," I announce confidently, already scrolling through the options.

He lets out a contented sigh as he rolls onto his side and wraps his arms around me, pulling me close. His body molds into mine, his head nestling against my chest as he makes himself comfortable.

I rest my cheek against his head as I put on *The Flintstones*.

CHAPTER

Eight

When we wake in the morning, I'm met with the familiar weight of Beckett still draped over me. His arms are wrapped securely around my torso, his leg still tangled between mine. He's staring absentmindedly out the window, his breathing slow and steady.

"Are you looking for your brain out there?" I playfully ask.

He shifts his gaze, resting his chin on my chest as his eyes meet mine. A small smile tugs at his lips. "Good morning."

"You know you can get out of bed while I'm still sleeping, right?" I tease.

"I did. I already had coffee, brushed my teeth, and peed."

"And then climbed back in bed?"

"You were cold."

"I may have been cold, but I'm all sweaty now," I groan, feeling the heat between our bodies. "I need to pee," I add, trying to wriggle free.

He lifts off me reluctantly, and I slip out of bed, making my way to the bathroom. When I return, he's already propped up against the headboard, his phone in hand, scanning what looks like an email.

I grab my own phone and settle in beside him, as I rest my head on his shoulder, scrolling through TikTok aimlessly. The quiet between us is comfortable until there's a knock on the door. I start to get up, but Beckett shoots me a look.

"Stay in bed. You're not wearing pants," he scolds, swinging his legs out of bed and presumably grabbing a tip from his coat as he heads to the door.

Funny how he says I can't get out of bed because I'm not wearing pants, when he's literally standing there in just his boxers. At least I have underwear and a shirt on. He opens the door, and a man nearly enters with a cart, but Beckett stops him, hands him some money, and the man leaves without a word. I sit up, watching as Beckett returns to the bed and lays out our breakfast on the small trays.

"May I get out of bed now, master?" I mock, pulling the covers off and walking over to join him. I grab a pillow and place it on my lap before lifting the lid from my plate. The smell of warm food fills the room.

We eat in silence, the only sound being the occasional clink of silverware. As I take a sip of my orange juice, it hits me—I'm supposed to meet Elliot for lunch today. There's no way I'll make it back in time. I should cancel... or maybe I could suggest dinner instead.

I get up, walking over to grab my phone from the nightstand. As I scroll through a few messages, the phone vibrates in my hand. It's Elliot.

"Hey," I answer mid first ring.

"Do you just want to meet me at the restaurant?"

"Oh, I'm not back yet," I admit, biting my lip. "I won't be home until after lunch. Do you want to do dinner instead—?"

Beckett reaches over and snatches my phone from my hand. "No," he says, ending the call without another word.

"Beckett!" I snap as he tosses my phone on the other bed. "What the hell? You're on your phone while we eat, but I can't be on mine?"

He just ignores me, his indifference making me even more mad.

"Beckett," I say again, this time jerking his phone out of his hand. "Yeah, how do you like it?" I challenge, glaring at him as his expression darkens. But instead of reacting with anger, he calmly picks up another bite of food and reaches for his phone, acting like nothing happened. His ability to switch between hot and cold drives me crazy, and it's infuriating how he pretends nothing ever bothers him.

I pull up the ExpressWay app and start searching for us a ride. "I'm getting us a ride out of here," I mutter.

"I already have us a ride coming."

I pause, narrowing my eyes. "Is your car fixed?"

"I have more than one vehicle."

My mouth drops open, then I snap it shut, shaking my head. Of course he does. "Then why was I driving you around all this time?"

After prolonged silence, I discern he doesn't plan on giving me a response. "Have you heard from the sheriff about my car yet?"

"Not yet."

"K." I flop back on the pillows and lift my arms above my head in defeat.

"What?" he asks.

"I'm carless… my job requires a car." It's just now dawning on me that I won't be able to work without one. I really hope the other driver had insurance, especially since I will need a rental until my car is fixed.

"It will work out," he says.

I don't know if he's meaning this to try to reassure me, but all it does is piss me off. He just said he has multiple cars, while my only car got ran off the road the night before last. "Wow, really rich coming from you," I say dryly.

"And that's supposed to mean…?"

"Nothing." I stand abruptly, stripping off my T-shirt as I begin dressing. Though we probably won't leave for a while, I still throw on my coat, then begin tidying up the room in quick, angry movements. I grab my phone and toss it into my purse, packing the rest of our things into my backpack. He remains seated on the bed, composing an email, seemingly unaffected by my mood.

I sling my bag over my shoulder and make my way toward the door. His voice cuts through the room, low and authoritative. "Where do you think you're going?"

I freeze, then glance back at him. "For a walk downstairs while we wait for our ride."

Beckett's eyes lock onto mine as he rises from the bed, moving toward me with purpose. He places his hand against the door, effectively blocking my way. "No," he says firmly.

"Move," I snap, gripping the door handle, but he stands his ground, his body a wall between me and the exit.

"You'll wait for me," he orders.

"No!" I try again, but his dark gaze doesn't waver. He leans in slightly, daring me to push him further.

"Fine. Then hurry up and get dressed. I want to leave," I relent, crossing my arms and pressing my back against the door.

He fixes me with one last penetrating look, finally stepping away, walking across the room to gather his clothes. As he pulls on his shirt, he checks the room, making sure we haven't left anything behind. Once he's satisfied, he approaches me again, holding up his T-shirt. "Can I put this in your bag?"

I turn around, letting him tuck the shirt into my backpack. He zips it up, then grabs the door handle. "Ready?" he asks, staring down at me.

I push off the door, stepping aside, letting him open it. As we exit, we run into two of the girls from earlier waiting by the elevator. They light up when they see Beckett, and more flirtatious smiles spread across their faces.

"Just ask him for his number," I mutter, rolling my eyes.

"She's just mad because her butt hurts from us having anal all morning. Isn't that right, babe?" he says, his voice dripping with sarcasm.

"Yeah, it does. How does *your* butt feel after I finally fit my entire fist in it, *babe*?" I smirk right back.

"It was such an accomplishment," he grins down at me, softly tucking my hair behind my ear.

The elevator dings open, and we step inside. Once we reach the main floor, Beckett walks over to the counter and starts chatting with the woman behind the desk, handing her back the phone charger.

Of course, he managed to smooth-talk her into letting him borrow her charger. All he has to do is bat those pretty gray eyes, and she would likely let him do anything he asked.

I wander over to the sitting area, slumping down onto the couch. I watch him talk with her for a while before he finally comes over and joins me. We sit there for what feels like an eternity, though it's probably only an hour, both of us silently scrolling through our phones.

"How much longer until our ride gets here?" I sigh, bored and restless.

"My driver, Preston, has been here since we came down," he says casually, still absorbed in his phone.

I sit up straight, staring at him in disbelief. "Excuse you?"

He gives a slight head tilt toward the window. "He's right outside."

I follow his gaze, and sure enough, a sleek black SUV is idling by the curb. "Beckett, are you freaking serious right now?"

"You've already seemed irritated with me, and you look comfortable sitting here. Plus, you were quiet for the last hour. You didn't complain one time," he grins.

"I can't believe you."

We step outside, and the cold immediately bites at my face. Beckett pulls open the door, gesturing for me to get in. I slide into the seat, still nursing my frustration, while he circles around to the other side, settling in next to me.

As we pull out of the parking lot, I blink in astonishment at how clear everything seems. Mounds of snow are pushed against the edges, towering like forgotten remnants of a storm, and the lot itself is nearly empty of cars in comparison to the first night we got here. The roads, which Beckett had sworn were impassable yesterday, are now nothing more than a patchwork of frosty ice and slick, hard-packed snow. It's far from the perilous, snow-covered mess he had described. I'd braced myself for inches of fresh powder, but now, staring at these clear roads, I can't shake the suspicion that things were never as bad as he insisted. Did Beckett exaggerate just to keep us there another night?

But why would he do that?

As we drive past the spot where both my car and the other guy's car slid off the road, I notice how new snow pressed up against the side has completely covered any evidence of the mishap. It's like it never happened. My mind drifts back to the woods—when I had to pee, and Beckett offered his pocket square. He'd tucked it in his coat afterward, without even flinching.

"Did you get your pocket square cleaned?" I ask, turning to look at him.

He just turns his head and gives me a smile.

"Did you throw it away?"

"No."

"Where is it?" I press.

He raises an eyebrow. "Why are you so worried about *my* pocket square?"

"*Your* pocket square that has *MY* pee on it," I shoot back a bit louder than I intended. Both of us look to the front as his driver glances in the rearview mirror at the mention of it, then looks back to the road, probably wishing he could unhear that.

"Should I give him my address?" I attempt to steer the conversation to something a little more normal.

"Why?" Beckett asks, turning to look at me.

I stare at him confused by the stupid question. "To take me home. I need to figure out how I'm going to work."

He lets out a dry, almost condescending scoff "You're not working in this weather."

"Well, I still need to follow up on my car," I insist, letting my frustration seep into my voice. "Can I at least get the sheriff's business card?"

"I'm already handling it," he says brusquely.

The dismissiveness grates on me. I lean forward, addressing the driver directly. "Sir, can I give you my address?"

He glances at Beckett again through the mirror, and Beckett cuts in. "I already know where you live."

The statement makes me pause. "How?"

"I did a background check on you. Had to make sure you weren't a murderer."

"And?" I challenge, raising an eyebrow.

"And, you've been driving me around, haven't you?" he leans back casually as if that answers everything.

When we finally pull up to my apartment, I'm surprised to find that he really did know where I live. I thought he was just messing with me, but here we are. I wonder what kind of search he did on me—and what all he found out?

The SUV comes to a stop, and I get out, leaving the door open as I grab my backpack from the seat. I pull out his shirt and stack of folders, setting them neatly on the seat. "Thank you for the ride, Preston." Then I step back to close the door. As I move to shut it, Beckett's already there, waiting.

"You're wearing my coat," I say, noticing he put on the coat I had borrowed the night we met.

"Take my other one," he offers.

"I want the eight-thousand-dollar one."

"The other one is twelve," he whispers.

My mouth hangs open as I process that. "But maybe I like this one." I reach out and grab the pocket of the coat, feeling the soft fabric between my fingers.

"Maybe I do too," he counters, his eyes never leaving mine.

"Why?"

"Because it smells like you," he says, completely serious.

How does it smell like me? I slept with it because it smelled like *him*. Ohhh. The realization that my smell transferred to it during the times I wore it and slept with it, all while the only thing I smelled was him.

I huff. "Fine. Keep *my* coat for now, but I'll be coming for it eventually." My fingers absently tug on the pocket, and it's only then that I become hyper aware one of us must've taken a step closer. We're now standing toe to toe, the space between us practically nonexistent. "I'm cold. Thanks for taking me home."

"You're welcome," he replies, staring down at me, his eyes flickering between mine, but before I can get caught up in whatever this might be, I step back, releasing the fabric of his coat.

I turn and head toward my apartment, but some instinct makes me glance over my shoulder. He's still standing there, rooted in place, watching me. There's something unsaid lingering in the air between us, something he looks like he might voice but doesn't. His expression is unreadable, that familiar mix of aloofness and something deeper that he always seems to wear so well. I give him a quick wave, my awkward attempt at a goodbye.

Inside my room, I drop my backpack onto the bed and start unpacking, trying to shake off the tension from outside. As I pull out my phone, it vibrates with a new notification. I glance down and freeze.

$1,500 — Beckett

My eyes widen, staring at the screen in disbelief. At first, I think maybe it's a typo—maybe it says fifteen dollars, not fifteen hundred. But no, it definitely says fifteen hundred. I blink, not sure how to process it. He's been paying for everything: the meals, the ride home, and now this? I wasn't expecting him to give me anything at all, especially since he's the one who was driving us home the other night. I wasn't even planning to ask for payment.

CHAPTER
Nine

I sit on the bathroom counter, the steam from my shower slowly disappearing now that the door is open. A towel is wrapped securely around my hair, while I'm dressed in only my bra and underwear. I was in the middle of putting on my bra when I discover my eyebrows need some serious TLC. I prop one foot in the sink, while the other leg is tucked beneath me. The top half of the mirror is still covered in a fog, but the bottom half has cleared just enough that I can lean in and get a clear view of the stray eyebrows I'm meticulously tweezing, one hair at a time. It would be so much easier if I could just get them waxed.

Chloe once convinced me to get our eyebrows waxed together. It was originally just supposed to be her, but she talked me into trying it. I warned them that my skin is really sensitive, and the woman assured me she'd be extra careful. She prepped the area, applying extra baby powder before the wax. But the moment she ripped off that strip, an audible gasp rang through the air—from the gal waxing me and Chloe. The stinging hit me like a wave, and I remember her leaning over, asking, "When you say your skin is sensitive, what do you mean by that?" I could only manage to tell her that my eyebrow really hurt.

When she handed me a mirror, she told me not to freak out, but I nearly had a heart attack. The skin where the wax had been applied was completely missing, leaving my eyebrow raw and bleeding. I had a scab for weeks afterward, and I swore I'd never get waxed again. I'd rather endure the sting of each stray hair being plucked away than ever have my skin ripped from my body like that again.

The ring light in front of me illuminates my face and brow area, allowing me to focus on every tiny detail. As I work away on my left eyebrow, my thoughts start to drift, the repetitive motion of plucking becoming almost meditative. It's quiet in here, and I should have brought my phone to play music, but I'm already balls deep in the mirror that I don't dare get down. Every now and again, I lean back to make sure it's shaped how I want, then go right back in.

Refocusing on any hairs I might have missed, I barely register the faint creak of the floor. Suddenly, a figure appears in the doorway, and I catch a glimpse of movement in the corner of my eye. My heart skips a beat, and a scream escapes me with no time to process what's happening.

In a panicked blur, I lose my balance, the tweezers slipping from my hand as I teeter on the edge of the counter. I feel myself falling, my body tipping sideways toward the garbage can, but before I nose-dive off the side, strong arms catch me. I stare up, wide-eyed, and find gray eyes staring down at me.

"You okay?" Beckett asks.

It takes a second to catch my breath, my heart still racing from the shock.

"What the fuck!" I bite out, my voice shaking as I cling to his arm while he sets me back on the counter. "Now I don't even know where my tweezers are!" I grumble as I peer around on the floor.

He leans down, grabs them, and hands them back to me, his other hand still on my waist.

"Didn't know you'd be so jumpy." His tone is light, as if he hadn't just almost killed me.

My adrenaline slowly starts to fade as I reposition myself on the counter in the same spot I was in.

"You could've knocked, you know."

"I called you multiple times," he counters.

"Well, I don't have my phone on me."

"That sounds like a *you* problem. Are you good if I let you go?" He smirks.

I throw a pointed glare at him in the mirror then lean back in to focus on the other brow. Beckett leans casually against the counter and wall, arms crossed over his chest, his legs stretched out in front of him. The position highlights the definition of his muscles, his tattoos peeking from beneath the rolled-up sleeves of his neatly pressed shirt. Despite my best efforts to ignore his presence, I keep glancing in the mirror at him.

Every slight movement I make stirs the air between us, sending a fresh wave of his cologne wafting toward me. The scent invades my senses in the best way, sending an involuntary rush of warmth to the very place I'm trying not to think about. His shirt clings to him in all the right places, the button-down perfectly fitted, sleeves rolled just enough to showcase the intricate tattoos spiraling down his left forearm. My gaze flickers to the subtle flex of his forearm, the muscles taut beneath the fabric. Each time I steal a glance, the urge to climb off the counter and trace every defined contour of his body with my tongue becomes harder to resist.

"You're distracting me," I mutter, the effort to concentrate making the tiny hairs of my brow blur into one indistinct line. I briefly consider closing my eyes and blindly letting the tweezers do the work, pulling out clumps wherever my tweezers may.

"I'm not even doing anything."

"You being here is distracting me," I narrow my eyes at him through the mirror, though my irritation is thinly veiled.

He pushes himself off the wall, moving slowly. He steps forward, closing the already minimal space between us. His arms rest on either side of the counter, boxing me in as he leans over. I feel him everywhere—though he isn't even touching me. His eyes lock onto mine in the reflection and I watch as he moves in closer.

"Want me to help? I'm incredible with my hands." I don't miss the implied innuendo, but his eyes remain fixed on mine, genuine and confident.

"I'm good," I murmur, forcing myself to look away, though the pull between us feels magnetic.

Every subtle movement he makes feels magnified. His hand inches forward, fingertips brushing my thigh, wrapping firmly around it. He carefully lifts my leg from where it's propped in the sink, guiding it down gently. The tweezers in my hand freeze mid-air, my focus shattered. I let him maneuver me, my body responding to his every move.

He turns me until I'm facing him, his movements unhurried. Now leaning against the counter between my spread thighs, our faces hover close enough that I could pucker my lips and they'd touch his. His hand extends, reaching out to take the tweezers from me. I'm so entranced by him that I release them without resistance.

His touch is gentle, one hand lifting to rest just above my eyebrow, his fingers pinching the skin between his thumb and index finger to tighten it. With delicate precision, he begins plucking away the stray hairs. As he works, I study his face, captivated by the details I hadn't noticed before. His nose is perfectly balanced, the thin bridge leading to subtly flared nostrils, giving his features a striking, sculpted appearance. His lips, full and inviting, seem almost too beautiful to be real. His skin is smooth, his complexion clear, and his own eyebrows are naturally well-shaped, effortlessly framing his intense gray eyes.

I watch him intently, mesmerized by his focus and the way he concentrates. The closeness between us feels charged, and when his eyes flick down to meet mine, he smiles. "What?"

"Nothing," I reply shyly, closing my eyes as a flush spreads across my face.

After a few moments of silence, I feel the lightest brush of his lips against my freshly plucked brow, and the soft sound of the tweezers being set down on the counter. Opening my eyes, I glance at the mirror and see that he has perfectly tidied my brow.

"Thank you," I say quietly as I climb off the counter.

"You're welcome," he replies, his voice equally soft.

I pull the towel from my head, letting the damp cool strands of my hair fall against my back. Reaching for my leave-in conditioner, I spray it through my knotted hair. "Why are you here, anyway? I obviously can't drive you anywhere," I tease, pulling a brush from the counter to work through the knots.

He steps forward, taking it from my hand, his fingers brushing against mine. He begins combing through my hair with slow strokes. "I talked to the sheriff earlier," he says as he combs through my hair. "Your car's being repaired, but they won't have a rental for you until next week. I figured I'd take you grocery shopping, make sure you have everything you'll need for the weekend."

I nod, appreciating both the update and his offer to take me to the store. As he finishes with my hair, I head toward my bedroom to get dressed. "Thanks," I call over my shoulder. "I was going to order groceries for delivery, but I'd rather go myself. I need to get out of this apartment. I was about to start counting the carpet fibers."

He follows me into the bedroom, settling onto my bed as he reclines against the pillows, his body sinking into them with ease. I mentally note how he looks like a perfect, permanent fixture for my bed. Shaking the thought, I move to the window and peer outside, checking how much snow has accumulated on the ground in the past three days since I last left my apartment—the day I got back with Beckett. There are a couple more inches on the ground, though the sidewalks have been shoveled at some point, now partially re-covered by another layer of snow.

The only vehicle in the parking lot that stands out is a large truck parked next to my empty space. I scan the area, expecting to see Beckett's SUV or his driver lingering nearby, but neither is in sight. My gaze lingers on the truck. Perhaps that's Beckett's truck, and he drove himself here? Something about that detail—the fact that he really hadn't needed me to drive him—makes me pause.

I notice Nancy standing outside in her faded robe, puffing on a cigarette while her tiny Chihuahua takes a dump right in the middle of the sidewalk, in the middle of everyone's path. She turns to head up the stairs, and her eyes meet mine through the window. "Put some clothes on, skank," she mutters without even breaking her stride.

"Pick up your dog's shit, Nancy, or I'll pick it up and smear it on your door handle," I call back.

Beckett comes up behind me, curious about who I'm talking to. Nancy stops and gives him a once-over. "Your girlfriend's a bitch," she says bluntly, then pats her leg to call for her dog to follow. "C'mon, Taco."

Beckett strides from the bedroom, and I turn to watch him go. I hear the front door creak open and catch snippets of his conversation with Nancy. I hope he's out there telling her she's trashy for leaving her dog's turd on the sidewalk, but he's polite, telling her he knows it's cold, but she can't leave it sitting there.

She says she'll be right back, then returns with a bag, picks it up, and disappears back upstairs. He turns, glances at me, then comes back in.

When he enters, I turn back around as he sits on the bed, leaning back into the pillows with a relaxed demeanor, his posture casual and at ease. I can feel his eyes following me as I head to the closet, grabbing a pair of jeans and a shirt before returning to the bed. Avoiding his gaze, I start to get dressed.

"Come here," he says, his hands reaching out to me.

I hesitate, unsure of what he wants. He sits up, takes my hand, and gently pulls me closer. His arms wrap securely around my waist, guiding me onto his lap. I probably shouldn't have gone so eagerly, but it's exactly where I want to be. Straddling him, I feel his grip tighten as he leans back into the pillows.

He's the first person I've ever been in such intimate positions with, and it's a new feeling—a welcomed feeling. Part of me wants to melt into him, to surrender completely, but the other part of me holds back, refusing to show him just how much he affects me. But I keep my cool, playing it off like this isn't a big deal.

"So, this will get us to the store how?" I remark.

"We'll get to the store," he tilts his head to the side as he stares at me. "I promise."

"Well, I'm sure you've been at work and out and about. I've spent days stuck in here. I'm antsy to get out."

"Are you not comfortable?"

"You are quite comfy, actually." I wiggle my body on his to emphasize my point.

Mental note: *Don't wiggle on him.*

He bites his lower lip, his hands sliding up my back as he pulls me to him. "Then relax for a bit and let me hold you."

I let out a small sigh and nuzzle my face into the crook of his neck, inhaling his scent. I manage to stay still for all of about five seconds but my impatience kicks in. I push against his chest, trying to sit up. "All better. Ready to go now?" I flash him a cheeky grin.

"Hmm-mm," he hums, shaking his head. His hand slips behind my neck, gently pressing my head back down onto his shoulder. I laugh softly but stay put, letting him win this round.

"Your belt buckle is digging into my stomach," I mumble into his neck, my lips brushing his skin without even thinking about it. I'm not even sure why my mouth is touching him like this, but it feels good.

"Want me to take it off?"

"No." I shake my head. "I want to go shopping."

He lets out a long, dramatic sigh, his hand clapping down on my butt. "Fine. Get dressed." He releases his arms from around me and splays them out on the bed.

I sit up, my mouth hanging open as I gape at him. "You made that way too easy."

His lips curve into a smirk as he flips me onto my back, his body pressed into mine. His forearms rest on either side of me, and his thumbs gently trace the arch of my brows. "Your eyebrows look really nice," he says softly, focused on the small movements of his hands.

"Thanks, I did them all by myself," I reply, a little breathless as I watch him.

His gaze drops to meet mine. "Oh yeah? No help?"

"Nope, all by myself," I repeat.

His face draws near, and I remain still as a statue as he gently captures my bottom lip between his teeth. The sensation sends a jolt through me as his teeth graze my lip, teasingly pulling away until it slips free. Without a word, he sits up and gets off the bed, standing at the edge. I'm so hot and bothered, sitting here panting as he just walks away. My head falls back, and I stare up at the ceiling.

I feel his hand wrap around my ankle, and when I lift my head, he's already guiding my foot into my pants. He bunches the fabric around both ankles, then offers me his hands to help me off the bed. I take them, and he pulls me to my feet, leaning down to tug the waistband up into place, buttoning and zipping them. Once he's done, I finish getting dressed and walk to the front door closet to grab my snow boots.

As I'm slipping them on, I glance over at Beckett, who's leaning casually against the doorframe. "Did you bring my coat back?" I ask, slinging my purse over my shoulder.

A grin tugs at the corner of his lips. "I put that coat in a very special place. But I did bring a coat." He gestures to one draped over the back of the couch.

"And where exactly is this 'special place' you speak of?"

He leans in, his voice dropping to a whisper. "My spank bank."

The mere thought of him playing with himself, with the possibility of me being the one he thinks about, nearly brings me to my knees. I imagine him clutching the coat, breathing in my scent the same way I did, as he fists himself. *I need that coat back.* "Point me in the right direction, and I'll retrieve it myself."

He laughs softly, straightening up. "I'll show you. Want to come over?"

I feel my cheeks flush, and it takes immense effort to remain composed. "I expect my coat back."

We leave my apartment, and the unknown truck out front is confirmed to be his when it unlocks as we approach. He pulls open the passenger door for me to climb in, then closes it once I'm settled.

The drive to the store is short, just a quick ten minutes from my place—faster if the roads are clear. Beckett grabs a shopping cart and casually leans on the handle as we browse through the aisles. We move from section to section, tossing items into the cart until I have the groceries I will need for the weekend—probably even for the upcoming week.

As we continue meandering through the store, we find ourselves in the toy section. He picks up a double pack of Nerf guns, inspecting them with a grin. I shoot him a raised eyebrow, silently questioning what he's doing. He seems amused by my reaction.

"If you even *think* about trying to step to me with one of those, I'll shoot the ever-loving shit out of you," I warn, trying to sound serious but failing miserably at hiding my own grin.

He wags his brows at me, then drops the box in the cart.

"Oh, sir, you're going to regret that," I say as I walk ahead. I grab a few more essentials—shampoo, conditioner, body wash—and toss them into the cart.

As we move through the aisle, I see a box of wax strips. Turning back to Beckett, I hold them up. "Hey, if I buy some wax strips, will you wax my butthole for me?"

Surprise flashes across his face as his chin jerks back, then he bursts into laughter, the sound echoing through the otherwise quiet aisle. "Sure. Why not?"

"Can I wax yours?"

Without missing a beat, he gives the same response. "Sure. Why not?"

I shake my head at his nonchalance as I place the box back on the shelf. Just as I turn to continue shopping, I hear the unmistakable sound of the box being plopped into the cart behind me.

"Beckett! That was a joke," I protest, reaching for the box of wax strips to put them back on the shelf. He's quicker, though, blocking my hand and snatching the box away. I try again, but he just holds it out of reach. Eventually, he tosses the box back into the cart with a thud.

By the time we reach checkout, the cashier's eyes are practically glued to Beckett. She hasn't stopped smiling since we approached the counter, and she chatters away, making small talk with him as she scans each item. I'm barely a footnote in the conversation, watching her light up with every word he says.

As she picks up the box of wax strips, I decide to ask. "Do you know if those hurt?"

She looks up, her eyes widening slightly. From the way her expression shifts, it's clear she hadn't even realized Beckett was with anyone else, let alone a woman. She recovers quickly, though. "I'm not sure," she replies. "But I don't think it'll be too painful. Just use ice on the area after each strip you pull off."

I turn to Beckett, rubbing his shoulder in a mock soothing gesture. "See, baby? Waxing your butthole won't hurt too much. We just need to apply ice after each strip," I say, batting my lashes at him dramatically.

"Well, that's certainly a relief," he sighs playfully, and the cashier laughs along with me.

When she finally tells me the total, I'm already digging through my purse, fishing out my wallet. Beckett smoothly steps up behind me, taps his card on the reader, and before I can shove his hand away, he's holding the receipt out to me.

"Beckett!" I protest as he pushes the cart past me. "I'll pay you back," I huff, chasing after him.

"I got stuff too," he says, as if that somehow balances him paying for everything.

"You got a toy." I point to the Nerf guns in the cart.

"*We* got a toy," he corrects.

"Boring toy," I mutter.

He slides an arm around my neck and pulls me closer, positioning me between him and the cart as we walk. "What would be a not-boring toy?" he whispers in my ear.

"Not Nerf guns. Maybe like… Barbies or something."

"I'll play Barbies with you."

"I don't own any. All we own now are Nerf guns."

After we load the bags into the back seat, he takes us out for dinner, then back to my apartment. Once we arrive, he helps me carry in the groceries, which speeds up the time I have to spend in the cold. I kick off my boots at the door and head to the kitchen to start putting things away. I hadn't expected he would stay or even want to, but when he removes his shoes at the door as well, I'm happy to find he must be planning to stay for a little while.

I grab the shower items and head to the bathroom to put them away. When I return to the kitchen, I barely round the corner just in time to get hit with a Nerf dart. It smacks me right in the chest, and my mouth drops open in shock as I stare down at the dart, processing what just happened.

Looking up, I see Beckett doubled over with laughter.

"Where's mine?" I ask, holding out my hand.

He pulls the other one from his pocket, where it had been partially concealed. Handing it to me, I take it, ready to shoot him back. I raise the gun, aiming straight for him, but he grabs the barrel, redirecting it. My shot goes wide, harmlessly hitting the wall instead.

"Cheater!" I exclaim, pulling back the top to reload. He grins, and before I can even prepare, another dart hits me.

We burst into laughter, and I quickly fire back, then take off running around the corner. I sprint toward my bedroom, trying to slam the door behind me, but he's too fast. He pushes through the door just as I shoot again, the dart grazing his shoulder before he scoops me up and tosses me onto the bed.

I'm still breathless, as he straddles me, my Nerf gun still in hand, though I'm fumbling to cock it. With a grin, he pins my wrists above my head with one hand, his Nerf gun resting lightly against my chest. "Any last words?"

I shake my head, pretending to surrender. His pointer hovers over the trigger, poised to fire, but with a quick move, I jerk one hand free and swat the Nerf gun from his grasp. It tumbles off the side of the bed and clatters to the floor.

The look of pure shock on his face has me dissolving into laughter.

He rolls off me, collapsing onto the bed beside me, still catching his breath. Turning his head, he lets out a soft sigh. "Wanna watch a movie?"

I meet his gaze and smile. "Sure, as long as it's not scary."

He flashes a mischievous grin and casually climbs off the bed, heading toward the living room. I prop myself up on my elbows, watching him leave.

As I join him, he's already scrolling through movies and immediately hits play on the first horror film he lands on.

"Oh, I see how it is, Buckets," I protest, reaching for the remote, but he holds it out of my reach. For a brief moment, I think he didn't even catch the fact that I didn't say his name correctly, but he hits me with a nickname just as fast.

"Relax, Broom. I'm right here," he says, lying down on the couch and pulling me with him until I'm tucked against him, his body spooning mine. His arm wraps securely around me, and for the first twenty minutes, I'm constantly covering my eyes, peeking through my fingers whenever the music builds with suspense.

When I can't take it anymore, I roll over onto my side and bury my face in his chest. He chuckles softly, the sound vibrating through him as he holds me tighter. His hand starts to rub slow, soothing circles on my back. "You're missing all the good parts."

"Good parts, my ass," I mumble into his shirt, refusing to look.

Whenever the movie quiets down, I muster the courage to peek, turning just enough to see but always ready to look away again. Then comes another jump-scare, and I'm back to pressing my face into him, but this time I stay put, settling into his touch as his hand drifts lower, rubbing my lower back in steady, calming strokes.

He lifts the hem of my shirt, just enough for his fingers to graze my skin directly. The warmth of his hand against my bare back erases any anxiety the movie might've stirred. For all I care, it can play forever—his touch melts away every trace of fear, and the eerie noises in the background barely register anymore.

By the time the movie ends, I peek up at him. "Play it again."

"You didn't even watch it," he says with a smirk.

"But I like the back massage," I whine.

"Get up," he lets out a soft laugh. I grumble but do so, reluctantly pulling myself from the comfort of his embrace. He stands, stretching, muscles flexing as he moves toward the front door and flicks the lock in place. My heart skips a beat as I follow behind to my bedroom, the quiet amplifying the thudding in my chest.

I watch as he unbuttons his shirt, revealing the familiar tattoos that wrap across his toned chest and arms. His movements are casual, but my cheeks heat up as I try to act nonchalant, slipping into a tank top and sleep shorts. It feels like it should be no big deal, yet my pulse races as I slide under the covers beside him.

We settle in the middle of the bed, our bare legs softly brushing under the sheets. The light contact sends a rush of warmth through me. Part of me knows I should scoot away, create some space, but instead, I stay put, craving more of that closeness. In fact, I want him to keep massaging my back.

"How do you want me?" I whisper.

His head snaps toward me, his gaze locking onto mine with an intensity that takes me by surprise. His head remains on the pillow, but something in his expression shifts. "What?" he asks, his voice low, almost... turned on.

"You practically said you would keep massaging my back."

Without a single ounce of humor in his tone, he says, "Face me, and I'll massage you."

We roll toward each other, and his hand slides up my tank top as he slowly starts massaging me. "Does that feel okay?" he whispers.

I nod. "Yes… Can I rub yours?" I ask shyly.

He smiles and nods back.

I shift closer, wrapping my arm around his bare torso. My fingers trail up his back, softly rubbing along his warm skin, feeling the smooth lines of muscle beneath my fingertips. His body responds to my touch, his muscles relaxing under the steady, rhythmic motion, mirroring the way he skillfully massages me.

"That feels so good. If I start moaning, just know it's entirely your fault," I say with a soft laugh.

"Same."

As the minutes pass, we begin to drift off, our fingers still working on each other as sleep takes us away. The night feels calm and peaceful. When I wake, the early morning light is dim, and it takes me a moment to register Beckett's presence—his weight is partially on top of me, his body warm and heavy, with his arm draped over my waist.

I blink away my grogginess, smiling when I remember our back rubs, and thread my fingers through his hair as I savor this. His breathing is still deep and steady, and with every exhale, I feel his breath… I feel his breath on my skin. I glance down, and it takes me a second to fully register the situation. When I do, my heart nearly jumps right through my bones. My tank top has shifted completely down during the night, and to my horror, my boobs are fully exposed. His head rests between my bare chest, his cheek pressed against me.

"Beckett!" I hiss in a frantic whisper, my voice a mix of disbelief and embarrassment as I scramble to pull my shirt back up. "Why didn't you wake me? My boobs are hanging out!"

He doesn't even look up from his phone as he casually scrolls through whatever he's reading. "That's nothing," he says nonchalantly. "When I woke up, my mouth was practically sucking on your nipple."

"What?!" I sputter, blinking in astonishment. "You sucked on my nipple?"

"Not that I remember." He keeps his eyes on his phone, responding without an ounce of shame. "But if you want me to, I can now."

"No!" I say, pushing on him, my face burning with embarrassment. He just rolls off as I quickly pull my shirt back into place. "Since you got an entire peep show and a suck on my nipples, you can go make us breakfast."

"Deal." He climbs out of bed, walking out of the room.

I gather myself before heading to the bathroom for a quick shower. As I'm drying off, Beckett waltzes in, heads straight to the toilet, and starts peeing.

"You didn't want to wait until I wasn't in here?" I ask sarcastically. Despite my best efforts not to, my eyes drift down, and I mentally chastise myself for looking at his penis… his beautiful, glorious penis.

He catches me looking and grins. "Breakfast is ready," he says as he finishes up.

I roll my eyes and turn back to get dressed, tugging my shirt on while he stands next to me, washing his hands at the sink.

"I don't know why you keep staring at my boobs when you spent all morning getting acquainted with them while I was sleeping."

He shrugs, grabbing a towel to dry his hands. "You have nice boobs," he says casually, then walks out of the bathroom.

I stand there, processing that. *He thinks I have nice boobs.* I shouldn't care as much as I do, and I try to suppress the smile tugging at my lips as I finish getting dressed and follow him out to the kitchen.

He's already set our plates at the table with everything neatly arranged. We sit down to eat, and I do my best to act like nothing out of the ordinary just happened.

CHAPTER
Ten

He stays the weekend with me, and even though we didn't do anything spectacular, it felt so easy and perfect. We pass the time curled up in front of the TV, immersed in a marathon of movies. At one point, I joke that he'll either need to wear a pair of my clothes—which I practically begged him to do—or he'll need to go home since he didn't bring any of his own. When he says he'd be right back, I throw myself dramatically across his lap, pretending I've lost all ability to move because I didn't want him to leave. He just laughs, rolls me off, and gets up. I follow him to the door, still pouting, dragging my feet like a petulant child.

As he walks to his truck, I stand at the doorway, arms crossed, making sure he knows how much I disapprove of him leaving. He catches my exaggerated frown and winks at me, which only makes me more determined to pout harder. But instead of getting into the driver's seat, he opens the back door of his truck and pulls out a neatly packed to-go bag. I just blink at him as he walks back, shaking my head in disbelief.

"I wanted to make you feel bad your entire drive home, and you had that this entire time?" I point at the bag. "My pouty lip almost fell off; I had it out so long."

Sunday rolls in, even lazier than the previous day. We remain draped across the couch—me on one end, Beckett on the other—letting the hours slip by as movie after movie plays. The quiet hum of the TV fills the room, but my mind starts to wander. I glance over at him, watching his relaxed expression, then blurt out, "Massage my feet."

He doesn't even look at me, just keeps his eyes glued to the screen, so I slide my toes up his shirt, pressing them against his stomach. His muscles tense immediately, and I smile at the reaction.

"Why are your toes always so cold?" he grumbles, grabbing my foot and finally begins to knead it with his hand.

I shut my eyes, releasing a pleased sigh, only to feel him shift. He swings his leg over mine, resting it across my lap. "Massage mine," he says with a smirk, shoving his foot near my face.

I push his foot away, since his long legs practically had it positioned right on my forehead. "Bend your leg then.

You're trying to make this kinky by having me massage you with my tongue, and we aren't there yet."

He chuckles and bends his knee like I asked. I grab his foot and start rubbing it, mimicking the way he's massaging mine. We fall back into a comfortable silence, with the movie playing softly in the background as we both relax.

When he takes my other foot and tucks it under his shirt, pressing it against his warm stomach, I smile. I press my toes into the muscles, feeling the way his abs flex under the touch before they eventually relax as my toes start to warm up.

The movie ends, and we sit quietly, letting the credits roll. Beckett breaks the silence, scanning the room curiously. "Why do you have so many llamas all over in here?"

I follow his gaze, taking in the various llama decorations and wall art around the room. "Oh, because I love surrounding myself with things I hate."

"Okay, wiseass," he mutters, then tickles the bottom of my foot. I squirm, trying to pull away.

"Why do you live in a sterile environment?" I counter, raising an eyebrow.

"You've never even been inside my place." He stares at me pointedly.

"Does the thought of having me in your home make you nervous?"

He laughs, giving my foot a squeeze. "Why? Because it would be like having a Tasmanian devil in a china shop?"

"Probably," I admit, knowing full well I'd likely destroy something expensive.

"All my possessions can be replaced. I'm not worried about you breaking anything," he says, just as a knock sounds at the door. He pauses and tilts his head in question.

"Relax," I squeeze his toes as I get up. "I ordered something."

I retrieve my package and head to the kitchen with him following behind. I tear open the box to reveal two blank canvases, a set of acrylic paints, and brushes.

"What are you painting, Picasso?" he teases, resting his chin on my shoulder as he peers down into the box.

"*WE* are painting," I correct. "I was going to paint a llama, but after your little remarks about all my llama stuff, I think I'll do a walrus or perhaps a squid. You like stinky things like that. And *YOU* can paint me a llama."

"I don't think you smell anything like a squid." He winks.

As I unpack the supplies, he observes me. While I tidy up the packaging, he places a soft kiss on my shoulder, then swats my butt as he picks up the paints and carries them to the table. I watch him walk away, noting he did that absentmindedly, without even a second thought—meanwhile, I'm left standing here, practically in a puddle of feelings.

We set everything up, laying plastic bags under the canvases to protect the surface. Actually, that was his idea, and now I'm thinking he did it because he expects me to make a giant mess. Once everything's prepped and we're settled in, we start painting. Despite my earlier joke, I end of sketching a llama after all, my brush moving fluidly as I lose myself in the process. Beckett, meanwhile, works on his own masterpiece: two llamas, one light blue and the other light pink, their noses touching in a kiss. It's the most adorable thing I've ever seen.

We keep checking our phones for reference, and I find myself loving his painting way more than mine. When he finishes, he writes "I'm with stupid" under the pink llama, with an arrow pointing to the blue one. Then, under the blue llama, he adds, "I am stupid," complete with another arrow pointing back at it.

"I was going to suggest these were new art pieces for your sterile condo, but now I feel like they're better here. I really want to keep yours," I say, and we both look at it and burst out laughing.

"No way—they're coming home with me," he insists, glancing between the two paintings.

"You don't even like llamas," I counter.

"No, but you do. The way to lure someone where you want them is with the things they already like."

"This is true. I especially like the pearls you put around her neck," I point out, noting the string of white pearls adorning the pink llama's neck.

"Thanks. He just gave them to her," he smirks, and I playfully hit his shoulder at the innuendo.

I grab the paintbrushes to start cleaning them in the sink, and he comes up next to me. I assume he's there to help, but then I feel him press a wet paintbrush against my cheek.

"Oh, that's precious," I say, flicking water at him as he tries to deflect the droplets. Grabbing my blue paintbrush, I advance on him. He holds up his hands in a gesture of surrender. "Oh, it's too late for that, Mr. Shaw. You started this."

He laughs and stops walking as I approach him. I hold the brush up and paint three lines on his cheek, then three more on his other side. "The best-looking kitty I've ever seen," I smile.

After we finally clean up the paint, I head to the bathroom and start stripping off my clothes, ready to wash off the rest of the mess. As I step into the shower, Beckett walks in and begins undressing too.

"You can wait until I'm finished," I call out.

But instead of listening, he pushes the shower curtain aside and steps in, pulling it closed behind him.

"Beckett!" I screech, covering my boobs, even though I know he's already seen them. I should probably focus on trying to cover my own cat, but I remain frozen when he stares down at me, biting his lower lip.

"We're saving the planet by conserving water," he grins, adjusting the spout so it hits both of us. "I've already seen you naked. No point in hiding—you naked is no secret to me." He bends down, his face hovering just inches from my thighs as he reaches for the washcloth I put off to the side. After wetting it, he gently presses it to my cheek, wiping away the paint.

"Yeah, well, me seeing you naked is still a secret," I retort.

"Then look. I don't mind," he says casually, holding the washcloth out to me.

I stare at it, realizing I'll have to let my boobs go. I chew on the inside of my lip, contemplating how I'm going to get through a shower while trying to cover myself the whole time.

"If you want your breasts covered, take the washcloth, and I'll keep them covered," he offers.

"With what?"

He holds up two large hands. I hit his chest, and he laughs as I jerk the washcloth from his grasp. I squeeze some face wash onto the cloth and turn toward him. I bring it to his cheek, carefully wiping away the paint. His eyes stay on mine the entire time, his expression softening as I clean him.

We proceed to wash the rest of our bodies, working around each other in the confined space. My backside brushes against him as I reach for my shampoo, not knowing he had moved in closer. The subtle contact sends a tingle through my fingers, and I do my best to keep them steady as I pour shampoo into my palm and massage it into my scalp, but even that feels slower and more sensual. I lather the shampoo through my hair and can feel him watching me with an intensity that makes me acutely aware of his presence.

I tilt my head back under the spray, letting the water rinse away the suds. My body arches slightly as the warm water rushes over my scalp, and I can feel the droplets gliding down my neck, over my chest, and along the curves of my waist. It's impossible to ignore how closely he's standing, and I worry I might let this go somewhere maybe I'm not quite ready for.

"You can take my towel and dry off. Just bring me a new one." I try my best to keep my voice steady as I tilt my head back, letting the water rinse out the last of the shampoo.

When he doesn't respond, I peek out of one eye. The expression on his face hits me like a jolt, and even though I don't look down, I know exactly what I'd see if I did. The thought alone is enough to make my nipples harden under the warm spray.

His eyes lock onto mine as he steps closer, the water pooling between us. His hands glide up my wet hips, trailing along my sides before wrapping around my back and pulling me flush against him. His warmth is everywhere, his breath hot on my neck as he rests his forehead in the crook of my shoulder. I loop my arms around him, gently cradling the back of his head. I feel his hardness pressing against me, and my body responds instantly.

It would be so easy—too easy—to let this go further. If he just tilted his hips a little more, he could…

God. What am I doing?!

That thought snaps me out of this trance I've fallen into.

"Are you finished?" I ask, my hand moving behind me, resting on the water knob, ready to turn it off.

He doesn't respond so I twist the knob, shutting off the spray. I reach for the towel draped over the curtain rod, feeling the cool air against my wet skin as he finally lets go of me. I wrap the towel securely around myself, but he steps in, gazing down at me.

"Share it with me," he murmurs in a low voice.

He scoops me up effortlessly, pulling back the shower curtain and stepping out of the tub. My legs wrap around his waist for balance, but the motion causes the towel to shift, leaving his hardness positioned against my very bare nether region. When he sets me down, our very turned-on private parts slide against each other, and the contact isn't nearly enough. Trying to gather my wits, I quickly turn away, grab a towel, and hand it to him, trying to focus on anything but the magnetic pull between us. Wrapping my hair in my towel, I head to the dresser and pull out clothes to wear to bed.

I hear him drying off behind me, and when I turn around, he's already slipping into bed, completely naked. I don't say anything, knowing he does that when he's cold. I finish getting dressed, pretending not to notice how my heart races in the quiet room. I slip under the covers, doing my best to ignore the warmth radiating from his body next to mine.

It's early Monday morning, and he's still here with me. The room is cloaked in darkness, the only sounds are the soft rustle of sheets and his steady breathing. I feel him stir beside me, his arm sliding around my waist, pulling me closer as he presses a gentle kiss to my shoulder. He pulls the blankets up over me, his careful movements telling me he's trying not to wake me. Half-asleep, I drift in and out of consciousness, but the warmth of his touch lingers, keeping me tethered to the moment as I slip back into dreams.

When I wake, the apartment is eerily quiet, a stillness that confirms I'm alone. I roll over, half expecting to see Beckett, but the space where he slept is empty. The sheets are rumpled, the faint imprint of his body still visible. It's the only evidence he was here. I reach over and grab the pillow where his head rested, pulling it close. His scent lingers, a mix of cologne and my shampoo, and I inhale deeply, letting it wash over me. I allow myself to indulge in the fantasy that it's him I'm holding, not just the pillow. My arms wrap firmly around it as I sink deeper into the lingering memory of his presence.

I stay like that for a good half hour, nestled in the remnants of pillow beckett, pretending he's still here, still holding me. But eventually, reality nudges me, and I force myself to sit up, stretching slowly as I slip out of bed. The cold air hits me, and I pull on a robe as I shuffle toward the kitchen.

As I fill the coffee pot, something on the counter catches my eye—or rather, the absence of something. I glance over and realize the canvases we painted last night are gone. I stop mid-motion, my hand hovering above the coffee maker, a sudden rush of thoughts filling my mind. Did he really take them? I can't quite picture Beckett hanging those silly llama paintings in his pristine home, or what I envision his home to be. But if he took them because he actually plans on hanging them, it makes me happy. The thought of another woman seeing them, wondering where they came from… Then the full comprehension of that thought—another woman being in his home—hits me, and I feel a sharp pain directly in my gut.

I spend the rest of the day trying to keep myself occupied, starting with laundry at the apartment's shared facility. Tenants have been known to steal other people's laundry, so I stick nearby, heading to the small gym attached to the laundry room while I wait for the cycles to finish. It's a decent distraction, and it keeps me from worrying about anyone walking off with the few clothes I actually have.

Once the laundry's done, I head back to my apartment with a full basket, folding everything and putting most of it away while imagining, *What would Beckett do?* He's a good little motivator, even though he has no idea he's being one.

The first day isn't too bad—I manage to stay busy, keeping myself entertained with small tasks around the apartment. By the time the second day rolls around, though, the restlessness sets in. I find myself pacing from one room to another, staring out the window, willing time to move faster. The four walls of my apartment start to close in on me, each hour dragging longer than the last. By the third day though, I'm ready to bang my head against the window, so restless my own thoughts begin to annoy me.

With no car and no real way to escape the confines of this place, I feel trapped. Chloe was supposed to be home in a couple of days, but she and her boyfriend, Tom, decided to go on a mini-getaway together. I'm happy for her, really, but there's a twinge of jealousy creeping in. At least she has someone to go on spontaneous trips with, while I'm stuck here, counting down the minutes to some kind of distraction.

She offered for me to go, mentioning Tom's roommate, Mark, was interested in going too if I wanted to, but that sounded lame. Then she suggested I invite Elliot, which sounded even more lame. If only she'd known about Beckett and floated his name, I probably would've jumped all over that.

It's been days since I've heard from Beckett, and the silence is starting to unravel me. I hate how much I care. I hate that I'm sitting here, wondering what's been keeping him so occupied that he hasn't even reached out or come back. I guess I could reach out, but what would I say? I could always use the excuse of asking about my car. I do need to know what's going on with it.

I lie on my bed, kicking my legs back and forth, scrolling through social media with a half-hearted attempt to distract myself, but it's not working. Just as I'm about to roll over in frustration, a sudden, sharp smack lands on my butt.

I whip around and there he is—Beckett, standing by the bed, looking absolutely irresistible in his crisp business attire.

"What are you doing here?" I blurt out, my voice betraying my happiness. It sounds almost like I'm annoyed, when in reality, I'm anything but. My heart's doing somersaults.

He climbs onto the bed, kneeling over me, his hands planted on either side of my head. His eyes lock onto mine as he leans closer. "I'm here to pick you up. We've got to deal with some insurance stuff for your car."

My eyes widen with surprise and relief, and I attempt to sit up, but his body is still hovering over mine, leaving no room. Our faces are just inches apart. "You're going to have to move if you actually want me to get up."

He grins and smoothly slides off the bed, giving me just enough space to scramble to my feet. Once I'm up, I'm a whirlwind of movement, diving toward the pile of clothes I never got around to putting away. My fingers frantically sort through them until I yank out a pair of jeans and a sweater. With quick, jerky motions, I pull the clothes on, struggling to zip my jeans, muttering a string of curses under my breath until the zipper finally cooperates.

I run my hand through my tangled hair in a weak attempt to smooth it, but it's a futile effort. I slip on my snow boots, catching a glimpse of Beckett in the corner of my eye. He's just standing there, looking amused. His calm demeanor only making my frantic energy feel more chaotic. I wonder if it ever stresses him out, having to witness me struggle through everything I do, while he moves about his day with grace and ease.

"Okay, let's go," I say, grabbing my bag and heading for the door.

"You're awfully eager," he comments as we walk to his truck.

"Unlike you with your collection of vehicles, my one and only car is getting fixed, therefore leaving me carless, and trapped here." His comment rubs me the wrong way, striking me as a bit tone-deaf considering he hasn't been cooped up in a 900-square-foot apartment for days like I have.

The ride is quiet, and I glance at Beckett, who seems like my remark may have bothered him. I wonder what he's been doing for the past three days, but I remind myself it's none of my business—just as I'm sure he feels what I do is none of his concern, hence him disappearing for days. As we pull up to his building, I stare in confusion. "Why are we coming here? You're going to come with me to meet with the insurance people, aren't you?"

"Of course," he says, pulling into his VIP parking spot. "My legal team is talking to the driver's insurance team," he explains. "Even though we didn't get hurt, they're offering a settlement if we agree not to take the driver to court. I agreed with their terms. Their driver is already going to serve time. They'll also cover the cost of the damages to your car and your rental."

"Sweet," I say, already liking the sound of this.

Once inside, Beckett leads me to a conference room where discussions are already underway, and we take our seats. The conversation quickly turns to legal jargon, and I find myself zoning out. "Do you understand any of this?" I whisper to him.

He nods, placing a reassuring hand on my leg.

I make an honest attempt at listening to the legal team ramble on. Bored out of my mind, I pull my phone from my pocket and open a farm game I downloaded while we were back at the hotel. This level is tough—I need to make 10 hamburgers, but all I have are 10 chickens when the game starts.

I dive in, quickly selling off enough eggs to get things moving. The clock's ticking down, and I'm tapping like crazy, selling off all the chickens once I've got enough cash to buy a cow, knowing this is where the real challenge begins. The cow's milk comes in slow, and I need it to churn into cheese before I can even start thinking about making those hamburgers. Storage is another problem; I have to juggle my resources carefully to make sure there's enough space to hold the finished hamburgers while I wait for the delivery truck to come back with my money.

Just as I'm about to beat my time so I can finally advance to the next level, Beckett slides a stack of papers toward me. He glances down at my phone, and his expression says he wants me to put it away.

"This is the farthest I've gotten. I'm about to beat my time," I whisper to him.

"Brynn, sign," he whispers back, his tone leaving no room for argument.

"Can you collect my hamburgers?" I ask, sneaking a quick peek at him, while frantically tapping the screen to make sure the cows have enough grass to keep producing milk.

Beckett shakes his head, a mix of amusement and frustration in his eyes. "You're going to make all my hair fall out."

After I finally beat the level, I grin at him. "Beat my score and upgraded my bakery," I announce, a bit of pride creeping into my voice. The rest of the table certainly isn't proud of my accomplishments as they all glower at me, looking utterly annoyed.

Oh well.

As I pull the papers to me, I gape at the settlement amount line, a figure that makes me pause.

"What does this mean?" I ask, my voice softening as I stare up at Beckett.

"That's the amount they're offering to settle with you," he says, cutting off any further questions by adding, "They'll still cover the cost of the damages and your rental."

"Are we splitting this?" I ask, still staring at the number.

"No, that's your amount. I settled mine earlier this morning."

I turn to him, covering my mouth so only he can see. "They're really going to write me a check for $25,000?" I ask, still in disbelief.

"Yes, as soon as you sign here." He points to the line.

"Do I have to suck their dick?" I ask, completely serious.

He leans in. "If you're in the mood, we can discuss that when there aren't six other people in the room. Sign so we can go." He points to the line again.

I sign, and moments later, they slide a check to me with my name on it. I stare at it, barely able to believe it's real, and I have to resist the urge to start kissing it right here.

I turn to Beckett, clasping the check in my hands. "Can you take me to the bank? I need to deposit this before I start thinking it's a prank. And we need to get out of here now or I might start making out with this piece of paper."

He grins, leading me out of the conference room and back through the building. The cold air hits me as we step outside, and I clutch the check, almost afraid it might disappear if I let go for even a second.

Once we're in his truck, he starts the engine but doesn't pull out of the parking spot right away. Instead, he turns toward me, resting his arm casually on the center seat, which is folded down as an armrest between us. "So, you mentioned something about making out?" His voice is slightly teasing.

I roll my eyes. "I never said that."

"Oh, but you did. You said you wanted to make out with the check," he leans in slightly. "But that check can't kiss you back, whereas I might be able to."

I feel the heat rise to my cheeks as I playfully hit his shoulder. "Just drive." I try to hide the blush spreading across my face. He puts his truck in reverse and pulls out of the parking lot, and we head toward the bank. The whole way there, I keep sneaking glances at him, scolding myself to stop each time I do.

The rest of the ride there goes by in a blur. Beckett follows me inside, and I'm grateful. I can only imagine the teller thinking I've stolen someone's check. Beckett would be sitting in his truck waiting for me as the entire bank is swarmed with police and S.W.A.T., then I'd be brought out in handcuffs.

Thankfully, that doesn't happen. The transaction is quick and smooth, and before I know it, the money is in my account—no questions, no complications. Well, except for Beckett putting his driver's license on the counter alongside mine. I notice the teller's eyes grow large as she looks between her computer, Beckett's ID, and then at him. I have no idea what that's about, but she hands it back to him and then mine to me, saying we are all set. Once we're outside, I pull up my mobile banking app, and when I see the balance, I blink in disbelief.

"I'm literally not even going to sleep for a week because I don't want to wake up from this dream," I joke as we head back to his truck. "Can I buy you lunch? I happen to have a little money." I wink at him.

"Sure, money bags, where would you like to go?"

"You choose," I say, leaning back in my seat, enjoying the feeling of financial security for the first time in my adult life.

After lunch, he drives me back to my apartment, and follows me in. "Your car will be fixed in about two weeks."

I shrug off my coat and hang it on the coat rack by the door. "What do we know about the rental?"

A look of confusion crosses his face as he leans against the doorframe. "You still want one?"

"Uhh, yeah. I still need to work."

"You could not work for the rest of winter and be fine," he counters, raising a brow.

I let out a short laugh, shaking my head at him. "You'd like that, wouldn't you?"

"I absolutely would."

"Well, I want to work because I'm bored out of my mind sitting here all day alone. Who do I need to contact to find out when one will be available?" I ask, pulling my phone from my coat and sitting on the couch.

He pushes off the doorframe and walks over to me. "I'll call on it and let you know. I've got to get back to work. Thank you for lunch." He leans over the back of the couch and kisses my cheek.

"Thanks for the ride," I say as he leaves.

As the door closes behind him, I sit there, staring at the empty space he's left behind. There's no part of me that believes he will try to figure anything out with my rental, especially since I know he doesn't want me driving in this weather. So, I decide to call around to figure out what's going on with it myself.

After nearly an hour of bouncing from one clueless person to another, I finally reach someone who knows what's going on. "Your rental has been ready for almost a week now," the woman on the other end of the line tells me.

A week? That can't be right. Beckett had said the rental wouldn't be ready for a few more days. Confused but eager to get moving again, I arrange for the car to be delivered. No sooner do the keys hit my hand than I'm out the door, excited to finally escape the four walls of my apartment. As I hit the road, picking up food deliveries, I feel a sense of freedom I hadn't realized I'd been missing. Strangely, with the pressure of relying on tips lifted, I find myself making better ones than ever. It's like the universe is rewarding me for just getting back out there.

After dropping off another order, I get into the car, my phone buzzing with Beckett's name on the screen. "Where are you?" he asks, his voice clipped.

"Doing deliveries, what's up?"

"Doing deliveries? How?"

"Well, Beckett," I say, unable to hide the sarcasm creeping into my tone. "My rental has been ready for almost a week."

There's a long, loaded silence. "It's starting to snow, Brynn."

"Yes, my eyeballs are currently looking at it," I quip.

"Where are you? I'll come pick you up."

"No. I'm working." I repeat. "I just accepted another delivery, so I need to get off the phone. Have a good night." I end the call before he can argue.

I wasn't even mad when I found out he hadn't mentioned my rental was ready. I wanted to believe maybe he kept it from me because he wanted to spend more time together or some shit. But now? Now that he's trying to keep me off the road like I'm some kind of reckless driver, it's starting to piss me off. It feels like another backhanded way of telling me I'm a crappy driver. How does he go from being sweet, to this? He's always swinging between sweet and controlling, and it's driving me crazy. And after he picked me up—what did he plan on doing with my rental? Putting it in the backseat of his truck?

I continue doing deliveries until 1 AM because I'm on a roll with tips. When I finally pull into my parking spot at my apartment, I see Beckett's truck parked next to mine. Getting out, I peer in his truck window and see him reclined in his seat, sleeping. Quietly, I circle around to the driver's side and gently tap on the window. He doesn't stir, so I try the door handle, and it opens with a soft click.

"Hey," I give his shoulder a light shake. "Come inside; it's freezing out here."

Beckett stirs awake, rubbing his face as he slowly follows me toward the apartment. We don't say much—both too tired for conversation. We head straight to my room, climbing into bed in silence. His warmth beside me is comforting, and I drift off almost immediately.

When I wake in the morning, I find his side of the bed empty. I assume he's left for work, but when I step into the living room, I jump, startled to see him on the couch, typing away on his phone.

"It's noon," I say through a yawn, heading to the kitchen for a glass of water. "Don't you have work today?"

"Yeah," he sighs, not looking up from his phone.

"So, what are you doing then?"

"Waiting for you to wake up," he says simply, finally locking his phone and turning his attention to me.

I walk over to the living room, flopping down on the opposite couch. "Why?"

His expression shifts, something serious crossing his face. "Do you know how many accidents there were between 5 PM and 1 AM last night?"

"No?" I respond, confused why he would even ask that. "If you're about to tell me how many there were and how unsafe it was for me to be out on the roads, save your breath."

He leans forward, his voice firm. "It's not safe, Brynn. You drive too fast, you take corners like you're in a race car, and you weave in and out of traffic like you're invincible. One wrong move in this weather, and you're going to get hurt."

"Give me a break," I roll my eyes. "It's how I earn money, Beckett. It's my job. Go back to your job and don't worry about mine."

"You're not going back out today. The snow hasn't let up since morning," Beckett declares with finality.

I feel the spark of defiance rise in me. "What are you, my dad now? You don't get to tell me what I can and can't do," I snap, standing from the couch to go make coffee. It's too early to argue without it.

"Maybe your dad should have done a better job teaching you when to use common sense," he bites back.

I whip around to face him, my glare like daggers. "You have about half a second to take that statement back," I warn, my pulse spiking.

"Brynn—" He steps forward, hands out, like he's trying to defuse the tension.

"No." I raise my hand, stopping him in his tracks. "You can go." I point toward the door, my voice shaking with anger.

He pauses, torn between standing his ground and respecting my space. His jaw clenches as he makes his decision. Without another word, he turns and walks out, the door clicking shut softly behind him.

A moment later, I hear his truck's engine roar to life and then him back out.

CHAPTER
Eleven

I lay sprawled on my bed, staring blankly at my phone, mindlessly scrolling through the endless stream of posts, but nothing is holding my attention. My thoughts keep drifting to the silence since Beckett left.

The sharp ring of my phone slices through the quiet, making me jump. For a split second, I think it's him calling to apologize—and disappointment settles in as I see it's my mom. I hesitate to answer; it's been weeks since we last spoke, long enough that she's going to make sure to turn it into a big deal. She always does.

"Hey, Mom," I answer, trying to inject some cheerfulness into my voice.

"Brynn," she says in that calm tone of hers. Then she whispers off the phone, "She answered," before resuming her call with me. "Your dad and I want you to come home for a visit. It's been too long."

"You can always come and visit me?" I turn it back around on her.

"Oh, honey, no. Daddy said he's buying you a plane ticket home. What day works best for you?"

"I'll have to let you know, my schedule is super full," I lie, trying to get out of it.

"Dad says tomorrow works good for us."

"I can't. I have to work."

"You don't work," she dismisses me with a wave of her words, then proceeds to talk to dad.

There's no point in even arguing with her because they don't believe I do anything right. They also never take no for an answer, so getting out of this trip is useless.

"Okay, honey, we just miss you and want to see you. Daddy bought you a ticket for tomorrow evening. He just sent you an email with the flight details. Josh will pick you up."

My stomach clenches at the mention of my brother. "Josh is home?" I ask, feeling a pang of dread. He's just as judgmental as they are, always full of opinions about my life and what I should be doing differently.

"He's been home for two days. He said he'll stay a couple more days so he can see you," she says, sounding overly happy.

As soon as I step out of the terminal, I scan the bustling crowd until I catch sight of my brother. Josh is leaning against the wall, sweeping over the steady flow of travelers. When our gazes finally lock, he straightens up, his expression shifting as he makes his way toward me with a purposeful stride.

"Hey, sis," he pulls me into a brief, firm side hug.

"Hey," I respond, as I wrap my arm around him. "Thanks for picking me up."

"No problem," he says easily, already reaching for my suitcase. He nods toward the parking garage, and we fall into step beside each other. We walk in silence, and I dread even being home. I almost feel a sense of annoyance that it's warm, knowing there's a snowstorm where Beckett is. I wonder what he's doing. I shouldn't have told him to leave. Well, he was leaving anyway, so it wouldn't have mattered whether I told him to go.

We reach Josh's car, and he tosses my bag into the back then slides into the driver's seat. Once we're on the road, with the familiar landscape speeding by, I glance over at him, trying to gauge his mood. I can't tell if he's just tired or if he's uptight over the conversation I was summoned here for.

"So… what are Mom and Dad up to?" I ask, keeping my tone light, even though my mind is miles away, back home with Beckett.

Josh shrugs, his focus remaining fixed on the road. "Nothing much."

I squint, unconvinced. "I don't believe you. They wouldn't drag me all the way home for 'nothing much.'"

He lets out a long exhale, gripping the steering wheel a little more firmly until his knuckles pale. "They're just…

concerned. They want to make sure you're thinking about the future, about what you're going to do. They want you to have some kind of direction."

Annoyance flares up in me. "Of course they are," I mutter, crossing my arms and turning to stare out the window. I don't say another word for the rest of the drive, letting the silence between us thicken.

As we turn down the familiar dirt road, the tires crunch softly over the gravel, stirring up small clouds of dust behind us. The road seems shorter than I remember, and I'm not quite ready when my childhood home comes into view. The large white Victorian-style house stands tall at the end of the road, its wraparound porch still holding the swinging porch bench I used to sit on with friends, late at night, gossiping about boys.

To the left, the big white barn stands tall. Growing up, it was red, but my mom always claimed it was an eyesore, so my dad had it painted to match the color of the house.

Acres of land stretch out endlessly around us. My dad inherited this land with my Uncle Ralph from their parents. While Dad pursued a career with the government, Uncle Ralph kept the farm alive, working the cornfields and maintaining the equipment that's older than I am. The arrangement always worked seamlessly—Dad never minded sharing the land, and Uncle Ralph handled the crops and workers, keeping the legacy alive. It didn't hurt that Dad and Uncle Ralph were practically inseparable, and my mom and Aunt Marla were just as close, making the shared space feel like one large, sprawling family estate rather than two separate properties.

When we finally pull up to the house, Mom and Dad are already waiting at the door, their faces lighting up when they see me. Mom rushes down the steps, down the gravel drive, toward the car before Josh even stops. She wraps me in a hug as she rocks us back and forth like she hasn't seen me in years, while my arms hang awkwardly at my sides.

"Brynn, sweetheart! It's so good to see you," she croons, squeezing me.

Dad joins in, his big hands resting on both our shoulders as he pulls us into a family hug. "We've missed you, kiddo."

I try my best to push down the irritation that I've been brought here as a sort of intervention. "Missed you too," I say, though the words feel a bit hollow.

As they usher me inside, the familiar scent of Mom's cooking fills the air. "I made your favorite—meatloaf," Mom announces as she hurries off to the kitchen to take it out of the oven.

"The last time you made me meatloaf, you told me my cat got run over," I halfheartedly tease. Though it's the truth. So now it really feels like this is going to be quite the conversation they flew me home for.

Dad chuckles. "Well, we don't have any cats that got run over, and last we checked, Granny is still in the nursing home, unless she somehow managed to sneak out," my dad says, making a stab at a joke.

"Oh, Harold," my mom scolds, shaking her head as she brings the meatloaf to the table.

Dinner tastes good, with a side of tension. I can see my mom and dad exchanging looks, trying to silently communicate with each other about talking to me, but neither seems to know how to begin. I wonder who will crack first and start this inevitable conversation about my supposed failures in life.

Mom is the first to speak, interrupting the silence. "Do you want some dessert?" she asks while I'm still chewing.

"No, thanks," I say, not wanting dessert. I didn't even want to eat, but I forced each bite down.

After dinner, we move to the sunroom. Mom pours tea for everyone as we settle onto the couches. The air grows heavier with the conversation we're avoiding, making it feel so uncomfortable I can hardly stand it. It's only made worse by the continued exchange of glances between my parents.

I let out a long, exaggerated sigh. "Just say it. Whatever reason you had for bringing me here," I blurt out, my patience finally snapping. It's more awkward watching them tiptoe around the conversation than hearing whatever judgment they're about to hand down.

They both blink at me in surprise, and then my dad clears his throat. "Brynn, sweetie, we're glad you're home," he begins. "But there's something we need to talk about."

"Obviously, we've established that with you flying me all the way here. You can just get straight to the point," I respond, already knowing how this is going to go.

Dad sighs, shifting in his seat like he's rehearsed this speech a dozen times. "Well, Brynn, there's no easy way to say it, so I'll just come right out. You're making poor choices, honey, and I hate to say it, but being a taxi driver isn't a safe or sustainable career. It's not something you can retire from, and it's not a long-term plan."

"And do you really think you'll meet a respectable man doing that?" Mom chimes in. "Wouldn't you be embarrassed to tell him what you do for a living?" Her expression sours, driving the point home.

Dad nods, picking up the thread. "We're just trying to make sure you're on the right track, sweetheart, and frankly, you're not. We need to figure out how to get you sorted out."

"I'm happy with my life, Dad. I'm doing what I want."

Dad shakes his head, half looking like he doesn't understand how he has such an idiot for a daughter. "You don't have a real job. Nobody will ever take you seriously. How will you ever build a future? One day, you're going to wake up in your seventies, still working, with no savings, no retirement."

"I literally have a *real* job."

Mom lets out a short, patronizing laugh and places her hand on Dad's arm. "Oh, I guess we were never informed. Where are you working now? We thought you were still doing that silly Taxi stuff. So, what's the job?" Her red-painted lips stretch into a wide smile as she bats her lashes in a knowing way.

"Thank God, not a taxi driver. You sure have strong opinions on those cockroaches. I drive for ExpressWay," I say matter-of-factly.

Mom looks exasperated. "Daddy is going to pull some strings to get you into school a couple weeks late this semester. You need to get your life straightened out. This is final. No more gallivanting around, Brynn. We've had it."

Hot rage settles in the pit of my stomach, but I force myself to take slow, deep breaths, trying to keep my composure.

When I finally feel a small bit of control, I respond. "No. If I wanted your help I would ask."

Silence settles over the room. Dad shifts in his chair, rubbing his hands together, leaning forward, his eyes softening just a bit, though his words are no less cutting. "Sweetheart, listen. No one worth anything is going to want to be with someone who doesn't have a solid career. The kind of people you'll attract? They're going to be the ones working dead-end jobs, crashing on friends' couches, drifting through life just like you're doing right now."

His words sting, but I hold my ground, unwilling to let their expectations dictate my choices. "Well, this has been a super delightful chat. Thank you for flying me out to tell me how big of a loser I am and how I'll eventually bring a loser into this family. Maybe one day we can even have loser kids," I stand from my seat. "I'm tired. I shall see my 'loser' self up to my room."

As I go to walk inside, my parents exchange a look and they both go to speak at the same time. "I'm over this conversation. Save your breath. You know, this could have been a phone conversation," I bite out as I walk away, letting the screen door slam behind me.

Once I'm upstairs, I peel off my clothes and slip into a tank top and shorts, then pull back the covers on the bed. How can they sit here and judge me like that? At least I'm not pregnant or in trouble. I have a job—maybe not the type of job they see as respectable, but I pay all my bills on time. I don't waste money on things I don't need. Some nights I skip dinner just to make sure everything's covered. And they want to judge me? I'm happy, and they can't even be happy for me.

My phone vibrates beside me, and I flip it over to look at the screen—it's Beckett. I let it ring twice, staring at the name flashing on the screen, debating whether I'm in the mood to talk to him tonight. I quickly decide my mood is soured and send it to voicemail. But the phone rings again almost immediately. Annoyed, I send it to voicemail once more.

By the third call, I answer on the first ring. "What?" I say, my voice sharper than I intended.

"Why are you ignoring my calls?"

"Why are you calling me?" I retort.

"Your car is ready. I can meet you at the rental shop then take you to pick up your car in the morning," he says, practically sounding like this is a business transaction.

"Its fine. I'll figure it out when I get home."

He lets out a sigh. "The roads are—"

I cut him off. "Relax grandpa. I'm back home."

"No, you're not," he says.

I stare around my childhood bedroom, which has been converted into a guest bedroom, thinking if I'm not here, I'm losing my mind.

"Pretty sure I am," I say sarcastically.

There's a brief pause. "When did you get home?"

"I flew in a couple hours ago."

"You went on vacation?"

I let out a bitter laugh, shaking my head even though he can't see it. "I wouldn't consider this a vacation."

"When will you be back?"

"Not soon enough."

There's a pause and then he asks, "Are you okay?"

I ponder that question. Sure, I'm okay, in the most basic sense. Just tired of everyone treating me like I'm a baby. My parents think I'm going nowhere in life, my brother agrees with them, and Beckett never misses a chance to criticize my driving. It seems like my driving is the root of everyone's problems with me.

The knock on my bedroom door, preceded by my brother entering, catches me off guard.

"Hold on, Beckett," I mutter, putting my phone down.

"Why are you so stubborn?" Josh asks, walking to my bed.

I blink, incredulous. "Me?!" I snap, sitting up straighter. "I don't even burden you guys with my life, and then Mom calls just to force me home so you all can do an intervention on me about how I'm a big ol' screw up."

"You're a freaking taxi driver, Brynn, that's disgusting," he spits out, his face contorted with disdain.

"Thanks, Josh. Not all of us aspired to be a lawyer."

"Mom and Dad are trying to pay for your college, and you'd rather waste these years doing this? Do you have any self-respect?"

"I don't want to go to college, and fuck you," I bite out.

He combs his hands through his hair in frustration, then lets out a sigh. "Why'd you stop doing photography?"

"I make decent money driving."

He scoffs, waving a hand dismissively. "You think you're gonna make a living off of driving? That's like a summer job, Brynn. Go to school and do that driving nonsense in your free time."

I cross my arms over my chest, then stare at him. I have nothing clever or witty to say. I'm just tired. "Are you done?"

"You drive me nuts. You were good at photography! You want a new camera? I'll get you a new camera! But it's time to grow up."

"What about you? Mom and Dad hate my job; they equally hate that you haven't given them a grand baby. You settling down yet?" I counter.

He stiffens, his jaw flexing. "I wasn't the one flown across the country so they could lay into me about how disappointed they are. That was you."

"You can close the door on your way out." I point for him to leave.

"We are trying to help you because we care. Open your eyes and see that," he says as he walks away.

I flop back on the pillows, letting out a huff as I stare up at the ceiling.

"Brynn." I hear Beckett's voice from my phone.

Damn it...

Picking up my phone, I half-hope I'd imagined hearing him, that maybe he'd hung up when I left him on hold. But no, he's still here. "Beckett," I reply, resigned.

"Was that your brother?"

"Yeah, you two would get along great," I mutter. "Maybe you should come on out for a visit. My family is really on a roll. They'd love to have another person on their side about my job."

"I'll come right now if you send me the address."

"That was called sarcasm, Buckets."

There's a pause but then he shifts gears. "You did photography?"

"I took pictures of shit, yeah."

"Why'd you stop?"

"Because I needed an actual job," I laugh, the bitterness creeping into my tone. "And said actual job is still not good enough for my family."

"Fuck 'em," he says bluntly.

I prop myself up on my side, phone still on speaker, when the screen switches to an incoming FaceTime. "Why are you FaceTiming me?"

"Just answer it."

Beckett's face appears on the screen as he moves around his closet, shirtless, getting ready for bed. He exits, and the lights flick off behind him. How fancy. He props his phone on his nightstand and pulls back the covers of his ridiculously large bed, one that looks like it stretches across half his room. Definitely a king-sized bed. He probably needs all that space for the orgies I imagine he has.

He settles in, turning on his side to face the screen, the soft glow of his nightstand lamp illuminating his face as he looks at me through the screen.

"Why is your bed so big?"

He gazes over his shoulder, then turns back to the phone and shrugs. "Gotta have a big bed since you're a bed hog."

"I've never been in your bed. So, you must have a lot of bed hogs in there."

"You're the only bed hog I want in my bed."

"Keep dreamin', Romeo," I laugh.

"You tired?" he asks.

"No, you?" Though I notice just how tired he looks.

"Maybe," he mumbles, struggling to blink away the exhaustion. His lids are heavy, and it's obvious he's losing the battle.

"Go to bed," I say, and he nods.

I grab my iPad and open my farm game. After a few moments, I glance over, only to find Beckett's eyes still on me. "That's not sleeping," I tease, returning my attention to the game. But even after a couple more peeks at my phone, he's still looking, half-lidded and quiet, like he's trying to stay awake.

It's only when I finally power down the iPad and roll over that I see he's drifted off. I stare at him for what feels like hours. I just watch him, his face relaxed in sleep, imagining myself there beside him, curled up behind him with my arms wrapped around his waist and my face snuggled into his back.

I realize I've never in my life felt these feelings, but my feelings for Beckett don't matter, not really. They won't change anything. I know this. I'm not naive enough to believe he's going to fall madly in love with me and we'll live happily ever after. But maybe it wouldn't be too bad to think about the possibility of giving myself to him. Giving *THAT* to him.

I can feel the exhaustion pulling at me, but I don't want to hang up. I don't remember drifting off, but when I wake up, the morning light is streaming through the window, and my phone screen is still on. I blink a few times, trying to clear the sleep away, and can hear Beckett talking.

His phone is propped up on his desk, angled toward him as he sits in his office. He's on a call, his voice steady and professional as he speaks. I take him in, my heart fluttering as I see him so focused and completely in his element. He's writing something down, then types on his computer, with the phone pressed between his shoulder and ear.

He glances at the phone, probably checking to see if I'm still asleep. When our eyes finally meet, he does a double take, not expecting to see I'm awake. A slow smile spreads across his face, softening his otherwise serious expression.

With a quick word, he wraps up his call then turns back to me. "It's about time you woke up. You were snoring so loud," he ribs.

"I don't snore," I shoot back, trying to sound indignant but failing to suppress a smile.

"How would you know? You were sleeping," he grins.

I touch my phone screen to see how long we've been on the call, and it's a little over fourteen hours. I wonder why he didn't just hang up on me when he woke up.

"How long did you plan on watching me sleep?" I raise a brow.

"I was just timing you to see how long you would sleep for. You weren't even bothered by the sun shining in your eyes."

"Why would I be. I was sleeping."

He leans back in his chair, swiveling side to side with his head resting comfortably against the backrest as he watches me. There's a long pause before he finally speaks again. "You should go shower," he suggests, though there's a playful edge to his tone.

"That's rude," I laugh, sitting up. "But yeah, I probably should."

"I should probably supervise, make sure you don't just hop in, dump shampoo on the floor, kick it around a bit, and call it clean."

"Ohhh, I see. You wanna see me nakey." I quirk my brow at him.

"Very much, yes," he nods.

"Naughty, naughty," I say, wagging my finger at him as I get up and walk to the bathroom. I prop my phone on the counter and brush my teeth, then floss. As I undress I don't try to make it sexy or appealing, just going through the motions of a normal shower. I hang my phone on the pop-socket holder stuck to the shower wall, knowing Beckett has seen this—after all, this is technically the third shower we've taken together, if you can call it that. His eyes stay glued to me, tracking every movement. I expected to feel self-conscious, but there's none of that, just a strange comfort in his steady gaze.

Once I'm done, I return to my room and prop my phone on my nightstand, then I towel off. I rummage through my suitcase and start digging through it to find something to wear, then toss the clothes on the bed.

"What happened to your back?" Beckett's tone shifts slightly, as he leans in to the screen.

Turning to the full-length mirror in the corner of the room, I twist to get a better look. A bruise is forming along my left ribcage, faint but noticeable. I reach up, trailing my fingers over it, but there's no pain.

"No clue," I shrug. "I probably have a poltergeist beating me up in my sleep or something." I grab my underwear and pull them on. I take my time dressing the rest of the way, moving slower than I usually would, enjoying the way his attention is entirely on me.

When I'm finished, I adjust my phone to face me while I sit on the edge of my bed to put my socks on. He hasn't taken his eyes off of me for even a second. I'm not even sure he has blinked.

There's a soft knock on the door, and then dad pokes his head in. "Hi, sugar. Mom and I will drive you to the airport. Some of Josh's friends wanted to head to the beach, so he can't take you." He lingers at the door not trying to come in any further.

I let out a condescending laugh. "Cool for him. Fine by me. I've got my earbuds fully charged so I can listen to music on the drive there."

Dad stands there, exhaling a long breath. "Wanna go for a walk? Or we could go fishing for a little while before we leave."

"You want to go fishing with me?" I ask, lifting a brow.

He chuckles. "It was Mom's idea to offer. She wasn't the one who took a fish hook to the neck fishing with you."

Beckett's sudden laughter echoes through the room, catching Dad's attention. His eyes get so big, and he slinks into the room, nudging the door open just enough to slide through then closing it quietly behind him. "Is that a boy on the phone?" Dad mutters, moving closer to get a better view of the screen. He leans in, peeking at Beckett, who casually lifts his hand in greeting, a small, amused smile playing on his lips.

Dad waves back, then turns his head toward me and mouths, "Are you in trouble?"

I chuckle, shaking my head. "No, I'm not in trouble. This is Beckett Shaw. He's, you know, really successful, has his life together—someone you'd be proud of. I just happen to give him rides sometimes."

"Ohhhh," Dad's eyes widen with approval as he gives Beckett a thumbs up.

"Oh my god, Dad. Not that kind of ride; I'm not a prostitute." I roll my eyes.

Dad motions for me to scoot over, then plops down next to me on the bed. "So, Beckett," he starts, grinning wide as he slings his arm around my shoulder, giving me a squeeze. "You've got your hands full with this one."

"Yes, sir," Beckett responds.

The next half hour is spent with my dad asking Beckett a million questions about his company, while Beckett patiently answers each one. I try multiple times to cut in so I can end the conversation Beckett is being held hostage in, but Dad waves me off each time.

I'm so bored I start picking at the wood on the edge of my nightstand. I hear Beckett start to laugh, and when I look up, he shakes his head like he knows what I'm doing, then says he needs to get back to work.

Dad goes on to invite him to go fishing sometime, and to my amazement—and mild horror—Beckett ACCEPTS.

"I'd like that," he says, leaving me speechless as the call finally comes to an end.

As soon as Dad leaves the room, I can hear him practically bouncing down the hallway, already eager to tell mom everything that 'she won't believe.'

BECKETT:
16 hours and 34 minutes.
You talk A LOT 😜

BRYNN:
I know. I need some water with all the talking I did...

I purposely hide in my room until it's time to leave. I even make a big production out of putting my completely dead earbuds in my ears just to make sure nobody tries talking to me. But that doesn't stop them one little bit. The entire ride to the airport is filled with Dad and Mom asking nonstop questions about Beckett.

I'm pretty sure they think I'm his chauffeur, and at one point my mom said she must have misunderstood because maybe he accidentally called the wrong number. She then proceeded to make up different reasons why I might be in trouble.

As I step off the plane and make my way toward the luggage carousel, the noise of the airport surrounds me—announcements echoing, people chatting, and the occasional beep of a cart rolling by. Now would be a fabulous time to not have dead earbuds. Then I wouldn't have to listen to all of this. I navigate through the crowd, scanning the rotating conveyor belt for my bag. Just as I spot it coming around the bend, someone bumps into me, jarring me from my focus.

Anger flares up, and I whirl around, ready to tell off whoever it is. But when I turn, my eyes meet Beckett's.

"Sorry about that," he says, his voice laced with amusement. "You're kind of taking up a lot of space. I'm looking for someone. She's about yay high, brown hair, hazel eyes, BIG attitude; You can't miss her."

"Haven't seen her. Maybe she's purposely avoiding you?" I quirk a brow, stepping forward just as my bag comes into reach.

"Not possible. She would never," he says, grabbing my bag before I can lift it.

"Yeah, I'm sure she wouldn't."

"We're parked right outside." He gestures to his truck, then reaches out, looping his arm around my neck and pulling me to him. I fall into step beside him, slipping my arm around his waist as we walk out into the snow.

"How'd you know what time my flight would get in?" I ask as he effortlessly hoists my bag into the back seat while I climb into the front. The truck is warm, and I sink into the heat, grateful for the relief from the freezing cold. My body had acclimated to the warmth back home, and now the winter chill feels even colder.

"Are you hungry?" he asks, pulling away from the curb."

"No, not really. Can we go pick up my car?" I turn to look at him, detecting the slight hesitation in his expression. He seems caught off guard, like he's reluctant to take me. Upon seeing how much snow is on the ground, I knew this was going to be an issue. After two days of relentless badgering from my family, I'm not in the mood for more of the same, especially not from him. He's the one person I've been desperate to see, the person I've been yearning to see for days now.

"You can just say no," I begin, ready to find another way to get my car. "I can find someone else to take me—"

Before I can get another word out, he's already shaking his head. "No, I'll take you," he says firmly.

We make a quick stop to return the rental, then I hurry back to his truck and climb back in. The ride to the repair shop is quiet, just the low hum of the heater filling the space between us. He's focused on the road, and I stare out the window. When we arrive, I reach for the door handle. "Thanks for the ride," I say, ready to head inside.

But instead of staying in the truck, Beckett kills the engine and steps out.

"What are you doing?" I ask, watching as he rounds the front of the truck.

"Coming with you," he says simply, holding the door open for me.

Inside the shop, the man behind the counter only addresses Beckett, ignoring me completely. He outlines the details about my car as if I'm not even there. I stay quiet, observing the interaction unfold. When it's time to sign the paperwork, the man slides the forms across the counter toward Beckett and offers him the keys. I reach out and snatch them away, causing him to look at me startled. I take the papers next, scribbling my signature, then slide the forms back to him, slapping the pen on the counter with a sarcastic smirk. Then relax my face, take my papers off the counter, and walk away.

We step outside, the cold air hitting my face as we walk toward our vehicles. I brace myself, already dreading how freezing my car is going to be, but at least I'll finally have it back. Beckett follows me to the car, his boots crunching softly against the snow. I slide into the driver's seat and start the engine, feeling the chill seep through the open door. As I settle in, Beckett leans against the doorframe, peering down at me.

"You heading home?"

"No," I reply, not bothering to sugarcoat it. "I'm gonna go work."

His expression instantly shifts to one of disapproval. "Brynn, it's not safe with these road conditions."

Annoyance flares inside me, everyone's opinions pressing down on me. I'm tired—so tired—of being shamed for the way I live. "Thank you again for the ride, can you please move," I say, trying to close my door.

"After we talk."

"Go judge someone else. I'm so tired of everyone judging me," I snap. "Both our vehicles are fixed. You no longer have to hover over me like I'm your charity case."

His chin jerks back in shock. "You have a bad attitude."

"And you're annoying," I retort. "So I'll take my bad attitude out of here, and you can take your annoying attitude away from me."

"Maybe take a nap and call me when you're feeling better," he releases my door and steps away so I can slam it shut. My adrenaline is racing as I back out, and I half want to peel out and cover him in snow, but I do the only adult thing I've probably ever done in my life—I drive away slowly.

CHAPTER
Twelve

I'm finally making mine and Elliot's date up, although I half forgot he existed until he called. The guilt that surged through me was enough to make me say yes. He didn't even call it a date—he said, "lunch sesh." I was so thrown by that phrase that I sat in stunned silence. He must've taken it as an agreement because he quickly told me to meet him at his work on Monday. I've written and deleted about a hundred different texts to cancel, but somehow I never sent any of them. So, here I am, actually going.

I put on a dark blue dress with black pantyhose and black ankle boots. I add my black wool coat, which falls just to mid-thigh, matching the length of my dress and providing me with both warmth and style. As Chloe and I like to say when it's really cold out, "It's nipples out," and it *is* nipples out, so I wrap a coordinating scarf snugly around my neck. My hair cascades down my back in soft, wavy curls, and I finish the look with a pair of elegant earrings that complete the ensemble.

I have no idea why I put this much time and effort into this when I'm still trying to think of ways to get out of it. Maybe I will meet *"the one"* while I'm on my way there, and then I'll be grateful I dressed up.

When Elliot texts me the address of his work, I pause. My eyes scan the message again and again. It's Beckett's building. Elliot works in Beckett's building. Elliot works for Beckett…

It's been two weeks since Beckett and I argued, and I haven't worked since. I've spent the time catching up with Chloe, doing everything to avoid thinking about him. Now, I'm heading right into his territory.

When I pull up to the building, a small part of me still considers backing out. I text Elliot to figure out what floor he's on. I don't like that he works here. I never knew this. Then again, it's never been mentioned. Why would it have been? Elliot and I never talk.

BRYNN:
I am here. Want to meet me down here?

ELLIOT:
Come on up. I am wrapping up. I am on the 14th floor.

Of course he's on the same floor. Why would he not be?

Getting out of my car, I head inside. When I get off on the 14th floor, the receptionist looks annoyed when I approach her desk. I doubt it's from her remembering me bringing food here since that was a while ago, looking half homeless that day.

"Do you have an appointment?" she asks in a clipped tone.

"I'm here to see Elliot Parker."

She taps away at her keyboard, her face never shifting from that annoyed look, then tells me to sit. I find a bench and do as she said, my eyes wandering around the busy office floor.

A moment later, I hear my name: "Brynn." I look up to see Elliot approaching, offering what could hardly be called a hug. His arms barely graze my shoulders, and the whole exchange feels awkward.

"Hi," I mutter, half-heartedly patting his back, trying to hide the discomfort on my face.

"Thank you, Savannah," he says to the receptionist as he starts walking away. I suppose I'm supposed to follow him, so I hurry after him to his desk.

He leads me to his cubicle that's a total disaster. Papers, empty coffee cups, and random clutter are strewn across every surface. My anxiety spikes just looking at it. Why would he want me to see how messy he is? He didn't even want to tidy up a little bit before he walked me over here? I would have rather swiped everything on the desk into the trash than have someone see my workspace look like this. The disorganization makes me itch to go home and start purging my own things, just to reassure myself that I'm not living like this big of a slob.

I stand in the aisle, fidgeting, wishing he had just met me downstairs. He tells me he'll be right back and casually suggests I sit in his chair if I want. I almost laugh at that; his chair is filthy, stained with what looks like spilled coffee. I'm not even sure why I find this irritating. He isn't doing anything wrong. I think I might be overly sensitive that I know this is Beckett's building.

As if fate really wants to make things worse, I look over, trying to distract myself, and spot a group of men walking by. My gaze falls on the person leading them—Beckett. He's focused on the folder in his hands, but when he looks up, our eyes meet. Time seems to slow, stretching into what feels like an eternity until he's fully out of sight. Maybe he didn't even recognize me. Honestly, I don't think he did.

What an actual loser.

I stand there, so uncomfortable, for at least ten minutes. When Elliot finally returns, he announces he's ready to go.

"Are you sure you have any lunch time left? I've been standing here for probably half of your shift," I mutter as I fall into stride next to him.

He chuckles. "We're good. My lunch doesn't start until I actually leave," he reassures me.

As we near the elevators, I spot Beckett standing with two other men. They seem to be wrapping up a conversation, given they haven't even pressed the button yet. Elliot smiles and reaches past them to push it.

Beckett faces us, but his expression is unreadable. No flicker of recognition crosses his features, and it throws me off balance.

Elliot turns toward me, rubbing his hands up and down my arms. "Do you have anywhere specific in mind for lunch?"

"I'm fine with whatever." My eyes drift upward, watching the numbers above the elevator, silently willing the doors to open and relieve the growing discomfort I'm feeling standing here.

The doors finally part, and just as Elliot steps forward, Beckett and his men move first, cutting him off. Elliot awkwardly steps back, gesturing for them to go ahead like it's no big deal.

"We'll catch the next one," he says to me. I nod, staring at my boots. My irritation builds at how rude I find this, since they didn't even push the button to call for the elevator, and now they're taking ours.

But just as the doors start to close, they open again, and Beckett's hand appears, holding them back. "There's room," he says.

Elliot beams, his face lighting up in gratitude. "Thanks so much, sir," he says, stepping forward eagerly. But I grab his arm, shaking my head in silent protest, not wanting to share such a confined space with Beckett.

"Come on," Elliot urges, oblivious to my discomfort, and strides right into the elevator, leaving me with little choice but to follow.

I step in, trying to stick to the far corner with Elliot, but the confined space only makes it harder to avoid the weight of Beckett now staring directly at me. He's probably trying to place where he's seen me before.

Dumbass.

"Mr. Shaw, your model of the Ark project is incredible," Elliot praises.

"Yes," Beckett agrees candidly.

Elliot seems way too eager for this conversation, like he's trying to impress him. It's almost painful to watch.

"Are you going to lunch?" Elliot asks Beckett.

"Yes," Beckett answers, his tone flat. "You?"

"Yes," Elliot smiles at Beckett.

"You should join me," Beckett says to Elliot.

I try to interject, my voice coming out at the same time as Elliot's enthusiastic response. "Oh, no, thank you—" I begin, while Elliot, completely ignoring me, practically glows with excitement, "I would be honored!"

I turn sharply toward Elliot, trying to convey with just a look, absolutely not.

"This is Mr. Shaw, my boss," Elliot says proudly, beaming like it's some grand accomplishment just to be standing in his presence.

"And Mr. Shaw, I'm sure, is very busy and doesn't want to spend his lunch time with us on our lunch *date*," I say through clenched teeth. I make sure to emphasize the word "date," trying to remind everyone why I'm even here.

"I insist," Beckett says.

"He insists," Elliot echoes with happiness. He's so happy you'd almost think Beckett asked *him* on a date.

"Well, I insist we don't," I say through gritted teeth, directing my frustration at Elliot.

"I can take you to dinner or something later, if you want," he says.

I blink at him, utterly dumbfounded. Did he seriously just say that? Without responding, I turn back to face the elevator doors, mentally checking out of this whole situation. All I want now is to get off this damn elevator. I'm going home, and they can enjoy a lunch date. Glad I dressed up for nothing. Well, that's not true. I certainly got to impress the piles of shit on his desk.

The moment the doors slide open, I practically bolt, striding ahead with purpose. Elliot's voice calls after me, but I don't slow down. "Wait, you're walking so fast," he snickers as he hurries to catch up.

I keep going, marching straight out of the front doors. Elliot stops and watches me go as I head toward the parking garage where my car is parked. I hear footsteps behind me, quickly approaching.

"Preston will drive us," Beckett says, wrapping his hand around my waist, steering me toward his SUV.

"I'll meet you guys there," I mutter, trying to break free from his hold, but he doesn't loosen his grip.

"No need." Beckett clutches the fabric of my coat on my hip and continues guiding me toward his waiting vehicle.

Elliot looks more than excited to be getting in the SUV. He hurries to the other side and hops into the back seat as Beckett holds the door for me to get in, which means I now get to be sandwiched between Beckett and Elliot in the back.

"Hey, Preston," I wave as I settle in the center.

"Brynn," he nods.

Elliot pats my knee a couple times in excitement, smiling so wide it takes up the entire back seat. I push my hand out, trying to get his hand off me, and feel Beckett watching Elliot touch me, and his body instantly tenses. I shift more toward Beckett, not wanting Elliot to do that again, bringing both my feet to Beckett's side and angling my knees toward him. I don't miss when he subtly spreads his knees wider until our legs are touching.

Elliot immediately launches into some long-winded conversation with Beckett and the guy in the front passenger seat, but it's painfully clear Beckett couldn't care less.

I shift uncomfortably, staring out Beckett's window, trying to tune out Elliot's rambling when my phone vibrates in my hand. Glancing down, I see a new text message from Beckett.

BECKETT:
Should I have Preston pull over and let him out?

BRYNN:
Yes

BRYNN:
Maybe you both can get out

BECKETT:
It's going to snow soon…

BRYNN:
> Do you plan on taking us far away for lunch. Maybe somewhere we can get caught in a blizzard and have to spend the weekend in a hotel…

BECKETT:
> I can make that happen…
> Wouldn't be the first time…

Rolling my eyes, I tuck my phone back into my coat pocket. I don't even know where we are going, but Elliot's incessant talking is driving me up the wall. My gaze drifts to Beckett, and unconsciously, I find myself staring at his hands resting on his thighs. There's a small cut on his knuckle, the skin pulled back slightly. It looks fresh—still red and swollen, like it hasn't fully scabbed over yet.

Without thinking, I reach out, brushing my fingertips lightly around the wound, careful not to touch it directly. I glance up at him, silently asking what happened.

He looks down at it, then back up at me. "I was putting a coffee mug away, and the shelf above decided to lower itself and grab my skin," he says with a wink,

"Does it hurt?"

"So bad," he teases, his voice dropping to a whisper, "except when you do that."

I continue tracing the swollen area, oddly mesmerized by the simple act of touching him, and I can't seem to stop. My hand lingers longer than it should, and when I slow my movements, he scoots his hand slightly closer, seeming to enjoy it. I take it as an invitation to keep going. As we finally pull up to the restaurant, Beckett takes my hand and opens his door, helping me out.

Once inside, it hits me again that this is a really upscale place, but at least I'm dressed appropriately for the occasion. Beckett removes his jacket and hands it to the hostess, while Elliot and the other man do the same. I stand there, waiting for Beckett to remove mine. He turns to me and wordlessly begins unwrapping my scarf, slipping it from around my neck then moving to my coat. His hands are careful, and I thank him softly as he removes it and tosses it to the hostess. It's only after the exchange passes that I realize how intimate it must have looked to Elliot, yet he remains completely oblivious, too wrapped up in the excitement of being here with his boss.

We're led to the table, and Beckett's hand finds its place on the small of my back, his fingers drifting just low enough that it feels both possessive and intimate. I want to hate it, but I love the way his touch feels. What nearly makes me halt in my tracks is when Elliot rushes ahead and claims a seat first, leaving Beckett to pull out a chair for me. Once I'm seated, Beckett sits next to me, positioning Elliot across from us. I almost avoid eye contact with Elliot, thinking I'll see the awareness of the situation on his face, but when I finally dare to look, his eyes are solely on Beckett. What baffles me even more is when he asks the man next to him to switch seats with so he can sit directly across from Beckett.

I've never seen him like this—granted, I've only spent a handful of awkward encounters with him, but still. Elliot dives headfirst into peppering Beckett with questions, each one more trivial than the last. It's obvious Beckett has no interest in the interrogation, and the irritation creeping across his face mirrors my own. The other guy who came with us seems to pick up on this, quickly jumping in to distract Elliot by starting a conversation with him.

I stare, practically dumbfounded at Elliot. He's quite the moron.

Beckett leans in, his voice low enough that only I can hear. "I have a dinner meeting tonight."

"Cool," I reply, a little flat.

The waiter arrives, and Beckett orders both our food and drinks, while Elliot orders exactly what Beckett ordered for himself, not even acknowledging that a seemingly complete stranger just ordered my meal.

While Elliot resumes his conversation with the other guy, Beckett turns his attention back to me. "I'll need a ride tonight."

I turn and look at him, and he meets my gaze. "No, you don't. You have Preston. Plus, you think my driving is scary. Anyway, you interrupted my date, so I'll make him take me on one tonight."

"I hate these dinner meetings. Please come," he says, staring at me.

"You want to know what I find so comical, Beckett? You ignored me for the past two weeks, you didn't even recognize me back at the office, and now you're asking me to drive you somewhere when all of our arguments are about my driving."

"*I* ignored you? How many times have you ever called or texted me first? Or shown up at my place? It should be pretty easy for you to remember because it's never. I was waiting for *you* to reach out for once. Do you think I wasn't checking my phone constantly or driving to your apartment every day, just to leave because I wanted you to reach out to me for once? But even you showing up at my work today was for someone else. And of course I recognized you, I thought my knees were going to give out when I saw you. I stood at the elevator, stalling until you came." His voice is low so nobody else can hear.

"So, it's somehow my fault? Because I didn't reach out? Why would I when every time we talk we argue over my job."

"I don't want to argue," he says, staring directly into my soul.

"Me neither," I turn back to look at Elliot and the other gentleman talking.

"8:00 tonight. Please."

I turn to look back at him. "Did you just use manners?"

"I did, and I will use them all night if you will come."

"Have you had dinner meetings at all in the last two weeks?"

"No." He shakes his head.

I was going to use the fact that he managed meetings without me as an excuse to get out of this, but apparently, he hasn't had any. "Why are you asking me to go? It's not like you would have, had I not shown up at your work. Which, by the way, I was unaware he worked for you," I whisper.

He holds up his phone, displaying the ExpressWay app with my profile and a requested ride for tonight that he put in four days ago.

I had alerts on my phone for requested rides, but I hadn't opened my app in a week, so I hadn't seen it.

"Please," he repeats with a pouty lip and then a smile.

"Manners and showing your veneers? Fine, I'll come, but you're paying me for the ride *and* my dinner."

His smile widens, and he bites down on his lower lip, looking completely happy. "I'll even pay for your lunch," he winks.

"Pretty sure that would make this *our* date if you pay."

He shrugs lazily.

"What time do I need to be at your work?" I change the topic.

"Meet me at my place at 8:00… please."

"Fine," I agree. "How late is this meeting?"

"Late."

"What's late?"

"11:00 or so," he squeezes my thigh under the table.

CHAPTER
Thirteen

This isn't a date. I know this isn't a date. I keep repeating the thought as I stand in front of the mirror, having spent two hours perfecting every detail. My hair is styled just right, soft waves framing my face and down my back, and my makeup is subtle but flawless. I smooth down the maroon dress I picked out, paired with black pantyhose and my favorite boots, and the same scarf and coat from earlier. Why am I putting this much effort into something that's not supposed to mean anything? I sigh at my reflection, trying to convince myself again that this is nothing more than a ride to a meeting.

BRYNN:
I am here.

BECKETT:
Come up. Not ready.

BECKETT:
I know it doesn't take 10 minutes to get up here...

BRYNN:
I'm just waiting for you down here. My car is nice and warm

BECKETT:
Come. Up.

I sigh, park my car, and enter the large building. It's funny—for someone who hates my driving, he's sure pushing the time limit on when we need to get to his meeting, which will inevitably make me have to speed to get us there. Actually, he never told me what time his meeting was or where it was. He just said meet him here at 8:00.

When I get off the elevator, his condo opens up to a large area. I was partially correct in thinking he lives in a sterile environment. It's huge inside, the dark gray marble floors gleam so brightly they almost look wet. It's spotless in here—so spotless, I get the urge to press fingerprint smudges all over the large mirror hanging in the entryway, just to break the perfection.

It smells amazing, like someone's been cooking for hours. As far as I know, Beckett lives alone, so I'm not sure why it would smell like someone's making food.

"In here," he calls out. I follow his voice to the kitchen, where I find him wearing an apron, stirring something in a pot. The sight completely throws me off.

"What's going on?" I ask, eyeing the way he moves between the stove and the counter. I've never pictured Beckett in a domestic setting like this.

"I'm cooking dinner," he replies casually as he continues to sauté whatever's in the pan.

I glance at the clock, feeling a wave of confusion. "We're going to be late for your meeting if you don't hurry. And didn't you say this was a dinner meeting? Who's all this for?" I drop my bag on a stool at the counter, then move around the kitchen to stand beside him.

He looks at me, his eyes briefly trailing over my dress before returning to his work. "For you."

"For me?" I blink. "What happened to your meeting?"

"I got the dates mixed up."

"Why didn't you text me and tell me?" I ask, feeling like I'm wasting his time.

"Because I decided I'd cook for you instead."

I squint at him, half-suspicious. "Are you sure this isn't some takeout you had delivered, and now you're just reheating it to impress me?" I tease, leaning over the stove to inspect the food.

"I'll have you know, my father is a chef," he glances over his shoulder at me, and then back at the food.

"Sure, sure. Where's your trash can?" I start opening random cupboards beneath the sink, looking for evidence of takeout containers.

He steps aside and opens a low cupboard I hadn't even thought to check, revealing neatly organized trash and recycling bins—both nearly empty, with no sign of any delivery boxes.

"Well, if you got the dates mixed up and knew we'd be staying in, why didn't you at least tell me to wear something comfy?" I walk back to the counter, unzipping my boots and taking them off.

"Want some boxers and a T-shirt?" He looks over his shoulder.

"No. I don't plan on staying long."

"Technically, you knew I would need a ride from 8:00-11:00, so I know you have at least three hours of time."

"That was before I knew you were tricking me."

"It wasn't a trick. You're still getting dinner—just better than what you would have had if we went out," he says as he starts serving our plates, carefully arranging the food.

He leads us to the formal dining room, and it strikes me how elegant and thought-out this setup is. The long, polished table is preset for two. He sets our plates down, pulls out a chair for me, then takes a seat in the adjacent chair. As he pours wine into the crystal glasses, he slides one to me and sits back in his chair.

"Elliot Parker," he says, staring at me while lightly swirling his wine. "How did you two meet?"

Hearing Elliot's name instantly irritates me. We were supposed to have a lunch date, but he gave it up so quickly just to have lunch with Beckett. Now this dinner feels an awful lot like a romantic date—but with the wrong person. I'm sure I'm the only one seeing it that way, but it doesn't make hearing Elliot's name any less annoying.

"My roommate, Chloe, she went on a date with him," I admit. "They came back to our apartment, and he told her he was interested in pursuing me instead. She said she didn't feel a connection with him and asked if I'd be willing to talk to him." The words spill out candidly.

"And? Is there a connection with you and him?"

"I think?" I say, unsure what to say. Elliot is attractive, and his curly blonde hair was the first thing I noticed—I've always had a weakness for curls. Chloe had described him as a "string bean" when she told me about her date with a cute guy, and when I saw him, it was slightly comical because he's tall and scrawny, just as she said. When she mentioned not feeling a connection with him, she joked that if they ever had sex, she could snap him in half like a twig. That seemed so funny at the time. I never considered the possibility of Elliot and I being intimate.

But Beckett… now that's a different story. Though I don't fully grasp Chloe's comment about feeling like she could break Elliot, I think I somewhat understand the sentiment. Beckett is 6'3" and lean, the kind of man whose weight I would love to have pressing down on me, whereas Elliot's weight would probably feel like a gust of wind blew past me. Beckett's hair is also a contrast to Elliot's—a dark brown, just slightly wavy, and always combed up and off to the side.

"That's a no," Beckett responds.

"No… I said yes."

"You said you think. When you have a real connection with someone, there's no doubt. You don't have to think about it or question it—you already know."

"Then yes. Elliot and I have a connection." I hate how even saying it makes the words feel strange on my tongue. I think about how messy his desk was, and it makes me wonder how messy his house must be. The idea of cluttered rooms and disorganized tables and counters fills my mind, but it's the thought of his bathroom that really makes me want to gag. Like has he ever cleaned his toilet? Would I be going to the bathroom late at night and find myself falling inside the pee-covered toilet bowl, right into the brown grime and filth? Only to need a shower, pull back the curtain, and find it covered in different shades of brown and orange mold and mildew?

"When you just spaced off, were you thinking about the deep connection you and he share?" Beckett jests.

"Are you feeling jealous because *you* want to have a deep connection with Elliot?"

He lets out a laugh. "The women from the hotel aren't here. You can drop the gay jokes."

"I don't know that you aren't gay," I retort, taking a bite of my food. "You're pretty enough to be," I add nonchalantly.

"You think I'm attractive?" he asks, slightly playful but with a hint of seriousness.

I freeze with the wine glass to my lips as I stare at him, not sure if he's fucking with me. But he genuinely looks like he wants an answer.

"I'm not going to fall for that. I'm not going to stroke your massive ego by telling you how attractive you are. You can have every other female do that," I say, taking a slow sip of my wine before setting the glass back down on the table.

He remains completely focused on me. "I want to hear it from you."

"Why?"

For a long while, he's silent, his gaze steady as if he's weighing his words carefully. "Because it's you," he finally says.

"Well, it doesn't matter what I think. And I certainly don't care what you think." I take another bite of my pasta.

He swirls his wine some more, then picks up the glass, takes a drink, and stands. "Want to watch a movie?" he asks, already making his way to the living room, turning the TV on without waiting for an answer.

"Sure. What movie?" I ask as I follow after him.

"I'll surprise you."

I stop, my breath catching in my throat when I see our two paintings hung in his living room. I forgot he took them, and I find myself speechless that he actually hung them up on the walls, along with his other thousands of dollars' worth of art.

"Sorry, those aren't for sale." He winks at me when I meet his eyes.

"I can't believe you actually put them up," I murmur, stepping in to admire them. "I want yours back, though," I say, turning my head just enough to catch his reaction.

"Sorry, no can do. However, you can come stare at them anytime you'd like."

"Yeah? Do I get like a key card or something to your condo?" I tease as I settle onto the couch.

"If you would like access, you can have access. But I'd prefer you come while I'm here."

"Because you don't trust me?" I quirk a brow at him.

"Because I don't want to miss a chance to be around you," he says, getting the movie ready.

"Are you flirting with me, Buckets?"

He turns the lights off and settles onto the couch beside me, leaning into me, one leg stretched across the cushions while the other stays on the floor. There's an effortless sexiness in the way he moves—he's so unaware of it, but it drives me wild.

He turns his head to look at me, and when I meet his gaze, he whispers, "To answer your question… yes."

I roll my eyes, trying to hide the way my pulse quickens just from him looking at me like that and admitting he was flirting with me.

We settle in on the couch, the room dimly lit by the glow of the TV. It only takes me about five minutes to figure out he put on a scary movie. My stomach twists with unease as the eerie music fills the room, signaling something terrible is about to happen on screen.

I lean closer to him, sinking into the cushions as I whisper, "I have to drive home in the dark. Why did you put on something scary?"

He gazes down at me. "You'll be fine. I'll protect you from the boogeyman," he whispers back.

As the tension in the movie builds, so does my anxiety. I pull my feet up onto the couch, curling my knees toward his chest. He shifts slightly into me, his arm draping over my lap, and I feel his fingers lightly gliding back and forth across my ankle and shin.

I try to watch, but every time something gory or suspenseful happens, I shield myself with my hands or look down, refusing to see what comes next. My heart races with every jump scare, my pulse quickening as the intensity builds. I hate how these kinds of movies make me sweat.

By the time the movie ends, I'm completely unnerved—my body tense and my mind racing with thoughts of what might be lurking in the dark.

"I can't believe you made me sit through that," I whisper, feeling a mix of annoyance and fear. I look up at him, and he's focused on the screen, still tracing gentle patterns on my legs, completely unbothered by the movie's ending. I sit there quietly, then huff, "I'm scared."

"Don't be," he says.

"That's easier said than done. You're not the one who has to drive home in the dark," I retort.

He stands up, offering his hand to me. "Come on."

"Thank you." I reach out, letting him guide me around the couch in the dark. Only I try to head toward my boots, and he tugs me the opposite direction.

"Where are we going?"

"To bed," he whispers.

I relax, thinking I won't have to drive home in the dark and then sleep in my room alone.

When we get to his room, he flips on the lamp on his side of the bed. I can discern the room from the viewpoint of his nightstand where he had his phone propped up when we were FaceTiming. He goes to the closet, coming back with a T-shirt. "This might be more comfortable than your dress. Unless you prefer sleeping naked. And no, I don't mean that in any sort of inappropriate way."

"T-shirt will be fine," I say, taking it from his hand and putting it on the bed while I make quick work of taking off my outfit. Then I slip on his T-shirt. As he starts to pull the covers back, I already know this is his side of the bed because it's closest to the door. So I hurry and climb in. He stares down at me, then climbs right in, grabbing my thighs and pulling them apart. Lying on top of me, he sits up briefly to adjust the blankets over us before lying back down.

"I was just kidding," I say as I giggle underneath him.

"Nope," he nuzzles his face in my neck. "You offered to be my bed."

His weight on me is exactly what I had expected it would be, but so much better. And then I feel it… his erection.

"Okay, get up," I say, pushing on his chest. He barely lifts up, and I scramble from underneath him. He plops right back down in the same spot, completely unfazed, while I sit here, feeling the tingle of heat between my legs.

Damn it.

When I wake, it's the same randomness we seem to keep finding ourselves in. We are a tangle of flesh, with my shirt once again somehow being pulled up and his face buried between my bare boobs.

"Are you drooling on me?" I murmur, feeling the wetness on my chest.

"Mmm," he mumbles, barely stirring, still half-sleeping, his grip tightening around my waist.

"Beckett, you're drooling," I repeat, lifting my head to confirm I do, in fact, have drool on me. "Beckett."

"Go back to sleep, I'm not ready to wake up," he groans, shifting slightly, his voice muffled against me. He lazily grabs the sheet with one hand and wipes my chest without even fully lifting his head, then promptly returns to his original position. His face nestling back into me.

"Hand me my phone," I say. But his only response is sliding his arms under me and squeezing.

Letting out a laugh, I relax back into the pillow and softly run my fingers up and down his tattooed shoulders. I close my eyes and let my fingers roam his smooth flesh. He groans when I begin massaging behind his ears, neck, and shoulders, and his hold on me begins to relax. I switch between massaging and softly brushing along his skin.

I know he works today—or I would assume he does. It's ten o'clock, and he doesn't seem fazed at all. Even while checking his phone, he keeps his face nestled in my chest. Once he's done scrolling through his notifications, he sits up and kisses right between my boobs. "Thanks for the massage, that felt amazing," he says, then rolls over and leans back against the headboard.

Climbing out of bed, I stretch my arms above my head, then strip off his shirt and lean down to grab my bra. Noticing I have a new text from Chloe, I decide to open it and send off a response. Plopping my phone down, I switch it with my bra and stand to put it on. Beckett is leaned back on his pillows, his head resting on his arm as he watches me.

"What?" I ask, feeling self-conscious.

"Come lay back down."

I smirk and shake my head. "I'm going home to shower. Someone drooled all over me."

"Let's shower then," he suggests as he stands.

"Why are you not at work?" I counter.

"Because I'm with you," he replies, moving in closer.

"Do you plan on working today?"

"If you sneak out on me, I will. But if you will stay, then no."

"If I stay, will you make me pancakes?"

He pulls me into an embrace, his arms wrapping securely around my neck while his chin rests softly on top of my head. I can feel the rise and fall of his chest as he holds me. I respond in kind, sliding my arms around his waist, pressing into him as we stand there in quiet comfort. His hold eventually loosens, and he presses a soft kiss to my temple.

"Yes," he murmurs, turning and walking out of the room, leaving me to finish getting dressed.

I fasten my bra and slip into my pantyhose, smoothing them down over my legs before pulling on my dress. I follow him into the kitchen and as promised, he's at the stove, making pancakes.

He's still in only his boxers, and his ass looks so round and perfect that I walk up behind him, wrapping my arms around his torso, wanting to feel his perky butt pressed against me. One hand comes down to mine, and he lifts it to press a kiss to my knuckles. When he shifts, I step back as he puts two pancakes on each plate he had put out.

We sit side by side while we eat. He finishes long before I do, but instead of getting up, he turns toward me, softly nipping my shoulder. I turn my head, meeting his gaze as he leans in once more with the intent to bite again.

"Why don't you make yourself useful and rub my back or something," I say.

His lips pull away from my arm, and he smiles. "Why don't you just worry about your breakfast and leave me be." He leans back in, biting closer to my neck.

"That's distracting."

His only response his a subtle "mmm" as his tongue brushes against my skin.

I gather every bit of willpower I have to bring the final bite to my mouth and chew while his tongue continues playing. As soon as I put my fork down, he rises from his seat, gathering the plates and carrying them to the sink. The sound of running water fills the kitchen as he quickly washes them.

I stare at him, stunned by the way he built me up like that, only to walk away like nothing happened. His grin spreads wider when I turn and gape at him. He closes the distance between us, holding his hands out to me. "Come on," he says, tugging me to my feet.

I shake my head, a soft laugh escaping. "I'm not tired. If you want to go back to bed, I couldn't sleep if I tried."

"Not bed," he murmurs. "Shower."

I find myself easily following, letting him lead me down the hallway.

CHAPTER Fourteen

'm surprised when I hear from Elliot. I've been reflecting a lot on what Beckett said, and I think he might be right. I don't think I feel a connection with Elliot… Okay, I know I don't have a connection with Elliot. I've talked with Chloe about it, but she insists it's my lack of experience making me feel like that, and I will feel like that with anybody until I'm comfortable with them. Yet, I've always felt at ease with Beckett—maybe too much so. Perhaps I only feel like that because I know there's no chance in hell he and I would ever date, making it easy to be myself with him since I don't need to impress him. That has to be what it is.

ELLIOT:
Guess what! We are going to dinner tonight.

BRYNN:
Is that you asking me to go or assuming I'd go...?

ELLIOT:
I assumed since I know you wouldn't have plans.

BRYNN:
That's awfully bold of you

ELLIOT:
That's inconsiderate of me to assume. Do you have plans already?

BRYNN:
No.

ELLIOT:
Awesome. I'll ping you the location

BRYNN:
Sure. There's something I want to talk to you about.

...He's just going to ping me the location? As in, he doesn't even plan on picking me up? This is exactly why I don't feel anything for him—things like this. He invites me to dinner but can't even bother to pick me up. If I were truly interested in him in a romantic way, this would actually hurt my feelings.

When the location comes through, I immediately Google it to check where it is. I scan the menu and the dress code to figure out what I should wear. It seems decently casual. Funny how Beckett's words from so long ago still have an effect on me regarding what I wear out in public.

I wait until the last possible second to even begin getting ready. There's no part of me that wants to be going tonight. After waiting longer than I should have, I decide I'm not even going to bother trying to fix my hair. I throw it in a messy bun that looks decent, put on mascara, and apply some subtle pink chapstick and call it good. I pull on distressed skinny jeans, ankle boots, a white top, and a warm cardigan over it. Then I wrap a scarf around my neck and saunter out.

Why are you even going to this? What kind of date is it where the person who initiated it doesn't bother to pick me up? He must not see this as a real date either. Maybe he's planning to use dinner as an opportunity to tell me he's not interested. That would actually make things a lot easier for me. I'm glad I brought cash—I can guarantee he's either going to want me to cover the bill or pay for my own meal.

I park, then sit here debating whether I should even go in. Maybe I should just tell him something came up. I start pulling up our texts to let him know I can't make it, but my stomach growls. Maybe eating isn't such a bad idea after all. Just as I'm about to put my phone back in my purse, a message from him pops up.

ELLIOT:

> Hey, just saw you pull in.
> I'm inside. Come on in.

So he saw me pull in and still went in without waiting for me? I'm so confused. This situation just keeps getting weirder and weirder.

As I walk in, I peer around at the crowded restaurant bar then see Elliot hold his hand out and wave so I can see him. Acknowledging him, I wave back and start walking toward him. He's sitting at a booth with a man and a woman. I have no idea who they are, but I'm instantly irritated to find that this is obviously a double date. As I approach, Elliot is radiating happiness, and it sinks in that he doesn't plan on ending anything.

Looks like I still have to handle that part too. I sigh, mentally bracing myself for this long-ass dinner. With a forced smile, I approach the other two, their backs turned to me, and feel my heart drop to my boots.

"Brynn, you remember my boss, Mr. Shaw, and this is his girlfriend, Rachel."

"Rachelle," she corrects, then waves at me. "Hi."

"Date," Beckett corrects. "She's just my date," he adds, taking a sip of his beer.

The way his arm is casually resting over the back of the bench behind her makes me want to reach over and snap each of his big ass bitch boy fingers. It's the same way he always has his arm when we're together, and it dawns on me that it was never anything special he was doing with me.

I don't even sit down. I just stand there, staring at them and then at Elliot, blinking in disbelief. "Did you say you needed to use the restroom?" I ask Elliot, narrowing my eyes at him.

"No, I'm good," he says.

"No, I'm pretty sure you absolutely need to use the restroom. Now." I stalk off, hearing him scramble after me.

As soon as we're near the restrooms, I turn toward him. "How dare you not tell me this is a double date."

"It's my boss. How could you be mad about it?"

"Because it's your boss! That's so weird, Elliot. Are you two besties now?"

"I wouldn't mind if he wanted to be," he admits.

"Did you not ask me to dinner for a date?"

"It's just dinner, Brynn," he says, as if he can't fathom why I'm upset.

I let out an exasperated scoff. "And you brought me and Rachelle to be the sideline observers to you and your boss's date?"

He looks taken aback by my anger, like it's completely misplaced.

I roll my eyes and go in the bathroom, leaving him standing there. I stare at my reflection in the mirror, trying to calm myself down. Why am I even upset? Beckett is allowed to date. But what the hell was he doing with me the other night?

He made me dinner, cuddled me on his couch, slept with me in his bed, made me breakfast, and then washed almost every inch of me in the shower aside from my vagina and butt. But he took his sweet time washing my boobs, claiming they took the longest to clean. I've never even let a guy see my boobs before him, let alone touch them, but I allowed it—and reveled in every second of it.

I find it so odd that Elliot acts like he wants to date Beckett, but proceeds to ask me out, and then ruins it. This is just making it so much easier for me to tell Elliot we've come to the end of our situation-ship.

It's fine. I'm a big girl. I can sit through dinner. It's just dinner, I tell myself in the mirror.

As I walk back, Elliot is talking to Beckett, and Rachelle is leaning in, whispering something in Beckett's ear. Beckett's eyes meet mine as I approach the table, and I immediately change plans. "I just forgot; I have to feed my cat. I can't stay. Sorry. Rachelle, it was nice to meet you." Then I turn to Elliot, "Emmett," and then to Beckett, "Bryce," before walking away and trying to keep my feet moving.

"You don't even have a cat," I hear Elliot call after me.

"Right, I meant my bird," I say, holding up my middle finger to him as I shove the doors open.

I barely make it through my front door when I burst into tears. I don't even bother turning on lights as I stumble to the bathroom, stripping off my clothes and stepping into the shower. The hot water hits me, mingling with the streams of tears, and I scrub at my face, desperate to wash away my makeup and the overwhelming sadness and jealousy clingy to me. I dig the loofah into my chest as if I could scrub away the ache lodged there, but it doesn't help. No matter how hard I try, I can't seem to get my emotions under control.

The loofah slips from my hand, hitting the floor with a soft thud, and I follow, sinking down until I'm sitting under the spray with my knees pulled to my chest. The water beats down on me, mixing with my sobs, and I allow myself to break completely. *Ten minutes,* I tell myself. *Just ten minutes of a good cry then I have to stop.* But when the time passes, my body isn't quite on board with it and proceeds to keep going, long after when my brain says that's enough.

My stomach is so twisted in knots I feel I might pass out. Then again, I was hungry when I got to the restaurant, and I'm still hungry, though eating is the last thing on my mind.

When I muster enough energy, I drag myself out of the shower and wrap a towel around me. I stand over the sink, letting my head hang, trying to focus on something—anything—to get a grip. I practice breathing steadily in and out. One breath at a time. Just make it through this breath, and then the next.

I pause, straining to listen when a faint knock echoes through my apartment. I can't discern if it's coming from another apartment or maybe Nancy, telling me to shut the hell up. I quickly put on a T-shirt and underwear, then toss my hair in a wet pile on top of my head. I wipe at my face, but the tears are already threatening to spill over again. Bracing myself, I open the bathroom door, only for another wave of tears to begin. My breath hitches in my throat, and I can't seem to hold it together.

Then, another knock—louder this time.

Someone's definitely at the front door.

I peer out the peephole, but it's being covered. That's not creepy at all. Turning and walking back toward my room, a knock rings out again. I stop walking and listen, trying to decipher who's on the other side of the door. I'm not in the mood to talk to anyone, so I keep walking, but then the door swings open. Beckett strides in with purpose, slamming the door shut behind him.

"Do you see the difference in how this feels?" he asks. "This is a connection, Brynn." He gestures with his finger between us as he stalks toward me.

His hands come to my face, cupping my cheeks, our eyes locking for a brief moment. Then his lips crash into mine. It's not just a kiss—it's a collision of everything him and I have been holding back. My hands grasp his forearms, giving him the deepest kiss I've ever given a man.

His lips are cold from being outside, and I bring the warmth of mine to meet his. When his mouth parts, I surrender completely, opening up to him. His tongue presses inside, finding mine with an urgency, claiming me, and I hand myself over on a silver platter.

When we pull part, his thumbs swipe away free-falling tears. The simple gesture only makes more fall, and I begin to sob. He pulls me into his arms, wrapping me in a hug.

"Where's your date?" I sniffle.

"Preston took her home."

My hands tighten on the back of his coat, not wanting him to leave. When he starts to release me, I squeeze harder. "Please don't go."

"I'm not. We're going to bed," he whispers back.

As I turn to lead the way, he reaches out and takes my hand. I don't bother turning on the light since the rest of the apartment is dark and our eyes are already adjusted. Plus, my curtains are open, letting the moonlight filter in, and he's also not a stranger to my room.

"I'm gonna go lock the front door," I tell him, wiping tears from my cheeks.

When I return, he's already lying in bed, so I walk to the other side. "You're on my side of the bed again," I comment, pulling back the blankets and sliding in.

"My side now."

I turn to face him, finding him lying on his back with his arm outstretched toward me. I nestle into him as he wraps his arms around me. I kiss his chest and rest my nose against his skin, trying to hold back my tears. He gently lifts my chin, and our eyes meet. Then, he leans in and presses his lips to mine, and I melt into him, letting his kiss take over once again.

When we finally pull apart, my eyes are heavy and swollen. He traces his thumb across my cheek, giving me a sympathetic smile, then pulling me close again, his hand soothingly gliding up and down my back.

"Hey Brynn, can I borrow your black dress—" Chloe's voice cuts off as abruptly as she stepped in my room, her eyes widening and mouth falling open.

I open my eyes and freeze, stunned and embarrassed. She wasn't supposed to be home for another day, and now daylight streams in, revealing a nearly naked man in my bed. I'm unsure how we always end up in these sleep situations, but here I am—lying flat on my back, Beckett half-sprawled on top of me, my shirt completely off, and his arm wrapped around my chest. His bent elbow pulls my breast towards the other one, while his face is nestled between them as makeshift pillows. My arms are wrapped around his neck, my face turned into him, showing I'm just as much a willing participant in this.

I watch, wide-eyed, as Chloe approaches my side of the bed, her expression shifting from shock to a barely contained smirk. She stands beside me, grabbing the edge of the blanket and lifting it slightly. "Oh, you've got some serious explaining to do."

I'm so focused on quietly demanding she give me back the blankets while tugging at them, I don't realize all the movement has woken Beckett.

Her grip on the blanket loosens, and her confident demeanor falters. "Hi," she squeaks out as her posture stiffens, an audible gulp about to be set free.

I turn to see his beautiful eyes open and fixed on her. He sits up, pulls the blanket over my chest, then reaches his hand out to her. "Hi, Beckett. You must be Chloe," he introduces himself.

She looks dazed as she shakes his hand and nods. He has rendered my outgoing, bubbly, fun-loving roommate utterly speechless.

"If you don't need anything else, you can go," he practically dismisses her.

"Beckett," I chide, swatting his chest.

He just reclines again, placing his hands behind his head.

Chloe, still wide-eyed, mouths "O.M.G." to me, and then walks out, grinning.

"What was that about?" I ask once the door shuts behind her.

"What?" he replies, unknowingly.

"Why were you so rude?" I push, lying back on the bed beside him.

He shifts onto his side, propping himself up on one elbow. "What was rude about that? We're in bed, your roommate is the one who barged in without knocking and started ripping the blankets off us. What if we had been in the middle of something?"

"We practically were. You literally looked like you were sucking on my boob," I accuse.

"And that's our business," he replies, completely unapologetic. "She doesn't need to know what goes on behind closed doors."

"She *knows* she wouldn't have to worry about walking in on anything," I say, embarrassed.

"She doesn't *know* that." He scoots closer, wrapping his arm around my waist and resting his head on my chest again, reclaiming his previous spot.

"She does…"

I can practically sense the very second the words sink in and he understands what I mean, because he suddenly stills. Then, just like that, he rolls over, pushes the blankets off, and climbs out of bed, dressing quickly.

"Beckett?" I ask, confused why he's acting like this. "Beckett? What are you doing?"

"I've got a lot of work to do today," he mutters as he begins buttoning his shirt.

I hurry out of bed, fumbling for a pair of pants and tugging them on. I toss open my closet door, grabbing the first shirt and sweatshirt I can find. "Why are you in such a hurry?" I call out as he heads toward the door.

I hear Chloe's muffled voice from the living room, attempting a greeting, but it's cut short by the sound of the front door closing.

I grab my purse and dash after him as she gives me a *what is going on* look. Catching up to him, I grab his arm, pulling him to a stop. "What's your problem?"

He ignores me and keeps walking, so I unlock my car and tug him toward it. "You're not walking. Get in, I'll drive you home," I open the passenger door for him and stand there waiting for him to get in.

He seems to contemplate, his jaw flexed, before reluctantly getting in. I shut the door and walk around to the driver's side, climbing in and starting the engine.

It's so silent, it's driving me nuts. "So, did you forget to feed your cat too?" I make an attempt at humor, but he ignores me.

The rest of the drive to his place is filled with uncomfortable silence. I pull up to the front of the building and stop. "Can I come up with you—" I start, but the words barely leave my lips before he's out of the car, the door slamming behind him.

"Jackass," I mutter, staring after him, trying to decide if I should follow. "What the fuck is his problem?"

Shoving my car in park, I chase after him. When I reach the lobby, I make a beeline for the elevator. "I need to get to Mr. Shaw's floor," I tell the attendant, my words coming out breathy and urgent.

He barely looks at me, shaking his head with a flat, "No."

"Please, if you just call up to him, he'll tell you I'm supposed to go up," I insist, but he just stares at me. Pulling out my desperation card, I blurt out, "He ordered me. I'm his prostitute. I don't get paid unless I sleep with him. I need money. Call him."

For a second, he hesitates. Then he picks up the phone, and I hear him tell Beckett there's a woman trying to go up. After a pause, he nods, hangs up, and says, "Sorry, miss. He's not expecting anyone."

Oooo, my blood is boiling. "Can you let me call up?"

"No, I'm afraid not."

Desperate times call for desperate measures. "What is that?" I point down the hall, and he falls for it, looking over. I grab the phone and press the button to Beckett's floor. The attendant lunges to stop me, trying to wrench the phone from my hand. "Just let me talk to him!" I growl, trying to wrestle free.

"Let go of the phone. Now," he demands, pressing his body against mine to take it, his arm wrapped painfully around me, pinning my hand with one, his full palm cupping my boob with the other.

"Those are my boobs that you're grabbing," I bite out. I try to release the phone, but he still has me trapped in his arms. "Get off of me, you fucking creep," I snap, jerking my hand out from underneath his.

When he finally lets go of me, his face is beet red from the struggle. I storm off, throwing a parting jab. "You might want to get your dude a chair—he just worked up a sweat," I call to the man behind the desk.

I decide to work for the next six hours because I don't want to go home and explain to Chloe what was going on. Besides, aside from sleeping, I have no clue what happened. What I do know is I don't plan on going back to Beckett's condo, ever. Especially now that two people in that building have felt my boobs. How can that worker even justify that full-blown squeeze he took? I know it wasn't a simple accident because I could fully feel him massaging it. I'm sure thinking I'm a prostitute justified his actions in his head.

When I finally do return home, I see Chloe's blinds spread and then go back into place. Cool, so she's been waiting for me. As I walk through the door, she's standing in the living room doorway.

"What happened with Elliot? Are you guys not seeing each other anymore?"

"Elliot is more interested in dating Beckett," I reply dryly, tossing my purse onto the entryway table with a little more force than necessary.

"And what led to that sexy naked man in your bed?"

I slump down onto the couch. "I planned on telling Elliot last night at dinner that I didn't even want to try to get to know each other anymore. But he decided to have a double date with Beckett and didn't bother telling me"

"And then... Beckett ended up in your bed after that because?"

"I don't even know," I turn my head to look at her.

"Your lips are swollen," she accuses.

"So are yours," I retort. She giggles and leans back on the couch.

CHAPTER
Fifteen

A week goes by.

I've gone over the conversation I plan to have with Elliot at least a hundred times in my head, trying to figure out how to end things, but no matter how I phrase it, nothing feels right. We've only been on a handful of dates, we text maybe once a week, and we've only kissed once. It's never been serious between us. If I had any lingering doubts, the kiss with Beckett erased them because that kiss was nothing like Elliot's. Maybe I don't even need to have a conversation with him. My relationship with Beckett seems deeper than mine and Elliot's and I don't owe Beckett shit.

Still, I remember Elliot mentioning once that he'd been ghosted and how awful it was. I don't want to leave him wondering what happened. I need to just face it and get this over with. So, I ask if I can stop by his house to talk. He hesitates, then reluctantly agrees, suggesting we meet at my place. I tell him I'd rather just drive to him. Once I receive his address, I start driving over.

As I pull up, I'm caught off guard—Jesus Christ, he lives in a castle or some kind of massive estate. I sit there, stunned, staring at the place from the driveway without moving further in. I double-check the address he gave me to make sure I'm at the right spot, and sure enough, I am.

What the fuck?

I watch as the front door swings open, and he walks out onto the front steps. His hands are shoved in his white dress pants pockets and is literally wearing a light blue sweater. He looks completely different than when I've seen him anywhere else. He looks like I just interrupted him playing a game of croquet.

Well, I can't back out now. As I pull up to the steps, he comes down and slides into my car.

"Do you live here?" I ask the most obvious question.

"I do," he says, looking back at his… palace, then back to me.

"Are you like the pool boy?"

"I'm like the son," he laughs.

Holy shit. His family is rich. Why does he work?

"I'm going to cut straight to the point. I don't think this is working out," I tell him honestly.

He sits there, looking completely blindsided. He starts to speak but stops, then tries again. "How can you even say that? You never even gave us a fair go?" he tells me, sounding hurt and frustrated.

"I'm sorry; I just don't feel a connection. I don't want to lead you on."

He lets out a long sigh. "Is this because of the double date thing? He's my boss; I need to impress him. Anyway, if you had waited even two minutes longer, we would have been alone. He got an upset stomach and had to leave."

"Did he say that?" I ask, now being the one caught off guard.

"Sort of. His exact words were, 'I have diarrhea and it's leaking out; I need to go.' Then told Rachelle his driver will take her home. After that, he threw cash on the table and ran out of there. The weird part is, I looked to see if he had an accident, and there was nothing on the seat. He smelled good when he left. I think he may have lied to get out of there, but I don't know why he would have."

This shouldn't bring me any kind of satisfaction, especially after he flew out of my apartment like a bat out of hell the other day and wouldn't let me come up to his condo. Still, it does make me happy. It makes me happy that he didn't stay on the date with Rachelle.

"This has nothing to do with the double date thing. Well, not entirely. I think it was crappy that you asked me to dinner and didn't disclose that little detail. But that's not why I don't want to continue dating," I admit.

"Does this mean you want nothing to do with me?" he asks, confused.

"We can be friends if that's what you're asking," I tell him honestly.

"I'm filthy rich, Brynn," he says, catching me off guard.

"Okay?"

"Does that change your mind?"

"Change my mind about what?" I ask, puzzled.

"About wanting to end things with me."

"As in, you believe I was only after you for your money when I'm finding out right now that you even have money? What a complete douchey-ass thing to question," I spit out.

"No no, that's not what I meant," he starts trying to backpedal. "I don't like telling people I'm dating that I'm rich because they will stay just for that. I didn't know if me having money changed your mind at all."

From what I'm gathering, he doesn't tell people he has money because he wants them to like him for who he is but is now trying to use the fact that he comes from wealth to keep me from ending things.

"It changes nothing."

"So, if I tell you about a date I go on, you will just, what, be happy for me?" he asks.

"Yes, of course."

"I just don't understand, Brynn. Why? I can't stand the thought of you dating someone else." He's still confused, which equally confuses me why he would even need to wonder how I could be ending things with him.

"I already told you, Elliot, I don't feel an… intimate connection with you." I hate having to admit that.

"We've never even tried. How can you say you don't feel an intimate connection when we haven't ever tried to have an intimate encounter."

"Elliot, I'm not changing my mind. I'm sorry. You know what? No, I'm not sorry. I don't see you as anything more than a friend. If you can't accept that, then that's your own problem."

He stares, completely bewildered at my words, then looks straight ahead. "Well, I don't have time to find a date for my company Christmas party this Saturday. Will you still accompany me?"

"No, Elliot. That wouldn't be a good idea," I answer honestly.

"I won't have time to find someone else in four days. You can't honestly hate me that much that you'd bail on me four days before the party."

I honestly forgot all about it. Still, why would he even want me to go to his work's Christmas party? "Try to find a date in the meantime, and if you can't, I'll go," I acquiesce.

Why did I agree to that? I'm well aware Beckett will be there. Not that it will matter—he hasn't even talked to me in a week, since he practically ran out of my apartment in his skivvies.

As I rummage through my closet, trying to find something suitable for the event, I have no motivation to even try very hard to look presentable. I had really hoped Elliot would have found a date for the Christmas party, but he claims he has been too busy to ask anyone. So here I am, begrudgingly preparing for an event I have no business attending.

I slip into a burgundy mini dress that hugs my figure, pairing it with black tights and matching burgundy heels. My hair is swept up in a sleek twist, and I keep my makeup simple, just enough to look polished without trying too hard.

I tell Elliot I will meet him at the venue, and he's been texting me every five minutes, apparently worried I'm going to stand him up.

BRYNN:
Relax, I'm parking now. I will see you soon.

ELLIOT:
Where are you?

BRYNN:
Walking to the front.

I make my way around the front of the building, bracing against the wind. The chill seeps through my coat, making me shiver as I turn the corner. There, standing with his arms wrapped around himself, is Elliot, shivering while waiting for me. I raise an eyebrow—so it takes me ending things for him to act like a gentleman and wait outside? Before, he would have just gone in, leaving me to wander around trying to find him.

"That worried I was going to stand you up, huh?" I quip as I walk up. "You do work with these people, don't you? It wouldn't have been weird if you came alone."

"It's weird. Trust me. The lunchroom will be swirling with gossip about the people who came solo. C'mon, let's get inside."

We step through the doors, and attendants immediately greet us, offering to take our coats and giving us tickets to retrieve them later.

Inside, the banquet hall is packed—easily over 200 people milling about, the tables draped in crisp white tablecloths with bold red placemats. The room is overly busy with the sound of conversation, laughter, and the clinking of glasses.

I've spent the entire night trying not to look for Beckett but find myself absentmindedly searching for him over and over. When I finally spot him, my heart plummets. He's chatting with a group of people, and there's a blonde next to him. Maybe she's just part of the conversation? Either way, I don't miss the way she stares at Beckett and keeps scooting toward him. Though, I notice him subtly step away with each step she takes.

"Come on, I'll introduce you to some colleagues," Elliot suggests.

"No, I'd rather not," I interrupt, not giving him a chance to pull me away.

"Why?"

"Because, Elliot, I'm not your girlfriend," I bite out, my nerves displaying how frenzied they are being in the same room as Beckett. Right now, all I want is to observe him from a distance like a scorned, stalker ex-girlfriend.

He seems taken aback, trying to process my sudden outburst.

"Sorry, I'd love to meet your coworkers," I apologize, attempting to soften my tone. He doesn't deserve me being a butthole because I'm fixated on Beckett.

I impress myself with my ability to act interested in anything these nerds are talking about. They all excitedly discuss computers, Dungeons & Dragons, and quite literally playing in "Cody's mom's basement."

I manage to sit through dinner, listening to their game-related chatter and role assignments. I want to bang my head against the table. I even consider ordering a strong drink but decide against it since I'm my own driver tonight.

I endure the entire evening, plastering on the fakest smile, acting like I'm having a good time, and all but celebrate as Elliot and his group of friends head toward the booth to get their coats. They continue discussing their game plans, and I can't stand a second longer of it.

"Hey, I'm gonna get out of here. I'm tired. Hope you had a good evening," I quietly tell Elliot.

"Thank you for coming, Brynn," he replies, pulling me into a quick side hug before waving goodbye.

I hurry to my car, fumbling for my keys as the cold bites at my fingers. I click my unlock button and climb in, rubbing my hands together in front of the heater, even though I know it won't be warm yet. My teeth chatter, and I can see my breath clouding in front of me as I exhale. I wish I had one of those automatic car starters so my car could've been warming up while I was inside.

Suddenly, my passenger door swings open, and Beckett gets in. I just stare at him, and all his audacity to come get in my car after he was a douche this last week.

"What?" I finally ask, unsure why he's here.

He just sits there, lost in thought.

"Okay? So, I'm leaving. If you don't need anything, can you get out?"

He remains silent, staring straight ahead.

"Pretty bold of you to show your face in my car again after the last time, when you were a total fucking dickwad and then denied me access to your condo. So, go ahead and think how that made me feel. Which, by the way, I was groped by your creepy elevator attendant," I bite out. "I'm leaving. Either get out or enjoy walking home from my apartment, because no matter what option you choose, this night ends with you being far away from me."

He exhales, leaning his head back on the seat, propping his elbow on the car door, running his hands through his hair, and leaving them there. I don't know if I should talk or leave him to his thoughts. I sure hope he can't hear mine, because I'm currently completely confused as to why he's sitting in my car.

"Do you need a ride?" I ask, my hand already moving toward the gearshift. "I'll drive you home."

"No," he replies, and I instantly ease my foot off the brake. "Preston's waiting."

I blink, trying to make sense of that. If Preston is waiting, why is he in my car?

The longer we sit in silence the more my irritation grows. "I'm going home. Can you get out?"

He finally does, slamming the door behind him.

"Jackass," I mutter, flinging my own door open, ready to give him a piece of my mind. But before I can get a word out, he's already on my side, striding toward me.

"Quit slamming my car d—" The rest of my words are swallowed as his hands cup my face, and his lips crash into mine.

He pulls back, just enough for me to catch a glimpse of the fire in his eyes, and then his lips are on mine again—this time with more urgency. I'm frozen, my hands hanging limply by my sides until my brain finally catches up. Grabbing the front of his coat, I yank him closer. His lips are even softer than I remember. When he pulls away, I stare at him in disbelief.

"That's a pretty lame kiss for the way you've been acting and the way you slam my car door every time you throw a fit."

His gaze flickers between my eyes, and before I can say anything else, his mouth captures mine—hungrier, deeper. This time, his tongue slips past my lips, and I melt into him. Our tongues rub against each other, frantic at first, but gradually slow as the kiss deepens, growing more passionate. He brings one hand to the back of my neck, pulling my face in, almost as if he's trying to hold me in place, afraid if he lets go, I'll slip away.

We stay tangled in each other, but my eyes flutter open when a vehicle pulls up behind mine. I try to see who just arrived, but their headlights are still on. Beckett doesn't seem to notice or care, but it feels really weird that they're just sitting there, gawking at us making out. I pull him with me as I take a step back, and then keep trying to tug him with me as I reach for my taser.

"What are you doing?" he whispers, bringing my mouth back to his.

"Getting my taser," I breathe.

"It's just Preston, baby," he reassures me, his lips reclaiming mine.

I pull away, glancing past him to confirm. The headlights flicker off, and sure enough, I catch sight of Preston.

"You should go," I manage to say.

He nods, but instead of moving, he presses his mouth back to mine, deepening the kiss.

"Go," I urge again, though my resolve weakens as he kisses me.

"Come home with me," he murmurs.

"Fuck no. I'm never going back to your condo."

His lips are back on mine, and he wraps me in his strong embrace. My fingers tremble from the cold, and my mouth is so numb it's becoming hard to move.

His gaze softens as he pulls away, then gently runs the back of his knuckles across my cheek and leaves me with one final delicate kiss. "Goodnight, Brynn."

"Goodnight, Beckett." I watch as he walks away.

CHAPTER Sixteen

It's been two days. Two days of non-stop thinking about Beckett—the way he touches me, the way he kisses me. God, I crave his mouth. My mind keeps drifting back to the Christmas party, to that woman standing beside him. Then, the look of defeat in his eyes when he slid into my car, only to slam my door minutes later. And still, we ended up tangled in another kiss.

I really need to get a grip. No more. I'm done with all of this. I can't see him without feelings trying to happen. I don't do feelings, and I certainly don't do feelings with him.

"Brynn," Chloe calls from the living room.

"I'm almost done," I shout back, quickly towel-drying my hair, trying to finish up.

Tonight we're having a movie night because she leaves for work in three days and will be gone for a week. It sounds like she's talking to someone, but neither of us is expecting anyone. Maybe Tom stopped by to see her. And if he did, that would mean our movie night is now a *me* movie night.

I catch a glimpse of my naked self in the mirror and laugh. Chloe somehow convinced me to go with her for a Brazilian wax—said it was a 'treat' for Tom. Of course, she talked me into doing it too. I was nervous, considering how my last waxing attempt ended with the skin from my eyebrow stuck on the wax strip. Thankfully, this time, no skin was ripped off. Chloe says this will boost confidence, but I've never been one to worry about that kind of thing. Honestly, I've always felt secure in myself. Maybe I've just never over-analyzed it. I like who I am, and I'm comfortable in my body.

I was mortified when the technician told me she needed to trim my bush down to even begin the wax. Chloe, of course, found it hilarious, asking whether I ever even bother to trim at all. I said no—I have no need to, and nobody to impress. It was even more awkward when I was asked to get on my hands and knees and spread my legs so she could wax… well, everywhere. I can't imagine why any guy would like what this looks like. It looks completely… bare.

I did see Beckett naked, though. He was perfectly groomed, neat in a way that makes me wonder if he had someone take care of that for him. Bending over, I spread my cheeks, wanting to see the back of myself. This is the first time I've ever seen my own butthole. I don't get why some people are so fascinated with that part of the body. It's just there—functional and unremarkable, but okay.

"Phone," Chloe calls out again.

"What?" I emerge from the bathroom with a towel wrapped snugly around my body. "What did you say?" I ask, distracted as I absentmindedly clean my ear with a Q-tip.

She grins, holding my phone out to me. "Phone is for you."

Confused, I start walking toward her. "Who is it?"

Her eyes gleam as she mouths, "Beckett."

"What?!" I mouth back, a rush of nerves hitting me all at once. "Why did you answer it?" My heart races, and I panic as I reach her.

"Here she is," she says into the phone, passing it to me.

I shoot her a playful glare, shaking my fist at her, snatching the phone from her hand.

"Hello?" I say, glancing at the screen to confirm Beckett is actually on the line.

"I have a business conference out of town. I need to leave Sunday afternoon, and we will return Saturday," he says bluntly.

"That's… exciting for you," I respond.

"It's going to be cold, so bring warm clothing," he adds.

I blink, trying to process. "Your car is fixed. Preston can drive you."

"And you have nothing going on, just make sure you're packed. We need to leave by 3," he says, then hangs up, leaving me no time to respond.

He seriously needs to work on his people skills. He's so rude.

Chloe raises a brow. "What was that all about?"

"He wants me to go on a business trip with him."

Her expression lights up instantly. "You have to! What if he wants to… you know," she winks.

"I'm going to get dressed. Have the movie ready," I give her a pointed look and then walk back to my room.

I'M JUST FINISHING UP MY HAIR AND MAKEUP, THROWING THE last few essentials into my suitcase, when there's a knock on the front door. My eyes dart to the clock—only twenty minutes left before I have to be out the door to pick Beckett up

The knock comes again, louder this time, but I ignore it, focused on cramming the last few items into my bag. Whoever it is can wait.

"It bothers me you never lock your front door when you're always home alone," Beckett's voice cuts through the silence, making me jump. I wasn't expecting anyone, least of all him.

"Beckett!" I exclaim, clutching my chest as if that'll steady my racing heart. "What are you doing here?" I sink down onto the bed, trying to catch my breath.

He stands in the doorway, a grin tugging at the corners of his lips, with his hands in his pockets. "I still have forty minutes before I even need to pick you up," I say, getting up and resuming my packing, shoving a few more items into the suitcase.

"You never agreed to come," he says, strolling over to the bed and peering into my suitcase. "I didn't know if you would have started packing yet."

"What kind of meeting attire should I pack?" I ask, still having my closet open.

He turns and lifts a brow, looking amused.

"You're dragging me with you wherever we are going, so I'm coming to your meetings too," I state firmly.

"Pack pajamas for all I care," he chuckles, flopping down onto my bed and stretching out, completely at ease.

"That was super helpful," I mutter sarcastically, pulling a dress off the hanger and carefully folding it, trying to avoid creasing the fabric as I tuck it into my suitcase. "Are there even stores where we're going?"

"I've never been to this hotel. But I'd assume there will at least be something nearby," he says.

Finishing up, I zip my suitcase, and he stands, pulling the handle of it and placing it on the floor.

"I've got it." I reach for the handle.

"Thanks." He laces his fingers through mine, as if that's what I meant. I roll my eyes as he picks up my suitcase, guiding me out of the room. The physical contact makes me feel giddy, and I'll follow wherever these butterflies decide to lead me.

I lock up behind us as he goes to his truck, parked right in front, and lifts my suitcase into the back.

"What are you doing?" I ask, confused.

"Putting your bag in my truck."

"Yeah, I see that. But why?"

He walks to the passenger side, pulls the door open, and holds out a pink mini tray packed with all my favorite snacks. I cross my arms, giving him a pointed look, waiting for an answer. Though, that purple bag of skittles is calling to me.

"It's mostly back roads," he finally explains, walking toward me. "Your car wouldn't make it." He places the snack tray in my hands, then, without warning, scoops me up into his arms.

"Beckett, what—" I don't even get the sentence out as he carries me to the truck and places me in the seat.

He takes my hand, kisses my knuckles with a grin, and closes the door.

I watch as he rounds the truck. "If I'm not driving and you are capable of driving yourself, why am I even coming?"

"Because I want to spend all week with you asking redundant questions," he says flatly as he buckles up.

"Oh, wait, I forgot something. I'll be right back." I leave the snack basket on the center console and hop out of the truck. It only seems fitting that I bring my "I'm with stupid" shirt to wear as a nightie since I will be with 'stupid.' I grab it from my dresser, quickly stuff it into my purse, and make my way back.

Beckett is already standing by the passenger door, holding it open when I approach. "Did you even get anything?" he asks, an amused look on his face.

"Yep," I reply.

He spanks my butt as I climb in, then closes the door behind me with a grin.

We drive out of town and onto the back roads, where the snow becomes denser, and the icy conditions worsen the deeper we venture into the mountains. The radio crackles with a weather alert, warning that conditions will continue to deteriorate over the next few hours. As we press on, the snow intensifies, causing him to slow way down.

I start to feel uneasy with the limited visibility and unbuckle my seatbelt without thinking. Before he can say anything, I push the center divider back upright, scoot in toward him, and quickly buckle back up. I lean into him, my hand gripping his thigh and my head resting against his shoulder.

"We're fine," he says soothingly, placing his hand on my leg in reassurance.

"Both hands on the wheel," I insist, and he immediately returns his full attention to driving. "Are we going to make it?" I ask, my eyes glued to the thickening snow.

"Yeah, we've got about an hour left," he replies. "If we had left any later, we might not have."

I close my eyes, letting the gentle rumble of the truck lull me into a quiet calm. I feel his fingers intertwine with mine, and I look up at him.

"I'm fine, baby, I've got this," he reassures me. I squeeze his hand in acceptance and try to relax again.

When we finally arrive, I take in the sight of a large hotel, its structure resembling a grand cabin, nestled in the snowy landscape. Despite the darkness, the snow-covered surroundings reflect a soft light, giving the whole scene a serene, almost magical quality. Down the road, about half a mile away, I spot what looks like a small town.

"What an odd place to have a conference," I remark, taking in our surroundings.

We pull up to the front of the hotel and he parks. "Wait here," he says as he gets out.

"I want to come with you," I say, holding his hand tightly.

"I'll be right back," he presses a kiss to my knuckle and walks inside. When he comes back out, he pulls my door open and holds his hand out to me. "Come on," he urges, waiting for me to step out. "It's cold, Brynn, get out," he adds impatiently, moving his knees back and forth with his coat collar pulled up around his neck.

I immediately get out and follow him in as two men hurry out with carts to collect our luggage. We head down a hallway to a restaurant, where we're promptly shown to our table. It's a booth, and I know how this is going to go. He begins taking my scarf off and then my coat, placing both mine and his on the opposite bench.

"Are we doing this again? Sitting on the same side?" I question.

"Always," he smirks.

"We're not about to be that weird couple that sits on the same side," I protest. "We already did this, and it gave me the ick."

He just stares at me, gesturing for me to get in.

"We look so lame," I peer around the packed room to make sure nobody is staring at us.

The waiter appears, giving me no time to even scan the menu. Beckett begins rattling off our order, and I stare, wondering how he knows what to choose since neither of us has even opened a menu. The waiter listens without question, jotting it all down like he's familiar with exactly what Beckett is ordering, and strides away.

"Why do you always do that?"

"Do what?" he responds casually, leaning back against the seat, his arm draped lazily behind me.

"You never let me order for myself," I point out, meeting his gaze.

"Do you not like what I chose?"

"I do, but I'm capable of ordering for myself."

He chuckles softly, his eyes dropping to my lips for a brief second before locking with mine again. "Next time, I'll let you order if it'll make you feel better."

"It would. But I still want to know why you always order my food. You've done it the entire time we've known each other."

A small shrug rolls off his shoulders as if he hasn't given it much thought. "I don't know. I just like ordering for you."

"Is it a control thing?" I ask.

"Does it feel controlling?" he counters.

"Yes," I say quickly, then realize I don't think it feels controlling at all. "Okay, no, not really," I admit. "Do you do it with everyone?"

"Only you." His eyes remain locked on mine.

"Because I seem so helpless?"

"No," he murmurs, brushing a strand of hair behind my ear then cupping my cheek. His thumb traces a slow line down my jaw. "Because I like taking care of you. Or maybe I just can't decide what I want, so I order two meals so I can share your food."

I roll my eyes, but the way he's looking at me makes my heart skip a beat. "Why do you keep staring at my mouth?"

He glances down again before answering. "Because when you're embarrassed, your cheeks turn pink, and I'm not wanting to embarrass you right now, so I'm trying not to kiss you."

"What if I said you could…"

"Can I?" he breathes out.

"Yes," I say shyly. Gone are the days when I care we're in a public restaurant. I want his mouth on mine, and I want it now.

He barely leans in when the waiter interrupts. "Careful, these plates are hot," as he places our dishes in front of us.

Beckett lets out a sigh as he removes his arm from around me.

"Can I get some ketchup, please?" I ask as the waiter prepares to leave.

When he returns with a small plate holding two white dishes of ketchup, Beckett snatches it as I go to reach for it, gives the waiter a curt nod of dismissal, and sets the plate next to mine.

"Okay… what was that about?" I give him a questioning look.

"He didn't need to reach across the table when I'm right here," he replies nonchalantly.

"Don't you feel like that came off slightly rude?"

"Not any ruder than him trying to hand you something over me." He begins cutting his steak.

I don't even catch myself staring at his plate until he cuts off a piece of steak and holds his fork in my direction. I lean over and take the bite he offers, smiling at how good it is. I hold out my hamburger, expecting him to refuse a bite, but he leans over and takes one. While chewing, he picks up his napkin, wipes the corners of his mouth, then gently wipes mine.

"Mr. Shaw?" a woman's voice coos as she approaches. Her face is familiar, but I can't place where I've seen her.

"These weather conditions are quite extraordinary," she says with a bright smile aimed at Beckett. "It's supposed to snow another foot by morning. Glad to see you made it safely."

Suddenly, it dawns on me—she's the woman who was standing next to him at the Christmas party.

"I didn't realize you were attending conferences with your father these days," Beckett says flatly.

"I figured, why not," she beams.

When Beckett remains silent, offering no further acknowledgment, she fidgets, searching for something more to say. "What floor are you on? We're staying in the Presidential suite," she adds, her tone shifting to something more suggestive as she subtly pops her hip, trying to appear seductive.

Without even glancing her way, Beckett replies, "Have a good night, Collette." The words leaving his lips dismissively.

She stands there in disbelief. Her eyes land on me, scanning me from head to chest with thinly veiled disdain. "You too," she mutters, then turns and walks away, her heels clicking sharply against the floor.

We eat in silence after that. A couple times, he offers me bites of his steak, and I accept, leaning in to take it from his fork. But the food that tasted amazing minutes ago now taste bitter, and I lose my appetite. Apparently, he feels the same, as neither one of us touch our food afterward.

He settles the bill and collects both our coats, taking my hand in his, leading me out. We head to the elevators and get off on the 4th floor. At our room, he opens the door with the key card and pushes it wide.

"Where's my key?"

"We only need one," he replies, stepping in behind me. He proceeds to do the same routine as before—sweeping the entire room, checking every corner as if on autopilot, making sure everything is as it should be.

The room is way more spacious than the last one we stayed in, with a cute little kitchenette as soon as we walk in, a table set for two, and a half-wall separating the kitchen from the bedroom area.

We again have a room with two queen beds, though I can almost guarantee it won't matter because he'll help himself into my bed anyway.

"What if I lose the key? Shouldn't we each have one?"

"I will have the key, and I don't lose things," he replies.

"What if I want to go wander around, and you don't feel like coming, and I lose it?" I challenge.

"You won't leave this room without me," he says.

"So, if I said I want to go play in the snow right now, you'd come?"

"Do you want to go play in the snow?" He arches a brow as he looks at me.

"Heck no. It's freezing out there." I point to the window where the snow is falling so thickly it blurs everything outside.

He chuckles and shakes his head, slipping off his shoes and tossing them aside.

"What would you do if you pulled back the curtain and saw a guy in a mask, holding a knife?"

He stops mid-motion, giving me a flat look. "I'd throw his ass out the window."

"What would you do if you tried, but the window was rubber and he bounced back at you and his knife stabbed you?"

"Brynn... go get ready for bed," he says, cutting off my ridiculous scenario with an exasperated sigh.

"I expect an answer when I get out of the bathroom!" I call out as I head toward the door, laughing at his expression.

I'm undressing while the shower heats up, and just as I step out of my clothes, Beckett walks in. I glance over as he unzips a travel bag that folds open into several compartments, each filled with toiletries and essentials, and hangs it neatly on the door.

"Well that's a neat little contraption." I examine it, noticing there are two of almost everything: male and female products, even unopened toothbrushes, razors and shampoo, conditioner, and body wash—not the cheap stuff the hotels provide either.

"Shut up! Did you get me shower stuff?" I ask, amazed.

"If that's all it takes to make you happy, your bar is really low," he says as he starts pulling out the female products.

"My bar might be low, but I wasn't aware you even knew how to be sweet," I counter, stepping into the shower.

"Buying shower products is sweet?"

"Yep, but I won't tell anyone you did that; it can be our little secret."

He may act like it's no big deal, but the fact that he thought about me and got those things means something. I doubt he personally picked them up, but it was still really thoughtful.

The steam swirls around me as I wet my hair under the warm water, and soon enough, the shower door swings open. He places the products I need on the little seat inside, then steps back.

"Thank you," I say.

After the shower, I towel off and head to my suitcase, digging out a pair of underwear. I quietly grab the shirt I stashed in my purse.

"Why do you have three suitcases?" I ask when I see his three large black suitcases next to my single one.

"Wouldn't you like to know?" he quips.

"I would. That's why I asked," I jest.

"It's for me to know and you to find out," he turns and winks at me.

I head back to the bathroom to finish drying off, then spray my hair with the same brand of leave-in conditioner I use at home. He remembered the kind I use and got it for me.

Reel it in, feelings.

While I'm combing my hair, he comes in, stopping when he catches a glimpse of my reflection. His gaze drops straight to my boobs in the mirror.

"My eyes are up here, Buckets," I say playfully, pointing my fingers at him in the mirror and making a sweeping motion upward.

He grins, locking eyes with me before turning back to his bag. Pulling out a toothbrush, he walks up behind me and wraps his arms around my waist, casually using the sink as though I'm not in the way. His other hand remains on my belly, holding me close as he begins brushing his teeth.

I lean back into him, watching his every move in the mirror. It's strange how captivated I am by him, how even the simple act of brushing his teeth can hold my attention. I could watch him do anything and still be completely entranced.

"Why don't you focus on brushing your teeth and less on staring at my boobs," I tease.

He grins and keeps brushing, though his eyes still wander. "You're just taking your sweet time so you can stare longer. No more for you." I grab his free hand and place it on my boob while draping his arm across the other. His toothbrush slows immediately, and he starts moving like he's in slow motion, exaggerating each brushstroke.

I shake my head, laughing as I pull away from his embrace. Once he finishes, he wipes his mouth with a towel and flashes me a huge, toothy smile—showing off those perfect white teeth—before heading back to the bedroom.

After slipping on my shirt, I step out of the bathroom and burst into laughter. There he is, standing by the bed I figured he'd claim, casually flipping through TV channels, wearing his "I am stupid" shirt.

He looks at me, then down at my shirt, and smiles. "Nice," he nods in approval.

I head to the kitchenette to grab my purse, then walk over to the nightstand between the beds to plug in my charger. The bedspread on the bed in front of the TV is already pulled back, a clear sign that he's taking that bed.

Grabbing my phone, I check the battery—82%. Plenty to play my farm game. But just as I'm about to settle in and pull the covers up, I feel his arms wrap around my waist. He pulls me into his bed, placing me squarely in the middle.

"What are you doing?" I squeal as he tucks the blankets around me. "You dropped my phone on the floor," I complain, leaning over to retrieve it.

"*I* did?" he asks sarcastically. "*I* didn't have your phone, *you* did."

When I lean back onto the bed, it feels like it's gotten smaller, and I end up practically sitting on his lap. "You're all the way on my side of the bed." I turn and he's sprawled right in the middle.

"Am I?" he asks, reclining comfortably, one arm tucked behind his head, still flipping through channels.

"Uh, yeah." I point to the wide-open space on the other side of him.

"Sorry," he grins, sitting up long enough to toss *my* pillows over to the other bed. Then rearranges his own, stacking them in the middle and reclining again with his arms propped lazily behind him.

My mouth hangs open at his boldness. He smirks, slipping an arm from behind his head and wrapping it around my shoulders, pulling me closer. "You're rude," he teases.

"Me!" I exclaim, flabbergasted.

"I figured you were going to say that to me, so I beat you to it."

"I *was* going to call you rude—because you are," I mutter, snuggling into his chest while scrolling through social media. His hand softly glides up and down my side, and every so often, he presses a kiss to the top of my head. I respond by placing a kiss on his chest.

When I finally lock my phone and place it on the nightstand, I nestle back into him, exhaling contentedly as he wraps me up in his arms.

CHAPTER Seventeen

Bundled up in our coats, scarves, and hats, a large group of hotel guests all set out together, a line of figures trudging slowly through the thick snow. The once-cleared roads are now buried under six inches. The cold bites at our cheeks, and our breath forms clouds in the frigid air. Our boots crunch in the snow as we make our way to town. It's not too far, but the snow makes every step feel heavy.

I cling to Beckett's arm, my fingers numb despite the gloves, and he holds onto me just as tightly. As we pass through the streets, the world around us seems muted, softened by the blanket of white. The few trucks that drive by move cautiously, their tires leaving deep grooves in the snow.

We stay in the middle of the road, knowing it's safer than the hidden sidewalks.

After what feels like an eternity, we finally reach the only grocery store in town. The aisles are busy with other people who had the same idea as us, and we quickly grab the essentials—snacks, drinks, water—anything that will keep us comfortable back at the lodge.

With our bags full, we step back outside into the cold. It's almost like a different world—the sky has darkened slightly, and the wind has picked up, blowing snowflakes into our faces as we start the trek back.

About ten minutes from the lodge, the flakes grow larger and heavier until it feels like we're walking through a curtain of white. Visibility drops, and the temperature seems to plummet with it. Snow clings to our clothes, and our hoods are now heavy with the weight of it.

Despite the increasing intensity, we push on, the lights of the lodge finally coming into view. The last few minutes of the walk feel like a race against the storm as the snow turns to a full-blown flurry. When we finally reach the entrance, there's a collective sigh of relief. We step inside, shaking off the snow, our faces red from the cold.

When we get to our room, I place the bags I carried on the counter and hurry into the bathroom to turn on the shower. My teeth chatter from how cold I am. When I step under the water, it feels cold, even though I can see the steam permeating the room.

The shower door flings open, and a very naked Beckett steps in, his teeth chattering too as he squeezes in next to me.

"Hey! I'm showering first," I protest, my voice shaking, not wanting to share the hot water.

"I'm cold too!" he counters.

We try to huddle under the spray, but it's not wide enough for two. Beckett wraps his arms around me and pulls me close, the water pooling between us then spilling over our bodies. When I finally stop feeling stiff from the cold, I unwrap my arms from around myself and hold onto him instead. We're still shivering, but it's starting to subside, and the cold no longer feels as painful.

When our temperatures seem to stabilize, we actually start showering. "Can you get me a washcloth?" I ask, giving him my best pouty lip.

He leans down and sucks said pouty lip into his mouth, releasing it with a pop before stepping out and returning shortly with two washcloths.

We go through the motions of washing our bodies, lathering and rinsing. I tilt my head back, letting the water rinse away the conditioner from my hair, then open my eyes and catch Beckett staring at me. His gaze sweeps over me slowly, taking in every inch of my body. Without meaning to, I look down and see his very large, very in charge, very erect penis.

I quickly shift my gaze up, and as soon as we lock onto each other, he steps forward, drawing me closer. My heart pounds in my chest, and the intensity in his expression matches the arousal I feel. His hand moves to my mouth, his thumb rubbing across my bottom lip before capturing it with his.

My arms wrap around his neck, my fingers gripping the damp strands at his nape. Our kiss deepens quickly, and he bends slightly, his hands sliding down to grip the backs of my thighs, hoisting me up as I clutch his shoulders tighter.

"Beckett," I whisper, a sliver of worry creeping in, afraid he might lose his footing and we'll both slip and die from head injuries.

"I've got you," he says confidently. I wrap my legs firmly around his waist as he presses his mouth to mine again.

My back is against the shower wall as he adjusts himself. His erection, which was near my entrance, now rests between our bodies—against my slit. The sensation sends a rush of nerves and excitement through me.

When he breaks away from our kiss, he trails a path down my neck. I gasp when he starts sucking gently, a moan slipping out before I can stop it. Embarrassed, I bite down on my forearm, trying to muffle the sound. But he doesn't let up; he bites down on the tender spot of my neck, harder this time, his teeth sinking in just enough to make me moan louder.

I feel the curve of his lips against my skin as he listens to my unrestrained reaction. Pleasure courses through me, and I plant one hand on the soap ledge for balance as my hips roll upward, pressing into him, grinding against his hardness. My breaths come in ragged bursts as I close my eyes, letting myself get lost in the sensations building between us. My clit has never been stimulated like this, and each brush of his shaft against me sends pure bliss spiraling through my core. I can barely think through the frenzy of desire. I crave more pressure. I bite my lip, desperate to push harder, to grind faster. The tension coiling in my belly intensifies with every shift of my hips, and I find myself chasing that high, my mind singularly focused on whatever this feeling is making my skin tingle.

Without warning, the water turns ice cold, shocking us both.

"Jesus!" "Holy shit!" we shout in unison as he quickly shuts off the shower and lowers me back onto the floor.

I fling the door open rushing to get out of the cold water that's still trickling toward the drain. I quickly grab the robes, tossing one at him while hurriedly wrapping myself up in the other. My skin prickles from the cold, and I shiver as I snatch a towel to dab away the lingering droplets on my legs. "I thought hotels didn't run out of hot water," I grumble, irritated that the moment was ruined by the freaking water temperature.

He looks equally frustrated, pulling his robe around him as he stalks out of the bathroom. While I'm still drying off, I hear his voice in the other room, speaking sternly with someone on the phone about the water issue.

When I emerge from the bathroom, he's climbing in bed in just his robe, pulling the covers up to his chin, trying to ward off the lingering cold.

I grab some pajamas and walk toward the bed, curious if he's going to sleep in his robe.

"It's too cold for that," he answers the question I was thinking.

Following his lead, I set my pajamas on the bedside table and climb in beside him, still wrapped in my robe.

"What did they say about the water?" I ask, pulling the covers up as I nestle beside him.

"Everyone in the hotel decided to shower at the same time, all with the water cranked up as hot as it would go." He shakes his head.

I nod. "Bitches."

We settle into the bed, both of us turning to face one another. I rest my head on my hands, watching him in the soft glow that filters in from the snow-covered night outside. His gaze meets mine, and he smiles softly.

He leans in slowly, his lips brushing against mine with the lightest, gentlest touch. His hand slides down the length of my leg, gripping my thigh and guiding it up over his hip, causing my robe to fall open.

"Beckett," I pull back just enough to catch my breath. My heart pounds, a flicker of anxiety knotting in my chest. I'm worried that if this keeps going, he might panic again like in my apartment, and we're stuck here with no place to escape for either of us if that happens.

"I know, babe," he whispers.

But I don't know if he actually knows.

"I'm a vir—"

"I just want to kiss you," he interrupts gently. "I won't touch you anywhere else."

"What if I want you to… to touch me?"

His lips brush mine again, slower this time, and he asks softly, "Has anyone ever touched you before?"

I shyly shake my head. "No."

"Have you touched yourself?"

"Yes… kind of… not really," I admit, the words tumbling out awkwardly.

"Have you ever had an orgasm?"

I bite my lip, feeling my cheeks flush with embarrassment. "I think so."

I'm such a loser. JUST LIE TO THE MAN. Save your dignity.

His nose nudges mine in a playful way. "Do you want to?"

"Yes," I blurt out, probably too fast.

"Good girl." His voice is full of approval, sending full-body shivers throughout every inch of me. "Tongue or fingers?"

The question catches me off guard, and I stammer, "I… I don't know."

"Do you use tampons?" he asks.

This feels like a weird, non-sexy question for the mood we're trying to set. "I'm not on my period," I respond.

His lips quirk up. "I know. I'm gauging my options."

"Is it one or the other?"

"No," he shakes his head.

"Surprise me," I whisper, unsure what to expect.

He gives a subtle nod, leaning in for another kiss, but this time, there's a different energy between us. My heart races as I feel him tugging at the strap of my robe. His hand slips underneath the fabric, the warmth of his touch trailing up my side. Then, it drifts lower, cupping the curve of my bottom. I revel in the way his jaw flexes, almost like he's restraining himself and then—without warning—spanks me.

A startled yelp escapes me—the sting of it surprising but somehow… strangely satisfying. A surge of tingling spreads through my body from the unexpected mix of pain and pleasure. His lips curl into a mischievous smile as he watches my reaction, before he lowers his mouth to my neck, trailing slow, heated kisses along my skin.

With a firm but gentle nudge, he guides me onto my back. His gaze is intense, and I feel completely exposed as he peels the robe open, letting it fall away. A gleam flickers in his gaze as he sweeps over me.

"Let me know if it's too much, okay?" he says softly, his voice thick with restraint.

"Okay," I nod.

His fingers trace a slow path along my side, every stroke sending ripples of warmth through me. Leaning down, he brushes his tongue over my nipple, and I exhale a shaky breath. Then his mouth fully envelops it, sucking deeply then pulling back with a pop.

"Is this alright?" he asks, his own breath coming in ragged bursts, mirroring my own unsteady rhythm.

"It was… until you stopped," I murmur, not intending to be funny, though it earns a quiet laugh from him.

With a mischievous grin, he returns to my breast, tugging gently while his hand slides between my legs. My thighs part instinctively, as my body's been waiting for this forever. The instant his fingers glide between my slit, a surge of intense pleasure floods through me, making my whole body tingle. He moves lower, gathering my wetness then traces back up. He presses firm circles against the spot I've felt ache before but never knew could ignite such overwhelming bliss. My hips rise off the bed, seeking more of his touch, and a moan escapes. My legs twitch, wanting to trap his hand in place, forcing it to never leave.

He continues, skillfully circling that tender spot, and I can't stop the moans that fall freely from my mouth. I don't even try to. Each movement brings a new wave of ecstasy, making me lose track of everything except the feeling building inside me. His finger slows, trailing downward toward my center, then back up. This time, as he dips lower, I place my hand over his, not wanting him to avoid going inside me. There's a growing ache and I don't just want him—I *need* him.

When he's finally just outside, he lazily circles my entrance, looking down at me. Leaning in, he kisses me, and as he pulls away, he watches intently while slowly stretching his middle finger inside my channel. My lips part in a breathless moan, my body instantly reacting to the new sensation. It's unlike anything I've ever felt—the way he fills me. A sound catches in my throat as my entire being focuses on the pleasure surging through me.

He keeps his eyes on mine as he slides his finger all the way in, then pulls back torturously slow. Once he's all the way back in, he teases me with the rhythm—just when I adjust to the feeling, he pulls out almost completely, only to push back in.

I bite my lip, my body arching into him, silently pleading for more of him, more of everything. My breaths become shallow and ragged, until he abruptly pulls out completely, leaving me empty and desperate.

"Wait… what?" I gasp, my head lifting off the pillow, a mix of confusion and need coursing through me. "I… don't think I finished…"

"You didn't," he confirms with a grin.

"Is that… is that it?" The disappointment starts to take over. It was feeling really good, and if that's all there is to it, I'd rather not build myself up for such a letdown ever again.

He flashes a knowing smile as he pushes the blanket down further on the bed. His eyes darken with hunger as he shifts between my thighs, settling his face intimately close.

"What are you doing?" I manage to ask, my chest rising and falling as I try to keep control. But then I feel it—an overwhelming rush of sensations. His soft, wet tongue presses firmly against my slit, moving in slow, deliberate circles on my clit. The euphoria is instant, a fire igniting within me, shooting through my entire body.

"Oh my god," I gasp as his finger slips back inside me, matching the rhythm of his tongue. My legs part wider, inviting him in, as his mouth works magic on me. Each suck, each stroke, sends me spiraling further into a haze of bliss, and all coherent thoughts melt away. My mind goes blank, lost in the euphoria, and I feel I may have died when he pulls out of me and joins a second finger with the first, stretching them both back in. There's a brief sting, but soon his fingers start moving in that same steady rhythm, and the discomfort melts away.

He picks up the pace, plunging deeper, rhythmically moving, each stroke building in speed and intensity. "Beckett, stop," I gasp, grabbing fistfuls of his hair, my body teetering on the edge. "Oh my god…"

My voice trails off as my body clenches around him, every muscle constricting as I lift off the bed, "I think I'm—" I pant, my body jerking as I try to pull away, the stimulation too overwhelming. His arm secures my thigh, holding me in place as his mouth presses harder, his tongue and lips continuing their blissful assault on me.

"Don't fight it, baby," he murmurs, sliding his free hand up my thigh. His fingers splaying wide as he reaches my lower abdomen, then applies firm pressure.

The orgasm that rips through me has me screaming so loud we've now become the couple echoing through the walls. My entire body breaks out in goosebumps, and my hips grind against his mouth as I ride out every last wave of pleasure.

He licks and sucks between my legs until the intensity has tears welling up. When he finally withdraws his fingers, I let out a soft moan. He crawls over me, his body hovering above mine, and kisses me deeply, his tongue sliding in tenderly.

"That's what you taste like," he murmurs as he pulls back. "Heaven."

He slips off the bed and heads to the bathroom, leaving me breathless and completely undone. I sit up, still in awe of how amazing that felt, but when I glance down, I see blood on the white sheets. Alarmed, I grab my phone and turn on the flashlight for a better look—there it is, definitely blood. Just as I'm processing it, Beckett walks out of the bathroom toward me.

"I'm not on my period, I swear," I blurt, staring at the sheets.

"I know," he says calmly, sitting beside me and pressing a soft kiss to my lips. "Lay back." He guides me down onto the pillows.

He carefully spreads my legs and starts wiping between them with a damp washcloth. I notice the towel he's using has blood on it, too. His fingers literally popped my cherry. Or maybe that sting I felt earlier was something being torn.

Beckett stands from the bed and walks back to the restroom. I sit up and there's no pain—just an insane amount of slickness between my thighs. I spread my legs a bit wider and peek down. There's no trace of blood on me—can't say the same for the sheets though. I swipe between my lips, feeling the wetness, and rub it between my fingers.

When I look up, Beckett is grinning at me. I'm completely mesmerized by my own moisture.

"Let's move to the other bed," he suggests, pulling the covers back on the fresh sheets.

"Chloe talked me into getting waxed. Does it look weird?" I ask, glancing back down.

He walks to the bed and climbs in on his knees, leaning over me, pressing his lips to mine. "Everything about you is perfect."

"Do you have a preference?" I look down again, knowing he's seen me at both extremes—with what was probably the world's biggest bush, and now completely bare.

"Yes," he replies with a smirk. "You. You're my preference." He slips his arms around my waist, lifting me off the bed and depositing me onto the other bed with ease.

The new sheets are cold against my skin, and I quickly gather my robe around my body, fastening the straps snugly. Luckily, the robe had gotten bunched beneath me during our little rendezvous just now, or it would've been stained with blood, not just the sheets.

"I'm really not on my period. I don't want you to think I tricked you."

"I know," he says reassuringly, pulling me close. "It's not my first rodeo," he adds with a smile. "You stretched a little when I put my second finger in, it's normal."

"Could you feel it?"

"Yes."

"Did you know it made me bleed?" my eyes widen.

"I saw the blood, yes."

"Why didn't you stop?"

"Because I'm an adult and blood from a woman's vagina doesn't bother me," he says coolly.

I WAKE HOURS LATER TO A COMPLETELY QUIET ROOM. MOONlight filters through the open curtains, casting a faint glow over Beckett. I stare at him, thinking how devastatingly gorgeous he is. Gently, I place my hand on his jaw, my thumb tracing along his cheek as I lean in, pressing a light kiss to his lips.

"Can't sleep?" he murmurs.

"Sorry," I whisper. "Did I wake you?"

"No." He shakes his head, then slowly opens his sleepy eyes, studying my face. "You okay?"

I nod. "Better than okay."

He winks as if he understands. Without saying more, he shifts beneath me, slipping his arm free from where it's been cradling me. His hands disappear under the blanket, and I watch, curious, until I discern what he's doing—loosening the tie of his robe.

"Come here. Sit on me." He pulls the blanket open in invitation.

I sit up as he tugs on the strap of my robe, slowly pulling it apart. I straddle him, catching a glimpse of his erection as he presses it down against his stomach. His hands guide me, and as I lower myself, his fingers slide between my folds, spreading them gently as I settle on top of him. The direct pressure against my clit is immediate and mind-blowing, reminding me of how incredible it felt in the shower.

"What should I do?"

"Nothing," he murmurs, his eyes locking onto mine as he intertwines our fingers.

It's as if he can sense every shift in my body, whether he's a mind reader or just knows exactly what he's doing. Just moments ago, I wasn't entirely sure where this was headed, but now, the evidence is undeniable—I'm dripping all over him. I pull my fingers from his and reach between my thighs, confirming I'm definitely drenched.

He bites his lip like he was waiting for my body to do that. His hands slide to my hips, adjusting my position as he starts to guide me, pushing and pulling, setting the rhythm. I match his pace, rocking back and forth, each movement becoming smoother as the slickness spreads over his length.

His hands find their way up to my breasts, his grip firm as he squeezes. Every roll of my hips sends a new wave of sensitivity through my clit, the heat inside me growing more rapidly by the second.

"I think I'm about to come again," I whisper, my voice trembling.

"Good," he murmurs, sitting up and pulling me into his embrace. His arms wrap around me securely, hands gripping both cheeks as he takes control, guiding me up and down along his shaft.

Our breathing syncs, both of us panting as we watch the rhythm of my hips sliding over him. I cling to his shoulders, digging into him as my orgasm builds, the tension coiling tighter and tighter until it snaps. A wave of ecstasy crashes over me, and my hips shudder uncontrollably, my cries filling the room as my knees begin to tremble. The aftershocks ripple through me, each one leaving me breathless, when suddenly, something warm splashes against my lips and chin, startling me out of my reverie.

I flinch, blinking in surprise, and meet his gaze just as he bursts into laughter, his moans turning into breathless chuckles. Confused, I raise a hand to my face, dabbing at the liquid, and stare at the evidence on my fingers. "Did you just cum on my face?"

His laughter deepens, and he leans back, clutching his stomach. "I'm sorry," he chokes out.

I shake my head, amused despite myself. Pulling off my robe, I wipe at my face, giving him a mock glare. "You just shot me in the face with your sperm," I repeat, watching his amusement only grow. "We will call us even since I came on your tongue," I add, hitting his leg as I get up and head to the bathroom, still hearing his laughter echo behind me.

After I wash my face, I fumble for a towel, and one appears in my hand. "Thanks," I murmur, drying off. When I lift my gaze to the mirror, I find him standing behind me, completely naked, his hands resting on either side of the counter, eyes locked on mine.

"What?" I ask, smiling softly at his reflection.

"You're so beautiful," he says earnestly.

A blush creeps up my cheeks, and I shyly reply, "So are you."

He leans in, brushing his lips against my shoulder before resting his chin there. "Ready for bed?"

I nod, smiling. "Yes."

"My first meeting is tomorrow at 10:30 for breakfast, then another at 3, and the last one is at 8:00."

"Okay."

He stands, takes my hand, and guides me back to bed. As we settle in, he wraps his arms around me, as we snuggle under the warm blankets.

CHAPTER Eighteen

I wake before him, my nerves already going haywire over the meetings today. I didn't really bring anything particularly businesslike or fancy for the occasion. It might not be too late to get out of going. But who am I kidding? I apparently enjoy making both Beckett and myself look stupid during these things. I'm surprised he doesn't force me to stay in the room while he conducts anything business-related.

I slip into a matching black bra and panty set I bought when Chloe was home. I definitely didn't think anything like last night would happen between Beckett and me, but Chloe insisted that every woman needs a few matching sets for when they "get lucky," and I caved and bought some. Since I don't have much to wear for breakfast, I might as well wear this. At least it gives the illusion that I've got something in my life together. Maybe I should throw on my see-through lace bottoms, so it REALLY looks like I have my act together. After all, nothing says "life together" like a fresh Brazilian wax.

I style my hair into loose curls and go for subtle makeup. I try a bold red lipstick but immediately feel like all I can see are lips, so I wipe it off. It leaves behind a nice pink stain, so I add some lip gloss on top. Surprisingly, it looks like I intentionally did it.

When I step out of the bathroom, Beckett is sitting at the edge of the bed, scrolling through messages—maybe emails, though I'm never entirely sure what he's up to. He glances up and does a double take, his gaze sweeping over me as a grin spreads across his face. "Wow, you look incredible," he says as he stands.

"Thank you, except this is about as good as it gets." I gesture to my current lack of outfit. "Yet, somehow, I don't believe this is appropriate for breakfast. You never told me what to pack for the meetings, so I don't have anything super elegant," I admit.

"It's just breakfast—you can dress casual if you'd like."

"Are *you* dressing casual?"

He stands and walks over, wrapping his arms around my waist. "Air kiss," he says, leaning in but stopping just short of my lips. "Don't want to mess up your sexy lips." He winks, then heads over to the closet. He pulls out a zipped suit bag and lays it on the bed. I perch on the arm of the couch and watch, just wanting to see his butt.

He looks over his shoulder at me, and I grin. "Drop the robe already, or I'm going to start catcalling you," I warn, eager to see him naked again. He playfully tugs the straps, letting the robe fall to the floor, then continues with the bag.

Damn, he's got a sexy ass. I'm so entranced by it that I can't help myself. I stand and walk to him, grab his hips, and bite his cheek.

"Jesus Christ!" he shouts, raising onto his toes and rubbing the spot where I bit him. "Let that intrusive thought win, did you?" he asks, wide-eyed.

"That was even better than I imagined," I laugh.

He grabs my arm, pulling me into him as he smacks my butt. He keeps his arm around my waist as he pulls out his suit with a navy blue tie and a navy blue dress behind it.

"Did you get me a dress?!"

"No, I was going to wear that to dinner." He tickles my side. Pulling it out, he holds it up for me to see. "Do you like it?"

"Yes," I say, staring at it.

He grins and removes the dress from the hanger, then takes a seat on the bed, opening the fabric for me to step into. His hands travel over my legs, hips, and sides, eventually pausing to squeeze my breasts before sliding it the rest of the way up. The dress fits like a glove. I walk to the full-length mirror and examine it from every angle. It's gorgeous—slightly casual but stunning.

"You look sexy," he says as he steps around me and pulls shoes out of the closet.

He returns to the bed, tucking in his white shirt and straightening his tie. Afterward, he sits down on the edge of the bed and starts lacing up his shoes. I take a seat across from him, spotting navy blue heels with a strap that goes across the top sitting next to him. He picks up my foot and places it on his lap, grabbing the first heel.

"I thought sneakers would look pretty with this dress." I try to sound serious.

"Sneakers would be more for dinner," he winks.

"Okay, Prince Charming, see if I'm Cinderella?"

Instead, he puts the heel down, lifts my foot, and playfully puts my toes in his mouth.

"Beckett!" I exclaim, laughing as I try to yank my foot away. "Why would you do that, freak!"

He grins as he pulls his lips away, wiping the wetness from my toes and slipping my foot into the shoe, fastening the strap. In one fluid motion, he puts the other shoe on, completing the task on that side.

"I could've gotten you a snack if you're that hungry," I quip.

"I'm better now; I just filled up on toe snacks." He stands, pulling me up onto my feet.

"I've literally never had someone put my toes in their mouth," I say as he retrieves his phone.

"I'm being greedy, taking all your firsts, I guess," he wraps his arm around my waist. "Plus, I recall you saying you wouldn't massage my feet with your mouth because our relationship wasn't to that point yet. I'm just letting you know, I think it is."

"Lucky me. We're gonna go to bed every night with you wanting me to massage your toes with my tongue," I joke. "Do I need anything?"

"No," he replies.

As I unplug my phone and start to walk toward Beckett, he takes it from my hand and sets it back down. "Probably best if you leave this here," he says casually.

Well, that's super lame. If this meeting is boring, I'll have nothing to distract me. Then again, I think the majority of the time he's given me those annoyed looks is for playing something too loud on my phone at inappropriate times.

We walk down the hallway toward the elevators with our fingers intertwined. The entire wall near the elevators is a mirror, giving us a full view of ourselves. He's dressed simply—no suit jacket, just his slacks, a white button-up shirt, and a tie. He pulls his phone from his pocket and tugs me in, angling it for a picture.

"Send that to me," I say, glancing at the screen. "I'd take my own picture, but I'm not allowed to bring my phone with me to professional functions," I quip.

He slides his hand down my back, stopping on my butt and giving it a squeeze. "Your ass looks incredible," he murmurs with a grin, giving it a light smack.

I slide my hand down the outside of his pants, ready to give his front a squeeze in return. Just as I do, the elevator doors slide open. My hand drops to my side, and I pinch my lips between my teeth, hoping nobody saw what I was doing. My mood instantly sours when I see Collette standing inside with two older men. They all light up when they see Beckett.

"Mr. Shaw, come on in; I think we can make some space," the taller man says, though the elevator could comfortably fit at least ten people.

Beckett offers a forced smile and places his hand on my back, gesturing for me to go first.

This situation is even more awkward than the elevator ride with the five enamored women at our first hotel. The taller man tries to engage Beckett in conversation, but it's obvious Beckett is uninterested. As soon as the doors open, I step out quickly, with Beckett effortlessly falling into step beside me. We head towards the banquet room, where around thirty people are already mingling. Beckett navigates the crowd with ease, greeting everyone smoothly, while I follow behind, unsure what I'm supposed to do.

When we approach the first group, I try out doing the stupidest bow, fighting back laughter. I felt like Mr. Collins bowing to Lady Catherine in *Pride and Prejudice.* By the end of breakfast, I'd be stunned if anyone took me seriously. The first man to offer me a handshake, I let my hand fall completely limp, wiggling it around in hopes he never wants to touch me again—especially since his "date" seems young enough to be his great-great-great-granddaughter, and she looks as uncomfortable at him caressing her butt as I feel watching it.

Beckett's lips brush my temple as he murmurs, "Stop," reminding me to fix my face. I realize my expression is one of visceral disgust, focused intently on the inappropriate way the man is touching this girl. My features contort with a scowl, eyes narrowing, and my nose crinkles as I physically push away the revulsion I felt.

From that point on, I mentally tune out the entire breakfast, mindlessly picking at my blueberry bagel. I don't even react when Collette and her posse sit with us.

When we head down to the 3:00 function, the banquet room is buzzing with activity as Beckett steps through the propped-open doors, pausing to scan the room. At the front, a stage dominates the space, complete with a podium and a massive projector screen looming behind it. The chairs are meticulously arranged in neat rows, divided into three sections with two wide aisles cutting straight down the middle, leading directly to the stage.

Of course, since Beckett insists on arriving fashionably late, the room is already packed. He holds his hand out behind him, and I take it, then guides me down one of the aisles, the chairs already filled with people who politely nod or smile in our direction. To my dismay, several of them recognize Beckett, their faces lighting up with familiarity as they greet him.

"Beckett! Good to see you, man," one of the men says with a wave.

"Hey, how's it going?" Beckett responds, slowing down just enough to nod back and exchange pleasantries.

The aisle feels endless as we continue walking past more and more people, each one offering a friendly hello. I try my best to smile politely, but with every step, I feel more uncomfortable. The last thing I want to do is make a scene, but being the center of attention while weaving through the row of seated guests is already exhausting. By the time we reach our seats and sit down, I'm already contemplating how soon we can leave.

"I just wish the aisles were a little smaller so we could have crowd-surfed to our seats," I tease when he looks at me. He smiles at my words and shakes his head, resting his hand on my lap.

Within minutes of us getting settled, the lights dim and the soft hum of conversation fades as the room quiets. A man walks onto the stage, and the projector screen comes alive with a logo, followed by his presentation slides. He steps up to the podium, his voice filling the space as he welcomes everyone.

As he speaks, people move along the walkways with baskets of brochures. Each person on the aisle takes a small stack and passes them down the rows. By the time the brochures reach me, we're smack dab in the middle, so I'm left holding a decent pile of extras. I place them on my lap, unsure what I should be doing with them. I debate putting them on the floor and kicking them under the chair in front of me, but I know I would get eye scolded by Beckett.

The first speaker wraps up, and soon the next person approaches the podium, while another round of pamphlets makes its way down the rows. My collection of extras grows even larger. This time, though, I take my stack and place them on the floor next to my feet.

When I sit back up, Beckett is dutifully listening to the presenter. I rest my wrist on his shoulder, trailing my fingers through the side of his hair, tracing down to the nape of his neck where I gently thread them through his soft locks, and lean in. "I want to suck on your tongue."

He meets my gaze and winks, then turns back to the speaker.

I glance around the room, taking in the sea of business suits, and wonder what the point of these conferences even is. My mind starts wandering, and soon I'm thinking about how all these men in here have… wieners. I stifle a laugh, suddenly aware I'm surrounded by a bunch of wieners. Then the thought hits me—I'm probably the only virgin in this room. Or maybe I'm technically not anymore? I bled when Beckett used his fingers. What equates to no longer being one?

My gaze drifts down to his hands, trying to mentally calculate if his two fingers hurt, just how many fingers would it take to reach his penis size. I bunch my fingers together, peering directly down at them, and he's definitely bigger than that. Then, I make a circle with my thumb and try it with each of my fingers, comparing the size. None of them seem to match his girth. I go back to using my thumb and middle finger, blinking in astonishment as I realize he might be even thicker than that. I switch back to my other hand, bunching my fingers again, creating a comparison between my two hands, and the more I think about it, the more I stare in disbelief at the difference.

Beckett reaches over, his hand making a circle as he rests it on my lap for me to see. As I stare at the circle, it's exactly his size, and I silently laugh as I put my fingers in the hole and take his hand, turning my head to stifle my laughter. Leaning into him, I realize he knew what I was doing. He leans back into me, playfully nudging me, and my eyes land on Collette. She's sitting directly behind us, and I hadn't noticed until now. She definitely saw me playing with his hair, and judging by her expression, she isn't thrilled.

Feeling uncomfortable under her gaze, I turn back around. I didn't bring my phone, so I have nothing to distract me. Well, technically, Beckett told me I wasn't allowed to bring my phone, while simultaneously putting his in his pocket.

Looking down, I see the outline of his phone in the pocket closest to me. Without giving it any thought, I reach over, slipping my fingers into his pocket to pull it out. Since his ankle is crossed over his knee, his pants give no slack. His attentions remains straight ahead, but he puts his foot down and stretches his leg out to give me easier access.

Unlocking it with a swipe, I click on the internet browser and type, *Is it safe to swallow gum?* Then, I search *Is it safe to swallow sperm?* Apparently, it is—and according to some sources, there are even health benefits. How random.

I close the search tab and head to the app store, downloading my farm game onto his phone. As I set it up, I create his username as "Buckets." When the game prompts me to play with friends from contacts, I see my own username pop up: "Snacks." I click add friend, but it notifies me that I'm not currently playing. I wonder how a dual game would go. I'll make him try it with me later.

I play for the rest of the presentations, handing him his phone back once everyone begins clapping at the conclusion of the last speaker.

When we return to our room, I dump the heaping pile of brochures on the kitchenette counter. I had no real reason to take them other than I couldn't spot the people with the baskets as we left. I thought about throwing them away, but too many people were around, and now we're back in the room.

When I emerge from the bathroom, Beckett is sitting by the window, rubbing the back of his neck. I walk over, slipping behind him and moving his hands aside, pressing my thumbs into the knots in his neck and shoulders. He lets out a deep groan, his head dropping forward as I work my way along his muscles.

Leaning down, I softly bite his ear and whisper, "I still want to suck on your tongue," then nudge my nose against his cheek.

"Oh yeah?" he mutters, sounding more relaxed already.

"Yes," I say softly, continuing to knead the tightness out of his neck.

"I want to suck on yours, too."

I don't press for said sucking because I can still feel how knotted his muscles are. I continue working him over for a solid hour until he grabs my hands, halting my movements and guiding me around to sit on his lap. I wrap my arms lazily around his neck as I smile at him.

"Tongue sucking…" he murmurs as he leans in, brushing his lips against mine.

I nod in response and initiate a deeper kiss.

By the time we head to the last meeting of the day, he's fully tense. His jaw is set, and his movements are stiff and deliberate. This is the one meeting during this conference that he's in charge of, which I'm assuming is why he's so on edge. Two of his colleagues came by earlier to discuss the meeting's agenda and it seemed like everything was organized and ready to go.

We're directed to a conference room where fifteen people are already seated. I notice Beckett is usually the last to arrive at meetings, while I prefer to be the first to feel comfortable.

As we walk to the front of the room, his hand remains on my back. He pulls out a chair for me, and I sit down promptly. Beckett starts his presentation confidently while the attendees review their packets.

I notice an older gentleman at the very end of the table appears annoyed by the packet and keeps grumbling. I can see Beckett looking at him repeatedly. Something about Beckett's demeanor has me standing from my chair and walking over to the man. I lightly touch his shoulder. Initially, he looks frustrated, but his expression softens when he meets my gaze.

"These packets can be tricky," I explain, flipping to the fifth page. "Each slide is included in the packet with additional details. It looks like Mr. Shaw is on slide 5." I offer a reassuring smile and squeeze his arm. "The packets are detailed and comprehensive, just like everything at Shaw Industries."

While Beckett continues with his presentation, I assist the gentleman with the packet. As others start to take interest, I guide them through it as well, ensuring everyone is aligned. I almost want to snicker because this is baby stuff—figuring out that the packet mirrors the slides, a clear method Beckett uses to present information to a group. I am quite possibly the dumbest person in this room, and I can piece this together on my own.

When it's time for questions, the man directs one at me, and I have no clue what he's talking about. But, like my mom and dad like to say, *fake it 'til you make it.* "What a great question. I'm sure Mr. Shaw can go into the nitty-gritty of these fine details." I wink at Beckett as I repeat the gentleman's question.

Once Beckett addresses him, I lean in and adjust the man's tie. "Let's hope this meeting wraps up soon; I'm starving." I give him a playful nudge, which makes him chortle

I walk back to Beckett. "I need to use the restroom. Do you know where it is?" I ask.

He points me in the direction, and I head out. That was a tough crowd; that must be why Beckett was so tense.

After I finish in the bathroom, I hesitate before re-entering the room. The lights are back on, and everyone is standing and chatting. Beckett stands by the man I had helped earlier, shaking his hand. They seem to be in the middle of an easy chat, but as soon as Beckett spots me, his expression softens, and the man turns with a broad smile.

"There she is—Brynn Pierce," Beckett introduces, gesturing for me to join them.

"Brynn Pierce, wonderful to formally meet you," the man says, extending his hand as I approach. "Rick Sullivan. I lost a contact this morning, so I'm only half-seeing today," he laughs warmly. "But I'm looking forward to working with both of you."

I shake his hand. "It's nice to meet you, Mr. Sullivan. I'm sorry to hear about your contact—that must be incredibly frustrating."

"Thank you, Miss Pierce. We'll talk soon. Bye-bye now." With that, he gives a polite nod and heads for the door, followed by a few others.

Beckett continues making his rounds, shaking hands and exchanging brief words with the remaining attendees. As the room begins to clear, he gives a final wave to the last group.

We leave and head to a different restaurant this time, one I hadn't seen on our first night. We're shown to a cozy round booth tucked into the corner of the room. I slide in first, only to find Beckett waiting behind me, still standing.

"You literally could have gotten in on that side but decided to wait for me to awkwardly scoot in," I grumble as I finally sit.

He smirks as he finally takes his seat beside me. "I don't mind waiting," he says, amusement dancing in his eyes.

"Oh, okay, Mr. Impatient," I tease.

"I just wanted to admire the view," he whispers, right as the waiter approaches.

The waiter introduces himself, then takes out his pen and notepad, ready to take our order. I sit quietly, expecting Beckett to place our order, but he gestures for me to go ahead.

"Oh, um, I'll have the 6 oz sirloin medium well, with a baked potato and house salad," I say, closing my menu.

Beckett hands our menus to the waiter, who gives a polite nod and starts to walk away.

"Actually, make it the 12 oz instead," I call after him, watching as he nods again, disappearing toward the kitchen.

"You put me on the spot, and then you didn't even order food."

"You said you wanted to order," he shrugs. "Now we're sharing yours."

I figured he was planning on sharing my food when he didn't order, hence my changing to a sirloin size I'd never finish on my own.

I lean back in my seat. "What's on the agenda tomorrow?" I ask, trying to gauge how our day will look.

"More meetings."

When my food arrives, Beckett isn't kidding—he takes my plate, cuts up the steak, dips it in steak sauce, and offers me a bite before taking one himself. This continues throughout dinner, to the point where I never get to touch my own plate, as Beckett feeds me every bite.

As we step off the elevator on our floor, he wraps his arms around me. "I'm ready for dessert," he grins, his lips brushing the side of my neck.

"Did you get us dessert?" I ask eagerly, turning to face him as he unlocks our door and pushes it open.

"You're my dessert." He tugs me to him until my chest is pressed against his.

"I too, would like to try dessert…" I bite the inside of my cheek.

"What's wrong?" he smiles as he keeps walking me backward.

"You can't make fun of me when I try."

He shakes his head, leaning in to kiss me softly. "Baby, I would never make fun of you. Not ever."

Without a word, we start stripping off our clothes, each piece of fabric falling away, revealing more of our bare skin to each other. My breath catches in my throat as I take in the sight of him, every muscle and line of his body accentuated by the dim light of the single lamp in the corner. He watches me with that intense gaze, following the movements of my hands as I slip out of the last of my clothing.

I've never done this before, never gone down on anyone, but the thought of doing it with him ignites something feral in me.

Beckett notices my hesitation and steps closer, his hand gently brushing my arm in a soothing gesture. "It's okay. You don't have to do anything you're not comfortable with."

But I want to. I want to feel him, taste him, and explore this new level of intimacy with him. I meet his gaze and give a small nod.

He sits on the edge of the bed, spreading his legs slightly, and I move to stand between them. His erection stands proudly. "I don't know what to do," I admit quietly.

His expression softens, and he gives me a reassuring smile. "Get on your knees," he murmurs, and I lower myself in front of him. He takes my hand, wrapping it around the base of his length. "Grab it like this," he instructs, his voice soothing as he shows me exactly where to place my hand. His fingers guide my other hand to mid-shaft, his hand wrapping around mine as he begins to show me how to stroke, slow and steady. It feels different than I was expecting. I guess I never realized the skin moved like that over the hardness.

"And then," he says, his voice low, "suck on it like a lollipop."

Leaning in, my lips part slightly as I move toward him. Just as I'm about to take him into my mouth, his voice halts me for a second. "Teeth are no good."

I nod in understanding, my heart hammering in my chest as I lower myself onto him. I start with a tentative lick at the tip, tasting the salty bead of pre-cum that's gathered there. As Google informed me earlier, this has health benefits. His reaction is immediate, a low groan as his hips twitch slightly in response. The sound emboldens me, encouraging me to continue.

I swirl my tongue around the crown, then explore every ridge and vein, savoring the way his body responds to me. His hand comes to rest on the back of my head—not pushing, just resting there. I take him deeper into my mouth, sucking gently.

I pull off, unsure if my hand at the base is meant to do anything else beyond holding him. "Can I touch this?" I point to his balls.

His head lifts, and he nods, sitting up again. He takes my hand, guiding it to him, letting me explore. I feel the shape of them between my fingers, and, well, okay, my health class failed me. I know they are referred to as "balls," but I didn't know there were actually two balls inside the sack. Then again, I spent my entire semester of health having my desk right next to the teachers because I could never concentrate and "talked too much." Jokes on Mr. Lattamer, I still never listened to anything he taught, and well, I'm learning more in real time than I ever learned in his boring class.

"They feel good." I continue rolling the tender skin between the two balls. "Would you like it if I did this while doing… that?" My gaze flickers between my hand and the length of him, still slick and waiting.

"I think I might." He leans back on his forearms, watching intently as I take him into my mouth again. His lips part, and from his expression he likes what I'm doing. I let out a small, amused hum, and when I do, his eyes roll back in surrender.

"What made you do that?" I whisper, wanting to do whatever it was again.

"The vibration... when you hummed," he pants.

I smile to myself, lowering once more, this time letting a soft, intentional hum vibrate through me as I take him in. His response is so good—his mouth falling open as a deep moan escapes him.

I can feel the tension in his body, the way his muscles contract as I work him over. His hand wraps over mine, guiding me in a lazy stroke as he teaches me the rhythm he likes. I follow his lead, my mouth moving in tandem with my hand, the motions becoming more fluid.

"That's it," he praises. His other hand fists the sheets beside him, his knuckles white as his control slips away. His praise fuels me, and I take him a little deeper, hollowing my cheeks as I suck, wanting to draw more of those delicious sounds from him.

I feel his body start to tremble, his breathing turning shallow and erratic. Sensing he must like what I'm doing, I quicken my pace, my hand and mouth working in perfect harmony. The room fills with the wet, rhythmic sound of my mouth on him, accompanied by his low, raspy groans.

"Fuck, Brynn." His hips start to move, rocking gently, meeting my mouth with each motion. He's careful with his thrusting, trying not to overwhelm me. I don't mind, though—I want to feel all of him.

His grip on my hair tightens slightly as a long, guttural moan escapes him, and he spills into my mouth. I take him in, swallowing around him as best I can. The sensation of his release is delicious. I don't stop, continuing until his entire body shudders with the aftershocks. Only then do I pull back, releasing him with a soft gasp. My lips are swollen, my heart racing, and my entire body tingles with the knowledge of what I've just done. I watch the heavy rise and fall of his chest as he comes down, spent and utterly undone.

He looks down at me, his eyes dark and filled with an emotion I can't quite place. He reaches out, his hand cupping my cheek as he leans down to press a soft, lingering kiss to my lips.

"Good job, baby, that was incredible," he whispers against my mouth.

I climb to my feet and straddle his lap. "Rate it." I stare down at him, biting my lip.

"One hundred percent. Ten out of ten. A+, five stars—would absolutely recommend," he declares, pulling me closer until our bodies are flush.

"You'll recommend?" I grin, my fingers tangling in his hair, tugging his head back. "I must be a natural. I guess I'll have to branch out, collect a wider range of reviews."

His arms tighten around my waist, and he growls as he flips me over in one swift motion, pinning me to the bed with ease. I let out a startled giggle, which quickly turns into a gasp as his weight presses into me. The sheets are cool beneath my back, contrasting sharply with the heat radiating from his body as he settles between my legs.

"I think *my* review is plenty. But if you're looking for a lot of feedback, I'll make sure to give you some every time you do that."

"I like that. Can you take your dessert now? My vagina is aching," I say candidly, practically dying with how turned on I am.

He nods slowly, his eyes never leaving mine as he moves down the bed. He positions himself between my legs, and I watch anxiously as his mouth descends between them.

CHAPTER Nineteen

The next three days pass in a blur of sameness. Each morning starts with a business breakfast, followed by meetings sprinkled throughout the day, with just enough time in between to catch my breath. The routine is relentless—awkward mingling with businessmen who all seem to have mastered the art of small talk, while I, on the other hand, specialize in making a fool out of both myself and Beckett. I half expect him to pull me aside and suggest that I stay behind for the next meeting or "sit this one out," but he never does.

Instead, he seems to gladly accept my presence, even when I can tell I'm out of my depth. Every time we head out for another meeting, he's there, offering a reassuring smile or a quick touch on my back, silently telling me I'm welcome. It's almost surprising how natural it feels, despite the tension I bring to these otherwise polished events.

By the last meeting, he sighs as he loosens his tie while we make our way back to our room. It was the last meeting of this trip, and I don't know why we don't just leave now or first thing in the morning, but I don't feel it's my place to question his business trip.

I wake up wrapped in Beckett's arms, his chest rising and falling against my back, his arm draped over my waist, pulling me close. He stirs behind me, shifting slightly as he nuzzles into my neck, his lips grazing against my skin in a lazy kiss. "Morning," he mumbles, his voice gravelly with sleep.

"Morning," I whisper back, sinking deeper into his embrace. We stay like that for a while, wrapped up in each other as his body heat seeps into me, shielding me from the early morning chill creeping through the room.

Eventually, he shifts, stretching his limbs and pulling away just enough to turn onto his back. I roll over to face him, propping myself up on one elbow as he rubs the sleep away. He looks peaceful—his hair a tousled mess, his cheeks still flushed.

He meets my gaze, a slow smile spreading across his face. "What are you smiling at?" he asks in a teasing tone.

"Just you," I say softly, reaching out to trace along his jawline. He catches my hand, bringing it to his lips for a quick kiss before finally pushing himself up into a sitting position.

"Alright, enough lounging around," he declares. He swings his legs over the side of the bed and stands up, stretching out the kinks in his back then heading to the closet.

He pulls out a suitcase and unzips it, rummaging through the contents and pulling out two pairs of snow pants with suspenders, along with a pair of fluffy earmuffs and two thick pairs of gloves. He's grinning like a kid on Christmas morning as he starts getting dressed, pulling on his snow pants and fastening the suspenders over his shoulders.

"What's this?" I ask, sitting up fully now, the blankets pooling around my waist as I reach for the clothing.

"Get dressed," he says, tossing a glove at me.

I catch it with a laugh. "What are we going to do?" I ask, climbing out of bed and dressing in comfy clothes, then putting the snow gear over them.

"You'll see," he replies with a smirk, zipping up his coat.

Once we're both bundled up, I grab a scarf and wrap it snugly around my neck. He steps forward and gently places the earmuffs over my ears, his hands lingering as he adjusts them. I look up at him, the closeness making my heart race.

"There's an ice sculpture show in town," he finally reveals. "Nobody can drive in this weather, but we can walk."

I like the idea of walking through the snow with him, bundled up in our warm clothes, feeling like it's the perfect winter adventure. "Exciting," I say, leaning up to kiss him. "Let's go."

The town is alive with people bundled up in scarves and hats, their cheeks rosy from the chill as they admire the ice sculptures lining the streets.

We stop at each sculpture, marveling at the intricate designs. Some are small and delicate, while others are towering, almost mythical creatures with details so fine it's hard to imagine someone used their hands to create them. I take pictures of each one, capturing the way the light reflects off the ice. Beckett poses with me in front of the most impressive ones, and we ask passersby to snap a few photos of us together.

As we continue down the main street, a group of children rush past us, their giggles ringing out as they race toward a nearby hill. My gaze follows them, and I smile when I see them sledding down. I glance up at Beckett, lifting my eyebrows.

"Absolutely not," he says before I can even ask, his tone firm but his eyes softening as he catches the look on my face.

I tug on his arm, giving him a pout. "Please," I draw out the word.

He raises an eyebrow, weighing the options, but I don't give him a chance to say no. I start walking backward, pulling him along with me, my boots slipping slightly on the snow-covered ground.

A resigned smile tugs at the corners of his mouth as he finally gives in. "Fine, but if I break something, you're the one carrying me back to the hotel and nursing me back to health."

"Easiest deal I've ever agreed to," I wink.

When we get to the top of the hill, a woman offers us her sled as she doesn't want to go again. I eagerly take it, thanking her profusely. "We'll bring it right back," I promise, but she just happily waves me off, telling us to have fun.

"Come on," I call out to Beckett as I plop down on the sled, then pat the spot behind me.

He hesitates for a split second. "I can't believe I'm letting you talk me into this." He sits down behind me with a huff, his long legs stretching out on either side of mine. I wiggle a bit, trying to get us positioned just right, and then use my feet to push us over the edge of the hill.

The sled takes off faster than I expected, and Beckett wraps his arms tightly around me, holding me close as we fly down the slope. The world blurs around us, nothing but white snow and the sounds of our laughter echoing in my ears. The wind whips against my face, and my heart leaps in my throat.

We reach the bottom far too quickly, the sled coming to a gentle stop in a powdery drift. I turn my head to look at Beckett, my cheeks aching from the smile plastered on my face. "Again?" I plead, the excitement making my voice pitch higher.

He shakes his head, but there's no hesitation this time as he agrees. We trudge back up the hill, and the second ride is even better, the sled seeming to glide smoother over the packed snow. By the third ride, we're practically experts, steering with subtle shifts of our bodies as we zoom down the hill.

After our fourth ride, breathless and a little dizzy from all the excitement, we return the sled to the woman. She's still there, chatting with a friend, and I hand it back. "Thank you so much," I say, still catching my breath. "That was amazing."

We wave goodbye, then retrace our steps back to the hotel. That's enough fun and cold for today. As we're walking, I feel something hit my back, and I turn to see Beckett laughing as he crouches down to scoop up more snow and make a snowball.

I let out a sinister cackle. "You have no idea what you've just done." I bend down and pack my own.

He takes his shot, trying to hit me again, and I duck, letting it barrel past me. I wind my arm back and put my full force behind my throw, striking him square in the face with a well-packed snowball.

The impact is so solid that it knocks him clean off his feet, landing him on his rear end with a grunt. I'm overcome with laughter as I approach him, extending my hands to help him up.

His eyes are wide as he stares up at me. "What the fuck was that?"

"You're the one who threw a snowball at me first."

"You're the one who blew off half my face with a snowball."

I smile proudly. "I played softball in high school."

"It felt like you put rocks in it," he quips.

"Maybe I did," I counter.

We cackle all the way up to our room, his nose and cheek swollen from the well-placed snowball. I feel a little bad, and I would offer to get him ice to hopefully minimize potential discoloration. However, given the chilly temperature, I reason the cold air will serve a similar purpose.

I go to the bathroom, stepping into the welcoming warmth of the shower. I enjoy the heat as I wait for Beckett to join me.

I know he will.

A smile spreads across my face as I feel the brief rush of cool air as he pulls open the shower door and steps in beside me. He wraps his arms around me, pressing a kiss to my neck. I turn in his arms, wrapping mine around him, and gaze up at him.

He leans in to claim a kiss, then pulls me into a snug embrace. When he releases me, he reaches for his body wash, beginning to cleanse himself. I follow suit, finishing the rest of my shower.

Once we're out, I towel dry, then pull on a pair of soft shorts and an oversized T-shirt, adding a cozy sweater for warmth. When I emerge, Beckett's already sprawled out on the bed, absently rubbing the cheek where my snowball made contact, the skin still slightly red from the impact.

"I'll be right back," I say, moving towards the door. "I'm going to get you some ice for your face."

He laughs softly, sitting up. "I'll come with you."

I shake my head but smile as he gets off the bed, slipping his shoes back on. Together, we head out of the room, making our way down the hall to the ice machine. The cool, dimly lit corridor is quiet except for the hum of the vending machines nearby. I grab a plastic bag and hold it under the ice dispenser, the cold cubes clattering into it. Beckett stands next to me, watching with amusement.

"What?" I ask, noticing the look on his face.

"Nothing," he grins. "Just glad you're holding up to your word."

"My word?"

"You promised to take care of me if you hurt me."

I tilt my head, raising an eyebrow. "No, I said I'd take care of you if you broke a bone. You decided to start a snowball war with me. You just didn't know who you were up against."

"You practically broke my nose. Any lower and you would have knocked my teeth out," he says, as the realization hits him that I probably could have actually knocked his teeth out. "You're dangerous," he muses.

I roll my eyes and grab the bag of ice. Holding the top securely, I twist the bottom to seal it, then knot it so it won't leak. "Here," I say, handing it to him.

When we return to the room, he flops onto the bed with a dramatic sigh, placing the ice bag over his face. I let out a laugh at how over-the-top he's being.

He peeks out from under the ice pack, his face mock-serious. "This is all your fault, you know."

"Am I getting a sample of what sick Beckett will be like?" I tease, crawling up him on the bed. I straddle his hips and look down at him, trying to feign seriousness. "I'm sorry, babe."

He peeks around the ice pack with one eye, a lopsided grin forming on his lips. We both start laughing. The ice crinkles as it shifts on his face, and I shake my head at how ridiculous it all is.

Without thinking much, I start rocking my hips against him, trying to jostle him on the bed. But the instant I start, the pressure and movement send a warm sensation through me. I slow down, testing it out again, feeling how good it is. I keep my pace deliberate, waiting to see if Beckett will stop me.

Instead, his hand finds my thigh, his fingers curling around it, gripping firmly. "You feel good," I murmur, letting my hips roll gently over him, feeling a building heat between us.

But then reality hits me—he's lying here with a giant bag of ice on his face, and I'm on top of him, getting my rocks off. I stop and laugh, climbing off him to grab the remote from the nightstand.

He lifts the ice pack just enough to protest, his eye following me. "Why are you stopping?"

I grin and shake my head. "It would be way sexier if you didn't have a giant bag of ice on your face."

He sits up and removes the bag. "Well, you're the reason I need the bag of ice, so you should be sympathetic."

"This is me being sympathetic," I say as I hand him the remote.

We spend the remainder of the day lounging in the comforts of our room. As night finally falls, we climb into bed to settle for the night. Once he switches off the light, the only sound is the soft rustle of sheets as he nestles into his pillow.

I scoot into him, pressing a soft kiss to his chest as I drape one leg over his, nestling it comfortably between his thighs. His arm wraps around me, pulling me closer, while his other hand traces lazy patterns along my thigh. He smiles in the dim light, his chest rising and falling steadily as I settle in against him.

"Beckett?" I whisper.

"Yeah?"

My fingers glide slowly across his chest, tracing the familiar contours of his muscles, gathering every ounce of courage I have, knowing if I don't say it now, I will chicken out.

"I want to have sex with you."

He literally stops breathing. The silence stretches on for so long I don't know if I just killed him. I lift my finger under his nose to see if there's any air, and when I finally feel the signs of life in the exhale he lets out, he still hasn't responded. "Beckett?"

"Yeah?" he replies, though his tone is still distant.

"Did you hear me?"

Another pause. Then, he clears his throat and finally says, "Yeah."

"… And?"

"And what?"

"What do you mean, 'and what'? Can we have sex?" The words come out sharper than I intended, and I brace myself for his answer.

After an agonizing moment of silence, he says, "No."

It feels like the floor just fell out from under me. "No? What do you mean, no? Why?" I ask, my voice tinged with annoyance and hurt as I prop myself up on my forearm and look down at him.

He hesitates, then says with unnerving honesty, "Because virgins are inexperienced, and it's not a good time."

The blow lands harder than I could have imagined. Anger flares hot in my chest, and I snap back without thinking, "WOW. Pretty sure you already took my virginity when you fingered me, but whatever."

I roll over, turning my back to him, staring blankly out the window. I'm stunned by his refusal. I thought he'd say yes, and I was mentally prepared to let him have me right now. Lying in bed with just my underwear and tank top on, I feel exposed, embarrassed, and vulnerable.

"You're mad at me because I won't take your virginity?" he asks in disbelief.

"No," I snap. "I wouldn't give it to you anyway."

"Then why bring it up?"

"Go to bed," I bite out.

"Babe—" he starts, but I cut him off, already feeling the walls go up around me.

"Go to bed," I repeat.

He rests his hand on my side, placing his chin on my shoulder. "Babe," he says more softly.

"You were a virgin once too, you know," I say tersely.

"A long time ago," he replies.

"And I've been a virgin for a long-ass time."

He softly trails up my arm in a soothing gesture. "Were you saving yourself for marriage?"

"No. I just never had the desire to have sex. There's no big religious reason or trauma. I'm awkward and usually find men off-putting. But you're different."

"Gee, thanks." He digs his chin into my arm.

"Do you have STD's?"

His head jerks back in surprise. "What? No. Why would you ask that?"

"I wouldn't judge you," I assure him.

"I don't have STDs," he says defensively. "Where is that even coming from?"

"Because you won't have sex with me. It would make me feel a lot better if you won't because you have herpes or something and you don't want to spread it," I admit.

"I don't have herpes."

"That's exactly what someone who has herpes would say," I raise a brow.

"Are you fucking with me?" He stares down at me in disbelief.

"Yes and no. I think that's a lame excuse to not have sex with me because I'm inexperienced. I can be taught. You can teach me. But you're refusing, and there has to be a reason." I pause, wondering if I've been reading way too much into him and me. I know he's out of my league. I've never initiated contact with him because I know my place. I also know eventually this will all end. I don't want to be the girl who chases after him while all the outside spectators say how bad they feel for the naive girl chasing after the fox.

"We can still fool around," he finally offers.

"No thanks. It was decent while it lasted," I retort. "As you already know, I'm 'inexperienced,' and 'that's not a good time.'" I swipe away the traitorous tear that slips free, putting forth my best effort to remain composed.

He lets out a heavy sigh and then rolls over, facing the opposite direction.

When morning comes, he's still on his side of the bed—a first for him—and it sends another pang of hurt deep into my stomach. The cold distance between us feels more palpable than ever. I slip out of bed quietly, careful not to disturb him, and begin dressing. Moving around the room, I gather my belongings, folding clothes and tucking everything away as I prepare to leave.

By the time he finally stirs awake, I've already packed my things and settled on the couch, swiping absentmindedly across my phone screen, playing my farm game. It appears we've entered a phase of mutual avoidance, which seems will bode poorly for the ride ahead, confined in his truck. I glance at him briefly, but he doesn't look back, and I know this drive is going to be an unbearable stretch of silence.

A bellman arrives to collect our luggage, and the ride down in the elevator is just as uncomfortable. I'm consumed by mortification for even suggesting the idea of having sex. Of course he wouldn't want to have sex with me. Virgins ARE inexperienced and I agree with him; it certainly wouldn't be a good time for him. I'm assuming he came to that decision after the couple of times we fooled around. Here I was, naively believing I was pretty good for being a beginner, while he must have been inwardly cringing so hard. I'm glad we established this now before I really started to get attached to him.

Our bags are loaded in his truck, and we're just about to leave when Collette and her dad approach us. "You're already headed the way we need to go. We rode up with the Fullers, and their car is stuck. Mind giving us a ride back," the gentleman asks.

I glance at Beckett, who hesitates. Finally, he relents and nods. "Yeah, sure."

We pile into the truck, and the first half of the drive is uneventful—almost too uneventful—until we stop at a gas station for a quick break. I head inside to grab a few things and use the restroom. When I return, my stomach drops—Collette is sitting in my spot up front. My blood boils instantly, but I force myself to stay calm.

Beckett emerges from the store behind me, and I slow my pace, waiting for him to fall in step beside me. "Have you had sex with Collette?" I ask quietly, but the question feels like I just pulled the pin from a grenade.

He stops dead in his tracks, his brows furrowing in confusion. "Not ever," he says slowly, as if trying to understand where that's coming from. "Why?"

I signal toward the truck, where Collette is now in my seat. "Just wondering why she's sitting in my spot."

He glances over at the truck, then back at me, trying to figure out if I seriously think he had anything to do with it. "And you think I told her to?"

I shrug. "Do you want me to sit in the back?"

He blinks, baffled by the question. "No, of course not."

"K," I say simply, turning away and heading for the truck without another word. I yank open his door and climb up into the seat, flipping up the center console so I can wedge myself right in the middle. Collette looks over, her eyes wide with bewilderment, but I ignore her. I'm not giving up my spot next to Beckett, especially not to her.

"That's awfully squished up there; why don't you come on back here, girlie?" Collette's dad offers me from the backseat, trying to sound friendly.

"No thanks, Pops," I reply, fastening my seatbelt with a firm click. I scoot closer to Beckett, hoisting my leg up and over his, letting it settle between his legs, making a point to get as close as possible. Out of the corner of my eye, I catch Collette glance down, followed by her fingers flying over her phone screen. Good. She can enjoy stewing. I don't even want to be this close to Beckett right now, but the satisfaction of making her uncomfortable is too tempting to resist. Especially since she shouldn't even be here with us.

Once we're back on the road, Beckett's hand rests between my thigh, close enough to my vagina to consider us more than merely friends, but definitely not touching me in an inappropriate way.

Collette's dad keeps up a steady stream of conversation the entire ride back, his voice droning on, but I'm not paying attention. I just wait until we can drop them off, and I can scoot over to my original seat.

The drive to my apartment is less than thirty minutes from the time we drop the excess passengers off, and it can't come fast enough.

Beckett is the one to break the silence. "I'd like to offer you a job," he says, his tone neutral but serious. "At my company."

"Okay," I respond.

He shifts slightly, keeping his eyes on the road. "Mr. Sullivan was so impressed with you. I'd like you to handle his account, or at least be the face to him."

When I just sit there, he turns and stares at me.

"What?" I say, meeting his gaze.

"Can you start Wednesday? That way, you can still have a couple days off to get ready."

"No," I reply.

"What day can you start?" he presses.

"I appreciate the offer, but I already have a job," I reply, keeping my voice steady. "Thanks, though."

"But you just said—"

"What did I say? *You* said you'd like to offer me a job. *I* said 'okay.' As in you may offer me a job. And I am declining your job offer."

He sighs, gripping the steering wheel a little tighter. "I'll give you time to think about it."

"No need," I respond sharply. "I've already made up my mind."

"Why are you acting like this?"

"Like what?" I snap.

"Like a brat," he retorts.

I can't help the laugh that escapes me. It's bitter, harsh, and I turn away, staring out the window, refusing to meet his gaze.

"You're still mad over the sex thing?" he prods.

"No," I lie, annoyed that he would bring it up when it's exactly why I'm angry.

"Then why are you mad at me?"

"I'm not mad at you."

"Good," he replies, his truck coming to a stop outside my apartment. He unbuckles his seatbelt and turns toward me. "Then kiss me."

I whip my head in his direction and give him a disgusted look, climbing out and heading to the back seat to grab my bag.

"So, you are mad at me?" He calls after me.

"Bye," I toss over my shoulder, unlocking my apartment door and slamming it shut behind me, locking him out both physically and emotionally.

CHAPTER Twenty

As I walk into the apartment, I barely have the door closed behind me when Chloe pops out of her room. "How'd it go?" she asks, leaning against the doorframe with a grin.

I drop my bag on the floor and sigh. "Beckett and I fooled around."

Her eyes widen with excitement, and she practically bounces on her toes. "No way! That's awesome! How was it? Give me all the details."

I hesitate, then let out a frustrated laugh. "It was incredible. Then he ruined everything when I bared my soul to him and told him I wanted to have sex, and he said he wouldn't sleep with me because I'm a virgin."

Chloe's enthusiasm instantly fades, and she rolls her eyes, crossing her arms. "Are you serious? Most guys would be all over that!"

"Not Beckett," I groan, making my way to my room. "He said virgins are 'inexperienced,' and apparently, it's 'not a good time.'" I flop down on my bed, staring up at the ceiling.

Chloe trails behind me. "Well, his loss then."

"He has a big weenie," I mumble, watching her as she walks over and sits on the edge of my bed.

Her brows lift and she purses her lips. "On second thought, you might've dodged a bullet. I don't know how fun that would be for a first time."

"I think I was starting to believe he wanted to date me or something. When he said that, it killed all those fantasies since it guaranteed we'd never be anything serious or long-term."

Chloe gives me a sympathetic look then perks up. "Tom's roommate, Mark, is still dying to have a double date with us." Her tone brightens, like she's just found the solution to my problem.

I groan and roll over to face the wall. "No thanks. Men suck."

It's Wednesday morning, and a sharp knock sounds at the door, growing more insistent by the second. Chloe strolls past my bedroom, her voice carrying through the hall. "Are you expecting someone?"

"No," I mumble, pulling the blanket over my head.

I hear her answer the door, muffled voices blending with the morning quiet, and then, suddenly, my blankets are ripped off me.

"What the fuck." I sit up, disoriented, only to find Beckett standing by my bed, looking devastatingly gorgeous in his suit.

"Get up, you're going to be late for your first day."

I groan and flop back down, pulling the pillow over my face. "Get out of my room."

Undeterred, he sits on the edge of my bed and delivers a swift smack to my butt, the loud slap echoing in the room. "Up. Now," he insists.

"Go away," I grumble, burying myself deeper into the mattress.

"I will lick your asshole if you don't start moving in the next five minutes," he threatens playfully.

I shove the pillow aside, glaring. "You're disgusting."

"I have a meeting at 10:30. I'm not leaving without you. Don't make me late," he says as he leans back on my pillows.

"Maybe she doesn't want a job with you," Chloe chimes in from the doorway, crossing her arms and staring pointedly at him.

"Good morning, Chloe. How are you?" he greets her.

"I was about to have morning sex until you banged on the door," she retorts.

"Don't let us stop you," he calls over his shoulder, then rolls closer to me, wrapping his arms around me.

"You better not have your shoes on my bed."

He nuzzles his face into my neck. "I took them off at the door."

"What kind of bipolar are you?" I ask.

"I'm not bipolar." He presses a kiss to my cheek. "I'm just highly motivated."

"You're not diagnosed bipolar." I air-quote 'diagnosed,' because this man is giving me mental whiplash with his back and forth.

"I'm not bipolar, period." He rolls me onto my back and partially lays on me. "You still hung up on the virginity thing?" He leans down, softly biting my neck.

"She won't have to be hung up on it long. My boyfriend and his roommate are taking me and Brynn on a double date this Friday. And he's fine with virgins," Chloe says, still standing there.

He glances at her briefly before throwing his leg over mine. "Thought you said your boyfriend was waiting for you," he says, almost dismissively.

"Just wanted to make sure you knew—her virginity isn't an issue for others," Chloe snorts as she saunters off.

"*Very* hung up on the virginity thing," he says, his teeth grazing my shoulder.

"Yes. How do you justify doing everything BUT having sex with me?"

"Do you not enjoy what we have done?" he asks.

"I do. And it made me want more. And you're refusing me," I say bluntly.

"What do you want right now?"

"To go to bed. So leave." I attempt to roll away from him.

"We have work." He nips my ear between his teeth.

"Can't. I have a lot going on this week," I lie.

"Mmhmm... your double date?"

"Yep," I say too quickly. In reality, there's no double date. Chloe made that up purely to mess with him, and it didn't even bother him.

"Then I can warm you up," he says with a smirk, completely unfazed by the idea of me with someone else.

Well, based on that response, I can piece together that Beckett views me the way I view Elliot—I couldn't care less what he does with someone else or who he sees. Beckett basically just said he's completely fine with another man hooking up with me. That's quite the punch to lay on me first thing in the morning. And now, to avoid further hurt, I decide to go along with him just to make him shut up.

I throw off the covers in a huge display of my unwillingness and get up, wanting to put an end to this conversation. If that means going to work, I guess I'm clocking in to a nine-to-five. "What am I supposed to wear? And don't you dare say, 'You can wear pajamas for all I care,' because this is your company, and I don't want to look like an idiot."

"Wear the blue dress you wore when we went to lunch."

"The one I wore for the date with Elliot that you interrupted?" I raise my brow.

"That's the one," he winks.

I grumble as we walk into Beckett's building.

"Oh, stop," he jibes.

"What? I'm so excited for this," I deadpan, keeping my face completely flat. "You're taking me to lunch," I say as we step in the elevator.

"Anywhere you want," he agrees.

He leads me to a large area with sleek, spacious cubicles, each with dual monitors and plenty of desk space. He walks me to one that is right at the edge of the corridor we just walked down, positioned with a wall behind it instead of the rows of cubicles surrounding each other. At least this one feels somewhat secluded.

"This will be your perch for now. I plan on getting you your own office, but until then, you can sit here and just look pretty."

I narrow my eyes at him, crossing my arms. "I hate that. Give me something to do."

"Play your little farm game," he offers, then turns to walk away.

"Uh-uh. Get back here, Mister." I walk toward him. "You dragged me out of bed to come here and work. Make me work, or I'll find myself something to do, and when you receive a call that your new hire has accidentally shut down your entire system and you find me tangled in the wires in the comms room, you'll have only yourself to blame." I narrow my eyes.

He lets out a laugh and shakes his head, knowing that scenario is a plausible possibility. "I've got spreadsheets I need created. Think you can handle that?"

"Maybe. I'm willing to try," I shrug.

"Come with me," he smiles, and I follow after him.

We head to his office, and I make an honest go at just staring at his firm ass as he walks. But as soon as we step through the threshold, I can't stand it any longer, I reach out grabbing two handfuls of his butt cheeks and squeeze.

"Brynn, you can't do that here," he laughs, prying my hands away.

"But those cakes look too good to leave alone," I grin.

He shakes his head as he powers up his computer, then opens his bottom desk drawer, pulling out a folder. It's filled with organized papers all covered in chicken scratch.

"I wrote samples of what I'm needing." He hands me the folder.

"Yuck, Beckett, is this your handwriting?" I crinkle my nose as I look through the papers.

He stares flatly at me.

Pulling my lips back, I realize what I said was rude. "Sorry… You would have made a good doctor," I add, trying to lighten my insult.

"Go work," he laughs, dismissing me to go back to my jail cell.

The morning crawls by painfully slow. Beckett keeps popping in and out of the office, taking me with him whenever he leaves, but it's all so monotonous. I've never been so bored in my life. At one point, I catch myself nearly nodding off from the endless flow of spreadsheets on the screens in front of me.

As promised, he takes me to lunch. He sits next to me, rubbing my shoulder the entire time. We went back to our routine of him ordering for me because, quite frankly, I enjoy not having to decide, and I find it sexy when he does it.

Around midday, Elliot walks by, doing a double-take when he sees me getting back to my desk. I try to act like I don't know who he is, but it's hard to miss his expression shifting to one of mild irritation as he approaches.

"What are you doing here?" he asks.

I look around, hoping he's talking to someone else even though he's standing at my cubicle. "Your boyfriend offered me a job," I reply, casually logging back into my computer.

Elliot's jaw tightens. "Tell him you changed your mind."

I turn and stare up at him in disbelief. "Oh, no thanks."

"I don't want to see the woman who broke my heart every day," he mutters, glaring at me.

"Well, lucky for you, your desk is wayyy over there," I drawl, pointing in the vicinity of his trash-infested area, "and my desk is wayyy over here. So it should be easy to avoid me."

"Are you wanting me back?" he asks, and I nearly snort.

"No, Elliot. I don't want you back," I assure him.

"But you got a job to be near me?"

"I know you can't actually believe that. But if, for some reason, you think you might enjoy convincing yourself that that might actually be why I'm here, let me reassure you—I forgot you even worked here until just now. Don't try to soothe your own feelings by thinking something so silly," I say, turning back toward my computer.

"Why else would you get a job where I work?"

"I got a job where Mr. Shaw works," I correct.

"Because *I* work for him."

"Have a nice day, Elliot." I pull up the spreadsheet I was working on and start trying to decipher Beckett's handwriting. This is some of the sloppiest handwriting for one of the most organized people I've ever met. I wonder if he's self-conscious about it, and here I was, talking shit to him. I need to not do that. Then again, he talks shit about my driving—though I'm not self-conscious about it.

It's sort of implied that I will most likely unintentionally hurt your feelings if you choose to surround yourself with me. Beckett probably didn't think twice about my comment.

"Can we have dinner and talk about this?" Elliot asks, and it startles me as I had already forgotten he was there.

"Elliot, this isn't your area. Go back to your corner," I say as I put in my earbuds. I watch as he saunters off, throwing a last look back over his shoulder, his face sad, and I'm almost positive I rolled my eyes at him. But I don't remember. Sometimes, my facial expressions have a mind of their own.

The rest of the day drags on. Everyone around me is working hard while I just sit here, ready to claw my eyes out. I created every document Beckett gave me, and I figured I would just do them all and bring them to him when I completed everything, but he insisted I bring them to him after I finish each one.

"Because you miss me or need to check my work?" I tease.

"Wouldn't you like to know."

"It's okay to just admit that you miss me," I glance over my shoulder with a smile.

Now, with nothing left to do, I find myself trying to avoid idly clicking around on the computer. I know how companies like this operate—they monitor every keystroke and mouse movement. There's no way I want Beckett seeing the random things I'd Google to pass the time, so I discreetly pull out my phone to keep myself entertained. Between mindless searches, I manage to conquer four more levels in my farm game.

Each time I beat a level, I take a screenshot and send it to Beckett with something along the lines of: "In case you wanted to see my progress," "Still bored," and "Let's go home."

His responses come back just as quickly: "Good job, baby," "Can't be bored when you're making such progress on your farm," and "We'll leave soon."

Just as I'm tossing a piece of popcorn into the air, trying to catch it in my mouth, the girl at the desk next to me leans over with a bright smile. "Hey, I'm Mandy," she introduces, her voice cheerful and friendly.

I turn and stare wide-eyed, wiping popcorn from my dress. "Brynn," I reply, taken by surprise. I wasn't expecting anybody to talk to me and had been throwing popcorn in the air, trying to catch it in my mouth. I planned on showing Beckett my new trick when he came to get me to leave, but my skills are nowhere near polished enough.

I've gotta say, though, she probably thinks I look cool—especially since the only piece I caught was the one that hit my mouth as she started talking to me. I think it would have missed if she hadn't startled me, causing me to jump right into the kernel.

"If you need anything or just want to chat, I'm always available," she offers.

"Thanks," I respond, then lean over in my chair to pick popcorn up off the floor.

"How do you know Mr. Shaw?" she asks.

I don't actually know if anyone is supposed to know the extent to mine and Beckett's relationship. Heck, I don't even know the extent to our relationship. So I decide to play dumb. "Who's that?"

She looks at me, confused, then subtly points behind me. I turn to see Beckett leaning on the wall, staring down at me.

"Ohh, *this* Mr. Shaw. I thought you said Mr. Shawl. That was my bad." Sometimes I wonder why I'm even legally allowed out in public. I have zero social skills.

Beckett gives me a half-smile. "Wanna head out a little early?" he asks, but already wearing his coat, cueing me that we are leaving now.

"God, yes," I reply eagerly, grabbing my purse and coat. "Bye, Mandy. See ya tomorrow!" I wave, hurriedly slipping into my jacket and following him out.

ON THURSDAY, I SPEND THE ENTIRE DAY PLEADING WITH BECKett to let me leave early, even offering a "blowie" as a bribe if he agrees. He smirks, turning me down every time, but suggests that I can give him one outside of work whenever I want.

Both Wednesday and Thursday, he's at my apartment by 9:00 AM to pick me up, ready to drag me to work, whether I like it or not. But by the time Friday comes, he has to be at the office earlier than usual for a meeting, so I drive myself. I'm already halfway there when my phone rings—it's Beckett.

"I'll come pick you up in a couple of hours so you can sleep in," he says.

"I'm almost at the office," I reply.

There's a pause, then he sighs, clearly annoyed. "Turn around and go home. I'll head over to your apartment and get you."

I can practically feel the tension radiating from him through the phone and I'd rather not start my morning off with that kind of negative energy. Plus, tonight, I have dinner plans with Chloe, so I'll need my car anyway.

"Yeah, yeah, yeah," I say, shrugging off his frustration.

"See you soon," he responds, then hangs up.

I'm walking down the stairs in the parking garage when I spot him heading toward his truck.

"Hey, Pookie," I call out.

His head snaps in my direction, his eyes narrowing with clear irritation. "I said I was coming to get you."

"And I told you I was already on my way." I approach him, grabbing the lapels of his coat and pulling him to me. "But if you want me to go home for the day, I absolutely will hold up my end of the bargain," I add with a playful wag of my eyebrows.

"Where are you parked?" he asks, ignoring my offer.

I point up toward the upper levels. "Somewhere up yonder. Can we take turns using your parking spot? That would be way more convenient for me," I quip.

"I'll get you a parking pass for the spot next to me."

"When does Preston drive you?"

"When I'm not driving you," he replies, taking my hand and pulling me toward the building.

He seems distant today, or maybe I'm reading too much into things. This has been the world's longest day ever, and it's now 6 PM, and we're still here. I don't actually know my official hours; I've only ever worked the same hours as him. So, while he's still here, I remain too.

I knock on the door to his office, waiting for a response. When I get nothing, I knock again. Still nothing. I push open the door and step inside.

There he is, sitting behind his desk, looking so effortlessly handsome that I'm hit with an intense surge of cute aggression. I want to walk over to him and strangle him, while simultaneously kissing every inch of him profusely.

He's scribbling away, focused on whatever notes he's making. As I step inside, he glances up briefly, then his eyes flick back to the paper. "Thought you had the place to yourself?" I smirk.

"I knew you were still here," he replies, not bothering to look up again, his hand moving quickly across the page.

"Well, there's your writing problem right there. You hold your pen weird," I tell him, noticing he's holding his pen between his pointer and middle finger. He ignores my comment and keeps writing.

I move to the side of his chair, draping my arms around his shoulders and pressing myself against his back. He places a kiss on my arm without pausing his work.

"What time are we leaving?" I ask, resting my chin on his shoulder. "Or, if it's okay with you, can I head out now?"

He stops writing, his posture stiffening as he leans forward to grab a stack of papers. Without looking at me, he pushes the stack toward the edge of the desk. "I need these filled out before you go. It shouldn't take more than an hour," he says, then resumes working.

"Sure," I say, leaning in and pressing a firm kiss on his cheek, holding my lips there. He's emitting grumpiness, and it's bothering me. When I pull away, he's still focused on his writing, so I press my lips to his cheek again and push harder. Still no reaction. I start pressing hard kisses along his face until I get near his lips. "Kiss me, grumpy pants," I tease. He barely turns his head, allowing me to press my lips to his. He at least reciprocates the kiss and gives me a pucker.

"Mmm. Your lips are soft." I lean in and kiss him again, then swipe my tongue across them. Satisfied, I stand up, ruffle his hair affectionately, and take the pile of papers.

As I hurry away, I cast a look back at him, knowing I've just irritated him further. His eyes narrow as he smooths his hair back into place. Returning to my desk, I find the office completely empty. It looks like everyone leaves between five and six, so I'm alone out here.

The "hour-long" task he gave me turns out to be more like five hours' worth of work. There's no way he actually expects me to stay and finish all of this tonight—that's nuts. I decide to give it an hour, like he'd said, and then head back to his office. When I get there, he's on the phone. I mouth, *Can I leave now?* But he holds up a finger, signaling for "just a minute."

I wait, but when I check back a little later, he's still on the phone, deep in conversation. By 8:30, he's still talking, and I need to get going. I had planned to shower before Mark and Tom picked up me and Chloe, but now that it's so late, I'll have to skip it and just meet them at the restaurant. I tried telling Chloe I wasn't in the mood to go tonight, but she insisted, saying we already committed. I even explained how this feels too much like a date, and she promised it's just a casual dinner with friends. She knows how I feel about Beckett, and we talked about how I don't want to lead Mark on.

Chloe reassured me that everyone's on the same page, and it'll just be low-key.

Taking a final peek into Beckett's office, he's still on the phone as I expected. Instead of bothering him, I stick the prewritten sticky note on his door: *That's the world's longest phone call. Hope your jaw doesn't fall off. It happens to be one of my favorite things in the universe. XO Brynn.*

I go back to my desk, grab my stuff, and head out.

I arrive at the restaurant and feel a wave of relief when I see that we are seated at a square table with individual chairs around it, so we don't have to sit in a booth together.

"Brynn!" Chloe exclaims excitedly as I approach. She stands up to hug me and then introduces me to Mark. I met him briefly a couple months ago, but this is the first time I'm going to be in a confined space with him.

Chloe and I chat and laugh effortlessly, while Mark casts lingering glances at me throughout dinner. If Beckett weren't in the picture, Mark would not only have a "shot" with me, but I would definitely date him. However, Beckett has me completely wrapped around his finger.

I hate how guilty I feel the entire drive home. I feel like I was being unfaithful to Beckett, even though I know he wouldn't want me to feel this way. I easily decide I don't like this feeling and resolve not to join Chloe, Tom, and Mark for any future dinners.

When I finally get home, exhaustion hits me hard. The day has dragged on, and all I want is to unwind. I step into the shower, letting the hot water cascade over my shoulders. Chloe went home with Tom, and I'm once again single and ready to mingle… with sleep.

Wrapping the towel around me, I pad barefoot toward my bedroom, nudging the door open with my foot. I toss my clothes into the hamper by the door and flick the light switch.

"WHOA!" I gasp, my heart leaping as I press myself against the doorframe.

Beckett is lying on my bed, feet still on the floor, as if he had just sat down and then sprawled out.

"Why do you do that?!" I huff, then head straight for my dresser, pulling out a pair of underwear. I'm about to make my way to the closet for a tank top, only Beckett is standing there.

When I try to move around him, he grabs my waist and pulls me flush against his body, kissing me deeply. My breath catches as he finds the knot in my towel, tugging it free and letting it fall to the floor.

"Mmm," I moan with a smile.

His lips press harder against mine, his kiss growing deeper as he lifts me and carries me to the bed. The world seems to blur as my back meets the soft mattress, his body hovering above mine. The weight of him straddling my thighs sends a wave of heat through me, pinning me down in the most intoxicating way. His lips drift from my mouth to my neck, each kiss leaving a burning trail behind.

I barely register when he grabs the underwear I had been clutching, tossing them carelessly across the room. My heart pounds, every nerve in my body tingling, wanting him touching me.

"Why'd you do that?" I manage to ask, my voice breathless as I prop myself up slightly.

His gaze locks onto mine. Slowly, he loosens his tie, the fabric slipping through his fingers before he tosses it aside. I'm captivated as he moves to his shirt buttons, undoing them one by one. The air between us is electric as I reach out, tugging his shirt free from his waistband. He grabs the collar and pulls it off, tossing it carelessly to the floor. My fingers trace the ridges of his abs, sliding up his chest and then back down.

His jaw flexes, but I can't tell if it's anger that drives him—or the same primal need I have to take his body. I want to taste him again. As his hands move to unbuckle his belt, the metallic clink fills the room. He climbs off my lap, letting his clothes fall away until he's completely bare.

Without breaking eye contact, he lowers himself, claiming my mouth in a fierce, hungry kiss, as he presses me into the bed. I feel the mattress dip under his weight as I shift, inching back onto my pillow while his body hovers above mine. His hands brace on either side of my chest, keeping him suspended, his face just inches from mine.

"What?" I ask shyly.

A slow, wicked smile tugs at his lips as he dips down, capturing my lower lip between his teeth. "Cute note," he murmurs.

"Thanks, I thought you might like that."

"It's taped to my computer."

My grin widens. "Perfect spot for it."

He kisses down my neck, pausing at my chest to brush his lips over each peaked nipple then continuing his descent. I arch beneath him, anticipation winding tighter with every kiss. By the time he reaches the apex of my thighs, I'm trembling, my body aching for him. His strong hands part my legs, and I bite my lip, holding my breath as he moves toward my center. His tongue teases me with a slow, sensual stroke that makes me buck toward him.

His tongue flicks over my clit with a delicate intensity, sending a shockwave through my entire body. I barely have time to catch my breath before his mouth seals over me, sucking hard, as his finger thrusts deep inside, curling with precision.

It's immediate. Brutal. Pleasure crashes into me with relentless force, my thighs trembling as I arch against his face. I gasp, my fingers threading through his hair and I pull him closer. I need him to never stop. He pushes me higher, his rhythm unyielding, and within seconds, I feel the coil inside me snap.

I'm gone. My back bows, a cry tearing from my throat as my orgasm rips through me, so powerful it's like he ripped it straight from my soul. My body quakes, and all I can do is fall apart under the merciless pleasure Beckett draws from me.

My body is still humming with the aftermath of my release, and he remains perfectly still, his lips pressed softly against my clit, allowing me to come down from the high without overwhelming me. His touch is patient, almost reverent, as he gives me time to let the intensity ebb away.

Slowly, my legs fall open, the tension easing out of my muscles. I drop my hands above my head, letting a warm glow settle over me. My breath finally evens out, and I feel him gently pull away. His mouth and fingers leave me, and I instantly miss the contact.

He moves up the bed, positioning his body between my legs, and as soon as his weight settles over me, I wrap my arms around his neck. He presses his lips to mine, before trailing them down to my neck. "How do you feel?" he whispers.

A lazy smile spreads across my face. "Good," I murmur. "Give my legs a second to remember how to work, and I'll return the favor." I squeeze my arms tighter around him. "Or, you know, you could always sit those fat cakes on my boobies and fuck my face," I add, biting my lip teasingly, letting him know that is actually an option if he wants.

He lifts himself onto his forearms, and I catch a flash of something new in his eyes. His hand slips between my thighs, and I feel his cock sliding down my center with ease then stop outside my entrance. My heart races as he leans back down, lips brushing mine again, his voice low and hoarse. "Want to back out?"

I shake my head, but it's not enough for him. He gives a half-smile, biting his lip. "That's not a word."

"I don't want to back out," I whisper, my voice steady despite the wild beating of my heart.

With a soft touch, his hand slides beneath my head, threading through my hair as he lifts me toward him, his lips crashing into mine in a deep kiss. His other hand finds mine, our fingers interlocking, and I feel the reassuring squeeze he offers before his hand trails down my leg, pressing mine firmly against his own.

Then, with painstaking slowness, he pushes into me. His cock stretches me in ways that make my body quiver, but he doesn't rush. He pulls back slightly before thrusting again, barely pressing deeper, yet each new depth feels like my entire body is being rearranged. My breath hitches, and I'm not sure what I feel other than my body screaming for more, my brain saying something too big is trying to enter me, and my soul trying to become one with his.

His breathing becomes uneven, and I relish the sound, aware of how deeply aroused he is. "Does that feel okay?" he pants.

I nod. "I think... it feels… tight." I glance between him and the space where our bodies are joined, wondering how it's possible to feel so full, like he's puncturing my lung.

He remains still, allowing my body time to adjust. But the longer he holds back, the more I need him to move. My hands slide down his back, tugging on his hips, urging him forward, and he responds with a slow, measured thrust. The sensation of him pushing deeper sends a sharp pulse of pain through me, and I gasp, but he immediately stops, brushing his lips against mine, his kiss soft and soothing.

The discomfort fades quickly, replaced by a mounting need that builds deep. He withdraws, only to ease back in with slow, measured strokes. His movements are gentle, each one pulling back just enough before pushing forward again. When he attempts to press deeper, there's resistance; like my body is struggling to accommodate him.

"Goddammit—that fucking hurts," I whimper, closing my eyes as the sensation overwhelms me. My hips feel like they're being pulled apart, and my mind can't make sense of the conflicting signals my body is sending. My brain feels like it's being scrambled; I can't tell what's pleasure and what's pain, as it's all morphing into one.

"Want me to stop?" he murmurs, his voice laced with concern.

"No," I gasp. "Just… maybe bring your smaller dick next time."

He chuckles softly, through his arousal

"Or maybe don't go so deep," I breathe out, offering a more serious suggestion.

"Got it," he whispers, his hand drifting down to rub my clit in slow circles. His thumb grazes over the sensitive nub, sending electric pulses through me. My whimpers turn into moans as my senses gradually start to drown out the discomfort. After a few strokes, he tries to go deeper, and the pressure returns, making me cry out from my body fighting against him.

He eases back, nipping my ear and I relax, then he tries pushing, and I can feel the resistance, then what feels like rubber bands of tissue snapping from the inside, causing me to cry out. "It doesn't fit," I gasp, a tear springing free as I press my hand between our bodies, trying to prevent him from going in further. I thought I could handle it. I handled the first nine inches he gave me, but these last fourteen are too much.

"It's okay," he whispers, leaning down to kiss my cheek. He stills inside me, waiting patiently. "I'll pull out as soon as you aren't clenching on me so tight."

"I'm sorry." The guilt immediately washes over me. I wanted this and made it so lousy for him.

"You have nothing to be sorry for," he reassures. "Just breathe. Relax, baby."

He props himself up on his elbow, and leans down taking my nipple into his mouth, sucking softly as his other hand works my clit. Both sensations distract me enough for me to relax long enough for him to withdraw, easing out of me with care. Even as he pulls away, I can feel the lingering ache between my legs, the discomfort refusing to leave. *Pretty pathetic of you, vagina, to still ache for that when you were being such a bitch, not allowing him all the way in.*

"Let's go to bed," he suggests softly, pulling back the covers and climbing to his feet.

I look at him, a bit confused. "Are you leaving?"

Instead of answering, he bends down to retrieve my discarded towel, using it to clean himself then flips off the light. Returning to the bed, he hands me a damp washcloth to clean myself up. Once I've wiped myself off, he folds the towel and holds it up. "You might want to sleep on this," he suggests, waiting for me to lift my hips before sliding it under me.

Once I'm settled, he pulls on his boxers and slides into bed beside me, his arm draping over my waist as he pulls me in. I feel the warmth of his body pressed against mine, his still-erect cock nudging my leg.

"Does it hurt?" I ask quietly, feeling bad that he's still so hard.

"It'll subside," he assures me.

"I just really confirmed your resolve for virgins, huh?" I murmur awkwardly.

He nuzzles his face into my chest. "Virgin? What virgin? I don't see any virgins in this room. But I'm going to have to use three fingers next time. You just squeezed my cock so tight it might bruise more than my face."

I giggle, the tension easing from my body. "So, you're gonna have a purple penis now?"

"Just the tip," he grins.

"Why just the tip?"

"Because that's all that got in."

I stare at him in disbelief, unsure if he's joking. "What?"

"Did you think you took the whole thing?" he asks, glancing up at me.

"At least half," I admit sheepishly. "I hear Chloe having sex all the time, and didn't know it would be that… painful. I thought it would feel more like your fingers—but we would both be enjoying it together."

He chuckles softly, brushing his thumb along my jawline. "My cock's a little bigger than two fingers."

"A little?!" I exclaim, unable to contain my laughter. "That's a big ass zucchini!"

"Why don't you eat it then."

"I will," I reply, making eye contact.

His grin softens, his fingers caressing the side of my face. "Let's just sleep."

He tucks his head against my chest as he pulls me tighter into him. His arms feel like an anchor holding me as we settle into the quiet intimacy of our bodies.

Hours pass and I wake to find us still wrapped in each other. My body aches with the desire that hasn't even began to subside. Nope, it's been steadily growing, a dampness between my thighs intensifying the need pulsing through me. I bite my lip, fingers stroking through his hair, feeling the way his breath fans against my skin as he stirs beneath my touch. I shift slightly, pressing my thigh closer to his leg, only to feel the bundle of nerves at my core light up as his leg presses harder against me.

The heat is unbearable, and I grab a fistful of his hair, tugging gently. His eyes flutter open with confusion. "You okay?" he asks, his voice thick with sleep, propping himself up on one elbow as he gazes down at me with concern.

"I'm really turned on," I admit. "Can we try again?"

His eyes lock onto mine, searching for any sign of hesitation. When he finds none, his gaze drops to my lips before rising back up. He nods, then slowly slides his boxers down, revealing his full arousal. He positions himself between my legs again, his body hovering above mine. I spread my legs wider, welcoming him, feeling the tension in the air shift as our bodies align.

He captures me in a deep, heated kiss, then trails down to my neck. His tongue creates a warm, wet path, igniting every nerve in its wake. His body presses closer as his hand slides down my side until he's gripping my thigh, then he moves between us, wrapping his fist around his cock. He slides it along my slit, teasing me with slow, torturous circles.

When he finally pushes the tip inside, a moan breaks free, and my body arches into him. The slickness between my legs makes his entrance easier, though the sharp sting of pressure lingers as he eases in. His thrusts are controlled, each one deeper but slow enough for me to adjust. His body trembles with restraint, holding back to avoid hurting me, yet with each thrust, I feel him pushing just a bit further, testing the limits of my body.

His deep grunts mix with my cries as I cling to him, needing him to keep going. He stretches me until I feel like I can't take anymore, yet I crave every inch of him. The fullness, the way he claims me so completely, sends my body into overdrive. The raw, primal need for him overwhelms me, and all I want is for him to stay buried inside me.

I tighten my legs around him as his hips drive into me, pushing us both past the edge of control. The room is filled with the sounds of our shared desire, and nothing else exists but the two of us, tangled in the unfiltered passion that courses between us.

When he presses back into me, reaching the depth we left off at, I feel my body's natural resistance, but there's no way I'm about to let this end again. Instead, I slide my hand between us, and for a second, he looks as though he's anticipating me stopping everything again, but I don't. My fingers find my clit, and I start to rub, my hips moving in small circles as I moan quietly. His gaze drops, watching me intently as his lips part with a subtle tremor in his breath.

Then his mouth is on my nipple, the heat of his tongue teasing in a way that has me teetering right on the edge. He's consuming me, making me unravel with every deep stroke and brush of his mouth. I feel like I might shatter from the way he touches me, so in tune with my body. Every movement feels perfectly timed, like he's taking me apart and putting me back together, one deep thrust, one gentle stroke, one heated kiss at a time.

"I need to push past this spot," he murmurs against my skin, his hips nudging that same place that won't let him deeper. "I can make it quick. It'll hurt for a second, but after that, it'll feel good—I promise."

I look into his eyes, then lean in, capturing his lips with mine, silently telling him to do it.

"I'm going to lift your hips off the bed just a little bit. Keep rubbing yourself," he instructs.

His hand slips under me, pulling my hips up, and I can feel him sliding out, then back in, rocking us gently, easing me into it. My eyes close tight, and I focus on the rhythm of my fingers on my clit, trying to relax into the sensations. Just when I think I've got the hang of it, he drives into me with a force that feels like fibers of my vaginal canal are ripped apart and stretched with a blunt force, as he tears past that barrier inside me. A sharp cry rips from my throat, my body stretching to accommodate him.

The intensity of it has me digging my nails into his back, but before I can fully process the pain, his mouth is back on my nipple, sucking hard, his teeth grazing over the sensitive peak. Gratification surges through me, drowning out the sharpness of the stretch.

He's so deep inside me, it feels like he's pressed into my ribcage. He's filling space I didn't know I had.

"Breathe," he purrs in my ear.

I release the breath I didn't realize I was holding, shaky and uncertain, as I struggle to remember how to do something so simple.

"You're doing so good," he soothes, and I feel my muscles start to relax. "In and out," he whispers, and I exhale a long, trembling sigh as the discomfort gradually melts into a deep, throbbing need.

He pulls back and thrusts in again, and I can't control the sounds that escape me—each movement draws a new euphoric cry from me. The tension between us hums with intensity as our bodies move in perfect rhythm. Every thrust is matched by a moan, not just from me, but from him as well, his low groans sending heat pooling deep in my belly.

It's beyond words. He feels so good, so perfect—better than I ever imagined. It's as if we're creating something entirely new, something pure and natural, just the two of us together. Every moment with Beckett feels like more than I could have dreamed, something entirely our own.

He adjusts, lifting my leg higher onto his hip, and the new angle makes me gasp as he sinks deeper. My cry is lost in his mouth as his teeth gently graze my lip.

My hips lift off the bed, meeting his thrusts, and he groans, our breathing growing heavier as the heat between us deepens. Our skin glistens with sweat, the room filled only with the sound of our bodies moving in sync, the raw tension building to a point that feels like it might break me.

I feel the telltale orgasm building in my core, the sensation coiling tighter with every moment, signaling how close I am. Beckett senses it too—he sits back on his heels, gripping my hips firmly as he moves faster, harder, driving deep with every stroke and I can't hold back any longer.

The release is blinding, my orgasm crashing over me in waves. My legs stiffen, and I cry out, clenching around him, my body pulsing with each thrust he delivers. He doesn't slow down—his movements become frantic, as he chases his own release. He's relentless, the tension between us tightening even more, until he finally lets go with a low, guttural growl.

He pulls out at the last second, and I feel the heat of his release spilling onto my stomach. His breathing is ragged, his muscles taut as he rides the last pulses of his climax. His eyes squeeze shut, and his jaw clenches as his body trembles, spent and satisfied.

With a shaky exhale, he removes his hand from his cock and rests it on my thigh, grounding us both in the aftermath.

"At least you didn't shoot that on my face this time." A grin tugs at my lips despite the haze still lingering in my mind.

His laugh is deep and genuine, wiping the sweat from his brow. "You look sexy with it dripping down your lips," he fires back.

I raise a brow, smirking. "Which lips?"

"I'll have cum dripping down every part of you," he promises.

I bite my lip, still feeling the pleasant aftershocks coursing through my body. "Feel better now?" I ask, trailing my thumb across his damp brow, satisfied to see the tension has left his body.

"You have no idea," he murmurs, leaning down to capture my lips in a soft kiss. When he finally pulls away, he climbs off the bed, taking the towel from beneath me, wiping himself clean, then tending to my belly.

Once he's finished, he lies back, pulling me into his chest, his arm wrapping around me possessively. I nestle into him, inhaling the intoxicating scent of his skin.

"Have you ever smelled something so good you want to eat it?" I press my nose back to the same spot.

He chuckles, the sound rumbling through his chest. "Yeah, I have."

"That's how I feel about you," I confess, inhaling deeply. "Your skin... it's yummy."

He gives me a playful squeeze. "Okay, Hannibal Lecter. Time for bed."

"Not until I've had my fill." I breathe him in again, overwhelmed by his scent. I've never smelled anyone so good in my life. "I'm gonna go get a fork and a knife and start eating you."

"Babe. Shut up." He laughs, pulling me in tighter.

When I wake in the morning, the room is overly warm. The covers are long gone, kicked off at some point during the night, leaving Beckett and me exposed. I turn my head and my lips curve into a grin. His body, still tangled up with mine, is relaxed—except for one very noticeable detail. His erection is fully on display, standing proud. I trail my fingers lazily down his chest, then walk them across his hips.

"Good morning, gorgeous man," I murmur.

With his eyes still closed, he smiles. "Morning."

I bite my lip as my fingers glide lower. "Actually, I was talking to him," I tease, letting my thumb brush lightly against the base of his shaft.

His laugh rumbles through the air, and he opens one eye to look at me. "I see where your priorities lie."

"He's the one who wants to tell me good morning."

"Tell him then," he says, his cock flexing.

Before things can escalate, the front door slams, and Chloe's voice rings out, "Honey, I'm home!"

Panic surges through me, and I scramble to the edge of the bed, trying to grab the blankets, but it's too late. She bursts into the room, looking like she got rode hard last night and put away wet, her hair tousled, and makeup smudged.

Her mouth falls open at the scene in front of her. "No way! Brynn! You guys totally fucked!" She grins, marching over to the pile of discarded blankets and tossing one in my direction.

I glance over at Beckett, who has one arm draped over his face, shielding himself from the sudden intrusion of light Chloe just flicked on. His other hand is trying—and failing—to cover his very obvious erection. Even with his large hand, it's not enough, and I quickly drape the blanket over him.

"Well, Mark was wondering if you'd want to hang out again," Chloe continues, entirely unfazed by the situation. "Should I tell him—"

"No," Beckett interrupts, his voice tinged with irritation. "You can tell him no."

Chloe smirks in my direction. "I'll tell him maybe. If he fucks like Tom, the second date will totally be worth it." She winks at me, then swats Beckett's leg. "I'll make breakfast. Looks like you've got a BIG problem to deal with first."

With one last cheeky grin, she flicks the light back off and heads out, calling over her shoulder, "Breakfast in thirty!"

I sit there, staring at the door when I feel Beckett's arm snake around my waist. "You heard her—we've got thirty minutes," he murmurs, his mouth finding my breast, making me gasp softly as my body responds instantly to him.

Exactly thirty minutes later, we emerge from the bedroom, both of us satisfied. Chloe's grin is one of pride, while

I feel nothing but blissful contentment and relaxation coursing through me.

We take our seats at the table, and Chloe quickly sets plates down in front of us. "Yum," I say, glancing up at her.

Beckett murmurs his thanks, already digging in as we settle into breakfast.

"Tom's taking me out again tonight," Chloe announces, setting her phone aside after sending a quick text.

"Where's he taking you?" I ask.

She shrugs. "Doesn't matter as long as we end up in bed."

"You dirty dog," I tease.

She grins, leaning back in her chair. "What about you? Are you working today?"

"I might," I answer, taking a sip of my coffee. "I haven't checked the roads or the app yet to see what it's like out there."

Beckett clears his throat, drawing both of our attention. "You have a real job now. You don't need to drive people around," he says, staring at me intently.

"I like doing it," I respond.

He doesn't break his gaze. "It's not safe, Brynn."

"It's fine," I insist, turning my attention back to my food, trying to end the conversation there.

"Nothing you say will change her mind," Chloe chimes in.

Beckett exhales sharply, letting it be known he's frustrated but unwilling to argue further. Leaning back in his chair, he watches me before speaking again. "I have a lot to do today," he says, his tone shifting. "I'll need a ride."

"Call Preston," I say, keeping my focus on my plate.

"I'm asking you," he counters.

"Fine. But if you try to take my keys and drive, I'm done. If you want me to drive, then let me do the driving," I warn him.

His jaw flexes, nostrils flaring as he exhales through his nose. "Fine," he agrees, pushing one arm against the table.

"What do we have to do?" I ask.

"Besides each other," Chloe quips, a playful grin stretching across her face as she takes a sip of coffee, her eyes flicking between me and Beckett.

"Cute," I give her a pointed look as I stand to go get ready.

In the bathroom, I apply a light layer of makeup, keeping it simple. I grab the curling iron and loosely curl my hair. Once I'm satisfied, I head to the bedroom, sliding hangers back and forth until I choose a fitted top and a sweatshirt. I slip into a pair of jeans and throw on a jacket over the sweatshirt. Even though there's not much snow outside, I pull on my snow boots. With my phone, keys, and purse in hand, I sling the bag over my shoulder and head out.

"Ready?" I call out, stepping back into the living room where Beckett and Chloe are lounging on the couch.

"Yes," he replies, standing up. "Thank you again for breakfast, Chloe," he adds, heading toward the door and pulling it open.

"Text me updates on where you guys end up," I tell her as we make our way out.

Beckett turns to me, his eyes softening. "You look beautiful," he says, leaning in to press a kiss to my cheek. "I need to head home to shower and change." His arms wrap around my neck, pulling me to his chest.

"Fuck no," I retort.

"The elevator attendant has been fired. The situation was dealt with," he assures me.

"He grabbed my boob," I bite back, feeling the anger flare up again. The memory of that creep fondling me still makes me want to go shove my foot up his butt.

Beckett's jaw tightens. "I know. I was on the phone when it happened. I'm sorry I couldn't get down to you fast enough. But the cameras caught everything. He tried to deny it, but we reviewed the footage and called the police. He was fired on the spot."

"Good," I smile, unlocking my car. He walks to the driver's side, and I stop in my tracks, giving him a pointed look. "No. You said you would let me drive."

He pulls the door open. "Relax, lightning McQueen, I'm opening the door for you," he says, turning back to look at me.

CHAPTER Twenty-One

We drive to his condo, and he takes my phone from my purse, shuffling through my music. He's lucky he's sexy, a sex god, and I'm driving, or I'd give him a monkey bump for touching my phone without asking.

When we finally pull into the parking garage, he casually points toward a spot near the elevators. "Park there."

"No. That says VIP parking. I'm not having my car towed," I shoot back, driving past the space.

"Babe, I'm VIP. That's one of *MY* spots," he explains.

I stop and look at him, then shift my gaze to my rearview mirror. His truck *is* parked right next to the empty space he pointed at.

"If my car gets towed, you're paying to get it back," I say, throwing my gearshift into reverse and stepping on the pedal as my tires squeal and I rip into the spot with far more speed than necessary.

"Jesus Christ!" he yells, gripping the center console and the dashboard. When I turn to look at him, his mouth is hanging open as he stares at me.

"Come on," I say as I climb out.

He sits in the car, gaping at me as I stand at the front. "Let's go, slowpoke," I call, waving him along.

Finally, he climbs out, walking around to inspect the side of my car for damage, then checks his truck. He gives me a wide-eyed look, shaking his head in disbelief. He sighs dramatically, wrapping his arm around my shoulder, pulling me toward the elevator.

He swipes his keycard for his floor, and the ride up is quiet, but not uncomfortable. I glance at him as he leans against the wall, and he gives me a soft smile. He straightens just as the doors open—his timing so perfectly on point.

"I'm going to grab a shower," he says, already heading down the hall toward his bedroom.

"Okay. I'll be out here packing my purse with all the expensive stuff," I joke.

"I'm too big to fit in your bag, babe," he calls over his shoulder and disappears into his room.

Once he's out of sight, I take the opportunity to look around in the areas I haven't seen yet. I walk down the long hall opposite the one to his room and go to the first door on the left. It's an office. A couple of travel magazines are fanned out on the corner of his desk, and a large bookcase covers the entire back wall. It's not fully filled with books; some shelves have decorations, and a couple have framed photographs.

I pick up the first one and study the people in it. If I were to guess, the older woman at the center of the group on the beach is likely his grandmother. Beckett has his arm wrapped around her, while another woman with a wide-brimmed hat and sunglasses hugs the other side. His mom and dad stand on either side of them.

The next picture I grab shows him standing at the front of a group of seven men, all lifting a bride face-first toward the camera. Beckett and the groom, both grinning so big, are at the front of the group, holding her securely while the others circle around her, lifting her up. His smile is infectious, and I smile myself, imagining the fun they must've had that day.

Setting it down, I reach for another photo. This one shows Beckett and a group of guys in hiking gear, trekking through the mountains with heavy backpacks. The landscape behind them is rugged and breathtaking, but my focus is on him—he looks so handsome, his face relaxed, eyes glinting in the sun. There's something about seeing him in these candid moments that makes my chest tighten just a little more.

I gently set the photo back and grab one that shows Beckett with a group of six guys dressed up for Halloween. I'm not sure what they were going for, but with the women's wigs, shirts tied halfway up their stomachs, booty shorts, and cowgirl boots, maybe they're going as slutty cowgirls? They're happy and so carefree, and I wonder what kind of friend Beckett is. I can't picture him just hanging out, relaxing with the guys as they give each other shit. However, it's something I'd love to witness.

"Finding anything interesting?" His voice startles me out of my thoughts.

I glance over my shoulder to see him standing in the doorway, freshly showered, a towel slung low on his hips, hair damp and tousled. Seeing him so casual and unguarded sends a little jolt through me.

"Nothing yet. Still snooping." I try to keep my tone light as I take in the glorious sight of him.

He walks closer and I revel in the way his shoulder muscles flex with each step. When he reaches me, he wraps his arms around my waist and rests his cheek on the side of my head. I point at the picture and then look back at him.

"Pageant queens," he states.

I let out a laugh and shake my head as I put the picture back down. "Your shower was too fast. I barely got to snoop. Are you sure you washed your balls?"

"Why don't you smell them and let me know."

"Well, that's an attractive thought. Were you getting worried about me being left unattended?"

"Not at all."

"And that's why you couldn't even take the time to get dressed?" I give him a playful once-over.

"I came to undress you," his voice drops.

I pull away from him with a smirk. "Nope. I'm working today. You needed a driver, and I'm all set to go," I say, strolling out of the room, making sure he watches me leave.

We spent the entire day hopping from store to store, filling bags with new work outfits and a couple of pairs of ballerina flats. Beckett pointed out that my snow boots weren't exactly business-appropriate, reminding me to swap them for proper shoes once inside the office.

At the register, I reach for my wallet, but Beckett is quicker, sliding his card to the cashier before I can even open my purse. "I've got this," he says, giving me a look that makes it clear there's no point in arguing.

"I have money now, remember? The settlement?" I remind him. "I don't need you paying for everything."

He leans in, his voice dropping to a whisper. "I'm using my portion. So technically, it's like you're paying for it anyway."

"If you just always plan on paying, I'm going to quit bringing my wallet."

"Please do. You don't need your money."

After a long day of shopping, we head to dinner. By the time we pull up to his place, I stop at the front of his building to drop him off. "Stay the night," he suggested, the words coming out as more of a statement than a question.

"No, sir. I'm going home, to sleep in my bed... alone."

"Do that tomorrow." His persistence is charming, but I'm not budging.

"Goodnight, Beckett," I smile.

With a resigned sigh, he opens the door, pauses for a second, then leans in and presses a lingering kiss to my lips. There's a brief hesitation before he pulls back and steps out, giving me one last look as he heads inside.

I watch him go and then pull away. No sooner than I'm on the road is he calling me. I'm not answering that. I just want to sing along to my music and drive home.

I walk into Shaw Industries on Monday morning, the lobby already buzzing with the usual hustle of people moving like sleep-deprived zombies, everyone clutching their lifeline of survival through the workday—their coffee. I make a quick stop at the coffee shop on the first floor and grab two coffees—one for me and one for Beckett. I grin when they hand me the cups labeled "Buckets" and "Broom."

As Beckett requested, I switch out of my snow boots for the new flats I got over the weekend, then take another look at our coffee cup names and snap a quick picture of them. I smooth down my dress and make my way to his office, his drink in hand. When I open the door, Beckett barely looks up from his computer.

"Morning," I say, trying to sound casual.

His only response is a curt nod attached to a clipped, "Morning," his eyes fixed on the screen. I stand there, debating whether I should yell, "RAHHH" really loud just to see if he jumps. But I tuck that intrusive thought into my back pocket for later.

"Good chat," I mutter, waiting for him to say something more. His fingers don't even pause on the keyboard, the rapid clicking filling the room as if he's purposefully drowning me out. I walk to his desk, set his coffee down, and kiss his cheek. Leaning my hip against his desk, I softly thread my fingers through the side of his hair, then trace my thumb over the curve of his ear. His typing slows, and I get a little reaction, but when I pull my hand away, he resumes typing. I wonder if he's upset because I didn't call him back when he tried calling after I dropped him off. Then again, he didn't exactly reach out after that one time either, so it's probably something else.

I get back to working on the stack of papers he had me filling out on Friday and manage to finish about half. I debate whether I should wait until I've completed all of them before taking them to him since he seems to be in no mood for people today, and I don't want to bother him while he's clearly busy. But I decide I want to see him, so I gather what I've done so far and head to his office to try talking to him again.

When I enter, he's still distant. At least he's been drinking his coffee. This time, he barely looks at me as he stands and grabs his coat. "I have a meeting," he mutters, striding past me without a second thought. I stand there, a bit stunned, as he walks out of the office without any indication that I should follow.

The rest of the morning drags on, my mind running in circles as I try to figure out what's going on with him. Is he honestly upset with me because I didn't call him back? Or is something work-related bothering him?

After lunch, I return to my desk to find a folder waiting for me. Beckett's chicken scratch is scrawled across the front: *Need spreadsheets created immediately.* I shake my head as I open it up and get to work.

When Beckett walks past, heading toward his office, he seems even more agitated than he did earlier. I try to keep my head down and focus on the task at hand, but my attention drifts when a tall blonde woman steps out of the office across the hall from the cubicles. She peers back at someone in her shared office space, then heads straight for Beckett's door.

A knot forms in my stomach, and I force myself to focus on my work, but my mind keeps wandering back to the look on Beckett's face, the coldness in his voice, and that smile on the blonde's face as she walks to his office.

She's in there for seventeen minutes. Yes, I timed it. No, I'm not ashamed of it.

Mandy's voice pulls me from my thoughts. "Do you like candy?" I hear her ask from behind me.

I turn to look, and she's peeking around our shared wall, holding a jar of mini candy bars. My first instinct is to start riffing with her by taking the entire jar, shoving it in my purse, and telling her, 'Thank you,' just to see how she would respond—but I decide against it.

"I'm good, thanks for offering."

"If you ever want some, I always have sweets." She jiggles the jar and scoots herself back into her cubicle.

I finally finish the spreadsheets Beckett requested and let out a long breath of relief, sliding the papers to the side. If I bring them to him now, he'll probably just give me more to do, and I don't necessarily want that. So, I'll milk my time and play a level of my farm game. As I'm about to start another, I catch a glimpse of Savannah, the receptionist, walking by. She's only ever back here when she's on her way to Beckett's office.

I don't really feel like going anywhere near him with the way he's been acting, so I figure maybe Savannah can bring the reports to him.

"Savannah," I call, standing from my desk and hurrying over before she can disappear down the hall. She looks surprised, maybe even a little confused, at me suddenly talking to her. I can't blame her; in our very few interactions, she has seemed to have a strong distaste for me.

"Hey, since you're going to see Beckett, can you give him these?" I ask, holding out the stack of completed reports. She just blinks at me, her confusion deepening as she stares at the papers in my hand. That's when it hits me—I called him Beckett, and she probably doesn't know him by anything other than Mr. Shaw.

"Uh, I mean, Mr. Shaw," I quickly correct myself. I keep my hand extended, hoping she'll take the papers.

Her expression softens and she finally takes the stack from me. "Sure," she says simply.

"Thanks," I respond, grateful for her help, and turn back toward my desk.

Within five minutes of Savannah taking the reports to Beckett, a Teams message pops up on my screen from him.

Beckett Shaw:
```
Please, don't have other em-
ployees deliver your work.
```

    Brynn Pierce:
```
    Got it
```

    Brynn Pierce:
```
    Can I slide the documents un-
    der your door? Your energy is
    a total buzz kill today.
```

Beckett Shaw:

You can deliver them to me as previously discussed.

> **Brynn Pierce:**
>
> Cool. I'll bring them to you at the end of the day.

Beckett Shaw:

You'll bring them as we've previously discussed.

> **Brynn Pierce:**
>
> What if I just tell you I haven't done any work all day and wait until the last ten minutes of the day to finish all of them?

Beckett Shaw:

It won't take you longer than twenty minutes to finish a report.

I don't know why he would want me going to his office every twenty minutes when he's acting like he can't stand me today, but okay. After finishing the last three documents, I saunter to his office.

"You might want to check my work. I input the information from my marshmallow bag and ignore the coffee stains—they were intentional. It gives them a little something extra…" I'm saying as I walk in.

Then I stop.

Beckett is sitting at his desk, typing away, looking as annoyed as he's been all day. Blondie is standing behind him. She smooths down her skirt, adjusts her top, and smirks at me like she's trying to imply they were in the middle of something inappropriate—which would have been believable if he didn't look like he wanted to jam a pencil in his eye.

"Seriously," Blondie scoffs, her smirk instantly transforming into a glare. "This is exactly what I mean," she shrieks.

"Don't just barge into my office without permission," Beckett snaps at me.

I stand there gaping at him. He literally just told me ten minutes ago to bring him these one at a time, and now he's mad I did? I stalk over to his desk and toss them on the corner. "Don't worry, I had the foresight to bring you all of them."

I turn and head for the door, stopping to lock eyes with him as I make an exaggerated show of flicking the lock in place on the door and shutting it firmly behind me. He wants to be a dick, then whatever.

Back at my desk, I gather my stuff and slip my snow boots back on. I don't even know my actual work hours, and since I never signed any paperwork, I'm not even sure I'm officially employed here. What I do know is I've had enough of his lame ass for one day.

I walk toward the elevator, press the button, and wait. From behind, I hear Savannah's phone ring and her answer it. She listens, then hangs up.

"Are you Brynn?" she asks.

Turning to look at her, I reply, "Yes."

"Mr. Shaw would like to see you in his office."

"Okay, thank you," I reply, then turn back and continue waiting for the elevator.

A moment later, I hear her phone ring again, and I know it's Beckett. She holds the receiver out toward me. "Brynn, Mr. Shaw is on the line for you."

The elevator doors open, and I step inside, hitting the button for the lobby. I have no plans to go back and talk to him right now. "Have a good day," I tell her as the doors slide shut.

I contemplate all night and morning whether I will even show up to "work" today. But I mindlessly dress and leave to make it on time.

I'm not entirely sure what I was expecting when I got to the office this morning—perhaps that I would go sit in my prison cell and get at least twenty levels completed on my stupid mobile game. But as I step off the elevator, Savannah informs me that Mr. Shaw requests I go immediately to his office.

I confidently march up to his office door and give it a firm knock, then wait. Silence greets me from the other side, so I knock again, a bit sharper this time to ensure he hears it. My mind starts wandering—maybe he isn't responding because him and Blondie are scrambling to get their clothes back on. I could barge in, but the last thing I want is to risk seeing him actually naked with someone else. But he's the one who called me to his office, so he should know better than to pull something like that when he's expecting someone else. Unless he wants me to see.

No way am I waiting around to find out who's in there with him. I turn on my heels and start heading back down the hall when his door swings open. I keep walking until I hear him say, "Brynn, get in here."

I've made it to Blondie's office, and she and the other girl stare at me. I give Blondie a smirk and a wink, running my hands over the front of my dress in a mocking imitation of her earlier gesture and turn back toward Beckett. He's standing at the door, looking pissed. First question answered—he is alone in there. Second question—he's definitely mad. This ought to be fun. He shuts the door behind me and wastes no time starting in on me.

"Where were you yesterday after you left?" he demands.

"I worked for my job at ExpressWay."

"Where were you last night," he changes his wording.

"Dinner," I reply coolly.

"With?" He doesn't let up.

"Is this like some sort of work requirement? I have to let you know who I'm with?" I roll my eyes.

"This is a *you* requirement. Who were you with?"

"My friend."

"Their name, Brynn."

"*Her* name is Rebecca. Do you want her phone number and social security number too?" I retort sarcastically.

"If you can provide that, it would make things easier for me," he deadpans.

"You're so ridiculous. What do you want?"

"For starters, we can discuss you leaving when I specifically ordered you to come back."

"You told me to bring you the reports once I finished them," I snap back.

"That doesn't mean barge in my office!"

"Maybe you should lock your door when you want to have alone time with one of your employees," I retort.

"I don't need to lock my office door. No one should enter without my permission," he snaps, looking so annoyed.

"Excuse me for not knowing. You told me to bring you my completed work after I finish it. I've been doing that, and it's never been a problem. If I needed to do something differently or I was doing something wrong, you should have corrected me the first time I did it. I left my telepathy at home, so unfortunately, I can't read your mind."

"Use common sense, Brynn. Don't walk in a closed room with the door shut." He stares at me like he thinks I'm quite possibly the dumbest person he's ever met.

"Every time I've walked in here the door has been shut. Maybe, if you conducted yourself professionally at all times, you wouldn't have to worry about someone walking in," I fire back.

"I can do whatever I want in my office," he spits out.

"And whoever," I mutter.

"What did you just say?" as if daring me to repeat the words he already heard but refuses to let slide. His voice is low, laced with warning, and I can see the fire flickering behind those eyes, demanding an answer he already knows.

I square my shoulders and hold my head up high, meeting his gaze with defiance. "You're clearly mad because I interrupted you getting your rocks off with your flavor of the day. I'm sure she'll gladly come back in here to finish the job," I bite back.

"You will NOT disrespect me," he growls, taking a step closer. "It's clear you've never had to conduct yourself professionally, but it's time you learn—or you'll be out of this job," he stares down at me, then turns and strides back to his desk.

"Fine by me," I reply, standing my ground.

He stops and turns back to me, his expression darkening. "Get out of my office."

"Sure. Want me to send Boobs back in here?" I add as I turn away.

"Leave!" he shouts, standing so abruptly his chair rolls back as he points for me to go.

"I obviously am." I throw my hands at the door to indicate that I was already practically out of his office. "Here, you can have this too." I turn and flip him off. I get the satisfaction I was looking for in the fury on his face when I give him that parting gift.

I'm seething as I storm away. I spot Blondie and her friend lingering at another employee's desk, pretending to be busy while keeping an eye on his office. She and the other girl snicker as I pass by.

"It hurts walking when he's finished, huh?" I clutch my stomach and wince. "Good thing he's covered in tattoos—otherwise, he'd be sporting some visible claw marks, am I right? That man knows how to fuck." I smirk as all three of their faces fall, but I just keep walking.

This is exactly why I don't do these nine-to-five jobs—I don't do well being treated like this, or being talked down to, or dealing with mean girl cliques. It's still early, and I have the entire day to turn things around. I keep my bag slung over my shoulder and head to the elevators, jabbing the button as I wait for it to arrive and take me the fuck away.

When the doors slide open, I step inside and pull out my phone. I open the ExpressWay app and accept the first ride that conveniently happens to be in this building. I meet the passenger out front and take her to her destination with the same quiet efficiency I use for all my rides. I'm glad she doesn't want to talk because I'm still so mad, my mind has sealed me off completely with my thoughts.

For the next three hours, I continue taking rides, setting my phone to "Do Not Disturb" to avoid any calls or notifications. As I drive home, my phone rings. I glance down, expecting it to be Beckett again—he's called me seven times—but it's Melanie, a mutual friend of mine and Chloe's.

"Heyyyy, bro," I answer. I started saying "bro" as a joke, mocking the people who use it, but somewhere along the line, I became the person who says it. I hate it, but it's become our thing when we greet each other.

"What's up, bro?" she laughs on the other end.

"Heading home. I just worked for three hours."

"Is Chloe working?"

"Yep."

There's a brief pause before Melanie asks, "I know this is super last minute, but could you pet-sit for me? I've got to leave town tonight and won't be back for a few days."

"Of course!" I say excitedly. "I'll run home, grab an overnight bag, and head your way."

"You're a lifesaver, thank you! Sorry again for the short notice."

Her house is stunning—in a quiet, upscale neighborhood about 30 minutes from where I live. She has two golden retrievers who are so precious. She likes to say they are boyfriend and girlfriend and has named them Booth and Bones.

She left me an envelope on the kitchen counter, stuffed with more than enough cash to cover my time here, so I can relax and not worry about work while I'm pet-sitting.

By the time I stretch out on the couch, Booth and Bones have already claimed their spots, each nestled on either side of me with their heads using my lap as pillows as they look up at me with those soft, trusting eyes.

"Well, I can't think of a better show to put on than *Bones*. Does that sound good to you guys?" I ask, stroking their soft fur as they snuggle up beside me.

Bones is my all-time favorite show. I've watched it so many times, Chloe has urged me to find something new. But why switch when every episode is so good? I decide to skip straight to my favorite episode—the one with the grave digger.

It's always fascinating to me how some actors can make their characters so convincing that you end up disliking them in real life. Take the actress who plays Taft—her portrayal is so compellingly despicable that whenever I see her in any other movie or show, I instantly think, *There's the bad guy.*

The dogs stir a few times, and I let them out into the backyard when they need to stretch their legs. Bones, the playful one, insists on fetch, dropping a soggy tennis ball at my feet over and over. I throw it until it feels like my fingers will fall off from frostbite.

Later, when I crawl into bed, I realize I haven't touched my phone since arriving. It's completely dead, so I plug it in and wait for it to power back up. Once it finally turns on, I see I've missed a call from Beckett. He isn't much of a texter—if he needs to reach you, he'll call or just show up in person, but you won't get a text. I, on the other hand, prefer texting over talking on the phone.

I wonder how Beckett anticipated our meeting in his office would go. He was the one who gave me specific instructions, and I followed them. I understand him saying I shouldn't have just walked in without getting permission, and he was correct—I've never worked a job like that, and I don't know what the proper way to do things is. He could have politely explained the correct way for me to bring him documents in the future instead of yelling at me. I didn't even want that job. He offered it to me, and I turned it down. Then he showed up at my apartment to take me to work. I wasn't thrilled to be there, but the only bit of peace I felt was knowing he was close by. I actually enjoyed that he wanted me to bring him my work so frequently because I love seeing him.

I get reheated when I think about the way Chelsea said "seriously" when I walked in—it made me want to slap her. And then he had the audacity to order me back to his office so he could reprimand me? Why did he ever even bother with me?

OUR MORNING STARTS WITH BOOTH BRINGING ME HIS LEASH and barking at me.

"Do you need a walk, bud?" I ask, gently patting him on the head. He responds with another bark. I guess we're going for a walk.

"It's cold outside," I say to him, hoping maybe he'll reconsider. But no such luck. He eagerly goes to the door, wagging his tail as he stares at me.

As we step outside, the chill in the air immediately bites at my skin, but Booth and Bones don't seem to notice. We take a long walk around the neighborhood, and I'm struck by how well-behaved they are. They seem so happy on the walk that I allow them to guide me in how long they want to walk.

Back at Melanie's, I flop onto the couch, grabbing the remote and putting *Bones* back on. Booth and Bones curl up next to me, their heads resting on my lap while I absentmindedly stroke their fur.

As I prepare a simple dinner, Booth and Bones observe with hopeful eyes, waiting for a morsel to fall their way. While my meal heats up, I also prepare theirs, their tails wagging eagerly. After dinner, we return to the couch, where I stretch out once more, content with the dogs nestled close by.

It's late in the evening and I think I hear my phone buzzing, so I get up to grab it.

"Well, hey precious, how's Florida?" I ask as I answer Chloe's call.

"For the love of God, Brynn, answer the man's calls."

"Who's?" I play dumb.

"You know who. He's so desperate he called me."

"That's weird," I reply nonchalantly.

We talk for an hour about her job and the crazy people that have been flying recently. Before she gets off the phone, she asks how many times he has called, and I hold my phone out and then answer, "Six."

"Good Lord, woman, call him back. See you soon."

I settle back into bed, snuggling with Booth, while Bones stands by the door, ignoring her food.

When my phone rings again, I know it's Beckett without needing to check. I let it ring a few times trying to decide if I want to fight tonight.

"Hello?" I finally answer after the fourth ring.

He lets out a long sigh on the other end. "Brynn."

"Beckett," I say flatly.

"Where are you?"

Is this really how he's going to start this conversation? Not addressing how he yelled at me, just jumping right in to asking where I am. "House-sitting for a friend," I answer.

Bones nudges the door open and stands there, staring at me. "Hold on a second," I say, setting my phone down.

I walk over to Bones, pointing to her food bowl. "Go eat and then come to bed," I tell her.

Once I'm back in bed, I pick up my phone again. "I've got to go," I say.

"Who's with you?" he demands.

"Nobody," I reply tersely.

"Who's there with you, Brynn?" he presses.

"Goodnight, Beckett," I say, frustration evident in my voice, and hang up.

Knowing he'll keep calling and feeling exhausted, I turn my phone off.

The next couple of days pass in a comfortable rhythm. Mornings start with long walks, with Booth and Bones always eager to explore. Afternoons are spent watching TV, with the dogs never straying far from me. The evenings are my favorite, though—just me and the dogs, curled up together in bed.

When I finally return home, I walk in feeling happy, knowing Chloe is already here. "Honey, I'm home!" I call out cheerfully, wheeling my bag inside and grabbing the stack of mail from the table by the door. "Well, these are all bills. How lame," I comment, sorting through them and stuffing them into my purse. "Not paying any of those," I joke as I turn around and stop.

Chloe, Tom and Beckett are all sitting in the living room.

"Beckett stopped by to see you," Chloe states the obvious, gesturing to where he sits on the couch.

"Nice. Let me get the door for you," I say as I grab the doorknob.

"No, thanks. We can talk in your room." He gets up and walks around the living room. "Come on," he adds when I just stand there.

I glare at Chloe, thinking, *What the fuck is he doing here? A little warning would have been nice.*

When we get in my room, I put my bag on my bed and unzip it, tossing the dirty clothes in the laundry basket by the door.

"Are you hungry?" he asks as he sits on my bed.

"I ate on my way home," I respond.

"Okay. Are you tired?"

"No," I reply.

"Well, should we address the elephant in the room?" he suggests.

"Sure."

He lets out a long sigh. "I want to apologize for how I acted at the office. I should have never talked to you like that."

I continue unpacking my bag. "Thank you. I apologize too."

"Why does it feel like you're still mad at me?"

"I just want to relax. I'm home after three days and want alone time."

"Were you not alone for the past three days?"

"Whether I was or not, I'm saying I want to be alone now."

He rubs his hands up and down his face before leaning over clasping them together, legs spread, and forearms resting on his knees. "Do you want to be alone, or you don't want to be around me?"

"Both equally," I reply.

"Do you want me to leave?"

"Yes," I respond.

He moves closer, his presence pulling me in despite my efforts to keep some distance. His lips brush softly against my cheek, then he lingers, not stepping back, and it makes me look up even though I try to resist. His gaze shifts between my lips and eyes, as though he's trying to read my thoughts, and then, without a word, his hand cups my face, his fingers tracing lightly down my jawline.

He lifts my chin, his touch tender, guiding me into a kiss so soft it's as if he's barely there. But that changes quickly. His lips press more insistently against mine, deepening the kiss. I respond in kind, matching his passion.

His hands move with purpose, finding the zipper of my coat and sliding it down. He takes his time, removing my sweatshirt, guiding the fabric gently up my stomach then lifting it over my head. As I stand there, letting him undress me, his fingers brush against my skin, making the moment feel intimate and electrifying.

With my clothes discarded on the floor, he steps back slightly, his eyes lingering on me with a mix of desire and tenderness. He begins undressing himself, moving methodically, each article of clothing falling to the floor. I watch, transfixed, my heart beating faster with every piece that comes off.

When we're both stripped bare, he steps toward me, his hands sliding over my skin, their warmth chasing away the coldness. He pulls me against him, his lips pressing back onto mine, guiding me slowly toward the bed. The heat between us builds with each step until I meet the edge of the mattress. I sink down onto it, scooting back, spreading my legs wide in an open invitation. He catches my gaze with a knowing smile and climbs over me, leaning in for another searing kiss.

His lips linger on my throat, sucking gently, just enough to make my breath hitch. His hand slides between my legs, fingers expertly finding my clit. He strokes it with the perfect amount of pressure, and a moan slips out, unbidden, and I arch into him. Every touch feels as though he understands my body more intimately than I do. His teeth graze my ear, his voice soft and intimate. "You're so wet."

"That's what you do to me."

He props himself up on his forearm, looking down between us as he reaches between my legs, positioning himself at my center. "Let me know if anything hurts, okay," he murmurs, his concern only making me want him more.

I nod, biting my lip as he slowly pushes inside, reveling in the familiar, welcomed tightness of him filling me. I exhale slowly, loving the feel of him moving deeper, my body gradually adjusting to him.

"That's it, baby, just keep breathing. You're doing so good," he soothes as my body begins to tense from the pressure.

His hand returns between my legs, stroking my clit again, coaxing my body into relaxing around him. I feel the tension melt away, and he begins to move—slowly at first, each thrust teasing. The slow rhythm feels incredible, and as his hips begin to quicken, pleasure starts to pulse through me, wave after wave of euphoria.

The intensity builds, and I cling to him, nails digging into his flesh as our moans fill the room. We're so consumed by each other that nothing else matters—not even the sound of my luggage hitting the floor in the chaos of our movements.

The door creaks open slightly, and Chloe's voice breaks through the haze, teasing. "I heard a noise—wasn't sure if someone was injured. But it looks like everything's perfectly fine in here," she smiles.

"Sorry," I apologize, but it comes out more as a breathy gasp.

I have an overwhelming need to sit on him, to feel him beneath me. I don't even know what to do, but I need to. Breathless, I ask, "Can I be on top?"

A smile spreads across his face as strong arms wrap around my back. In one fluid motion, he rolls us over until I'm straddling him, my legs on either side of his hips.

Well, fuck, this is an entirely new sensation. It feels different than when I was on top of him at the hotel with his cock like a hotdog between my lips—but this, inside me—it's so good.

I lean forward, planting my palms firmly on his chest as I begin to move, my hips rolling slowly at first.

When I descend, his hands grip my hips, holding me down, keeping me seated on his shaft. My core clenches and releases rapidly in response, my hips begin gyrating on him in a slow, steady rhythm.

Holy fucking shit.

Sex feels good.

This. This feels incredible.

My eyes roll back as my hips continue to rock back and forth on him. His hands slide to the sides of my ass as he pulls me up, then pushes me back down.

Okay, damn, that's good.

He helps with the motion until I have it and move with ease. His hands release my hips to their own accord and slide up my body, grabbing handfuls of my boobs, and he groans beneath me.

My body begins to stiffen, the familiar heat pooling in my belly. I hear him moan beneath me, his grip on my breasts tightening. "I'm gonna cum if you don't slow down," he growls, his voice strained with arousal.

"Me too," I gasp, my hand slipping between us to eagerly circle my clit.

"Do you wanna stay on top, or should I take over?" His voice is urgent, thick with need, but it doesn't matter because the rush hits me before I can answer. My orgasm crashes over me, powerful and unstoppable. My knees shake, squeezing him close as my orgasm rips through my entire body, and I tremble as I moan his name.

He follows right behind, hitting my leg repeatedly with urgency, but no words come out as his body tightens the same way mine did—his muscles rigid beneath my touch. His hands grip my thighs, his breath catching in his throat as he releases, until he stills, sagging limp into the pillows.

"Fuck," he rasps, wiping the sweat from his brow. "I came in you."

I try to remain calm to keep him from wigging out. "I'm on birth control," I say, thinking it'll ease the tension.

He shakes his head, still catching his breath. "We still need to get you a morning-after pill. It's better to be safe."

The mood shifts, and I feel the euphoria fading fast. I pull off him, slipping out of bed. "Way to be a buzzkill," I mutter. "I'm gonna take a shower. Join me if you want," I add, as I head to the bathroom.

I shower quickly, after I realize he doesn't plan on joining. When I return to my room, he and his clothes are gone. I check outside, but his truck and SUV are nowhere to be seen. Then again, I didn't notice either when I got home, so I assume Preston drove him. He left—just like that. No goodbye, no explanation. It feels like the air has been sucked out of the room.

Feeling the sting of disappointment, I get dressed and make my way into the living room, trying to act like everything is fine. But when I walk out, it's not just Tom and Chloe sitting there—Mark is there too. Great.

"We were just starting a movie. Come join us," Chloe says, her eyes full of sympathy as the entire room turns to look at me.

I hesitate, feeling the awkwardness creeping in. "Did Beckett say anything when he left?" I ask, more to Chloe than anyone else.

She shakes her head. "No."

I can only manage a sigh before heading to the farthest corner of the room. I settle into the chair by the back patio door, feeling isolated and out of place.

"Hey Brynn," Mark greets me.

"Hey," I say.

Mark is lounging on the loveseat, while Tom and Chloe are cuddled up together on the couch. Chloe puts on *Saw*, and it only takes about three minutes for me to absolutely hate it. I pull my legs up under my sweater, tugging the fabric over my chin as I squint, trying to avoid the worst of the gore.

The front door opens, and all eyes shift as Beckett strides in. He doesn't say a word to anyone, just walks straight toward me, placing a pill and a bottle of water in my hand. "Take this," he says.

I look down at the pill, then back up at him, my blood starting to boil. "Are you fucking kidding me." I bite out.

He stares pointedly at me. With a scoff, I begrudgingly pop the pill into my mouth and swallow, with everyone staring at us. "Morning-after pill," I announce sarcastically, glaring at Beckett. "He came in me but apparently couldn't let us finish our orgasm before he sprinted to the store."

I stand up abruptly, shoving past him as I yank the front door open. "Go," I say coldly, as I point.

He sighs in annoyance but steps around me, heading outside. As soon as he's gone, I slam the door shut with more force than necessary, twisting the lock until it clicks loudly, making sure he knows I've locked him out. I storm off to my room, closing the door behind me with a sharp thud. His headlights linger outside for what feels like an eternity until I finally hear the sound of his car pulling away.

I'm not mad at him wanting me to take the pill. I'm mad that he forced me to take it in front of my roommate, her boyfriend, and his roommate. That was humiliating. All he had to do was wait for me to come out of the bathroom, and I would've gone with him to the store. But no, he was so freaked out about coming inside me that he bolted out of here without a second thought. Hopefully, he grabbed some condoms while he was there, because he's not going in me bare again.

I fall asleep to the sound of Chloe's moans and the unmistakable slap of skin against skin, only to wake up to the same noises in the morning. For two days, their moans have been my new nighttime lullaby. And this is now the second night I just want to call Beckett and tell him to come slap my skin.

His reaction was weird, and I deserve an explanation. But I'm not going to call and beg for one. He can give me one when he decides to quit being an asshole.

It's Chloe's last day home and then she leaves again, and I honestly can't even be mad when she chooses to spend her last day home with Tom.

In the early morning, she slips into my room, gently kissing my cheek. "Love you, see you in no time." While Tom waves at me from the doorway.

"Miss you already," I call to her.

I try to drift back to sleep, but the emptiness hits me, gnawing at my insides. It's always like this when Chloe leaves—a sudden, consuming loneliness that wraps around me like a cold blanket. The room feels bigger, quieter, and far too empty. Finally, I get up, get dressed, and pull up the ExpressWay app, hoping to drown the loneliness in work. The first food order request that pops up is from a restaurant nearby, and I accept it, eager for the distraction.

As soon as I step into the restaurant, the warmth hits me—soft lighting, the low hum of chatter, and the comforting aroma of food. I walk to the front, telling the hostess I'm here for an ExpressWay pickup. She politely asks me to wait a few minutes while they finish preparing the order.

As I stand there, I let my eyes wander, glancing over the tables, absently noting the couples and groups enjoying their meals. Then, something—or rather someone—catches my eye.

Beckett.

He's seated at a table in the back, casually leaning back in his chair, his attention focused solely on the woman across from him. She's laughing at something he said, her long dark hair cascading over her shoulders as she tilts her head back. The sound of her laugh sends an icy chill racing up my spine. She's gorgeous, and the easy familiarity between them intensifies the pain in my chest.

I watch, frozen, noting a familiarity in the way he smiles at what she's saying. This isn't their first time meeting. My hands clench at my sides, my nails biting into my palms as I struggle to keep my composure. The pang of jealousy hits me harder than I expected.

I'm overwhelmed with the urge to storm over there, grab a cup of water, and throw it in his face, shouting, "It's been less than 48 hours since you were inside me, and now you've already moved on?!" I know Beckett probably dates other women—we were never exclusive—but seeing it up close and in person is different. He sure moved on fast. It feels like a punch to the gut, leaving me nauseous and disoriented. I want to look away, to pretend I haven't seen anything, but my eyes stay locked on them, almost against my will.

"Here you go, miss." The hostess's voice pulls me out of my daze. I barely register her speaking as she hands me the bag of food.

"Thanks," I mutter, barely able to form the word. My chest tightens, and the pounding of my heart drowns out the sounds of the restaurant. All I want is to leave—to escape.

I don't dare glance back as I walk past the windows, afraid that if I do, I'll see them again, see him with her. The thought alone feels unbearable. I reach my car and climb inside, the need to get far, far away overwhelming every other instinct. As I sit there, I grip the wheel contemplating peeling out of there like a bat out of hell, but then I pull up Beckett's contact on my phone. I hesitate, my thumb hovering over the block button. Then, with a deep breath, I press it and tuck my phone back onto the dashboard, the address for the delivery flashing across the screen.

I pull out of the lot, the weight of what I've just done sinking in. Just as I glance in the rearview mirror, giving a mental goodbye, I see Beckett standing there in the middle of the parking lot, phone pressed to his ear, his other hand in his hair, staring after me as I drive away. My stomach clenches, nausea creeping in, but I keep going.

I don't even remember dropping off the delivery, because I can't seem to shake off the nausea in my stomach. It doesn't matter he's on a date—why should I care? But no matter how hard I try to convince myself, the image of Beckett with that woman is burned into my mind, and I know it'll take more than just a drive to forget it.

CHAPTER Twenty-Two

Today is the first day in a while that the sun is shining, and it actually feels warm despite the snow on the ground. I made sure to wear my winter jacket because I had planned on spending the day doing food deliveries, but after seeing Beckett, my motivation crumbles.

Seeing him on a date was about as great as the thought of shoving a cactus in my butt and then going bull riding. He sure gets around. Which would explain why he's so good in bed. But I'm determined not to let myself cry. Instead of going home and moping, I just go for a drive. The thought of working sounds awful, and Beckett would be the person I'd want to call and complain to about my feelings, but he's the reason for my frustration.

As I pass by a park, I make a sudden decision to pull in at the last minute. I find an empty parking spot and sit there for a few minutes. The park is massive, with sidewalks cleared and salted, but the ground remains covered in snow.

Reaching over to the passenger seat, I grab my gloves and pull them on. After removing the key from the ignition, I tuck it into my coat pocket and step out of the car.

There's a walking path that goes all around the park, and on the outer edge, a lake. Benches line the opposite side of the path, where people can sit and admire the lake or lean on the iron fence that separates the park from the water. I choose a bench that looks dry and cozy up in my coat as I gaze out at the frozen water.

I just wish I could stop thinking about Beckett. I don't understand him. Some days, I feel like he might want more than whatever we're doing—more like an actual relationship with me. His seemingly constant desire to have me around makes me think he must want something more. He even offered me a job with him, which I thought was to be closer to me, only to have him treat me poorly.

I've never even initiated contact with him; I've always left that up to him. He's the one who keeps showing up, insisting on rides he doesn't even need. I wonder if I somehow brought this on myself, but deep down, I know I'm not to blame.

I briefly entertain the idea of filling up my car with snowballs and pelt them both as they leave the restaurant. Oh, the satisfaction I would feel seeing the shock on their faces. He already knows how accurate my aim is—his date could find out too.

For a split second, I consider calling him and just saying, "What the fuck?" But he'd probably come up with some excuse—maybe that she's a long-lost cousin, and when I walked in on her sucking his dick, he'd claim she just slipped and he doesn't know how his pants came down.

My thoughts are interrupted by a chocolate lab who nudges his face into my lap, his tail wagging excitedly.

"Hi, Buddy," I reach out to pet him.

"Roscoe," a man calls out.

As he comes closer, I smile, indicating it's okay. His cheeks and nose are tinged pink from the cold. He's wearing a black beanie, and winter jacket, a gray scarf around his neck, and jeans paired with black running shoes.

"Sorry about this; he doesn't usually approach strangers like this," the man says, looking a bit embarrassed. "Roscoe, what's gotten into you? Where are your manners?" he lightly scolds my newfound friend.

"No worries; he must have good taste." I continue to stroke the dog's head.

"Come on, Roscoe, leave the pretty lady alone," the man says, reaching for Roscoe's collar.

"Lady!" I feign offense. "Did you hear that, Roscoe? Your dad called me old," I joke, still petting him.

"My apologies, I didn't mean it like that," he smiles. "What's your name?"

"Brynn," I reply, continuing to pet Roscoe. He's now fully resting his body against my legs, leaning his head back onto my lap, his tongue hanging out as he pants contentedly.

"Brynn," he repeats. "I'm Grant," he introduces himself, extending his hand.

"Hi, Grant," I respond, shaking it. "I think you no longer have a dog. It seems like he belongs to me now. Isn't that right, Roscoe?" I bring my face to his, and he licks my nose.

Grant gestures towards the bench. "May I?"

"Please," I say, motioning to the spot he pointed to.

"I've never seen you around here before," he comments, crossing his legs and intertwining his hands between them.

"Oh, really? I see you here all the time." I glance over at him, waiting for his reaction.

He looks at a loss for words as he sits there, just blinking.

"Just kidding! I rarely come here."

He lets out a laugh as he looks at me. "I'm here almost every day with this big guy." He pats Roscoe's back. "We jog here in the summers and play fetch in the winter." He holds up a tennis ball.

"Well, I'll have to come back sometime just to say hi to my new friend," I gesture toward Roscoe.

"Of course, Roscoe is the ladies' man. Nobody wants to be friends with me, only my dog," he quips.

"Can you blame them? Look at this little love."

"He's somethin'," he agrees, crossing his arms at his chest as he leans back.

"I like his little snow boots." I look down at his little dog shoes.

"Gotta protect his paws," he leans over to inspect the shoes. "But he does look pretty awesome with them, right?"

"I've never seen anything cooler," I nod. "Although, he might be even cooler if he wore little socks underneath."

"He hardly keeps his shoes on—socks would be a lost cause."

"I don't even like wearing socks myself, so I understand."

"Who does?" He raises his shoulders in a playful shrug.

"Definitely not Roscoe, you never even let him try them on," I joke.

"She's gonna make us get you socks, Roscoe." He pets his dog's head. "Well, we should probably get going. Maybe we'll see you here again," he adds, standing up.

"Maybe," I reply, waving at Roscoe. "Bye, Roscoe."

Roscoe slowly stands and trots after Grant as he signals for him to follow. With a final wave, Grant walks down the path, and I watch them disappear.

Well, that was pleasant.

I stay for another twenty minutes, soaking in the quiet before finally getting up and heading back to my car. The drive home is silent, and it's only later that it hits me—I never bothered to turn on the radio.

The next day, I return to the park, arriving an hour later than yesterday, hoping to avoid bumping into Grant. I don't want him to think I'm purposely seeking him out. The parking lot is nearly empty, and the whole place feels deserted—perfect time to sit and wallow in my own self-pity.

I sit on the same bench, staring at the frozen lake. When I reach into my coat pocket for my phone, I realize I've left it in the car. Annoyed, I settle for watching the ice, deciding to stay a little while longer.

Just as my self-imposed time limit nears, two men approach. One sits on the bench beside mine, while the other takes a seat right next to me—exactly where Grant had been the other day.

A wave of fear washes over me as I berate myself for leaving my phone in the car. Out of the corner of my eye, I notice them gesturing to each other, and my anxiety spikes. The man beside me speaks first, breaking the silence.

"Are you here alone?" he asks, his voice too casual for comfort.

When I don't answer, he shifts closer, resting his arm over the back of the bench. "You alone?" he repeats, glancing at the other man.

"Leave me alone," I say firmly, keeping my gaze fixed straight ahead.

The stench of cigarettes wafts off him, making me even more uneasy.

"You're coming with us," he says, nodding in the direction of the bathrooms.

"No thanks," I say, trying to stand, but he grabs the hood of my coat and yanks me back down. Fear courses through me, causing my body to tremble.

"Oh, I think you are," he leans in so close I can feel his breath burning into my pores.

"And if I don't?" I challenge, my voice surprisingly steady.

"Try it," he smirks.

I mentally run through the karate moves Josh taught me when I was younger, wondering if my current state of fear would allow me to smash each of their Adam's apples into the back of their spines.

Just then, a voice calls out, "There you are, sweetheart. I told you to wait for me by the truck." I look up, and I don't think I've ever felt so much relief flood through me as I see

Grant approaching. It takes all my self-control not to leap up and run to him.

"Sorry, I just wanted to rest for a second," I say quickly as the man lets go of my coat. I nearly run to Grant, throwing my arms around him. He pulls me in tightly, his hand rubbing up and down my back in a soothing motion.

"Was he just holding onto your coat?" Grant asks, eyeing the two men.

"No," the man who was in fact holding my coat responds defensively. "She sat down between us, and her coat got caught on my hand."

My mouth falls open, and I gape at him. "That's awfully bold of you to sit there and lie like that. You think I'd intentionally come sit between two homeless losers who reek of Pall Mall cigarettes and sweaty balls? You're delusional to the high heavens, you freak."

Now their mouths hang open as they look at each other and then back to me. Surprise, I'm not done yet. "Also, your little bit about forcing me to the bathroom—let me guess, little ol' me was the one who was threatening you both to drag me there?"

The stinky motherfucker narrows his eyes at me before grinning, revealing a mouthful of blackened teeth. "You asked for it."

"How so?" I step forward, my anger flaring, but Grant quickly puts his arm out, stopping me.

"C'mon," he says, taking my hand and pulling me away.

I follow, then turn back, "By the way, you need to brush your fucking teeth. It looks like you've been eating potting soil," I say, my face twisted in disgust.

Grant's eyes widen in surprise, but we keep walking. Apparently, now that I feel protected, I grew a pair of balls. If I had ended up in that bathroom, I would've fought like hell, knowing full well what they were planning on doing to me. The only reason my mouth is so confident now is because Grant is right here.

As we continue down the path towards the parking lot, Grant glances back at them. They're still watching us, standing and talking among themselves. I see Grant spit into the snow—a silent act of defiance as he glares back at them.

We walk the rest of the way to my car in silence. As we reach the parking lot, Grant finally breaks the quiet. "Roscoe's going to be so disappointed he didn't get to see you."

"Why isn't he with you?"

Grant laughs lightly. "I feel like I should come up with a good excuse," he glances over at me with a sheepish grin.

"Why?"

"I don't want to seem like a stalker... not yet, anyways," he quips.

I give him a reassuring look. "You just saved me from who knows what. You can tell me anything right now and I'd be relieved."

He exhales, looking ahead. "I drove by to see if you were here. When I saw a car that was here yesterday, I parked to see if it was you. I watched those guys walking up to you, and something about it didn't feel right."

I stop walking and tug on his arm, making him pause. When he turns toward me, I wrap my arms around him, hugging him tightly. "Thank you." I finally let out a breath that felt stuck in my throat.

He hugs me back. "There's no need to thank me. I'm just glad I got to see you."

We start walking again, and this time he casually drapes his arm around my back as we step off the curb. It's a simple gesture, like he's making sure I don't slip on the pavement, but he doesn't move his hand away even after we reach my car.

I'm grateful for him saving me, but I feel a tinge of pain that it's not Beckett touching me. Why can't I just get over him. This is so pathetic. While I sit here sad, he's probably pumping his sperm into that chick, jokes on her when he shoves a pill down her throat

"This is me," I say awkwardly, stopping next to my door.

"Well, I will make sure you are fully in your car and leaving before I leave," he assures me.

"Thanks," I say, climbing into my car.

"Hey… would you want to exchange numbers?" he asks forwardly. "Try to catch a time for you to see Roscoe again," he quickly adds.

I hesitate, staring up at him. Then, in the spur of the moment, I agree. "Yeah, sure."

He pulls his phone out of his pocket and adds me.

My chime sounds from where my phone sits in the dashboard holder, and I tap the screen to see a new text.

UNKNOWN:

Here's my number. Roscoe's dad (Grant)

"Thank you again, Roscoe's dad," I say awkwardly, looking up at him.

"No need to thank me." He puts his hands in his coat pocket. "It's freezing, go," he urges.

As I reverse out of the parking spot, I catch a glimpse of him climbing into his truck, pulling up right behind me at the stop sign. I give a small farewell wave as I merge onto the road, and he returns it with a casual wave of his own.

When I get home, I hurry inside and feel relaxed when the warmth washes over me. I waste no time shrugging off my coat, hanging it in the closet by the entrance, then kick off my boots at the bottom.

Making my way to the bedroom, I strip off my clothes, replacing them with a pair of soft, worn-in shorts and a loose tank top. I smooth out the blankets on my bed, tucking them just right, before sliding under them.

My phone rests on the nightstand, so I pick it up and see a new text from Grant:

GRANT:
Roscoe needs to see you. He told me himself. I hear there's a park that has a nice walking path. Interested?

BRYNN:
Okay

GRANT:
6:00?

BRYNN:

GRANT:
> See you tomorrow. Goodnight.

BRYNN:
> Goodnight

I'm still holding my phone, wanting to smile, but the ache in my chest keeps me from doing so. I want to hold Beckett. As I fall asleep, I clutch my pillow, which still smells like him, pressing my face into it. His face is my last conscious thought as I drift off.

The next day, I arrive at the park ten minutes early, hoping to beat him there. But to my surprise, he's already here waiting. I park next to his truck, and he's looking down, likely at his phone.

I step out of the car and walk around the front, spotting Roscoe almost immediately. His tail starts wagging furiously, his whole body vibrating with excitement as he lets out a few eager whines, paws dancing in place. Grant looks up from his phone, quickly tucking it into his pocket as a smile spreads across his face.

Standing on the curb, I wave at them, and Grant returns the gesture. He opens the truck door, but before he can even step out, Roscoe practically launches himself over the seat, bounding straight toward me.

"Hi, buddy," I greet him, crouching down as his wet nose presses into my face. His excited licks come fast, and I can't help but laugh, wiping at my cheeks as he continues his enthusiastic greeting.

Grant approaches, and I rise to my feet, sweeping my hair out of my face. "Hi," I say softly, offering a little wave.

"Hi," he greets me, taking my hand. "Not that you need any help winning him over," he adds, as I shift my gaze down to find a dog treat in my palm.

I give it to Roscoe, and his excitement amps up another level, tail wagging faster as he devours the snack.

Grant tosses a tennis ball down the walking path. "Go get it, Roscoe!" he calls, and the dog races after it. We fall into step beside each other, following the direction of the ball.

"I see you're both wearing gray shoes today. Do you coordinate your shoes together?"

He looks down. "Thank you for noticing. He insisted," Grant jokes.

"I feel left out that nobody told me we were wearing gray shoes today."

"It was terribly inconsiderate of us. Since we didn't include you, you can choose our colors for tomorrow." As Roscoe bounds back with the ball, his tail wagging in triumph, Grant tosses it down the path again.

"Tomorrow?" I question.

"And the day after that too. Although you don't get to choose our colors every day."

"What makes you think I'd even come again?" I tease lightly.

His expression softens, his confidence shining through as he meets my gaze. "I'm hoping you will."

We leisurely walk down the path, and though it's nice, everything feels wrong. Beckett is much taller than him, and though his presence was all-consuming even without touching me, I don't like how close Grant walks next to me. His arm keeps brushing mine to the point I clasp my hands in front of me to stay out of his reach. But he still manages to scoot in even more.

Each time he throws the ball for Roscoe, I take a small step aside, trying to create some distance. But without fail, he closes the gap again, as if he doesn't notice—or maybe doesn't care. The tension is subtle but persistent, and I find myself more on edge than I want to be.

As the walk progresses, I start to relax. Grant is decently funny and a good conversationalist. I think he finally picks up on the fact that I don't want to be touched, because he backs off. About an hour into our walk, he seems distracted. I can hear his phone vibrating nonstop in his pocket, and he subtly silences it repeatedly before suggesting we call it a night, which I happily agree to.

CHAPTER
Twenty-Three

For the next several days, we meet up and spend hours walking and talking. The conversation flows more naturally with each passing day, and our walks gradually stretch longer. He's been a welcome distraction for my brain, though she's consumed by Beckett. I'm so egregiously jealous of the woman he was on a date with that anything to keep me preoccupied from thinking about it is good.

"I'd really like to take you out sometime," he says, standing in front of me as I unlock my car door.

"Why?" I ask confused.

His brows lift in surprise, but then he smiles. "Because I enjoy talking to you, and I'd enjoy doing it somewhere warm… and with food. You do like to eat, don't you? It's just casual, Brynn," he quickly clarifies, as if sensing my hesitation and not wanting to give me the wrong idea.

"Oh, okay. Sure. And yeah, I like to eat," I respond, feeling pretty lame saying that.

"Alright. I'll be in touch."

He shuts my car door, and as I start pulling out of the parking lot, my phone starts ringing. I answer it when I see his name on the screen.

"Do I have a taillight out?" I ask, thinking, that must be why he's calling me when I can still see him in my rearview mirror.

"I'm actually pretty hungry. How about dinner tonight?"

I sit at the stop sign, staring back at him through my mirror as he watches me. *It's just dinner, Brynn, nothing else. You have just dinner with Beckett all the time. Go.*

"Sure," I finally agree.

"Okay," he says sweetly. "Text me your address, and I'll pick you up at 8:00."

After we hang up, I quickly send him my address and rush home. I jump in the shower, then do my hair and makeup, trying to get ready in time. Is this a date? It has to be, right? I wonder if Beckett and I ever actually went on dates. No, not really. He never officially asked me out for dinner. We just ended up eating together, as if by chance. Everything with him has been by chance. Even when it felt like a date—like when he sat next to me in a booth—it wasn't ever acknowledged as one. He certainly never saw it that way.

"Ugh!" I groan out loud, trying to shove Beckett out of my thoughts. I hate that I miss him. I hate that I want to call him just to hear his voice.

But you blocked him, dumbass.

I refuse to let my mind wander to thoughts of him being intimate with the woman I saw him with the other day at the restaurant. Now, all these thoughts of him are making me feel sad. I wish it was him coming to pick me up. Instead, he's probably balls deep in another woman.

Why did you have to ruin your mood, Brynn? I scold myself.

When I hear a knock on the door, the uneasy feeling in my stomach intensifies, but I push forward and open it. Grant stands there with a bouquet of flowers in his hand, offering them to me. I take them with a quick thank you, setting them on the kitchen table. Flowers have never really been my thing. I don't even know what to do with ones that aren't already in a vase. Now, they'll inevitably die in that bag.

Grabbing my coat from the closet, I slip it on and step out, locking the door behind me.

"You look beautiful," he says with a warm smile when I turn to face him.

"Thanks."

We head to the restaurant and talk easily. As dinner progresses, I find myself enjoying being out of my apartment. Grant is engaging, witty, and knows how to keep the conversation light and fun. Yet, every so often, I glance down at my plate, only to look up and feel a small pang of disappointment that it's not Beckett sitting across from me. But just like that, Grant pulls me back into the present. He says something that makes me laugh, and once again, the unease fades.

When we arrive back at my apartment, Grant leaves his truck idling as he parks. I hesitate, unsure of how to end the night. With Elliot, it was always an awkward hug where we barely touched; Beckett, though never on dates would just do whatever Beckett wanted, and Grant appears to be content just letting me get out.

"Would you like me to walk you to your door?" he asks.

"Sure," I say, instantly regretting it, worried he might expect a kiss or something. As we reach my door and I unlock it, he waves goodbye and begins to walk away. I'm impressed—so impressed apparently that the words that fall out of my mouth aren't words my brain even agrees with. "If you're not busy, do you want to come in and watch a movie?" I offer, hoping with every ounce of my being he says no.

"I'd love to."

I put on the first non-scary movie I can find, and we settle in. He casually drapes his arm on the back of the couch, not making any moves, which helps me relax. As the movie goes on, I find myself leaning into him, and his arm eventually rests around my shoulder. I close my eyes, letting myself imagine it's Beckett holding me instead.

"This movie is kind of boring," he whispers.

I stare at the screen, having no clue what's going on because it's so boring it couldn't even hold my attention. "I agree." I turn my head to look at him. "Should I put something else on?"

He hesitates, seeming to consider it, then shakes his head, his gaze flickering to my lips before moving back up.

He's going to kiss me. Please don't kiss me.

I full blown start to panic and don't know how to get out of this situation. My mind races for a solution, and the only thing that comes to me is to let him kiss me, all the while imagining it's Beckett. His kiss is gentle and soft, but it's not Beckett. He doesn't have Beckett's taste or scent... because he isn't Beckett.

What if he tries to have sex with me? How would I get out of that?

When he finally pulls away, he smiles. "I should head home," he murmurs.

"Yes," I agree.

I lead him to the door, unsure of what to do next.

"Roscoe and I will be at the park tomorrow around 6:00 if you'd like to join us for a walk," he offers.

"Maybe," I respond, opening the door as he steps outside. "Thanks for dinner."

"Anytime," he replies, sliding his hands into his pockets and heading briskly through the snow toward the parking lot.

For five days in a row we meet at the park for walks.

I get home each time, conflicted with how I feel. It's nice spending time with someone and just talking. He's a better conversationalist than Elliot ever was, but not better than Beckett. Nobody is better than Beckett. I am so overcome with emotions that I pour myself a big glass of my gas station wine and down it, followed by another. By the time I'm feeling fuzzy and carefree, I get a text from Grant:

GRANT:
Wanna watch a movie?

NO! God no.

BRYNN:
> Sure

Okay. So I'm a rare breed of stupid.

And here we are again, just like that. This time, I let him choose the movie, figuring it couldn't possibly be worse than the one I picked. But it is. Somehow, it's even more boring, and it takes all of two minutes for the weight of my wine-induced haze to creep in, taking all my morals and flushing them down the toilet. The kiss that starts off innocent enough quickly turns into something else entirely. My pants disappear faster than I can process what's happening, his body is over mine, pushing into me.

I hate every second of it. The way he feels inside me is wrong. I hate how slow he's moving. I hate the stretch of someone who isn't Beckett. The stretch that would normally send waves of pleasure through me feels like a foreign invasion. It isn't Beckett, and my body knows it. I hate him whispering in my ear, telling me how tight I am. I hate his attempts to kiss me, so I turn my head, squeezing my eyes shut.

I try to escape, letting my mind conjure images of Beckett. His beautiful smile fills my thoughts, his touch, his scent, everything that made me feel alive. For a brief second, I pretend it's him—just so I can get through this. Grant's voice pulls me back to reality, and I force myself to nod, to say something, but my mind is far from present. I almost trick myself into enjoying it, but even then, it's not real. Not with him.

When he's finished, he heads to the bathroom to dispose of the condom, while I quickly pull up my pants and mentally berate myself. It didn't even last as long as it does with Beckett, and now my vagina feels almost swollen. My body must be punishing me for being a tramp.

He's been in the bathroom for so long, and I'm pretty sure he's on the phone with someone. I tire of waiting for him to come back, so I lie on the couch.

As I drift in and out of groggy consciousness, it gradually dawns on me that I'm in bed, gazing out at the darkened sky. I have no idea how I ended up here. A familiar scent fills the air, and I bury my face deeper into Beckett's pillow.

I feel a gentle touch between my legs and place my hand over his. I hear the sound of a wrapper being opened and my pants being lowered. He presses into me from behind, moving slowly in and out of me until he moans out with his climax.

Did he even put it all the way in?

I feel him shift behind me, his movement so subtle at first that I don't fully register it. His arms slide around my waist again, and instinctively, I turn to face him, ready to hold Beckett. But when I glance up, it's not Beckett. Grant is there instead, his eyes shut, and a peaceful smile on his face, oblivious to the mess of thoughts racing through my mind.

I just let Grant put his dick in me AGAIN… this time in my sleep, thinking it was Beckett. Actually, I don't think I was able to participate in that at all. It happened so fast I can barely register if it truly did happen. Realizing I thought it was Beckett, I try to recall if I was moaning his name but can't remember. I must not have been if Grant's still here with me. I don't even think it lasted long enough for me to moan at all. This is now twice that I've slept with him and twice I didn't get off.

Fuck!

I practically ignored him for the next few days. Okay, I fully ignored him for the next few days. It took that amount of time for my vagina to not have the aching reminder that a man had been inside me—a man that wasn't Beckett. By the time I finally decide to respond to his messages, he asks to take me to dinner. With zero groceries in my kitchen and no desire to go shopping, I agree.

He picks another upscale restaurant, the kind with dim lighting and a wine list that probably costs more than my rent. I really don't want to think about how much this meal is going to cost. I haven't been able to sleep much recently and have been working a lot more, so I can pay this time, or at least for my own meal.

I'm not feeling it tonight, though. From the moment we sit down, I'm distant. My mind wanders, and I've barely heard a word he's said. Instead, I focus on pouring myself glass after glass of wine, letting the familiar buzz numb the exhaustion that's been gnawing at me. Eventually, he catches on and tells me to slow down, but I barely acknowledge him.

While we wait for dinner, I pull out my phone and get lost in my farm game, tapping mindlessly at the screen. He's still talking, still trying to engage me in conversation, but his words feel like background noise. The more I drink, the more his voice becomes a low, irritating hum that grates on my nerves. I feel his hand brush my arm, a gentle attempt at connection, but I shift away.

Dinner is the same. He tries talking while I drink more wine and eat, not bothering to participate in this conversation.

I'm just about to beat this level when the bill arrives. I fumble through my purse, searching for my debit card. "You covered last time. Let me pay tonight," I insist.

"Absolutely not," he says firmly, his hand casually landing on my thigh. He rubs up and down with this possessive familiarity, and before I can argue, he's already reaching for his wallet.

"I insist." I reach across the table to shove his hand away. "I want to pay."

Just as I'm about to protest further, the waiter arrives. Grant quickly pulls out his card and hands it over.

"Why won't you let me pay?" I ask, feeling like now I owe him sex again or something.

He leans forward, catching my hand in his, planting a kiss on my knuckles. "Because I asked you out. My treat," he says simply, with the kind of smile that suggests he's not used to hearing no.

With a resigned sigh, I thank him and pull my hand away.

The waiter returns with the receipt and card, thanking us for dining. As I rise from my seat, Grant helps me into my coat, still playing the part of the gentleman.

But that's when it happens. My eyes drift across the room, and there's Beckett. His presence pulls the breath from my lungs in an instant. He's seated with a small group, but he's solely focused on me, the sharpness in his gaze cutting through the space between us. His jaw is set, and his fist are clenched on the table. My heart stutters in my chest, and I swear my legs might give out.

"Brynn," Grant's voice snaps me back to reality, humor in his tone as if oblivious to the pain that just ripped through me. "Let's go." He grabs my hand, and I almost flinch, my mind still fixated on Beckett's cold stare.

I rapidly blink and turn to look at him. "Yeah... sorry," I mutter, my voice trailing as I follow Grant toward the exit. I can still feel Beckett's eyes boring into my back.

The cold air slaps me as soon as we step outside. The streetlights and the dim glow from the restaurant are the only things cutting through the dark. I can see my breath rising in the frigid air as Grant hands the valet his ticket.

"Did you bring this cold weather tonight?" he teases, pulling me in while we wait for his truck.

"Yes," I reply through chattering teeth, "I wanted to make sure my bones felt like they were shattering from the cold."

When we pull up to my apartment, Grant leaves his truck idling. "I need to head home. Thanks for coming to dinner."

"Yeah. Bye," I reply quickly, giving him a half-hearted wave as I retreat inside.

The instant the door closes behind me, shame washes over me. I feel dirty, as if I'm betraying someone who was never even mine to begin with. It feels like I'm cheating on Beckett, and it makes my stomach churn.

A knock on my door startles me, and I hurry to answer it, knowing that though Beckett and I will probably fight right now, we will also be together. And Beckett *will* make sure I get off. As I swing the door open, my joy vanishes when I see Grant standing there.

"My night freed up. Can I come in?" he asks, his teeth chattering from the cold.

Confused, I stare at him. "I... guess," I murmur, stepping aside to let him in.

I sit on the couch, feeling a pang of guilt and discomfort, hoping that Grant will just decide to leave. But exhaustion starts to overtake me, and I'm barely aware when he whispers, "Come on," taking my hand and guiding me to the bedroom. Once again, my loose ass legs fall open for him. I suppose it's fine since this time it lasted about 11 seconds.

He falls asleep immediately afterward, and I lie there, staring at the ceiling, overwhelmed with a profound sense of emptiness. I can't stay in here any longer. I slip away to the bathroom, the emotions crashing over me like waves. Sitting on the cold tile floor, I lean against the door and let the tears flow silently. My sobs are soft, but each one feels like a knife twisting deeper into my chest. Beckett and I were never together, so why does his absence feel like such a deep wound? Why does he have this inexplicable hold over me? He doesn't want me—he never did. The epiphany hits harder with each tear, and my quiet sobs soon turn into angry, frustrated cries.

I collapse into a lying position on the bathroom floor, feeling the chill of the tiles against my side, wishing for the floor to simply swallow me whole. The rawness of it all consumes me until I eventually fall into a fitful sleep.

When I wake, I have a sore back and kinked neck. I sneak back to my room, dressing in a sweatshirt and pajama pants before crawling into bed beside Grant. Thankfully, he remains asleep, leaving me in the quiet solitude of my own thoughts, twisted between the remnants of the night and the shadows of my heartache. I shouldn't drink anymore—it really makes me emotional.

In the morning, I wake up to find he's already getting dressed.

"Good morning, sweetheart," he greets me, his eyes lighting up.

"Are you leaving?" I ask, sitting up and yawning.

"Yeah, I need to check on Roscoe," he replies, leaning over to kiss me. I turn my head, offering him my cheek. He doesn't appear the least bit fazed by it.

"I'll call you later," he says as he leaves.

I rummage through my purse, find my AirPods, and put them in, turning on some music to drown out the silence. I'm trying to avoid aggravating Nancy—she's always banging on the floor whenever I play music too loud, and I really don't want to deal with her today. My headache is bad enough without her being a bitch, I don't need her adding to it. I start by washing the dishes and cleaning the kitchen counters. I fill the sink with Pine-Sol and hot water, then grab the Swiffer and start mopping the floor, as if scrubbing away the grime could cleanse me of the lingering sense of filth from last night.

What did we even spill in here? I scrub at a dirty spot that doesn't want to come off. Frustrated, I remove the swiffer towel and use my hand to scrub at the spot until it finally disappears. Once it's clean, I stand up and turn to put the towel in the mop water, only to scream in fright when I find Beckett standing in the doorway of the kitchen, leaning against the wall, watching me.

"What the fuck, Beckett," I bite out as I rip my AirPods out.

"I knocked for the last five minutes," he says, walking over to the counter, pulling out a chair, and sitting down. "You really need to lock your door," he adds.

"Noted," I reply, dunking the Swiffer rag into the water.

He grabs my phone from the counter and begins scrolling through it. I stomp over to him, trying to grab it from him, but he's already unblocking himself from my contacts. "Well I see your phone still works," he remarks.

"Yes, it works just fine," I admit, slipping my AirPods back in my ears.

I continue mopping the kitchen when I bump into him.

"You're in my way," I snap.

He reaches down, yanking my AirPods out of my ears.

"Hey!" I shout, reaching for them. "Give those back!"

He traps me against the stove, his body close enough to feel the heat radiating off him, his hands braced on either side of the counter, boxing me in. His silence is deafening, his jaw clenched tight, nostrils flaring with every breath he takes.

"What?" I ask, suddenly feeling self-conscious.

He scans my face as if I've committed some unspeakable crime. "You reek," he snarls, his tone laced with contempt, as though the very sight of me disgusts him.

"I showered last night," I reply, feeling heat rise to my cheeks.

Without warning, he reaches out, his thumb rough as it swipes across my lower lip, the gesture so unexpected it makes me flinch. His eyes darken as he turns on his heel and storms out of the kitchen.

"Your entire apartment smells like him," he spits over his shoulder, yanking the door open and slamming it so hard the walls tremble in its wake.

For the next two days, silence fills the void he left behind. Each time my phone buzzes, I snatch it up with the faint hope that it's him, only to feel that familiar pang of disappointment when it's not. He's not coming back. He's made that perfectly clear.

While waiting to pick up an order for delivery, my phone chimes again, and this time, I hesitate, heart clenching as I glance at the screen.

GRANT:
Hi, sweetheart. Hope you're having a great day.

GRANT:
Can I call you later?

BRYNN:
Okay

That was the last text I received from Grant today. As I get ready for bed, I remember him saying he was going to call, but I didn't hear from him. We weren't supposed to meet at the park, so I dial his number just to make sure he's safe. It goes straight to voicemail. That's odd.

When I wake up, I check my phone and have nothing.

Surely he didn't wind up murdered or something, right? By four, when I still haven't heard from him, I start weighing the possibility that maybe he did get murdered.

> **BRYNN:**
> Wanna meet at the park at 6:00?

Another hour ticks by with no response, so I text him again.

> **BRYNN:**
> Earth to Grant.

As more hours pass, unease really starts to creep in. The only plausible explanations for his silence seem to be that he either got murdered or Beckett said something to him. But that's ridiculous—Beckett wouldn't do that.

Before heading to bed, I call once more. It rings half a ring then goes straight to voicemail. He literally ignored my call on purpose.

> **BRYNN:**
> I'm actually starting to think you've been murdered.

In the morning, I wake and still don't have anything new, but at this point, who fucking cares. I get dressed and get ready to work since the roads are finally clear today, which means I get to drive fast. Slinging my bag over my shoulder and grabbing my keys, I pull open the door only to find Grant standing there, hand raised mid-knock, holding coffee and donuts in his other hand.

"Good morning," he says, chipper as ever. "I brought you coffee and donuts." He extends them toward me.

I should slam the door in his face, but instead, I stare blankly at him.

"Can I come in or…?" He waits for a response.

"I'm leaving."

A flicker of irritation crosses his face before he easily masks it. "So, where are you headed?"

"I feel like the better question here would be, where have you been?" I fire back.

"Work's been busy, and my sister's in town. I'll make it up to you." He tries again, offering the coffee and donuts.

"I don't need you making anything up to me. Just weird you were sending my calls straight to voicemail. You were the one who said you'd call."

"I'm sorry. I got caught up in work and family. It won't happen again."

"Cool." I move past him, and he steps back. Locking the door behind me, I head straight to my car without a glance back.

"Sweetheart, come here," he chuckles, trailing behind me.

"I'm going to work. If you want to come by later to explain, fine. But right now, I'm leaving."

He catches up, reaching out and taking me by the arm. "Give me two seconds now, please. My sister is in town. I will be spending time with her," he answers apologetically.

I narrow my eyes at him. "And tomorrow?"

"I'll let you know once she leaves, and we can do anything you want. Unless you want to meet her? We can all go to dinner if you'd like."

"No, it's fine, spend time with your sister."

"Are you sure? I'm sure she would love to meet you," he presses.

"Positive," I say firmly, tugging my arm from his hold.

As I'm getting comfortable on the couch, a text from Grant pops up. I open it to find a picture of Roscoe, his tongue hanging out the side of his mouth, looking completely content.

GRANT:
[image]

BRYNN:
Aww 🖤

GRANT:
Miss you

In the morning, I check my phone but still nothing new. He's acting strange. If he's like Beckett and prefers not to text, he could just say so. Or if texting is his thing but phone calls aren't, he could mention that too. Out of curiosity if he will respond, I send a simple one-word text.

BRYNN:
Morning

The whole day passes without a reply. How long did he say his sister would be in town?

When my phone rings, I answer it accidentally without it being able to finish the first ring. I was distracted trying to lay down grass in my farm game.

"Hello?"

"It didn't even ring on my end. Were you trying to call me too?" Chloe's voice comes through.

"Oh hey. No, I was being a farmer."

"They changed my flight. I'll be home on Sunday instead," she says, reminding me I'm supposed to pick her up from the airport.

"Okay, no problem."

"Well, don't worry about picking me up, Tom says he wants to. Oh, speaking of the devil, he's calling me. I'll see you on Sunday. Love you," she says before hanging up.

I eagerly count down the days until Chloe's home. I know she'll want to spend most of her time with Tom, but I can't wait to see her.

Two days pass, bringing me closer to seeing Chloe. I'm so bored out of my mind, but I don't have the motivation to go work. I'm lying on the couch when a call comes in from a random number. I don't answer, but I do a quick Google search to try and see who it is. When nothing comes up, I decide to call it back. The call goes straight to voicemail, which seems strange—especially since it doesn't let me leave a message.

As I pull the phone away, I realize I accidentally called Grant. I hang up so fast, staring at the screen, hoping he didn't notice the call.

Sitting there, something about it nags at me. Why did it go straight to voicemail like that? Grant is always on his phone—there's no way he'd let it die. I search online for answers, and everything points to the same conclusion: he blocked me.

Just to be sure, I call the phone company. They confirm it—going straight to voicemail usually means you've been blocked, unless he switched phones.

Giving it one more go, I call again, and it goes straight to voicemail once more.

Funny how he would block me after he was just inviting me to meet his sister. I go to my bathroom and do a fast makeup and hair routine and then get dressed, leaving my apartment.

CHAPTER Twenty-Four

My nerves are shot as I step out of the elevator, barely noticing Savannah as I walk past her, not bothering to ask permission to head back.

"Ma'am, you can't just walk in here like that," she calls after me, her voice full of warning as she hurries after me.

I stride toward Beckett's office, throwing open the door without knocking. "Your receptionist is fucking annoying," I snap, shutting the door behind me and turning the lock.

"Let me call you back," Beckett says into the phone, then hangs up. He pushes away from his desk, stands, and walks to the door. He opens it a crack, speaks quietly to Savannah, assuring her that everything is fine, then closes it again.

"You could have just told her you were here to see me," he says as he walks back to his desk. "She would have called me, and you wouldn't have needed to cause a scene."

"Why?" I scoff. "So I can stand there like an idiot while she looks me up and down? No, thanks."

"Okay, well, since you're here, what can I do for you, Brynn?" he asks, settling back in his chair.

"Did you say something to Grant?" I ask, crossing my arms.

He leans back, resting his chin on his fingers, his expression unreadable. "Why would I do that?"

"Exactly!" I press, my voice rising. "WHY would you do that?"

"I didn't say anything to him," he replies casually.

"Right, so he blocked me for no reason?" I demand, stomping over to his desk.

"Who cares? He's a piece of shit."

"He's the piece of shit? Should we discuss *you*?" I bite out.

"He's married, Brynn." He unlocks a drawer and pulls out a folder, tossing it onto his desk.

"Fuck you, Beckett. You're so pathetic, you know that?"

He gestures toward the folder. "Open it."

I walk over and grab the folder from his desk. When I open it, I slump down into one of the chairs on the opposite side of him. Inside, I find a marriage certificate—Grant's marriage certificate. There are also photos from Grant's wife's social media page, with the latest status from last night showing them at dinner. My gaze fixes on her very pregnant belly.

Tears stream down my face as I flip through the pages. I've been sleeping with a married man, one with a pregnant wife who travels for work. I feel like I'm going to puke. My hands tremble as I stare at the pictures, unable to form words.

"Brynn," Beckett says, walking over to me and reaching for the folder.

"Don't," I snap, standing abruptly. "You've done enough." I turn to leave.

"Brynn, wait," he calls, catching my arm.

"DON'T TOUCH ME!" I shriek, hurling the folder. Papers scatter across the floor.

I wipe my tears away as I flee from his office.

I barely make it to my car as I begin to completely unravel, collapsing into the driver's seat with my forehead pressed against the steering wheel as sobs rack through me. How could I have been so blind? All the signs were there, glaring at me, but I chose to ignore them. The first time we met, he kept glancing at his phone like someone was incessantly texting or calling him. The second time, he shoved his phone in his pocket so fast when he saw me waiting outside his truck. When he stayed the night, he tucked his phone under his pillow like he was hiding something, and it never stopped buzzing whenever we were together. What a lying, cheating bastard. Every alarm bell had gone off, and yet I ignored them all.

I thought I was just trying to forget Beckett, to ease the ache of seeing him with someone else. But now, all I've done is create more hurt—my own, and maybe worse, a pregnant woman's. I've been complicit in her pain, even if I didn't know. The realization grips my chest, choking me with guilt, and the tears flow harder. I wish I could rewind, undo it all, confront Beckett at that restaurant like I wanted to instead of letting my feelings spiral out of control. Maybe then I wouldn't have gone to the park, wouldn't have let myself fall into Grant's mess.

Lost in the storm of emotions, I don't hear the footsteps approaching until my car door is pulled open. The comforting scent of Beckett fills the car. He crouches down by the open door, reaching for me, and though I resist at first, the fight leaves me as quickly as it came. I collapse into his arms, letting him hold me as I sob into his chest.

He holds me for what feels like hours, letting me cry into his chest while he remains beside me. His legs must be aching by now, but he doesn't let go. I'm a wreck—my sobs loud and broken, my breath coming in shallow, uneven bursts. He doesn't rush me. He just holds on, his hands warm and steady, letting me pour everything out.

When my tears finally start to ebb, I pull away, feeling the rawness in my throat. Beckett meets my gaze, his expression soft, and he reaches up, wiping away the last stray tears on my cheek with his thumbs.

"Beckett?" A woman's voice cuts through the air, breaking the fragile moment between us. I glance up, my stomach twisting. It's her—the woman from the restaurant, the one I saw him with.

Of course. Just when I thought I couldn't feel any lower.

She stops in her tracks, looking between us, and offers me a sympathetic smile. "It looks like a bad time. I'll meet you inside," she says softly, her eyes lingering on me before she turns, giving us space.

I push against Beckett's chest, needing to escape the weight of it all. "I need to go," I mutter, my voice hoarse. He stands and steps aside, letting me pull myself together just enough to get the door shut.

As I drive away, I glance in the rear-view mirror, catching a glimpse of him watching me leave, as she walks back, her hand resting on his arm in a comforting gesture. It's a scene that plunges the knife in my gut even deeper.

I. Hate. Men.

The following day, I don't even bother getting out of bed until the afternoon. Most of the night was spent crying into my pillow—yet again, all because of Beckett. It's painfully clear that he and that woman are obviously in more than just a casual, one-date type of situation, and that hurts.

Eventually, I force myself out of bed, refusing to let the entire day slip away in a haze of self-pity. Lying around all day isn't going to fix anything. I throw on some clothes, hop in my car, and drive to the nearest coffee shop. Grabbing a drink, I head back out, trying to figure out my next move, as if doing something—anything—will make me feel less like my life is unraveling.

I sip my coffee and pull up the ExpressWay app, scrolling through to see what jobs are nearby. But when I glance up, I do a double-take. There, walking toward me, is Grant—with his arm wrapped around his very pregnant wife's shoulder. The shock on his face tells me he spotted me first.

Rage surges through me, and I freeze, locking eyes with him as they approach. His wife notices me staring, whispering something to him while he murmurs a response. I take a deep breath, forcing my fury down, and press my lips into a thin line.

"Hi, Grant," I say, struggling to keep my frustration in check.

They stop in front of me, and his wife looks at me, confused. I relish the discomfort on his face.

"I'm Brynn," I introduce myself, extending my hand to her, my eyes never leaving his. "And you are?"

"Vivian, Grant's wife," she says, shaking my hand, still bewildered. Her gaze darts between me and Grant. "How do you two know each other?"

"Yes, Grant—how do we know each other?" I can't wait to hear what he comes up with.

His face turns pale, and he stammers. "We, uh, need to get going, sweetheart," he mutters to his wife, desperate to get out of this.

"Sweetheart?" I repeat with a mocking laugh, watching him squirm under the weight of his own lies.

As he pulls her away, she glances back at me, offering a polite wave. She clearly is unaware of the shit storm he's managed to get us both in.

I can't help myself. "Oh, Grant, is your sister still in town?" I call out, voice dripping with sarcasm.

They come to an abrupt stop, and he tries to keep her moving, but she's confused. "Sister? He doesn't have a sister," she says, turning toward me. "You must have him mixed up with someone else."

I raise my brows. "Oh right, my mistake. Does he even have a dog named Roscoe?" I ask, laughing bitterly.

Her features twist into total confusion. "Yes, *we* have a dog named Roscoe. I'm so sorry—who are you?"

I can feel the heat of anger burning through me. "Have a good day," I say, continuing on my way.

I am so angry.

I can't even focus on work today. That poor woman is over there getting ready for the birth of their baby while her husband is cheating on her. It's disgusting. How many other women has he been with? We always used protection, but I need to get tested to make sure he didn't give me anything.

By the time I get home, I put on a movie and wallow in my misery. I curl up on the couch, letting the sound of the TV fade into the background as my mind races. Then my phone rings, sending a jolt through my body. It's Grant. I ignore it, but he keeps calling—again and again.

I'm done. I pull up his contact info, block his number, and delete everything. Every message. Every trace. I refuse to have any reminder of this colossal mistake.

Not even thirty minutes pass before there's loud, insistent banging at my door. My heart races as I open it to find Grant shoving his way inside.

"Get the fuck out of my apartment!" I snarl, my voice shaking with fury.

"Let me explain," he pleads, desperation in his eyes.

"This ought to be good," I say sarcastically, crossing my arms and glaring at him. "Please, go ahead."

He shifts uneasily. "Yes, I'm married. We aren't happy. The first time I've felt happy in years is when I'm with you."

"Get the fuck out." I point to the door.

"Brynn, please don't do this. Things can be different now that you know," he says, moving toward me.

"Get out!" I shout, pulling my door open, my heart thundering in my chest.

"We need to talk about this," he insists.

"Leave now, or I'm calling the police," I warn.

"Just talk to me, sweetheart."

This motherfucker.

My hand twitches, ready to slap him, but before I can, Beckett strides through the open door. "She said leave!"

Grant's face contorts with anger as his gaze darts between me and Beckett. "Who the hell is this?"

"The man left to pick up the pieces after a cheating piece of shit like you. Get out," Beckett repeats, stepping closer, his jaw clenched.

"Now," I add, my voice firm.

Beckett moves beside me, slipping his arm around my waist protectively.

Grant shakes his head in disbelief. "Unbelievable, Brynn," he spits, storming toward the door. "This isn't over. WE are not over!"

I start to shout something after him, but Beckett pulls me back. "He's not worth it," he says, his voice low as he gently takes my hand from the doorknob and shuts the door behind us, locking it.

I turn away, but Beckett grabs a fistful of my hair at the nape of my neck, pulling me toward him. His mouth crashes against mine, and all the anger and frustration melt away as

I give in to the heat between us. My soul feels like it's finally home.

He lays me down on the bed, his eyes dark with desire as he yanks my shirt over my head, tossing it aside as the cool air prickles against my skin. In one swift motion, my bra is off, and his hands roam freely, exploring every inch of me.

Clothes are thrown carelessly across the room as we undress, leaving a chaotic mess. When he lowers himself onto me, I gasp at the beautiful feel of him inside me. His rhythm is relentless, every thrust is deep and powerful, making my body writhe beneath him.

He slams in and out of me with such force that our moans and pants fill the room. I lose myself completely, realizing how much I've desperately been missing this. The sound of our pleasure drowns out everything else, even the pounding on the ceiling from Nancy, who must be awake and annoyed.

All that exists is Beckett—the way he moves, the way he fills me. Every nerve in my body is electrified by his touch. It's everything I've been missing, every desire I've suppressed crashing over me in waves of euphoria. The undeniable connection between us, and the sheer bliss of finally being with him again, consumes me. He brings me to the edge, and I willingly surrender.

I'M PERCHED AT THE KITCHEN COUNTER, LAZILY TRACING around the edge of my coffee mug. My eyes are heavy, staring blankly at the wall, waiting for Beckett to emerge from the bedroom. I can hear the faint sounds of him stirring, the subtle rustle of him getting dressed, and the soft thud of shoes hitting the floor. A few moments later, he appears, buttoning his shirt and tucking it into his pants with practiced motions.

"Morning, baby. You're up early." His tone is casual. "I've got to head out to work, but I'll be back as soon as I'm done. Unless you want to come along?"

I turn slowly to face him, a lump forming in my chest. "Beckett…" His name feels so heavy on my tongue. "I don't want to have any more contact with you. Please, leave me alone."

He freezes, his hands stilled in the middle of fastening his belt. His brow furrows, confusion flickering across his face, but he continues, as if convincing himself he misheard. Once finished, he looks at me, his eyes searching mine. "What's this about?"

A bitter scoff escapes me. "You're just as bad as Grant." My voice hardens. "That woman at your work? She's the same one I saw you with on a date. The date I stumbled on when I was picking up an order. The date that made me spiral, making one bad decision after another just to forget you."

His expression shifts, something like disbelief flickering across his face before he laughs. "A date?"

"Yeah, funny, right?" I snap, pushing myself up from the counter. "Just leave. Don't bother contacting me—I've already blocked your number. If you ever cared about me, even a little bit, prove it by staying away from me. Please."

The space between us suddenly feels suffocating, like the room itself is closing in. I brush past him, heading toward the bedroom, desperate to create distance. My heart hammers in my chest as I walk, each beat echoing in my ears. I just need time to think, to breathe. But he doesn't let it go. I hear his footsteps behind me, trailing me until I shut myself in my bedroom. He stops on the other side, releasing a frustrated sigh. "Brynn, I wasn't on a date."

I press my back against my door, waiting for him to offer an explanation—something, anything, that might explain all of this. But there's nothing. Just silence.

"Baby, come out and talk to me," he says, his tone unnervingly calm. I close my eyes, the ache in my chest deepening. There's a pause. I can hear him exhale heavily, and then the quiet sound of his steps retreating. The air shifts when the apartment door opens, and a moment later, it closes with a final click, sealing the end of whatever this was.

THREE WEEKS CRAWL BY.

Each day more agonizing than the last. Grant keeps showing up every other day during the first two weeks, pounding on my door, begging for forgiveness, pleading for another chance. It takes calling the cops to finally get him off my back. Stupid little bitch boy. His wife must be days away from giving birth, and he's spending his days groveling at another woman's doorstep, asking for a second chance to be his side piece. Fucking dick hole.

I've found that evenings are the hardest for me. The silence feels unbearable, so I utilize that time to work, picking up ride after ride just to avoid being alone with my thoughts. Friday nights seem to be the prime time for drunken chatter, as people pile into my car, slurring their words and telling me about their messy lives. Conversations blur together—loud, tipsy voices filling the car with laughter, complaints, or confessions.

Sometimes, though, there's nothing but silence. Some passengers don't want to talk, just ping me their location through the app, and by the time they climb into the back seat, it's a quick double-check of the address before we drive off in shared quiet. It's in these still moments, when no one speaks, that the unease starts to creep in. The absence of noise leaves too much room for my thoughts to claw their way to the surface. I hate the quiet, the way it makes me confront everything I'd rather push away.

As the next address pings on my phone, I gape at it briefly, right as the passenger slips into the back and closes the door with a soft click. I stare at the screen, my mind blanking out, unable to focus as my chest constricts. The destination stares back at me, mocking me—the same hotel Beckett and I stayed at during the winter storm. Memories crash over me, sudden and overwhelming. I can't go back there. Not now. Probably not ever.

"I'm not driving there. Sorry," I manage to say, though my voice feels shakier than I'd like.

"I'll pay extra," the passenger mumbles from the backseat.

I peer in the rearview mirror, trying to make out his face beneath the hood. He's slumped down, barely visible, and for a second, he's just another shadow. But I can't do it. "No. There are other drivers out tonight who will take you there," I say firmly, ending the ride with a tap on the screen.

"Please," he murmurs, his voice almost desperate.

My already thin patience snaps. "Dude, no," I say more sharply, twisting in my seat to face him. "You need to get out—" But then he moves, and everything seems to slow down.

He raises his head, and the instant I see his face, my blood runs cold. My heart slams against my chest, my breath catching painfully in my throat. Bloodshot eyes meet mine, familiar and haunting.

It's Beckett.

"What... what are you doing?" I stammer, my voice barely audible, caught between shock and disbelief.

"I don't know anymore," he murmurs, his voice cracked and hollow, like everything inside him has shattered. The rawness in his tone hits me hard, knocking the air from my lungs. "I tried, Brynn. I really tried to stay away."

I swallow hard, my throat tight as a whirlwind of emotions surges through me—frustration, grief, and an aching need for him that I've tried to bury. "Let me take you home," I offer softly.

He doesn't reply. Instead, he sinks further into the seat, his gaze distant, fixed on something far beyond the window. Defeat clings to him, heavy and unmistakable. The silence stretches between us as I pull up to his condo. Beckett steps out, but rather than disappearing into the night, he circles the car.

I barely register the sound of the door opening before he's leaning in, his hand sliding to the back of my head, pulling me toward him. His lips crash against mine in a kiss full of urgency, a flood of unspoken feelings pouring out. Both of us desperate, and without thinking, I deepen it, my hands fisting into his jacket.

All the emotions I've fought so hard to bury—pain, confusion, longing—surge to the surface, and in this fleeting moment, everything unravels. He unfastens my seatbelt with swift ease, reaches for my purse, and gently tugs me from the car. His lips find mine once more, and I don't even try to resist. When he whispers, "Come up," I nod without hesitation, knowing full well how reckless this is. But the need to be close to him, after everything that's happened, overpowers any sense of reason.

The click of my car door shutting behind me feels final, and the keys disappear into the doorman's hand as we step inside the building. The hum of the elevator fills the silence between us, and I catch his eyes just as he lifts me. It's intoxicating—the intensity of being near him again, the magnetic pull we both keep falling into.

My back hits the cold metal wall of the elevator as his mouth claims mine once more, his kiss urgent, filled with everything neither of us can say aloud. My arms wrap around his neck, and I cling to him, not wanting to let go.

Once we stumble into his condo, he moves quickly, almost frantically as he undresses me. Silk sheets meet my skin as I sink into the bed. My heart races as I watch him strip out of his clothes just as fast, his movements impatient. As he climbs onto the mattress, the pounding in my chest grows louder. We want each other, and we're not taking our time doing it, but with these actions, there's an undercurrent of unease.

Before he's fully between my thighs, I blurt out breathlessly, "Can you use a condom?" My words breaking the heated silence. His body stiffens, and I see the shock flash across his face, his eyes widening as if he can't believe I asked that.

His chin jerks back in surprise. "Brynn," he says, his voice almost sounding hurt.

"We've both been with other people, and I don't feel comfortable not using one."

He exhales sharply and rolls off the bed. He searches through the drawers of his nightstand with growing impatience, then stalks to the bathroom, and finally the kitchen. Every second that passes feels heavier, but I'm glad I'm putting my foot down. If he doesn't have any available, he either used all of them or he was going without one with her—which makes me want to cry, considering that's the only way he ever was with me. I just kind of assumed that him going bare was something special we were sharing together. I can't believe I'm just now realizing I never even had him show me proof he was clean.

When he reappears, he's still fully erect, his irritation barely contained. "I don't have any," he mutters, his jaw clenched. "I'll call Preston and have him run to the store."

"It's fine," I reply, sliding off the bed and reaching into my purse. I pull out two condoms, tossing them to him. He catches them, his eyes narrowing as he stares at me, something like anger flashing across his face as he tears into the foil with his teeth.

"Get back on the bed," he growls, his voice rough, and without question, I do exactly as he commands.

I watch him as he rolls the condom on, his movements precise, though something about this feels distant. He reaches for a bottle in his nightstand, dripping lube along the condom, even though I know I'm ready. The amount he's using has me wondering how rough he's planning to be, since he's making sure he's soaking wet. He's about to create a slip 'n' slide out of me, and it's like he's focused more on control than our connection.

When he finally positions himself back between my legs, he grabs my knees, forcefully spreading my thighs apart. He stays kneeling, lining himself up, and when he slams into me, the impact is so powerful it propels me forward. A strangled moan from deep in my throat escapes as I reach out to grab his arms for stability. The mixture of pain and pleasure is so overwhelming, it takes me a second to wrap my head around what just happened.

His arm wraps around my leg, his fingers digging into my thigh, while his other hand presses down on my bladder. His hips move fast and relentless, each thrust is filled with an intensity that makes it clear—he's angry. He's hurt. And somehow, he's releasing all of it into me. And I might release my pee all over him if he keeps pressing down on me like that, even though it feels incredible.

It's not just his aggression I feel—there's something inside me too—my own frustration, my own longing. It all mixes together. His hips grind deeper into me, keeping him buried as I clench around him.

"You're gonna make me pee," I gasp, grabbing at his hand pushing down on me, trying to pull it away. I needed to use the bathroom before we even started, and now I really need to use the bathroom, or he's going to force it all out.

He abruptly pulls out, wraps his arms around my back, and flips me over onto all fours. His knees knock mine apart, spreading me wide, then lines himself back up as he drives into me. My arms stretch out, gripping the silk sheets like they're the only thing grounding me.

A fistful of my hair is yanked back, my head arching as his other hand wraps around my throat, squeezing with a pressure that sends a thrill through me. It's something I never imagined in a million years I'd want, yet here I am, rocking back against him with growing urgency. The tighter his hold on my throat, the more I lose myself in the feeling, pushing against him, hungry for more.

He pulls me upright onto his lap, his rough voice commanding, "Ride me." I wrap my arms behind me, around his neck, rolling my hips against him, driven by a primal need to feel every inch of him inside me. His hand comes down hard on my clit, the sting sharp but immediately followed by a rush of pleasure that leaves me trembling. He groans against my skin, then sinks his teeth into my cheek possessively.

"You let another man touch my pussy?" he growls, gripping my throat harder, causing my face to flush.

His fury and passion make my movements more desperate. "Did you come all over his cock like you do on mine?" His voice is fierce, and the question is laced with anger, igniting something raw inside me. Tears burn the corners of my eyes, threatening to spill, but I can't stop my hips from moving.

When he finally releases my neck, I gasp for air, only for him to slap my nipple, a sting that sends a whimpered moan slipping free. Before I can catch my breath, he's back to squeezing my throat. "Answer me, Brynn. Did you let another man make you feel good? Did you come on someone else's cock?" His voice is harsh as he delivers another stinging slap to my pussy.

I can't seem to get enough of it. My silence seems to fuel him. His fist tightens in my hair, yanking me closer as he delivers another harsh slap to my nipple, causing me to cry out. "No," I scream, the desperation clear in my voice—a plea and a confession all at once.

"No what?" he demands, his hand tangling even tighter in my hair.

"He never made me come," I pant, my words broken by ragged breaths. "I've only ever come for you."

He reacts with a forceful shove, pushing me back down onto the bed while still clutching my hair. His thrusts are relentless and intense as he drives deep into me. My screams mix with his groans, our bodies colliding with a frenzied need.

I did want him to slap my skin… and he's definitely doing a good job of that.

"Rub your clit," he orders.

I comply immediately, my fingers moving instinctively. The combination of his powerful thrusts and my own touch sends waves of ecstasy through me. I feel the intense pleasure build, and as we both reach our climaxes simultaneously, our moans rise and blend together, riding the crest of our shared release.

When we finish, I collapse onto the bed, my chest heaving for oxygen. Beckett abruptly pulls away and strides toward the bathroom. Through the mirror, I catch his reflection as he tears off the condom and throws it in the trash. The bathroom door slams behind him, the jarring sound making me flinch.

He's making his regret in what we just did palpable. I sit up, my heart racing now for an entirely different reason as I gather my scattered clothes, dressing with trembling hands. I grab my bag, slinging it over my shoulder, and hurry to the elevator. It opens right away, and I press the down button repeatedly, holding my breath until the doors close and the elevator is in motion.

At the lobby, the receptionist offers me a polite smile. "Can I have my keys?" I ask, my voice thin. She nods and disappears into the back, but the seconds stretch into agonizing minutes. My heart races as I shift from foot to foot, trying to ignore the cold sweat trickling down my spine. Why is this taking so long? By the time she returns, I all but snatch the keys from her hand, muttering a rushed, "Thanks," before rushing through the front doors.

I barely make it outside when I see the doorman look behind me and I glance back to see Beckett rushing toward me in nothing but his boxers, his face red with anger. "What the hell are you doing, Brynn?" he demands.

I stumble back a step, startled by the sight of him. "Beckett, it's freezing out here. Why aren't you dressed?"

He reaches out and grabs my arm, pulling me back inside.

"Beckett, stop!" I protest, trying to wrench my arm free from his grasp. The doorman keeps his focus forward as he holds the door for him, while the receptionist remains staring at her work as if she can't see the commotion unfolding.

We reach the elevator, and as the doors open immediately, Beckett pulls me inside with a determined stride. "Beckett, let me leave!" I insist, struggling against his hold.

As the elevator dings to a stop at his floor, he yanks me out and only lets go once we're inside his condo, the doors sliding shut behind us. I tear my arm free, glaring at him as he paces across the room, running a hand through his hair like he's on the verge of losing it.

"FUCK!" His roar fills the space, echoing off the walls of the hallway, his expression wild with untamed emotion.

"What is your problem?" I shout back, my voice cracking under the weight of my own anger.

"YOU! YOU, Brynn! YOU ARE MY PROBLEM!" his voice echoes through the condo, raw with anger. He storms into the kitchen, his footsteps pounding against the floor.

"Then quit bothering me!" I snap back.

He whirls back toward me, his fists balled at his sides, his body vibrating with barely contained rage. "YOU BOTHER ME! You're in my head, constantly. I want to kill that bastard for touching you! I want to rip apart every guy who dares look at you! I think about you every second of every damn day. You—" His voice trembles, dropping to something almost broken. "You're in my dreams, tormenting me, haunting me when you're not there. When you're not mine."

I take a step back, throwing my hands up in disbelief. "You just fucked me—had me on the verge of peeing all over your bed, and then you stormed off like you couldn't stand the sight of me. So I left, and you drag me back here."

His eyes flash between hurt and disbelief, as if I'm the one who doesn't understand. "You let another man fuck you! *You're mine, Brynn!* And his hands were on you! You put a barrier between us!" His voice cracks, his chest heaving as he spits out the words.

"You think just because you're sexy you can fuck around with anyone you want? Then get mad when I have sex with someone else too?! I slept with *one* other person, Beckett, and I didn't even want to! I feel dirty for it. All I wanted was you! I'm not like this, and I'm not going to participate in being one of the many women you sleep with!" I yell back, my voice trembling with a mix of hurt and anger.

His brow furrows, his expression shifting from anger to confusion. "What are you talking about?"

"You're a man whore, Beckett! It's trashy!" I snap, turning to leave. I pull my keys from my pocket, but he grabs my hand, attempting to pull them away from me. I yank my hand free, sending my keys clattering across the floor.

We stare at each other, then we're both diving for them. I manage to snatch them up first, but Beckett is relentless; he grabs my leg, pulling me back toward him. In a tangle of limbs, he rolls me onto my back and pins me down, reaching for my keys.

"Get off me, you huge beast!" I growl, twisting beneath him, every muscle straining as I cling to the keys.

His hand shoots out, pinning my wrist above my head. "Calm down." His frustration pours off him in waves as he tugs at my other hand, trying to pry the keys free.

"Get off me and let me leave!" I shout, my voice cracking with desperation.

"No!" he exclaims, his eyes burning with a fierce intensity. In one swift motion, he wrenches the keys from my grip and sends them skidding across the floor, the metallic clatter filling the room.

"Why?!" I cry out, thrashing beneath him, my attempts to escape growing more frantic.

"Because I want you, Brynn. I don't want anyone else—just you. And I need you to want only me." His voice softens, and his gaze drops, like he's waiting for me to say something. His breaths come in short, uneven bursts as his eyes search mine.

Then his lips crash into mine, fierce and hungry. I want to push him away—my brain screams for me to fight—but I can't. As soon as he kisses me, I melt. I kiss him back, and when he pulls away, I chase his lips, angry that he dared to stop.

"We need to talk, Brynn. We need to figure this out." His voice is a low rumble as he looks down at me.

"Fuck you," I snarl, the words spilling out, raw and venomous. "Kiss me. Now."

His lips curve into a smirk, but he obliges, pressing his mouth against mine once more. My mind spins, caught between anger and how turned on I am. "Take my pants off," I breathe, my legs wrapping around his hips.

"Talk to me first," he murmurs between kisses, his hands still pinning me, but softer now.

"Have me, and we'll talk," I reply, trying to free myself.

Just then, the elevator doors glide open, and out steps *her*—the woman from his date, the one I'd seen at the parking lot of his work. Her expression is a bizarre mix of curiosity and joy, her eyes gleaming as she strides toward us.

"I could hear you two screaming from the lobby," she says, her voice light.

My entire world crumbles around me as I stare at her in shock, the absurdity of the situation hitting me hard, and then I let out an incredulous scoff.

Beckett's grip tightens as I jerk my arms again, thinking if I'm fast enough, I can get them free.

"Oh you son of a bitch! I'm gonna kick your dick into your brain, you motherfucker!" I snap, my voice strained as I try to break free from his hold.

He looks over at the woman with an infuriatingly calm expression. "I had her settled down. She's usually much more pleasant after we've had sex," he says casually, like I'm some sort of wild animal that he's tamed. "But apparently, I didn't fuck her hard enough."

"Beckett has told me so much about you," she says with a smile, standing back a few feet, slightly bent over, as she... I don't know... greets me?

"Can't say the same about you," I retort sharply. "Get off me, Beckett!" I struggle against him, the effort only making me more frantic. "You're just going to stand there and watch your boyfriend harass another woman?" I yell toward her, my voice cracking as I push against his weight.

"Boyfriend?" They both say in unison, their voices tinged with surprise.

Beckett's laughter is sudden and jarring. He leans down, his breath hot against my neck as he bites down, his teeth sinking into my skin. I gasp in shock and pain—and, unfortunately, immediate pleasure.

"What the fuck?" I shout, my voice breaking as he sucks hard on the spot he bit.

"You either calm down, or I will fuck you right here," he growls in my ear.

"You wouldn't," I challenge.

"Try me."

I freeze, my breathing ragged from the struggle. I stare at him, the intensity of his gaze making my heart race. I'm stiff and unmoving, but then, slowly, I start to relax, the fight draining out of me.

"Brynn, this is my sister, Blake," he says, still holding me down, his voice softer now.

"Older sister, actually," she corrects.

He smirks at me. "By two minutes. Twins. She likes to make sure everyone knows she was born first."

I let out a nervous laugh, but they both remain serious. My laughter dies in my throat as I look between them. It's clear now—they share the same gray eyes, the same nose, the same full lips. Blake is the feminine counterpart to Beckett's more rugged masculinity. She's the woman from the picture with Beckett on the beach, the one I assumed was a family photo.

Heat rises in my cheeks, a flush of embarrassment and confusion.

I know I'm not learning right now that the giant train wreck that is my life was all because of me thinking he was on a date with his freaking sister!

"Can you get off me?" I whisper into Beckett's ear, my voice barely more than a breath. I'm not even sure he hears me at first.

"I'll go start getting dinner dished up," Blake says as she heads towards the kitchen, carrying takeout bags. "Beckett specifically told me what to get you, so if you don't like the food, blame him," she calls back, her laugh echoing slightly in the hallway.

"You are such a douche," I mutter.

He smirks as he leans down, giving me a soft kiss. "You're the douche for not answering my calls," he murmurs against my mouth, referring to the day I saw them together.

"You could have sent me a text," I bite back.

"I could have," he acknowledges, "or you could have come over like an adult and let me introduce you properly. We were in the middle of discussing you, after all."

"Why?" I blink.

He grins. "I'm going to get off you now." His voice drops to a calm, matter-of-fact tone. "We're going to eat dinner, because my sister has been dying to meet you. Then, we're going back to bed, and I'm going to fuck you without a condom because I haven't been with anyone else since I met you. And before that? It had been almost a year." His gaze holds mine, as he adds, "Tomorrow, we're going on a real date. A proper, *actual* date." Then he places a soft kiss on the tip of my nose.

I remain still, trying to process the whirlwind of emotions his words stir up. A faint smile tugs at the corner of his lips as he releases my wrists and slowly stands. He extends his hands toward me, offering them gently. I take hold, and he pulls me to my feet.

"Good girl," he says as he spanks my butt.

"Stop it." I swat his hand away.

He pulls me into a hug. "Any time away from you is hell. If you feel the same, I never want to be apart again."

"I feel the same." I hold him tighter.

When we finally pull apart, he gazes down at me, all traces of anger evaporating. He leans in and kisses me. "These bags under my eyes will thank you," he teases.

"Our eye bags were contending to see whose could be bigger," I quip.

He takes my hand, lacing our fingers together as he pulls me toward the kitchen. Blake's face lights up when we enter. Her smile is so genuine that it catches me off guard, and then she's wrapping me in an unexpectedly warm embrace.

"I'm so glad you're real," she says softly, her voice full of sincerity.

When she pulls back, she scans my face. "You're even more beautiful than he described—and those adorable pictures you two took together," she adds, her gaze flicking toward Beckett. She raises her brows at him, then gives him two enthusiastic thumbs up before grabbing two plates from the counter and handing them to him.

"He's so serious all the time," Blake says with a laugh as she loops her arm through mine, gently guiding me toward the table. "When he wouldn't stop talking about you, I knew I had to meet you. Now, I know *his* version of how you two met—I want to hear your version."

Beckett, meanwhile, opens a bottle of wine with a satisfying pop, the rich scent filling the room as he pours us each a glass and sets the bottle down.

We gather around Beckett's round dining table. I sit between him and Blake, who leans in a little closer, her body turned toward me, her legs crossed as she studies me with open curiosity. "I feel like I already know so much about you from what Beckett's told me. But I'd love to hear everything firsthand. So, you work for my brother now?" She twirls her fork around her noodles as she takes a bite of her food.

I smile, meeting Beckett's gaze. "No, he fired me," I reply light and playful as I dig into my own food.

Blake coughs and takes a sip of her wine, her eyes widening. "What?!" she exclaims, her gaze darting to Beckett for confirmation.

Still chewing, Beckett shoots me a smirk and swallows before responding. "I didn't fire her. She threw a fit and walked out, refusing to come back."

"Oh, so I'm still on the payroll?" I arch a brow as I spear another bite of food.

"You don't need to be on the payroll to have a job. You don't even have to work for me. You could just come and be with me all day," he says, nonchalantly taking another bite of food.

"So, you're offering to pay me for doing nothing?"

He leans in, grabbing the leg of my chair and pulling it towards him. "What you do with your pussy is definitely not nothing," he murmurs, giving me a tender kiss.

Blake lets out a soft chuckle. "Is she your whore?"

"If she wants to be," Beckett replies with a grin, his eyes locked on mine.

I meet his gaze. "I will be if the pay is good enough."

"Move in with me and I'll cover everything," he offers, his gaze steady.

Blake gives an exaggerated sigh, then chimes in, "Take her on a proper date first, Beckett."

He shoots me a wink. "I am, tomorrow."

Blake's eyes dance with mischief. "Be a proper gentleman and make sure you take her home after dinner."

Beckett leans back in his chair, his voice dropping to a deeper, more suggestive tone. "A proper gentleman," he murmurs, "would make sure she's thoroughly satisfied at the end of the night."

I cross my arms and tilt my head toward Blake. "I agree with your *older* sister. You should take me home after dinner. Maybe—if you're lucky—after the third date, I'll let you take me to bed."

"I'm not fully satisfied tonight," he leans in, grazing his lips along my arm.

"Oh? Why not?" I flirt.

"Because…" His voice dips lower. "I didn't make you pee all over my bed."

CHAPTER Twenty-Five

I've been told that true happiness makes the world drift by like a dream? I've found that.

A week passes in pure bliss as Beckett and I become practically inseparable. Time blends together in a haze of affection, laughter, and quiet intimacy, our routine as natural as breathing. This morning, just before he heads off to work, he presses his mouth to mine, his hand resting at my waist. "I'd like to take you on a date after I get off work today."

You don't even need to ask me that anymore. Just say when, and I'm there."

By mid-afternoon, he tells me he's getting off early and coming to pick me up. I wait by the window until I see him pull up and rush to the door, opening it without giving him a chance to knock.

"Were you watching for me?" he smiles.

"Maybe," I reply playfully, stepping outside and calling a quick goodbye to Chloe and Tom.

He doesn't waste a second, pulling me into his arms, his lips meeting mine in a tender, lingering kiss. "Did you have a nice day?" he asks, sweeping my side bangs away from my brow.

"Yes, but you already know that—we were on FaceTime."

"Well, we weren't during the drive over." He leans in for another quick kiss.

"Did you have a nice day at work?"

"I did. I got to see boobies," he grins, giving my butt a light slap then taking my hand and leading me toward his SUV. I notice Preston in the driver's seat today, which feels like a welcome shift—it means Beckett and I can sit in the back, completely absorbed in each other for the ride.

He opens the door for me, and I grab a handful of his crotch as I climb in. "Thanks," I murmur, settling into the seat.

Just then, Chloe comes running up, hauling my luggage behind her. "Wait, you forgot this!" she calls out, hurrying toward us and handing the bag to Beckett.

"Uh... what?" I trail off, confusion settling over me as I watch him take the luggage from her hand like he was expecting it.

"Thanks, Chloe," he says, then turns back to me with a broad smirk.

"What's going on?" I ask, trying to make sense of my luggage in his hands.

"We're going on a date," he smiles.

"I know that. But why do you have my luggage?"

Because we're going away on a weekend getaway date," he reveals.

"Go! Have fun, Brynn!" Chloe encourages, excitedly.

"Are you serious?" I ask, climbing out of the SUV and jumping into Beckett's arms.

I WAS THOROUGHLY USED AND ABUSED IN THE MOST DELICIOUS way all weekend. Beckett took me to Sandals Royal Caribbean, and it was absolutely stunning. I couldn't stop going on and on about how incredible everything was, and he promised to plan another trip for us—next time, at least a week.

When we return home, I expect Beckett to have Preston drop me off at my place, but instead, we pull up in front of his condo. I glance at him, raising a brow. "I really need to go home so I can do laundry," I mention as he steps out of the car.

Beckett ignores my comment entirely as he comes around to my side and opens the door. "Let's go shower," he says, reaching for my hand and pulling me out of the car with playful insistence.

Without further protest, I let him lead me inside. As we enter his condo, we head straight to the bathroom, our clothes quickly discarded as the steam begins to rise around us. The warm water immediately envelops us, a soothing cascade that washes away the weekend's traces. Beckett steps behind me, his hands sliding around my waist, pulling me flush against him. His touch is tender yet possessive.

His lips find my neck, leaving a slow, heated trail, and I lean back into him, my body melting under his affection.

"I thought you said we were showering," I say softly.

"We are," he replies, in a whisper against my neck.

"Then what are you doing?" I ask, my breath hitching as his hands begin to explore, sliding down my stomach and slipping between my legs.

"Showering with you." He nips at my jaw.

His fingers press gently between my lips and I gasp. Each slow touch sends a surge of tingles through my body, the tension building until a deep ache settles in my core. I grip his forearms tightly, my body quivering under the spell of his skilled hands.

When he finally presses inside me, a soft moan escapes, my body arching into him. My head tilts back against his chest, and I close my eyes, completely lost in the rhythm he creates with his hands. His mouth never leaves my neck, his kisses matching the movements of his fingers as they work me over, pushing me higher with every stroke. My hips move with him, seeking more of the pleasure that he so skillfully delivers.

As the bliss crescendos, I cling to Beckett, my fingers digging into his slick skin as my breaths come faster, each one more ragged than the last. My world narrows, dissolving into nothing but the moans spilling out. Every muscle tenses as I reach the peak, my body trembling in his hold until I finally clutch the wall, utterly spent.

Afterward, we step out of the shower, our skin still tingling from the steamy water. We dry off, wrapping ourselves in towels. My movements are slow and languid, reflecting the blissful haze that surrounds me. I pause, taking in the clothes scattered haphazardly across the floor. A quiet laugh escapes me as I realize I have absolutely nothing to wear. Turning to tell Beckett, I find him already emerging from his closet, holding out a T-shirt and a pair of boxers.

I quickly slip into his shirt, the fabric carrying his scent with it. His boxer briefs sit a little loose on my thighs, but I fill out the back comfortably.

"Come here," I say, holding open the waistband of his boxers. "Try and fit in these with me."

He looks over at me and just stares, then starts laughing as he slides on his own pair.

As he walks past, I grab the waistband of his boxers, pulling him backward toward me. He just needs to stop long enough for me to slide in the back. "Stop walking, babe, I just want to see if we can both fit."

He turns around and slings me over his shoulder, slapping my butt as he carries me out of the room. I laugh, holding on to his butt cheeks as he strides to the foyer, where he finally sets me down. My laughter fades as I glance around and see our luggage neatly lined up by the door. I look from the bags to Beckett, who's casually grabbing his own.

"Why didn't you tell them to leave my bags in the truck?"

"We're going to do laundry," he says simply. He heads down the hall toward the laundry room, calling back over his shoulder, "C'mon, let's get it done."

With a tired huff, I trail behind him, my body heavy with exhaustion. After we load the laundry, I let out a long yawn, barely able to keep my eyes open. I make my way back to his bedroom, slipping under the covers. I sigh wistfully, melting into the most comfortable bed I've ever had the privilege of sleeping in. I drift off, vaguely aware of him slipping into bed behind me and wrapping me in his arms.

When I wake, I blink away the remnants of sleep. I stretch lazily, realizing that Beckett must have gotten up at some point. The bed feels much bigger without him. I sit up slowly, rubbing the last bit of grogginess from my eyes, and spot a clean pair of my clothes neatly folded on the bench at the foot of the bed.

My heart swells at the simple gesture. I stare at the folded clothes, finding it so precious that Beckett's hands carefully folded them. He had little thoughts while he did it, his brain making the conscious decision to lay out a pair for me to change into when I woke. I slip into the fresh clothes, and as I move toward the door, I notice that the rest of my things have already been packed back into my luggage.

I pad down the hallway, drawn to the soft glow spilling out of Beckett's office. When I step inside, I find him fully dressed, his focus glued to the computer screen in front of him. His broad back faces me, and the sight of him working so intently makes me smile. I slip my arms around his shoulders from behind and press a kiss to the side of his neck.

"Hi, babe," he murmurs, tilting his head to meet my lips, his voice warm and welcoming.

"What are you working on?" I lean in a little closer, letting my cheek rest against his as I glance at the screen.

"Nothing now," he replies, turning his chair to face me, his eyes soft as they meet mine. "I finished all our laundry."

"I saw. Thank you. Sorry I fell asleep—jet lag."

His hand reaches for mine, giving it a squeeze. "I laid with you for a while."

I raise a brow. "Were you being good?"

"Ish," he winks.

"I'm disappointed. I was hoping you said you weren't good at all."

His grin widens as he stands, his arms wrapping around me, pulling me flush against his chest. "Let's go get back in bed, and I'll show you how *not* good I can be."

I softly push him away, my hand resting on him. "Maybe later. I want to check in with Chloe."

His face falls a little with clear disappointment in his eyes. "Spend the night with me tonight? I can take you home tomorrow."

"No. I want to check in with her. She leaves for work in two days." I poke his chest, then grab his hand and tug him toward the door.

As we pull up to my apartment, my heart drops into my butt. My bedroom window—it's boarded up. The sight freezes me, and before Beckett can even bring the truck to a complete stop, I'm out of the passenger seat, sprinting toward the front door.

"Babe, wait! Let me go first!" Beckett calls out behind me, but his voice barely registers as I race toward the door. Every worst-case scenario floods my mind, each one more terrifying than the last. Did someone break in and hurt Chloe? Is that why I never got a call about what happened? What if she was kidnapped? I must have been the intended target, since my window was the one broken out. What if Beckett had been with me when my window was smashed out, and he was injured? Ohhh, I'd kill the motherfucker.

My fingers shake as I fumble with the keys, and I curse the fact that Chloe always locks the door. The thought sends my pulse into overdrive, panic gripping me—until I hear the lock disengage with a familiar, comforting click. Relief washes over me, and I now thank the locked door—thank the sound of protection—maybe even safety.

"Chloe!" I yell, shoving the door open with a force that makes it slam against the wall.

Inside, I find Chloe, Tom, and Mark in the living room. Chloe looks up as I enter, her tense expression softening as soon as she sees me. In an instant, she rushes into my arms, and I pull her into a fierce hug, holding her tightly.

"Are you okay?" My voice cracks with the fear pumping through me.

"I'm fine," she answers, though I can see the frustration etched in her expression. "Some jackass threw a rock through our window!" She shakes her head in annoyance. "I already called the police. They took the rock for prints and snapped pictures of the shoe print by the window."

I'm shocked this happened, and even more frustrated that it was bad enough to involve the police. And instead of fixing the damn window, the apartment complex slapped a freaking board over it... in the winter.

"And you're sure you're okay?" I ask, holding her at arm's distance as I look her over for any signs she's not telling the truth.

I imagine myself being flattened under a massive boulder, or how surprised the culprit would have been if he threw the rock through my window and I picked it up and hurled it right back. Or if he threw it and I was fast enough to reach through the broken glass, and jerk him inside, and beat him up, then rip his undies up his butt and catapult him back out into the snow.

Chloe nods, but the light in her eyes dims as she continues. "I'm just so glad you weren't here. The rock was massive. It landed right on your bed." Her voice wavers, and a sense of dread knots in my stomach. "The cops said you could've been seriously hurt if you'd been there."

"And they don't know who did it?" I ask, my concern deepening, but also, fuck that person.

"No. They think it might've just been kids messing around or something." But there's doubt in her eyes—she doesn't believe it was random either.

"Were you here when it happened?"

She hesitates, glancing over at Tom as her cheeks flush slightly. "Tom and I were… in bed," she admits sheepishly.

My gaze flicks to Tom, hoping to see how he's fairing in all of this, but my attention quickly shifts as I catch Mark staring, and it's far from subtle. My first instinct is to hope Beckett hasn't noticed, but as I look up, I know he has. His jaw is clenched, his expression hardening in that all-too-familiar way when something—or someone—rubs him the wrong way. After everything we've been through, especially with Grant, he's extra sensitive to anyone paying too much attention to me. I get it. It's not like I don't observe the endless parade of women who swoon over him wherever we go. If I let that get to me, I'd be on a warpath all the time.

I slide my arm around his waist and lean into him for comfort. "Thanks for saving me from getting hurt," I murmur. His arm wraps protectively around me, but he remains focused on Mark.

"Let's grab some of your things and head back to my place," Beckett says. It's more a command than a suggestion, and I can feel that he's worried.

I shake my head gently. "No, I'll be fine," I reply, trying to sound more confident than I feel. "Plus, I have a cattle prod next to my bed," I grin.

Chloe steps forward, squeezing my hand. "Brynn, I think Beckett's right," she says softly. "It gets freezing in here, and that board isn't keeping the cold out. I've already packed a bag—I'm staying at Tom's for the next few days. But let's grab lunch tomorrow and catch up, okay?"

I hold her concerned gaze, her expression pleading with me to take this seriously and not give push back. Then I glance back at Beckett. His stare is fixed on me, silently telling me there's no real choice here. He's not letting me stay.

Twenty minutes later, I've packed my essentials, my bags sitting by the door as I take one last look around. It feels strange, leaving like this, but there's no use fighting it. I grab the handles of my suitcase, rolling it out. I packed way more than I should for staying just a couple of nights, but I don't know what all I might need. Beckett smiles every time I grab more stuff and cram it in my bags. He even joked that we should just get a moving truck to come finish clearing out my room.

As I make my way to my car, Beckett steps in front of me, his frame blocking my path. "No, baby. You're riding with me."

I stop short, huffing. "I'm not leaving my car here. This doesn't feel random—it feels like I was targeted. Someone purposely aimed at my window, and I don't want to come back to find my car vandalized."

Beckett's lips press into a thin line. He's quiet, thinking it over, but then he lets out a sigh of defeat. "Fine. I'll follow you," he relents. "I don't need you rear-ending me," he teases.

I laugh and shrug. "Deal."

When we arrive back at his place, I make a point to pull into his two empty spots diagonally, making sure to take up both of them. As I step out of my car, I flash him a big grin and give him a thumbs up. He rolls his eyes, smiling as he lowers his truck window.

"Can I stay like this or nah?" I shout.

"Nah!" he yells, still grinning. I slide back into my car to reposition it, pulling out and then easing into the spot backward to make room for him. He backs his truck into the space beside me, shaking his head as he climbs out.

"At least you didn't try to sideswipe my truck this time," he quips, draping an arm around my shoulder.

I nudge his side. "Ahhh, that's the real reason you wanted me to go first—you didn't want me backing into your precious truck!"

He gives me a look that says he's not denying it as he grabs my luggage. He wheels it up to his condo and straight into his closet like it's found its new home.

I WAKE TO THE SOUND OF WATER RUNNING. THROUGH THE OPEN door, I see him step out of the shower, steam curling around him as he wraps a towel around his waist. His movements are calm and unhurried, as he stands in front of the mirror, lathering up to shave before work.

For a moment, I lie there, just admiring him. This man is delicious; I could eat him for breakfast. I stretch beneath the soft sheets, then decide to join him. Slipping out of bed, I walk over, my feet barely making a sound on the warm floor. As I approach him, I lift my shirt and press my boobs against his back as I wrap my arms around his torso from behind, resting my cheek against his warm skin. He looks at me through the mirror with a small smirk, and I reach out to tug at the towel. It drops to the floor, pooling around his feet.

"Oops," I whisper, my hands gliding down the hard planes of his chest, moving lower to cup his glorious man jewels. A wicked grin tugs at my lips as I lean in and sink my teeth gently into his side, biting down just enough to make sure he feels it. I suck on the spot until I'm sure it'll leave a mark.

When I finally pull away, his eyes are on me as my teeth graze against his skin one last time. Slowly, I step back, letting my eyes linger on the perfect, sculpted lines of his body. I savor every inch—the broad, muscular shoulders, the tight, defined back, and of course, his sexy ass. He just stands there, pretending to be unimpressed.

He shakes his head, as he carries on shaving, completely unfazed by my antics. Smirking to myself, I head toward the closet, intending to find something to wear. But as I step inside, I pause, confusion pulling at me. My bags are still neatly packed, just as he left them, tucked away in the corner. Yet, next to them is an unexpected sight—a section of his closet is now empty, where his things once hung. In their place are a few of my vacation clothes, perfectly organized, along with some other random items from my room.

There's a half-full bottle of one of my perfumes, one of my sweatshirts, a couple of books—and most notably, Ursula.

Grabbing her, I head back to the bathroom where Beckett is still carefully focused on shaving. I lean against the doorframe, holding Ursula up in front of me like a piece of incriminating evidence and raise a brow. "Are you a klepto, babe?" I shake Ursula in his direction, my voice laced with playful accusation.

He glances over his shoulder, a gleam of humor in his eyes.

"You stole her from my apartment. What do you have to say for yourself?" I demand, wagging my finger at him with mock seriousness, trying to keep a straight face.

He laughs softly, turning back to the mirror, the sound rich and unbothered as he continues shaving. "I was keeping her safe," he teases, the words making my heart flutter despite myself.

I quirk a brow, shaking my head as I point out, "And my clothes too? Conveniently forgot to pack them back in my luggage before you knew I'd be coming back, huh?"

He just smiles, completely composed, as he keeps his attention on the mirror as he drags the razor across his jawline.

I walk up behind him, unable to resist the urge to touch him, as he rinses his razor and dries off his face. "What time will you be home today?" I ask, softly rubbing my hands over the firm muscles of his ass. Then grab two handfuls, squeezing hard with a playful aggression.

"Damn, babe!" he blurts out, standing a bit straighter, clearly surprised as he grabs my hands and pulls them away. "I'll be home around five," he manages, shaking his head in amusement.

"I'm meeting Chloe for lunch, and then I'll hang out at Tom's until you get back. Can you text me when you're home, and I'll head over?" I lean into him, pressing my body lightly against his.

"Just come back after lunch."

I tilt my head at him. "Are you going to meet me here?"

"No," he shakes his head.

"K, how will I get in?"

"Your key card is in your purse," he answers smoothly, leaning in to press a kiss to my cheek then heading for the closet.

I follow him, a familiar neediness tugging at me today, stronger than usual. *Lucky him.* He has a round plush bench in the middle of the room, and I lie down on it, letting my head hang upside down off the side. "Come try to choke me with that thang," I point to his dick.

He looks down at me, amused, as he pulls his work shirt on. "Behave."

"I don't want to," I pout, my voice full of need. "You're mine, mine. I can be as naughty as I want now."

He drapes his tie around his neck, and his eyes soften as he walks toward me. "I am yours, always." He bends down and presses a kiss to my lips, lingering just long enough for me to want more.

I reach up, my hand sliding between his legs, wrapping around him with firm intent. "Choke me with him," I demand, more seriously this time, pulling him down to his knees in front of me. The shift in the air between us is electric. He complies, a quiet groan escaping him as I stroke him slowly, enjoying the feel of him in my grip.

I bring him to me, swirling my tongue over the tip, teasing him before pulling him deeper into my mouth. I take my time, testing my limits, knowing he's too big to take all at once, but the challenge only fuels me as I choke him down inch by inch. His breathing hitches as I work, and I feel him tense as my hand moves faster, urging him on.

His hips begin to rock gently in sync with the movement of my hand and mouth, and the sound of his moaning fills the air between us, low and deep, setting every nerve in my body on fire. I can feel the tension building in him as I work him over, flicking my tongue and sucking, loving the power I wield over his body and the way it reacts to me.

He leans forward, his hand trailing down my stomach, slipping beneath the fabric of my underwear. His fingers expertly find their way between my slick folds, sliding easily to my entrance before plunging two fingers deep inside me. The sharp intensity of the sensation sends a jolt through my body, making me buck against him, a moan slipping free as his fingers curl in just the right way.

Reaching up with my free hand, I pull him in, gripping the curve of his ass, urging him deeper. The pressure in my body builds with every passing second as I take him into my mouth, stretching my jaw wide to accommodate his size. My lungs burn for air, and my jaw aches from the strain, but I'm too consumed by my raw desire for him.

I pull my legs back, opening myself up to him, my hips rolling in sync with the rhythm of his hand. He knows exactly how to work me over. I'm trembling as I continue to take him deeper, my mouth working him as much as I can.

His breathing grows ragged, hips stuttering as I feel the pulse of him against my tongue as he spills into my throat. His hand pauses, letting the sensation wash over him as he rides the final wave of release. When he finally pulls out, I wipe my lips, feeling the wetness smeared across them. He doesn't give me time to catch my breath or gather my thoughts as his hands are already wrapping around the inside of my thigh.

With a single fluid motion, he spins me around on the bench to face him, his eyes blazing with hunger. My underwear is jerked off, and his mouth is on me, finding my most sensitive spot. I gasp, a sharp breath that barely captures the intensity of what I'm feeling. His tongue moves in slow, torturous circles, his mouth devouring entirely as he sucks on me.

His fingers plunge back inside me, their rhythm perfectly in sync with his mouth. Each deep stroke is unrelenting, hitting the spot that makes my back arch. The way his tongue works me, coupled with the expert strokes of his fingers has my orgasm building faster than I can keep up with.

Within seconds, I'm teetering on the edge, the pleasure so intense it blurs my senses. His mouth never leaves me, while his fingers curl inside me, pushing right where I need them to. That's all it takes—my body seizes, and I scream out his name, the orgasm crashing through me so violently that I lose all sense of time. I can't stop trembling, my hands gripping the bench frantically as he holds me steady, letting me fall apart completely.

As I step into the restaurant, the warm scent of freshly brewed coffee and pastries envelops me. I scan the room until I spot Chloe, already seated and waving me over. I weave through the tables and slide into the chair across from her. We order our regular drinks and food as we settle in to catch up.

I've been so caught up in my own misery, and she with Tom, that I haven't had a chance to fill her in on all the details about Grant, or to tell her about Beckett and me—our little getaway or how wonderful things have been now that we are… officially a couple, I guess. He's never said we are, but I'm assuming with the whole "I never want to be apart again" talk, it means that we certainly aren't just friends.

"How's Tom?" I ask, taking a cautious sip of my drink. The rich, smooth coffee hits just right, and I roll my eyes from how tasty it is.

"He's alright," she replies chewing on the inside of her cheek. "Obviously worried after everything that's happened." Then her tone shifts, becoming more serious. "Actually, there's something I wanted to talk to you about."

Well, that doesn't sound like it will be followed up by anything good.

"Tom asked me to move in with him," she says, her hands curling around her mug as if for comfort. "He's already buying his house, and whatever I pay in rent will go toward his mortgage. It's way better than paying money to the greedy assholes at our apartment."

Her words land like a punch to the gut, but I force a smile, determined to hide the hurt. "So, you're moving in with him?" I ask, my voice tight as I swallow the lump forming in my throat. I focus on her happiness, even though it stings.

"I wanted to talk to you first," she says quickly. "And... we'd like to offer you one of the extra rooms at his place. Rent would be cheaper since we'd split it four ways."

My heart pounds in my chest; the idea of not living with her catches me off guard. "But our lease isn't up for another seven months," I reply, trying to wrap my head around the situation. Maybe by then, things would change. Maybe they won't even be together.

Chloe gives me a hopeful look. "We just wanted to see what you thought. Plus, with the whole window incident, we could have some leverage to get out of the lease early. I don't even feel safe going back, Brynn. I really don't want to live there anymore."

After my window is fixed, I begin splitting my time between my apartment and Beckett's place. Even on the nights I tell him I'll stay at my own place, he still shows up after work and spends the evening with me. I'm thankful for his presence, especially since strange things keep happening. Each time I walk through my front door, an involuntary grumble escapes me. The once-comfortable space feels different now—almost suffocating. I'm starting to understand how Chloe feels—there's a part of me that doesn't even want to be here anymore either.

One evening, as I make my way toward my bedroom, something feels off. My bedroom door, which I always keep closed, is slightly ajar. I stop in my tracks, a wave of unease creeping up my spine, and my instincts kick into overdrive. The logical part of my brain is screaming for me to giddy up on out of here right now, while the stupid part convinces me I'm overreacting and that I'll be fine.

Slowly, I push the door open, stepping inside with caution. Everything appears untouched—nothing seems visibly out of place—but I can't shake the feeling that something's different.

In the weeks that follow, that eerie feeling only deepens. I start noticing small, almost imperceptible changes around the apartment. Little things I might have overlooked before now seem glaringly obvious. My clothes, for instance—they're not where I left them. One afternoon, I left a basket of laundry sitting by the bed, and when I returned, it looked as if someone had rummaged through it. Even worse, a pair of underwear was missing from the load.

At first, I try to brush it off. Maybe I'm overreacting, being paranoid. My mind could just be playing tricks on me. But as the days pass, more unsettling things begin to pile up. A chair is subtly out of place, just enough to make me doubt myself. The throw blanket I know I folded neatly is now crumpled up on my bed. With each small incident, the pit of anxiety in my stomach gets bigger. I want to believe it's nothing, but the growing dread makes it impossible to ignore.

The breaking point comes when I go to lay down for a nap one afternoon. As I sink into bed, I discover something that makes my soul leave my body—my pillow is warm. Someone had been here, in my bed, recently.

CHAPTER Twenty-Six

Exhaustion is settling in, but I push through, determined to complete one more delivery before heading home to finally crash. Just as I'm loading the car with my final order, my phone buzzes with a call from Beckett. I ignore it, figuring I'll call him back once I drop this order off. As soon as I'm driving again, my phone goes back into Do Not Disturb mode. As I'm walking back to my car from dropping off the last order, my phone rings again, Beckett's name flashing on the screen.

"Hello, grandpa," I answer with a teasing tone, mocking his tendency to worry about my driving.

"Oh, thank God!" His voice practically bursts through the phone, filled with so much relief that it makes me pause.

"What?" I laugh, but there's a sharpness in my voice now, a creeping sense that something's wrong.

"Brynn, your apartment building is on fire," he blurts out, his voice strained and heavy with panic. "I was driving by and saw the smoke. I've been trying to reach you for the past twenty minutes."

The world tilts around me, and I feel like I'm suspended in a nightmare. My hands grip the steering wheel tightly as my mind races, trying to process what he's just told me. *My apartment. On fire.* The words echo in my head, and then the reality of the situation hits me with a staggering force.

Without a second thought, I slam my foot on the gas, my car launching forward. The streets streak by in a blur of headlights and shadows. Panic grips me, my heart pounding so violently it drowns out everything else. I weave through traffic, barely detecting the angry honks and shouts, my mind fixated on the burning image of my apartment.

When I finally skid to a stop on my street, a suffocating dread envelops me. The road is blocked off by a wall of emergency vehicles, their flashing lights casting a strobe-like pattern on the smoke-filled air. Thick, black plumes of smoke rise into the sky, choking out the last of the sun and curling around the upper floors of my building, which are now engulfed in flames.

I pull over and stumble out of the car, my legs feeling like they're made of lead. Each step toward the scene is a struggle, my breath caught in my throat as the full impact of the disaster crashes down on me. My eyes widen in disbelief, my world reduced to the hellish inferno before me. The realization is brutal and immediate—everything I own is being devoured by the fire.

Beckett rushes over, pulling me into a tight embrace as I stand frozen. People rush around, their voices a jumbled cacophony of panic and sorrow, but it all sounds like an echo through a tunnel.

Beckett's voice reaches me in fragments, his words lost amid the blaring sirens and the frantic shouts. He guides me toward his vehicle, but I remain focused on the firefighters battling the relentless blaze. My mind races through the images of what I'm losing—my clothes, my books, that ridiculous "I'm with stupid" shirt, and the bed where I gave my virginity to Beckett. Every single possession I owned is in there, being reduced to ashes, and the weight of that loss feels like it might crush me.

Chloe had been adamant about getting renter's insurance when we first moved in, and I know logically that our belongings can be replaced. Yet, knowing that doesn't ease the crushing weight of loss that presses down on me now. It feels like a part of my life is being consumed by the flames, and the devastation is almost too much to bear.

"Anyone got marshmallows?" I mutter, the words slipping out before I can catch them. The joke is dark and in poor taste, but it's the only thing that keeps me from completely falling apart. I force a laugh, trying to cling to some semblance of humor amidst the wreckage. "At least I didn't go grocery shopping yesterday. If I had, the food would probably be cooked by now," I add, searching desperately for a silver lining.

Beckett slides closer, his hand resting gently on my thigh, offering silent comfort. We sit there, the reality of the situation becoming painfully clear.

A police officer approaches the SUV, his face serious but softened by an air of kindness. Beckett rolls down the window, and the officer leans in. "I'm gathering information on the tenants and making sure everyone is accounted for. Which apartment was yours?"

I swallow hard, forcing my mind to focus despite the whirlwind of emotions. "Apartment 2B," I manage to say. "My roommate, Chloe, is a flight attendant. She's away for work."

The officer nods, scribbling down the details. "Do you have somewhere you can stay?" he asks.

"She's staying with me." Beckett steps in, his voice firm and reassuring.

I glance at him, then back at the officer, and nod. "I'm staying with him," I echo, the words feeling strangely detached as they leave my lips.

The officer hands me his business card, his face a mixture of concern and professionalism. "I'll be in touch, but if you need anything in the meantime, give me a call," he says, his voice steady but urgent as he gestures toward the incoming sirens in the distance. "We need you to clear the road—more firetrucks are on the way."

I nod, not really processing his words, my gaze drifting back to the roaring flames. Preston pulls the car around, stopping next to mine, and I barely notice as Beckett steps out. He moves quickly, grabbing my purse from the front seat, locking the doors with a quiet click. His voice reaches me, something about my car being brought to the condo within the hour, but I can't focus.

Beckett instructs Preston to take us to the store, and my frustration tries bubbling over. "Take me back to your place, please," I say, my voice taut with barely contained anger.

"We'll be quick, babe," he tries to reassure me, but it only makes me feel more on edge.

"Beckett," I snap, my tone so sharp both he and Preston look stunned, caught off guard by my intensity. "Your options are to take me home or take me in the car. I'm stressed out and need a release. Now."

Surprise flickers in his eyes as he stares at me, then quickly shifts his focus to Preston. "Take us home."

Preston nods, and we head back to Beckett's. The elevator ride feels unbearable, each floor crawling by like time has slowed just in here. I can't keep still—my thumb taps relentlessly on the railing, and I shift my weight from one foot to the other, watching the numbers.

"Damn it, why is this elevator so slow?!" I'm done waiting, and he knows it. I'm in motion, driven by a desperate need to escape the tangled mess of anger, frustration, and profound loss. Beckett's eyes meet mine with a knowing look, his own urgency mirroring mine. Our lips clash together right here in the elevator. He lifts me, and I'm already unzipping my jacket, then fumbling with the buttons of his shirt.

We barely make it to the bedroom before we're clawing at each other's clothes with the need to release everything pent-up. When he tries to ease me onto the bed, I refuse, grabbing his shoulders and pushing him back. "No, you lay down," I demand, and he obeys, his body sinking into the mattress.

I climb on top, positioning him beneath me, then lower myself onto him. I welcome the intense stretch. Even when my body tries to resist him entering me, I don't care. I push past the discomfort, forcing him inside me, even though the slight sting reminds me I probably should've used lube. But he doesn't seem to mind; his eyes are closed, his nostrils slightly flared, and that's all I need to keep going.

I move with purpose, my hips rolling in a steady rhythm, trying to drive away the crushing reality. "Fuck!" I cry out, the first burst of pleasure ripping through me. But then the enormity of everything I've lost hits me. The fire, the destruction, the complete obliteration of everything I owned—my belongings, my memories. It all crashes down on me.

"Fuck!" I scream again, my voice breaking, the raw emotion finally spilling over as I ride him, trying to drown out the grief with every desperate motion.

Beckett's grip tightens around me, his body moving in perfect rhythm with mine, but there's something deeper in the way he holds me—a silent attempt to comfort me. The more I scream, the more my anger swells, and I let it all out, purging the hurt and frustration through the physical release.

"FUCK!" I shout, the rawness in my voice displaying the pain beneath the fury. "Harder," I gasp, my breath ragged, desperate for more.

He pulls out and flips me onto my hands and knees, slamming back into me, his arm curling around my throat, pulling me against him as he drives into me with a force that feels like he's puncturing vital organs, It's brutal and unforgiving, and in this moment, it's the only thing that makes sense. It's incredible.

When it's over, we collapse together, our bodies entwined and spent. The fierce anger that drove me dissipates, leaving behind a hollow ache. I bury my face in Beckett's chest, feeling the last remnants of adrenaline drain away, leaving me utterly exhausted. He strokes my hair, just holding me as I finally let the tears fall.

After a long, tear-filled night and the deep, heavy sleep that follows, I wake with the same sadness. I turn to Beckett and tell him I need to call Chloe—there's no delaying this conversation. She has to know now. When I reach her, she's in the middle of connecting flights. I break the news, detailing just how bad things are. The situation is so serious that even her boss insists she take the next flight home to handle everything.

As soon as Chloe arrives home, Beckett and I meet her and Tom at the apartment. Chloe's face mirrors mine when I first saw the inferno. What's left behind is no less devastating. The building is blackened, and all the cars that were parked out front have fire damage. We can't go inside because the structure is too unstable—but we manage to peer through the gaping holes where the windows once were. The sight of the charred remains hits just as hard as the flames when I originally arrived at the scene. Everything we own, every part of our daily lives, has been reduced to a heap of rubble and ash.

Chloe's earlier words echo in my mind: *maybe this will give us the leverage to finally break the lease.* She was only talking about a broken window then, but now we don't even have an apartment. It's safe to say our lease is more than over.

Amid the destruction, there's a small glimmer of relief—our insurance will cover the losses. Chloe and I have already agreed to split the payout evenly. She's planning to move in with Tom, and she asks if I want to join them.

Beckett and I look at each other, and I know this is a serious conversation he and I need to have. I'm not sure if he's ready for this kind of step—to have me move in with him full-time. And I would completely understand if he wasn't.

"Let me discuss it with Beckett, and I'll let you know," I offer her a half-hearted smile.

"No need," Beckett inserts. "She will live with me. She was already practically moving all her stuff anyway," he winks, referring to how I'd overpacked to stay with him after the window incident.

"Okay, klepto," I tease.

"Don't act like my sticky fingers didn't do a little good," he quips.

After hugging Chloe goodbye, we agree to catch up tomorrow. I have a feeling she's eager to blow off some steam with Tom the same way Beckett helped me let out my own frustrations.

He opens the truck door for me, and I turn to him, wrapping my arms around him, grateful for him always being so amazing. "Thank you for being a thief and stealing Ursula," I say with a pained smile, knowing I would have lost her to the fire too if he hadn't taken her. My smile fades, and tears well up in my eyes as I remember everything else that was lost. "My 'I'm with Stupid' shirt burned." My voice breaks as I say the words.

Beckett's expression softens instantly. He gently wipes the tear that slips down my cheek. "Let's go home," he says, giving my butt a light pat as I climb in, and he closes the door behind me.

When we get back, Beckett asks if I want to cuddle and watch a movie. I agree immediately. I settle on the couch, waiting for him to join me, but when he finally comes walking out, I freeze. He's wearing lounge joggers—and his I'm Stupid shirt.

"I know you're lying." I stare at him, half-tempted to get up and rip the shirt off him just to strangle him with it.

"Not at all," he replies with a playful smirk.

"Okay," I say, rising to my feet. "So you woke up today and chose violence." My words drip with sarcasm as I turn to storm off. I just cried over my stupid shirt, and he chose to wear his in front of me less than an hour later to flaunt that his didn't burn.

He reaches out and grabs my arm, halting me from leaving. I turn, my glare meeting his unbothered smile, and when he tugs on the hem of my shirt, I see red.

"Oh, Buckets, I'm about to paint this wall with you," my voice is barely steady as I try to keep my composure.

He bites his lip as he looks down at my mouth, then back up to meet my eyes. "We're going to watch a movie and cuddle," he says innocently. "I thought we could wear these." He pulls out whatever is hanging from his pocket and holds it up—*my* I'm with Stupid shirt.

"What?!" I exclaim, my eyes widening in disbelief.

"I stole it," he admits, looking a little sheepish. "I figured I didn't have to hide it anymore, since it's making me look so good right now. But honestly, I'm kind of disappointed you didn't notice it was gone sooner. I've had it since the conference."

A laugh escapes me as I jump into his arms, wrapping my legs around his waist. "You little bitch," I whisper, grinning. "What a risky little game. I almost kicked your ass."

"I'm aware. You made my knees wobble a little when you stood up so aggressively. You pushed the couch back at least four inches."

Our movie was short-lived. We made it at least five minutes in before heading straight to bed, where we stay tangled together, skin to skin, wrapped in each other's arms.

When I stir in the morning, I'm startled to find Beckett still beside me, his arm draped protectively across my waist.

"Good morning, gorgeous," he murmurs, his lips brushing the back of my neck.

I blink, confused. "Why are you still home?" I ask as I roll over to face him.

He reaches around me and gives my bare butt cheek a light smack. "Get dressed. We're going for a drive," he says mischievously as he slides out of bed.

"Where are we going?" I ask, following after him.

THIRTY MINUTES LATER, WE PULL UP TO A SPRAWLING TWO-STORY house. The truck's engine rumbles to a stop in the driveway, right in front of the massive staircase leading up to the front door. My eyes widen as I take in the size of this place—it's enormous.

"Did you bring pantyhose?" I ask, lifting the center console to peek inside. Beckett gives me a confused look, his brow furrowing until I lean closer and whisper, "Aren't we going to rob these suckers?" I point a thumb at the house.

He bursts out laughing, shaking his head as he climbs out of the truck. He walks around to my side, offering his hand to help me down.

As we start up the wide steps leading to the entrance, the heavy front door swings open, revealing a woman with a smile that brightens when she sees Beckett. "Mr. Shaw, it's so good to see you again," she says warmly, extending her hand to Beckett like they're old friends. Her gaze then shifts to me, and she remains just as polite as she offers her hand.

"You have a beautiful home," I say softly, my gaze sweeping over the towering ceilings and pristine decor as we step inside. The space is so polished, elegant, and far removed from anything I'm used to. Even Beckett's condo is so nice that sometimes I feel completely out of place being in it. I wonder if he mentioned that I'm a walking disaster waiting to happen and that I'll probably break all kinds of stuff in here.

She looks slightly confused but quickly lets out a soft giggle, her expression smoothing into one of practiced politeness. "Feel free to explore at your leisure. I just need to make a quick call, but I'll be right outside if you need anything." She excuses herself as she closes the door behind her.

I shoot Beckett a questioning look, but he merely flashes a grin and guides me further into the house. As we wander, exploring the never-ending space, he casually asks, "How would you like to live in a house like this?"

I pause, looking around, imagining it. "I'd need a massive ballgown—one of those big, poofy ones, with high heels and a giant crown. I could walk around pretending I'm a princess," I joke. "Can't you just picture me making a grand entrance down the staircase?"

"I can see you taking one step in heels and tumbling the rest of the way down," he teases, turning to look at me with a smirk.

"Word." I playfully smack his arm.

We move from room to room, taking in the details of the house. When we reach the master bedroom, I wag my brows at him, a mischievous grin spreading across my face. "You're thinking about being naughty in here, aren't you?"

He smirks, leaning in just close enough to make my pulse quicken. "I'd be naughty with you in every room of this house."

We continue upstairs, discovering a home theater and a sprawling open room with gorgeous wood floors that gleam under the sunlight pouring in from the windows. At the far end, I spot a set of double doors leading to a balcony. I walk over, imagining all the potential of the space. "This room needs to be green," I say with conviction. I tell him that I'm going to paint my art room green, imagining the balcony doors open all day while I try my hand at painting.

"Why green?" he asks, tilting his head curiously.

"Doesn't it just feel like a green room?" I gesture around. "I'd fill it with paint and spend my days creating total trash, then force you to hang my masterpieces all over our house.

I'd even make a special painting for your office at work," I add, stepping in to kiss him.

He nods, kissing me back. "I like this idea."

"You should," I whisper seductively, "because it's going to be a collage of dicks."

He bursts into laughter, shaking his head. "Are we back to the dick jokes?"

"Maybe."

"So, what do we think?" The woman asks as she enters the room.

"It's beautiful," I admit, genuinely impressed by the home.

"Would you want to live in it?" Beckett asks, catching me off guard with the question.

"With her?" I ask, suddenly wondering if he's attempting to introduce me to some weird shit.

"No, babe. I want to buy it for us—if you like it."

I let out a surprised laugh, giving him a playful nudge. "We're not moving here, Beckett."

He turns to the woman, offering her a polite smile. "We'll be in touch."

Once we're in the truck, Beckett glances over at me, his brow creased. "You didn't like the house?"

My mouth falls open in bewilderment. "I loved it," I admit. I truly did. It was stunning, but I'm practical. I can't afford a house like that, ever, and I'm not going to play make-believe with Beckett over it.

His brow furrows. "You loved it, but you don't want it?"

"I love it, but I can't afford anything like that. And I'm certainly not going to leech off of you."

"It's not leeching. We're together, babe. This is us building a life together."

"I can't live off you for free."

"Okay, then you can pay part of the mortgage," he suggests, trying to keep his tone light.

I scoff. "You think I can afford part of that mortgage?"

He chuckles softly, turning the steering wheel as he pulls out of the driveway. "No, we'd split it fairly, based on each of our incomes and the total mortgage amount. That way, it's equitable for both of us."

I cross my arms, staring over at him. "I'm listening."

"I'd need to run the numbers to get an exact amount, but if I were to give you a ballpark figure, your part of the monthly bills would be about one."

"One?" I raise an eyebrow. "You mean one thousand?" I clarify.

"No, I mean one dollar," he deadpans.

"That's so dumb," I laugh, thinking he's just fucking with me.

He meets my gaze with a serious expression, not breaking his focus.

"A dollar, Beckett? You think I can only afford a dollar?"

"I'm going to buy the house outright. There won't be a mortgage. If you want to contribute something to make yourself feel better, you can pay whatever you choose. You don't need to worry about money—or your job," he narrows me with a firm gaze.

I roll my eyes. "You're adorable, babe. Can we get lunch?" I ask, effectively dismissing the conversation.

Chapter Twenty-Seven

I slump into the booth by the window of a small coffee shop, staring out at the snow falling in soft drifts outside. The rest of my time is spent scribbling out my bills, trying to figure out how much it would cost to live on my own. I haven't used any of the insurance settlement from the car accident yet, and with the fire settlement check coming soon, I know I'm not in a dire situation. But I don't want to live outside my means, and I want to stay on a budget of what I'm currently making. I'm not enjoying the reality of how expensive it's going to be. I grip my pen, the pressure of it nearly bending the cheap plastic.

Lost in thought, the sound of a voice breaks through the haze. "Do you know who I am?"

I glance up, startled, blinking at the woman standing in front of me. She looks vaguely familiar, though I can't quite place where I've seen her. She's older—mid-40s, maybe—and her eyes hold a strange intensity.

"I don't believe so. Have a good day." I try to keep my voice polite but distant, hoping that would be enough to send her on her way. I turn back to my papers, pretending to focus on the numbers, willing her presence away.

But instead of leaving, she pulls out the chair across from me, lowering herself down. Her eyes never leave me, and the silence stretches out so painfully, I want to slink down from the chair to the floor and crawl out of here.

"Oh sure, go ahead and sit," I mutter sarcastically, sitting up straighter as the wooden bench beneath me starts to feel hard and uncomfortable. She just stares, chewing on the inside of her cheek like she's thinking something over. It's unnerving. I notice her swollen belly—she's pregnant. It looks like she was due about three weeks ago.

I try to focus back on my papers, but any hope of concentration is gone. I don't have the patience for this. "Are you needing this table? Or are you... short on cash for coffee?" I ask, my voice edged with sarcasm. My gaze flickers between her belly and her face. She looks severely uncomfortable. She also probably shouldn't even be drinking coffee this far along, should she? And why is she here, staring at me like that? Is she in trouble? Maybe she needs a ride to the hospital, but the thought of a baby being born in my car makes me realize I would rather carry her to the hospital than to get afterbirth in my car.

I'm about to ask her if she's okay when she finally moves, her hand slipping into her coat pocket. Slowly, she pulls something out and holds it up—a pair of underwear, right there in the middle of the coffee shop. I blink rapidly, my attention shifting to the fabric dangling from her fingers, then to the people around us, half-expecting someone to start staring.

"Are these yours?" she asks, her voice steady, but there's something off in her tone—distant, like she's on autopilot.

I glance at them, recognizing the style but knowing I haven't seen mine in some time. "No," I say, shaking my head slowly. Then, because my brain decides to fall back on sarcasm in times of crisis, I add, "And even if I was unsure, which I'm not, you're definitely not the right gender to have possession of my underwear."

She doesn't laugh. She doesn't even blink. Her eyes remain locked on me, hollow and detached. "Is there a reason my husband would be?" she asks, her voice so quiet it barely carries, yet each word hits me like a punch straight to the gut.

I feel the blood drain from my face. Her husband. Holy shit. *Grant.*

The world tilts for a second as my heart thunders in my chest, the pieces falling together with brutal clarity—like a cruel jigsaw puzzle I never wanted to solve. I open my mouth, but no words come. I already know where this is headed, but I need to ask, as if hearing the answer will somehow undo it all. "Who's your husband?" The question sounds weak, shaky. I'm stalling, hoping for a reality that isn't coming.

"You know who my husband is," her voice sharp and brittle. Her gaze hardens, locking me in place. "Are you still sleeping with him?"

My throat constricts. "I didn't know he was married," I manage to say, my voice small and shaky. "I swear, I didn't know."

She sighs heavily, her eyes drifting down to her swollen belly. Her hand moves over it slowly, her fingers stroking the fabric of her coat like she's offering herself comfort more than the baby. "I know," she murmurs. "He's done this before. Told me he'd changed. That this was his way of proving he'd never be unfaithful again. But... here we are."

I feel a pang of sympathy for her. What a scumbag to cheat on his wife. This poor woman has to deal with so much pain. I can't even imagine how difficult this must be for her. I hope I never find out what this pain feels like.

"I'm sorry," I whisper, even though the words feel pathetically inadequate—meaningless in the face of everything she's had to endure.

But she doesn't answer. She just sits there, staring down at her hands, lost in her own private hell.

"We thought having a baby would solve our marital problems," she continues, her voice wavering. "But now he barely even touches me. I knew something was wrong after you talked to him that day. He swore he wasn't cheating, but he vanished afterward. He told me he went to your place to tell you he never wanted to see you again. Was that another lie?"

I feel trapped between the truth and the mess Grant has left in his wake. "He did come to my apartment, but not to say he never wanted to see me again," I answer honestly. "But I haven't been with him since."

Her eyes lock onto mine, searching for some form of truth she can hold on to. "Then why did I find your panties in his brand-new coat pocket?" Her voice cracks as she asks, the rawness of her pain cutting deeper into the guilt I already feel.

"I don't know." I struggle to find an explanation that makes sense. "I honestly don't know how that happened."

She takes a deep, shaky breath, and her tears spill over, streaming down her cheeks. She looks up at me, desperation in her broken gaze, as if I hold the key to easing her agony. "I'm speaking to you as a woman, as the mother of his child," she says, her voice trembling. "If you're still involved with my husband, I need you to end it. Please."

Before I can even muster a reply, she pushes herself up from the table, her sobs breaking through the quiet of the coffee shop. Every head in the room turns toward us as she rushes for the door, vanishing into the snow.

It looks like I just made a pregnant woman cry in public. But honestly, that's the least of my worries. I want to know how my underwear got in his pocket. How is that even possible? The whole situation feels unreal, like I've been yanked into someone else's nightmare. I gather my thoughts and hurry out of the coffee shop, making my way to Beckett's office.

As I approach the building, Beckett is just arriving back, heading toward the front entrance. I call out to him, waving to get his attention.

"Beckett!" I say, catching up with him. "You won't believe what just happened. I was at the Human CentaBean getting a coffee, and Grant's wife showed up. She sat at my table and accused me of still seeing Grant! She even had a pair of my underwear with her."

Beckett's face darkens with irritation as he processes this. "Why the hell did Grant have your panties?"

"I don't know!" I reply, anxiety creeping into my tone. "I think he might have been going into my apartment when I wasn't home. There were subtle signs—things out of place, clothes missing from my laundry basket. One day, I came home tired and found my blanket not folded how I left it, and my pillow was still warm. I had been gone for four hours."

Beckett's expression shifts to one of frustration. "Why are you just now telling me this?"

"I thought I was being paranoid," I admit.

His brows furrow as he studies me. "Has Grant tried to contact you since everything happened at your apartment?"

I shake my head. "No, he hasn't reached out at all." I thought he had moved on from whatever we were. Well, we weren't really anything. I was the unsuspecting homewrecker, too caught up in my own foolishness and heartbreak to acknowledge all the glaring signs that Grant was being a snake.

Beckett watches me, raising a brow. "What about at work? Any accidental run-ins? Have you seen him anywhere?"

I hesitate, thinking back over the past few weeks. "No… I haven't noticed him. But then again, I've been pretty distracted."

He leans in, looking thoroughly annoyed. "How long ago did all this start?"

"A couple of weeks," I answer, my gaze dropping as I think back. "His wife said the underwear was from a coat he'd just bought and had only worn once. So… do you think he's been carrying them around this whole time?" I feel a shiver of discomfort crawl up my spine. The thought of Grant walking around with my underwear in his pocket grosses me out. "Ew, what if he has a pair of my used underwear?" I wrinkle my nose in disgust. Suddenly, another horrifying thought hits me. "What if he even has a pair with, like, poop skids?" I blurt, trying to lighten the mood.

"Yuck, babe."

I grin teasingly. "You love my skiddies."

He shakes his head, his eyes crinkling at the corners. "I don't check your panties for marks, but now you've got me thinking you should probably just throw them away right after you wear them if you're unsure of your ability to wipe properly."

I chuckle at his response, taking his hand in mine as we walk to his office. "You don't think he had anything to do with the fire, do you?"

"No. The fire started in the top unit. Apparently, they were cooking drugs there."

I gasp, stopping mid-step. "What! I was living in a drug lab? Could I have gotten a contact high?"

Beckett smirks as he arches a brow. "Did you *feel* high?"

"I've actually never been high before, so I wouldn't really know," I admit, shrugging.

"This doesn't surprise me at all," he says, sitting at his desk.

"Want me to try to find some drugs and we can get freaky?" I wag my brows at him.

"You don't even need drugs to be freaky," he deadpans.

I wink at him. "Thanks."

I start to feel that needy feeling creeping in, and I have an urge to smother him with affection—or annoyance; he can decide. Grabbing the arm of my chair, I scrape it across his floor, dragging it to his side of the desk. Once my butt hits his chair, I turn around and plop down, satisfied I'm close enough. When I look at him, he's leaned on the arm of his chair, his chin resting on his knuckles, with his pointer finger tracing along his cheek, staring at me.

"What?" I ask, grabbing his arm and wrapping my arms around his bicep, squeezing while clenching my teeth. "I want to bite you," I confess as I lean in and sink my teeth into his bicep.

"Babe!" he exclaims, gently pushing my head back.

"Shh. Just go with it."

"Want me to bite you back?"

"Ooo, kinky," I grin.

I spend the next two hours showering him in my love: tousling his hair, licking his hand, biting his lip, nipping his ear, trying to undo his shirt, rubbing his crotch, and turning his chair toward me so I can bend over from my chair and wrap my arms around his waist. I guess the word he used is I'm being "annoying," but I'm sure what he really meant is that I'm being cute.

I tell him I'll get out of his hair and let him try to work because my overly affectionate, overly annoying mood isn't letting up, and I know he does need to work. I laugh when he readily agrees, walking me back to my car.

"If you prefer I stay, I can come back up—"

"I prefer you go home and wait for me to get off," he teases, kissing me as I start my car.

"Put your wiener in my mouth, and I'll have motivation to leave faster," I say, pinching his flaccid dick.

He laughs, shifting his hips to pull himself free from my fingers. "Babe. Go home."

"See you in a bit," I say with a bright smile, waving as I drive off.

I start to get that uneasy feeling in my stomach, the kind that tells you something's off. Glancing in the rearview mirror, I identify the same car has been behind me for the last few turns. At first, I chalked it up to coincidence, but now it feels intentional. The driver keeps a steady distance, like they're trying not to draw attention, but I can tell they're following me.

It's hard to make out the person behind the wheel, thanks to the dark windows and the glare of the sun. It's definitely not Grant's truck, but that doesn't mean it's not him. The car moves when I move, turns when I turn.

I switch lanes, testing the waters, and they do the same a few seconds later. My grip tightens on the steering wheel, heart picking up speed as I try to figure out my next move. Should I go home? Should I drive somewhere public? I don't want to lead them to Beckett's condo. I take a deep breath and turn on my blinker, heading toward a more crowded area, hoping that whoever's behind me won't dare follow. But the car stays glued to my tail.

Deciding to get to the bottom of this, I head straight for a nearby park—Grant's and my park, to be exact. I whip into the parking lot so fast that my car skids on the ice, fishtailing wildly. The dumbass behind me gets a front-row seat to the whole thing. The lot is mostly empty, so I drive all the way to the other side, watching to see if they follow. Sure enough, they do.

I throw the car into reverse and shoot back out of the lot, but they stay right on my tail. At the next entrance, I pull back in, speeding through the lot toward the same spot I was just in. I try to whip into a parking space, braking hard, but the ice takes control and spins me sideways, slamming me right up against the curb.

It would've been kind of impressive if the spots weren't supposed to be forward-facing. But now, my car's stuck. Looks like I'm not going anywhere for a while. If this dumbass gets close enough, I'm going to tell him he has to push the back of my car to help get me unstuck, since it's his fault my car is stuck on the curb now, anyway. But, the car doesn't come back.

The sidewalks are cleared of snow, but the grass is still blanketed. I keep my phone in hand, recording a video just in case something happens. If nothing does, I'll just delete the footage later. I manage to jog for about a minute before I'm winded—clearly, I'm more out of shape than I thought. I switch to walking for a couple of minutes, then pick up the pace again. As I jog past two girls filming a TikTok dance, I call out, "Your sock's untied," chuckling inwardly at my own humor.

On my return lap, a runner approaches and says, "Your shoelace is untied." I roll my eyes, thinking my earlier joke wasn't as funny as I thought. Turns out, he was being literal. I realize it as I step on the loose lace, trying to lift my foot to run. My other foot is already in motion, and they trip over each other, sending me crashing to my knees, then my hands, and finally flat on my stomach. But my face manages to avoid much damage, aside from my chin that scraped across the pavement too. I literally should just start log rolling off the side into the water.

I can already feel the sting of imminent blood and dread, looking at the damage. My phone lies just out of reach, its popsocket still open, the camera perfectly positioned to capture my fall from grace.

"Brynn, are you okay?" I hear Grant's voice before I even see him approaching.

"Get off me," I snap, shrugging him away as I roll into a sitting position. Staring at my knees, I see my leggings are torn to shreds, and my knees are definitely bleeding. The asphalt has left its mark on my skin. My palms took the brunt of the fall—now covered in blood. I wipe them on my sweatshirt, hoping to get a better view of what I'm working with, and well, it's not great.

"We need to get you to the hospital," Grant says, reaching for me again.

"Yeah, you're gonna need a hospital too, you slimy, stalking, two-timing, cheating, corn-nut-breath-smelling, puny imbecile," I say, grabbing my phone angrily as I stand. "You think I don't know you broke into my apartment and stole my underwear? I fart in those, you nasty underwear bandit."

"They were clean," he retorts.

"'They were clean,'" I mock. "Stay away from me!" I shout.

"HEY!" A voice calls out, and I look up to see three police officers approaching us. They have their hands on their holsters but haven't drawn their guns yet. "Put your hands where we can see them!" they command, and I immediately raise my hands. Grant follows suit.

"Did he hurt you?" the female officer asks.

"No," I admit.

I watch with a sense of satisfaction as the officers handcuff Grant. It's a small victory after everything that's happened, though I'm not sure what they are arresting him for.

"We have an ambulance on the way. Come with us so we can get you checked out," the officer says, and I follow her, glancing back at Grant. He looks furious as they search him, and when our eyes meet, I can't help but smirk before turning away.

"You can put your hands down," the officer reminds me. It dawns on me that I'm walking with my hands still raised.

As we reach the parking lot, I see the ambulance pulling in. The paramedics quickly get out and open the back doors, inviting me to sit inside so they can assess my injuries. I follow them and take a seat in the back of the ambulance, where a female and a male paramedic are ready to check me over.

"I'm pretty sure I just got road rash," I say, feeling self-conscious about the commotion over my fall.

"We'll need to cut your pants just above your knees," the female paramedic informs me as she pulls out scissors and starts cutting my leggings off up to mid-thigh.

"Now I look like a cyclist," I joke, but everyone remains focused and serious.

The officer climbs into the back of the ambulance, saying she needs to ask me some questions. I find myself recounting everything in detail, as if I'm involuntarily spilling my entire life story to this poor cop. I mention that I was recording a video of my jog, and the officer proceeds to play the footage. I can see the video showing me stumbling and falling face-first onto the pavement while I contemplate my life choices, followed by Grant approaching me.

Out of my periphery, I spot Beckett rushing out of his truck and charging towards us with a look of panic. An officer steps in to stop him, but Beckett side-steps him and nearly dives into the ambulance. "What happened?" His eyes are huge as he takes in my current state.

"Sir, you need to step out," the female officer in the ambulance says, trying to put my phone down and stand in his way.

"It's fine. He would be my one phone call," I interject, wanting them to know it's okay for Beckett to be here.

Everyone looks a bit puzzled, so I clarify. "Do people still get to make a phone call when they're in jail?" I try to lighten the mood despite the situation.

"You're not getting arrested," the officer says, settling back into the seat. She gestures toward Beckett and asks, "Who is this to you?"

"My ball and chain," I quip.

Beckett sits down beside me, shaking his head. "Why were you here? What happened? You were supposed to go straight home."

The officer holds up a hand. "Let me handle the questions, sir."

"I have proof that Grant was breaking into my apartment," I explain to Beckett, hoping he won't be as mad. "He admitted it, and I recorded the whole thing."

Beckett looks at me, confusion and concern etched on his face. "You came here to see if he would follow you? Why would you do that?" His hand comes to my face, lifting my chin to assess the damage. Then his gaze drops to my hands, which are now bandaged. "Christ, did he hurt you?"

"The only thing hurt here is my ego," I admit, glancing down at my bruised and scraped knees.

"And your car," Beckett nods to the parking lot. "Why is it smashed into the curb?"

I shake my head. "I'll tell you after you help push the back to get it unstuck."

I'm quite positive every single person in this ambulance thinks I'm the biggest idiot they've ever met. And I have to agree.

Once the paramedic finishes wrapping the last bandage around my scraped knees, I give my statement to the officer, replaying every painful detail. Each word feels like it's tugging at the bruises on my body. The adrenaline is long gone, leaving behind a raw ache in my limbs, making every step toward my car incredibly slow. My legs are heavy, my skin—or lack thereof—burns with each movement, and all I want is to curl up somewhere safe and disappear.

Just as I reach for the door handle, Beckett steps in front of me, his strong hand wrapping around my waist. "No way." His arm tightens around me, gently pulling me away from the car. "Preston can come get your car. You're coming with me."

The stubborn part of me wants to protest, but sense wins out. I shouldn't be driving, and I don't need to act big and tough in front of Beckett. He's my safe place. Plus, I'm pretty sure my rims are bent around the curb, so even if I wanted to be Billy Badass and try to drive, I don't think I could move my car.

Back at his condo, once we're settled in bed, he demands to see the video I took. I hand him my phone, and he watches every second of the footage with a frown. The video captures me stumbling and falling, then lying face-down on the pavement. Beckett's hand covers his mouth and nose in distress. His reaction makes me burst into laughter. He looks at me with a mix of horror and exasperation, which only makes me laugh harder.

"Maybe we should get you checked for second-hand drug inhalation after all," Beckett suggests, still staring at me with concern.

I lean back against the pillows, a reckless grin spreading across my face. "Want to have sex?"

"Yeah, but I'm really worried, babe," he admits, handing my phone back to me.

I take it and place it on the nightstand. "About what? Do we know if Grant was ever actually processed and booked into jail?"

"He was," Beckett confirms.

I grab my phone again and search for Grant's mugshot among the recent arrests. Seeing his booking photo brings me a surprising amount of satisfaction.

OUR NIGHT PRACTICALLY SUCKED. MY KNEES AND HANDS STILL burn from the fall, and the sharp sting makes it impossible for me to be on top. Every time Beckett touches me, he hesitates—his hands are too gentle, his movements too slow, like he's afraid I'll shatter. He asks if I'm okay, again and again, until the tenderness becomes suffocating. I can see the concern on his face, but instead of comfort, it only frustrates me. Neither of us can focus, and the tension builds like a wall between us.

Eventually, we give up, lying side by side, both of us achingly aware of the desire we can't satisfy. Silence stretches across the bed, heavy and uncomfortable. I close my eyes, but sleep takes its sweet time.

Morning feels no better, but Beckett accompanies me to the police station. My body feels stiff, and I'm more sore today than I was right after the fall. The detective—a no-nonsense woman with short, graying hair and tired eyes—sits across from us, her hands folded neatly on the desk, jumping right into briefing us.

"We searched Grant's phone," she says, her voice as steady as her gaze. "It appears he had numerous videos and photos of you, taken while you were around the community. Can you tell us more about your relationship with him?"

I nod, trying to stay calm. "I met him at the park a while back. We went on a couple of dates, but then I discovered he was married."

The detective raises a brow, her expression sharp and unyielding. "And the sexual nature of your relationship?"

Heat rushes to my face, and I fight to keep the embarrassment at bay. "I didn't know he was married," I repeat, the words feeling so dirty on my tongue.

Her eyes soften and shoulders relax. "Were you aware that he recorded the two of you having sex?"

The floor drops out from beneath me, and I just blink in rapid succession. "Excuse me? He... recorded us?"

"Yes," she confirms. "He had two videos."

Shock ripples through me. I look at Beckett, whose expression shifts from concern to rage in an instant, his jaw flexing. "Were these videos posted anywhere? Sent to anyone?" he demands.

The detective shakes her head. "Not that we can tell."

Beckett's grip on my hand tightens slightly, but he remains silent.

She continues, "We don't think Grant will be a problem any longer, but it would be wise to get a restraining order just to be safe."

I nod in agreement. Beckett squeezes my hand again, and we move through the motions, signing papers, filing forms, my mind elsewhere—back to the videos.

"Did you see the videos?" I turn to her just as we reach the doorway.

She falters, unprepared for the question, but finally nods. "Yes."

"Did I at least look good?"

The noise that comes from Beckett's throat makes me want to laugh. I glance at him and the detective, both of them staring at me like I've grown a second head. Beckett's eyes widen in disbelief as he gapes at me.

He clears his throat and shakes his head. "She gets utterly inappropriate when she's stressed. WE don't need to know how she looked. Thank you for your time." He places a firm hand on my back, guiding me out of the room, his head still shaking in disbelief.

I shrug as we walk down the hallway. "If there's a possibility that I have porn videos floating around the internet, I at least want to know if I look good."

From behind us, the detective's voice cuts through. "You looked bored. Rolled your eyes for the minute it lasted."

After handling the necessary paperwork for the restraining order, we leave the station. Beckett walks beside me. I can tell that he's mad, but he's doing his best to act like he's not.

Chloe's finally back in town today, and I've been keeping the recent drama with Grant under wraps to spare her the stress while she was away working. But I know I can't avoid it forever. Maybe I'll call her tomorrow. Or wait a few more days until my palms and face don't look like they've been through a shredder.

Beckett and I are lounging on the couch when the sound of his elevator doors opening makes us both turn our heads. Blake steps out, looking effortlessly put together, as always. She walks toward us with her usual grace. The look of horror on her face when she sees me is almost comical.

She tries numerous times to ask what happened, but each time, Beckett shuts her down with a firm look or a quick change of subject. I can see she's getting irritated every time he does it, the way her eyes dart between us.

Finally, after realizing Beckett won't budge, she shifts tactics. "Do you work tomorrow?" she asks him.

"Yeah, I've got meetings all day."

She doesn't hesitate, turning to me with a smile. "Perfect. Then you and I are having lunch, just the two of us."

We settle into the small café, and Blake wastes no time. She leans in, eyes wide with concern. "Alright, spill. What in the world happened?"

I find myself staring down at my plate, pushing my salad around aimlessly with my fork. I don't mind sharing the details—I just don't know where to start. I want to make it clear that she bears no responsibility for what went down. This isn't her fault. It was my own jealous immaturity that set everything in motion.

"Beckett told me about Grant. That was his name right? Is he the one who did this to you?"

"Technically, no. I did all this to myself." I gesture to my injuries—my bandaged hands, the bruise on my face, and the scrapes on my knees.

Blake's expression shifts slightly, her brows furrowing. "I bet Beckett was furious when he found out Grant was following you. When Beckett's PI texted him about your stalker showing up at the park, he called the cops right away. He must have sensed something was off."

"PI?"

"Oh, yeah," Blake waves it off as if it's nothing. "Private investigator. Beckett hired him just to make sure you were safe. He was probably worried sick."

I nod, forcing myself to hold it together. Beckett was the one having me tailed. *I knew I was being followed;* I just assumed it was Grant. Well, he was too. I had two people following me. That's annoying as fuck.

I don't want Blake to think I'm bothered, so I push through lunch with a fake light-hearted conversation.

I'm consumed by anger during the entire drive home, each mile amplifying my frustration. I picture myself storming into Beckett's office, striding right up to him, and slapping him across the face. The thought sends a rush of adrenaline through me, a flicker of satisfaction igniting in my mind.

I can almost see his expression—shock and confusion painting his features as he watches me, mouth hanging open, completely blindsided, with no clue what brought that on other than the fact that he obviously pissed me off somewhere along the line.

As soon as I step back into Beckett's place, I move on autopilot, my emotions swirling too intensely to form coherent thoughts. I start throwing clothes into my suitcase, haphazardly packing half my belongings into the car. The rest? He can toss them or leave them in the lobby for me to grab later; I don't care.

I'm so mad. It's not even just directed at him. I'm mad at myself for allowing his actions to dictate my feelings. His "date" with someone else ignited this chaos, and now, with the added annoyance of him hiring a private investigator, I feel cornered. I put myself in danger by confronting Grant in the park, fueled by reckless emotion rather than clear judgment. Maybe I'm missing my brain. Or at least the critical thinking part, because damn, I'm dumb as fuck.

The only time I suspected that I was even being followed, I assumed it was Grant—only; wasn't it? Sure, the PI was following me, but Grant was at that park. He knew that I was there and came at just the right time after I had fallen. That's too much of a coincidence. He had to have been watching me too.

I call Chloe and ask if the offer still stands of me staying with her for a while, and she eagerly agrees. When I get to Tom's, her mouth falls open as her and Tom both ask if I'm okay.

I had forgotten the state of my appearance—my bandaged hand—and though I probably should have kept it on longer, I took the bandage off my chin because I felt ridiculous.

"I was on my way here when the doctor's office called and asked if I could come in today instead. If you're not busy, will you come with me?" I ask Chloe, not wanting to go alone. My appointment was supposed to be tomorrow to have all my wounds checked out, and Beckett was supposed to come with me, but that's definitely not happening. So, this works out a lot better for me.

"Yes, oh my god, what happened?" she asks, sounding panicked.

"Come with me and I'll tell you everything."

In the waiting room, I recount every unsettling encounter with Grant. I start with our first meeting and how it began from the chaotic incident at the restaurant when I saw Beckett with someone else—the pain and rage I felt that he was moving on from what I thought we had, only to discover he was with his sister. I talk about the confrontation at his office and the shock of running into Grant and his pregnant wife. I share how I became convinced Grant was following me and decided to confront him at the park. As I show her the video, her face shifts from curiosity to horror, mirroring Beckett's reaction.

"How is it that you've managed to avoid men and all this drama for twenty-five years, and now you have more problems than I've ever had in my entire life?"

"No shit. Ridiculous, huh?"

"Is Grant still in jail?"

"No, he was released. Beckett has been keeping me updated—probably with the help of his stupid PI." I grimace at the fact he was having me followed, more so because Beckett thinks I'm helpless. Now that I think back, I wonder how long I was being followed because just a couple days ago, I was trying to throw away a napkin and dropped my phone in the trash, having to take the lid off the garbage and dig through it to find my phone. That was certainly the highlight of my day, and I can only imagine Beckett's reaction if he heard that I was digging in a garbage along a busy sidewalk in broad daylight. Without any context, I probably looked like I was scrounging for food.

After my doctor's appointment, Chloe drives us back to her house. Every part of me aches from the wound cleaning and fresh bandaging.

I settle into the guest bedroom for a moment of quiet, but it doesn't last long. I wander downstairs to find Chloe and Tom in hushed conversation. I can only guess she's filling him in on my latest mishaps. When Tom catches my eye, he offers a sympathetic smile before excusing himself, leaving us alone.

"Am I being too hard on Beckett?" I huff as I slump onto the couch next to her.

"No! He can't just have you followed like that," she says, confirming I'm not being overly dramatic.

When Beckett's name flashes on my phone for the fifth time, I hesitate before finally answering, my pulse already racing. His voice comes through frantic as he says, "Does he have you?!"

"Who? Grant or your PI?" I snap angrily.

There's a long silence on the other end. "Babe—"

"Don't 'babe' me," I interrupt. "You were having me followed! Who even are you?"

"Just let me explain—" he starts.

"No, Beckett. I just dealt with a stalker, and that shit is creepy. You want to do that bullshit, go do it with someone else," I say, my heart racing as I hang up the call.

And then I cry.

And cry.

For three days.

And for three days, Chloe sleeps in bed with me, holding me all night.

Two miserable weeks drag by, my heart crumbling more each day. The longer I'm away from Beckett, the more my mind tries to make excuses for him and justify how what he did was okay. I mean, it does show how much he cares for me, right?

"Is it weird that I kind of find it sexy that he hired someone to make sure I was safe?" I murmur, laying my head on Chloe's lap while she plays with my hair.

"Yes, Brynn, that's very weird. Never admit that out loud," she says. "We are mad at him, don't forget that."

I want to be mad at him. I do. I don't like that he still treats me like a child, but I like that he cares about me. Or at least I thought he did. Maybe he never really did.

"If it wasn't for him hiring a private investigator to follow me, the cops wouldn't have gotten there and arrested Grant," I tell her, almost defending Beckett's actions. No—*DEFINITELY* defending his actions. Had it not been for the PI, I would probably have been arrested for hurling Grant over the rail into the water.

I should be upset. I have every right to be. Yet, as I lie here, I wonder what he's doing. I ache to call him, to be in his arms. This is probably another one of the times where he's waiting for me to contact him. But he's the one who messed up. Not me. I shouldn't have to call him. And he hasn't tried even once to contact me.

CHAPTER Twenty-Eight

wake up determined to keep my life as normal as possible, so I jump straight into work, tackling orders as soon as I finish getting ready. It does keep me busy for the first couple hours—enough to push most unwanted thoughts away. Whenever a delivery brings me near my apartment, I drive by. Each time I approach, I pray it won't really be burned, or at least not as bad as what I remember. But when I see the charred remains, I just stare.

I wonder what kind of drugs someone would be cooking to cause such a massive fire. I keep hoping no one got caught in it. There haven't been any reports of casualties so far, at least that's a relief. I wonder how Nancy and Taco are faring in all of this. I wouldn't mind hearing her bang on the ceiling one more time, curled up in bed... with Beckett.

My phone vibrates on my dash, Chloe's beautiful photo and name lighting up the screen. "Hello, my darling," I answer, giving our apartment a final look, turning around to leave.

"Hey, I need you to pick something up for me and then come home," she says, sounding a bit off.

"Sure. What do you need?"

There's a pause before she finally says, "A pregnancy test."

My heart skips a beat. "You're pregnant?!" I almost shout. I'm thankful she can't see me because my jaw practically fell to the floor.

"I don't know. That's why I need you to get a test and bring it to me."

Apparently, Chloe and I wanted to make sure this year was jam-packed full of so much drama that it could fill us up for years to come—perhaps even competing with each other for who can out-drama the other. I thought for sure I would win this battle, but pending the results of this test, Chloe might have me beat by a mile.

I head to the store and pick up two boxes of pregnancy tests, the plastic bag rustling as I carry them. When I step inside the house, I call out, "Chloe?"

"I'm in here," she responds weakly from the bedroom.

She's still lying in bed, looking pale and sweaty, with a bowl placed nearby. "You look green," I say, trying to gauge her condition. "Are you okay?" I realize that commenting on her appearance might not be the most supportive approach.

I don't remember her looking this bad last night. How had I not noticed she was sick? Actually, I haven't left my room for two days. And for the two days, Mark has been bringing me dinner on a tray, saying I should really eat something.

Chloe stirs beneath the covers. "Just give me a test," she mumbles, her hand emerging to push aside the blankets in a weary motion.

I open one of the boxes, hand her a test still sealed in its packaging, and offer it to her. She slowly rises from the bed and shuffles toward the bathroom. I follow closely behind, ready to offer support no matter what the results might be.

She caps the test, slipping it back in the packaging, and hands it back to me. I take it from her and carefully set it on the counter, each passing second dragging by as we wait. After she washes her hands, she walks over to me, wrapping her arms around my waist. I hold her, feeling completely nervous for her.

"If it's positive, will you be okay?"

A heartbeat of silence passes before she responds. "Yeah."

Maintaining our hold, I reach behind me to grab the test. As I extract it from its packaging, my breath catches in my throat. Two vivid pink lines stare back at me. "How many lines mean positive?" I ask, trying to keep my voice calm.

"Two lines mean positive, but we need to wait three minutes for the result to be definitive."

I mentally count the lines just to make sure I'm seeing them correctly. One... two. "I don't think we need to wait," I say gently, "because there are already two pink lines."

Chloe pulls away suddenly. "What?!" she exclaims, snatching the test from my hand. Her gaze locks on the small window, her jaw hanging slightly open in disbelief. "Holy shit," she breathes. "I thought I was just being dramatic."

"Does Tom know?"

Her head shakes slowly from side to side, her trembling fingers coming to rest on her quivering mouth as she covers it. "No," she whispers, "I'll tell him when he gets home."

"When do you have to leave for work?"

She lets out a heavy sigh, tearing her eyes away from the small plastic stick in her hands. "I was supposed to leave yesterday, but I had to call in sick because I was vomiting. Now I don't even know what to do."

We retreat to the living room and sit in silence, waiting for Tom to get home. She stretches out on the couch, her head resting in my lap. "Will you play with my hair?" she asks softly.

I oblige, my fingers gently threading through her greasy hair. "Chloe?"

"Yeah?"

"You need to shower. Your hair is so greasy it's making my fingers wet."

"I'm pregnant," she says with a small smile. "You have to be nice to me."

"I'm being as nice as possible. But your hair is making me want to hurl." I try to word it delicately, not wanting to hurt her feelings, but then we both start laughing.

"Dick," she mumbles. "Then massage my back."

I comply, letting us sink into silence once again. She cries softly, and I don't say anything, knowing that she's probably working through the fact that she's becoming a mother and all the changes it will bring. If she wants to talk, I am here for her. But for now, I will just offer my silent support and reassurance.

When the garage starts to open, she sits up abruptly, her eyes widening with panic. "Okay, this is fine. Tell me everything is fine," she repeats to herself frantically, trying to calm herself. "Tell me everything is fine."

"Everything will be fine," I assure her. "I'm gonna go back to my room," I tell her, preparing to give her privacy.

She reaches out and grasps my hand. "Stay. Please," she implores, her voice filled with desperation.

"Okay," I acquiesce, settling back beside her as we wait for Tom.

Tom walks in and smiles when he sees her. "You still feeling pretty bad?" he asks tenderly, leaning down to kiss her.

Chloe nods, her hand shaking slightly as she pulls the pregnancy test out of her sweatshirt pocket. Tears well up as she hands it to Tom. His expression goes from confusion to surprise, and then realization dawns on him. His eyes shift between the test and Chloe, until he finally covers his mouth with his hand as tears fill his eyes. He sits next to her, wrapping her in a hug. After a brief pause, he pulls back, a smile breaking through his tears.

"We're having a baby?" he asks, overcome with tears of joy.

"Yeah," she nods, her voice quivering.

"This is wonderful," he says, hugging her again.

Tom is seven years older than Chloe, so I can't understand why she was worried he would react negatively. He handles the news exactly how I expected a mature man in his thirties would—especially since they have talked about starting a family several times.

When Mark arrives home, they share the exciting news with him too. His face lights up with happiness and he jokes about needing to plan for a move because he has the second biggest room in their house—perfect for a nursery. Chloe laughs and tells him he can stay as long as he wants; they would love to have a live-in nanny anyway. The room fills with laughter, but I know that once the baby arrives, Chloe will probably take all the help she can get.

The next morning, Chloe books a last-minute cancellation at the doctor's office for that afternoon. Although she is relieved to have an appointment scheduled, there is an underlying sense of anxiety. When Tom emerges from their bedroom dressed and ready to go, it's clear how much he's already stepped into the role of protector. He holds the door open for her with gentle care—just like Beckett used to do for me. There's tenderness in the way he helps her into their SUV, making sure she's comfortable and his hands never straying far from her back or holding hers gently.

I notice the parallels between Tom's actions towards Chloe and Beckett's previous behavior towards me. My heart twists with the memory and I feel a twinge of longing for that kind of attention—his attention. That deep-rooted sense of being cared for. Tom keeps focusing on Chloe, his expression overflowing with pure love. Each time he looks her way, it's clear he's cherishing every moment.

As we drive to the appointment, I sit quietly in the back, observing them through the gap between the front seats.

Tom's hand never leaves hers, his thumb stroking over her knuckles in a soothing rhythm. Chloe leans into him, her anxious breaths gradually calming. There's something so genuine, so unwavering in the way he supports her that evokes a wave of admiration mixed with a tinge of bittersweet yearning for what I once had.

As we enter the doctor's office, I start to feel nervous for her even though I know she's excited. The waiting room is filled with couples and expecting mothers at various stages of their journey. Tom and Chloe are still holding hands as they go to check in at the front desk. I find a seat in the corner and wait for them to join me.

"I can't believe this is really happening," Chloe whispers as she sits next to me.

I give her shoulder a reassuring squeeze. "You're going to be an incredible mom, Chloe."

Tom beams with pride, looking every bit the expectant father-to-be. "Yes, you will be," he adds, giving Chloe's hand another gentle squeeze.

When Chloe's name is finally called, we all rise together. As we walk down the hallway, I take in each framed photo on the walls—tiny newborns cradled in their parents' arms, families frozen in moments of pure bliss. It feels almost surreal to think that soon, one of those faces could be theirs.

The nurse leads us into a cozy examination room, and Chloe is handed a light pink gown. "You can change into this, and the doctor will be in shortly," she says before slipping out.

Behind the privacy screen, I can hear the rustling of fabric as Chloe changes into the gown. Tom and I settle into chairs by the examination table, his knee bouncing slightly betraying the nerves he's trying so hard to keep in check. "Can you believe we're about to see the baby?"

"I'm so excited for you guys," I reply with a smile. "Do you want me to record both of your reactions to seeing the baby?"

"Do you mind?"

Chloe emerges from behind the screen, now dressed in the gown and climbs onto the examination table. Any nervousness she had earlier seems to have melted away, replaced by a calm anticipation. "Okay, let's do this," she says, taking a deep breath.

The door opens, and the doctor walks in with a friendly smile on her face. "Good afternoon, everyone. Ready to see your baby? We should be able to get an estimate on how far along you are."

We all nod eagerly, and then the doctor chats with Chloe as she prepares the ultrasound equipment. She asks her how she's been feeling and makes small talk to help put her at ease. Tom holds her hand, his thumb stroking the back of it in a soothing motion.

I pull out my phone and begin recording, making sure to capture both Chloe and Tom's reactions along with the ultrasound machine in the background.

The doctor smiles gently and says, "Alright, let's take a look," as she applies warm gel to Chloe's stomach. The soft hum of the ultrasound machine fills the room, and the wand glides effortlessly over her belly. The monitor flickers with static, and we all hold our breath. Then, as she adjusts the wand, the image sharpens and slowly, a tiny form emerges on the screen.

In that instant, the room falls completely still. Every breath, every thought is focused on the delicate life dancing across the monitor. It's so small, but undeniably there—a tiny figure, jumping off the jelly walls. The delicate curve of a head, the faint outlines of arms and legs, and the beating heart. It's breathtaking.

Chloe's eyes are glued to the screen, wide and glistening with emotion. "Wow." Her voice breaks as tears slip down her cheeks. She's no longer just Chloe—she's this tiny human's mom.

Tom's eyes brim with awe and love, his features softening as he leans in, as if being closer might make it all feel more real. "That's our baby." His voice catches, and though he swallows hard, the emotion still rises, tears pooling and glistening in the dim light of the room.

A lump forms in my throat, and I feel my heart swell as I try to steady my phone, capturing every precious second. The happiness radiating from Tom and Chloe is infectious, and I feel incredibly lucky to witness this.

"Why does it already look so big?" I ask. I thought it would look like a bean or something. This actually looks like a fully formed baby.

The doctor nods in agreement as she begins taking measurements, gliding the wand over Chloe's belly. "The baby does look bigger than I was expecting," she notes, studying the screen carefully. "Let's see...ah, you're further along than expected. It looks like you're already 16 weeks," she says in a stunned tone. "And... I can see the gender. Would you like to know, or would you prefer to keep it a surprise?"

Chloe and Tom look at each other, answering together, "No." Chloe adds, "The baby was surprise enough. We want to know the gender."

The doctor chuckles at their synchronized response and adjusts the wand slightly, pointing to a tiny spot on the screen. "If you look here, between those tiny legs…you're having a girl."

Chloe gasps, her hand flying to her mouth in disbelief. Her eyes snap to Tom, who's already grinning from ear to ear. "A girl? We're having a daughter?" she repeats, her voice cracking with joy.

"We're going to have a daughter," he says, his voice filled with pride. He leans down and kisses Chloe's forehead, whispering something to her that makes her smile even wider.

I'm smiling so hard my cheeks hurt. "A little girl! This is amazing. She's going to be so loved."

Chloe nods, her face wet with tears, but laughter bubbles through her sobs. "I can't believe I didn't know sooner. How did I miss this?"

The doctor wipes away the gel from Chloe's belly. "It happens more often than you'd expect," she reassures them both with a kind nod. "Some women don't experience many early symptoms, and by the time they notice, they're already well into the second trimester. But everything looks great. She's healthy, and you're doing wonderfully."

Chloe wipes her cheeks with shaky hands. "I've been having really bad morning sickness only recently. That's not usual, is it?"

The doctor's reassuring tone and kind words put Chloe at ease. "Morning sickness varies for every woman," she explains. "Some experience it early on, and for others, it hits later. It's all within the realm of normal."

Exhaling a long, relieved breath, Chloe rests a protective hand over her stomach. "Thank you," she says gratefully to the doctor.

Tom can't seem to stop smiling as he helps Chloe sit up. "We need to start planning for everything—nursery, names, baby shower… I can't believe we're going to have a little girl," he says in awe.

Chloe wipes away the last of her tears. "It's all happening so fast, but I'm so happy. I can't wait to meet her."

Over the next couple days, nursery items are delivered to the house. We've been busy preparing the nursery for Chloe throughout the week, staying up really late to build the furniture. But once I'm in the comforts of my own bed every night, I cry myself to sleep. Beckett hasn't even tried once to call me. Asshole.

I swipe away my tears, thinking about the times when we were good, when we were happy. And I fall asleep to a happy me and Beckett.

CHAPTER Twenty-Nine

When I wake up, the remnants of sleep cling to me, gently pulling me back into a dream state. For a fleeting moment, I smile, unaware that Beckett's absence still looms over me like a shadow. The realization of another day without him begins to creep in, but I try to hold onto that warmth a little longer.

Every day, my stubbornness solidifies. I refuse to make the first move, and his silence feels like a clear message. Maybe I should take the hint. Today feels heavier, laden with an urge to curl up and cry, but I push against it. I won't let myself be reduced to tears.

As I step out of my bedroom, I catch a faint sound, almost like Beckett's voice echoing through the air. I must still be half-asleep, even though it's early afternoon.

"I won't go away, Chloe. I will come back every day until you let me talk to her."

The door clicks shut, followed by a soft lock. Chloe rounds the corner, halting, as if I've stumbled upon a secret. "Good... morning... well, I guess it's the afternoon now," she says, looking like a child caught with her hand in the cookie jar.

"Who's at the door?" I ask.

She brushes past my question, her eyes scanning the fridge for ingredients. "Wrong house," she replies casually. "Want breakfast or lunch?"

"Sure," I respond, sinking into a chair at the island counter. "How's the morning sickness?"

Her face lights up. "Better today! My doctor suggested preggo pops, so if you see me with suckers all day, that's the reason," she says, rummaging through the fridge for ingredients.

I'm assuming my subconscious is missing Beckett badly today. That's why I was hearing him. I hesitate, staring at his contact, debating whether I should call him—my finger hoverers over the call button, sliding up and down the screen, caught in a cycle of indecision. Then I behold the red words: 'Unblock Caller.' UNblock. He's blocked... from my end.

"Chloe..." I lift my gaze to her as she starts cracking eggs. "Did you block Beckett?"

A flicker of hope ignites in my chest, a small ember that maybe, just maybe, he hasn't been ignoring me.

Her face fills with guilt as she sighs, preparing to say something. Just as she looks up, her eyes dart behind me, and she gasps. The egg slips from her hand, splattering across the counter.

"What?" I turn to see what's caught her attention.

And then I see him—Beckett standing at the back door, looking devastatingly handsome yet weary. The entire wall is practically a window, giving a view of the sprawling backyard. "I'm not leaving," he states, and my heart skips a beat.

"Damn him," Chloe mumbles under her breath, storming around the counter with a fierce determination as she yanks open the wide sliding glass door.

Before she can say a word, Beckett reaches out and guides her aside, his eyes locked on mine.

"I'm not leaving," he repeats, his voice rough with emotion. "I can't do this anymore. I need you. I want you to come home. No more games, no more distance."

I swallow hard. "Have you tried to call me?" My voice wavers, barely holding back the tears that threaten to spill. I convinced myself he was done with me—that the silence meant he had moved on. Each day he didn't call felt like another confirmation. But when I saw his number was blocked, I knew he had been trying to contact me.

"Every day, about one hundred times," he replies, inching closer to me.

"You've been here?" I rise from my seat.

"Every single day," he confirms. "I understand why you won't let me see her, Chloe. You're protecting your best friend, and I thank you for loving her enough to do so. But I love you, Brynn. I loved you the moment we met, I love you today, and I'll love you tomorrow. Just talk to me. Please," he pleads, now just a foot away from me.

"I don't even know what's real anymore," I whisper, caught in the whirlwind of emotions swirling between us.

He takes a step closer until we're toe to toe. "Then let me tell you," he says desperately.

"I'll give you guys some space," Chloe says, excusing herself to her bedroom.

We sit on the couch, an uncomfortable distance between us. I stare at the floor, my hands clenched together, while Beckett's gaze weighs heavy on me. The silence stretches until he finally speaks.

"How far back do you want me to go?"

"The beginning," I meet his gaze.

He takes a deep breath, glancing towards the window before settling back on me. "I saw you in your car... something about you just pulled at me. I had Preston follow you. We followed you for hours. Even through dinner with your friends. I sat at the table next to yours so I could listen to you talk. I was so drawn to you, I can't explain the pull I felt." He pauses, running a hand through his hair. "We followed you home, then waited outside your apartment the next morning. When you left, we followed you again."

His words should probably make me feel uneasy, maybe even freaked out. But they don't. Not in the slightest. In fact, they only reinforce the deep connection I've always felt with him.

"We watched as you sat outside someone's house, waiting for your passenger. The way he yelled when he finally came out... I could hear him from the next house over, cursing as he threw his stuff into your car. I wondered why you didn't drive off right away. Suddenly, you sped forward and slammed on your brakes, causing your passenger to slam into the back of your seat before quickly buckling up. It was then that I realized…"

He looks at me, his eyes dark with memory. "I knew I had to get closer. At the red light, we pulled up beside you. You looked annoyed, and I could see him still talking, still getting under your skin. You kept glancing at us... I told Preston to leave enough space, figured you were trying to cut us off. But then—" He hesitates, his jaw clenching. "As you know, we were hit at the light."

He takes a breath, searching for any reaction. "When I saw you drive off, I was furious, but when you pulled right over, I took my chance. Got in your car. I knew better than to make the same mistake as your previous passenger, and I buckled up right away. Everything kept working in my favor," he admits. "I had a buddy that was a sheriff—he set up that roadblock. There wasn't actually a wreck, but the roads were getting really bad, so he texted me and said we needed to hurry before we all get stranded out there. The drunk driver... that was the only thing we didn't expect."

I look at him, my mind spinning as I try to comprehend why he went to such lengths for someone he didn't even know. All those chance encounters, the times we ran into each other—it wasn't fate. He had orchestrated every one of them.

"I thought if I could spend enough time with you alone, maybe the pull you had on me would fade. I expected that we'd hook up at the hotel and was dumbfounded when you not only never slept with me, but you acted so uninterested.

Every day after, I spent convincing myself you weren't interested in me. I told myself I'd let you go unless you made the next move first, but you never did. God, it pissed me off that you never ever tried reaching out, not even once. The seconds dragged into endless days of no contact. I kept thinking, 'This is it, I'm done,' but then I'd cave. I'd find another excuse to see you, to be near you, because… I couldn't stand the thought of losing that spark between us. But you never gave me anything to hold onto."

"Did you plan on bringing me to the hotel just to try to sleep with me?"

He blinks, caught off guard by the question. "What?"

"You forced your way into my bed, but you never tried to sleep with me. You literally slept with me but never… 'slept' with me. That's confusing."

He looks down, then back at me, his expression softening. "That first night in the hotel, we were both freezing. I figured we'd be warmer together, and honestly, I just wanted to be close to you. The second night… you were tossing and turning so much, I thought if I laid on top of you, it might calm you down. It worked. Your shirt rode up while you slept, and I couldn't help but stare. You were so beautiful, so perfect."

His voice falters for a second. "After that, every time we slept together, the same thing would happen. You'd start moving, and I'd… lay on you to calm you. That first time your shirt rode up, it was an accident. But after that… I helped it along."

"You were intentionally pulling my shirt up?" My eyes widen in surprise, I decide I like that he did it. As I stare, a smile starts to form.

"Based on your reaction the first time it happened naturally, you didn't try to gouge my eyes out or kick me in the dick, so I did it again… intentionally. And you never had a negative reaction, so I kept doing it."

"Why did you never just tell me how you felt?"

"Why do *you* never tell *me* how you feel?" he counters.

"What about the double date with Elliot? That was such a dick move."

"I'm slightly fuzzy on the details," he starts, rubbing the back of his neck. "Elliot and I were in the elevator. I wasn't really paying attention to him until he mentioned taking you out on a date. That's when I invited myself along." His brows furrow slightly as he recalls the scene.

"Rachelle is an old friend," he continues. "I asked for her help because I couldn't bear the thought of you going on a date with him. She agreed to play along, saying 'If you want her that badly, I'll help you get her.'"

I raise my eyebrows. "And Chelsea? You practically gave me a verbal lashing when I came to your office."

He sighs, looking remorseful. "She had just complained about employees barging into her office without knocking, saying there was no respect in the workplace. I assured her I'd address it and then you walked in. She said, 'This is exactly what I'm talking about,' and I reacted poorly."

I sit there, blinking. Chelsea isn't someone who would just allow someone to walk into her office unannounced and not say something if it bothered her. Could she have known I was going to his office? Did she set me up? That's sure how it feels.

"And the PI?"

His face hardens. "Grant had a history of stalking and as soon as I found out, I hired someone to keep an eye on you while you were working. I needed to make sure you were safe. I won't apologize for it because the PI is the reason the police showed up when they did. He got them there in time to arrest him."

I sit here, absorbing everything he's told me. I've already decided that, no matter what, I'm going to forgive him for hiring a PI. He's always hated my job, and deep down, I know he just wants to protect me. I didn't expect the rest of it, but I'm choosing to accept it—because I accept all his quirky, creepy, and stalking-of-his-own tendencies.

"You have to chill," I give him a pointed look.

His response is instant and firm. "No."

This catches me off guard, and I blink as I stare at him.

"I'm in love with you. I can't 'chill' when it comes to you."

I chew on the inside of my lip, mulling over his words, and then I smile. "You creepy, sexy motherfucker," I say as I dive into his arms and kiss him.

He holds me tight, his arms wrapped around me. "Will you come home now?"

I shake my head, meeting his gaze. "That's not my home."

"Babe—"

"I want that house."

He smiles and leans up, capturing my lips again. "Put your hand in my pocket," he says between kisses.

I hesitate, then nod, biting my lip as I lean in to kiss him again, sliding my leg over his, my fingers reaching into his pocket toward his cock. I hope he knows I can't jerk him off from inside his pocket, but I'll try my best. Instead of what

I expect, I feel something unfamiliar—paper? Confused, I ignore it, trying to move the pocket over more to his dick.

He lets out a laugh. "Just pull out the item instead of pushing it to the side. I wasn't asking for a hand job."

A pout forms, but I obey, digging a little deeper. My fingers close around a small object, not just a piece of paper like I thought—metal. I pull it out and stare, blinking at the shiny key in my hand, with a note attached: *Welcome Home.*

Looking up at him, confused, he smiles. "I didn't know what shade of green you wanted for your art room, so I bought every shade of green the store had," he says, his eyes glazing over with moisture.

EPILOGUE

Two years later

The sun shines brightly over our backyard, bathing everything in a warm golden glow. A perfect day unfolds, the kind that feels almost too good to be true. The air is filled with laughter and the sweet scent of blooming flowers, mingling with the faint sound of music drifting from the speakers.

A colorful arch of blue balloons on one side and pink on the other stretches across a large part of the yard, a whimsical pop of color that captures the essence of our celebration. Behind it, the sprawling trees stand with their leaves dancing in the gentle breeze, creating a picturesque backdrop for our baby shower gender reveal.

I wear a pink dress that highlights my growing baby bump. At five months along, I feel radiant. The theme of the baby shower is for everyone to dress in colors reflecting their guess for the baby's gender. Beckett stands beside me, looking effortlessly handsome in a crisp blue button-up shirt paired with a pink tie. He says he doesn't care what gender the baby is—just for him or her to be healthy.

The party planners scurry around, putting the final touches on the decorations. Chloe and Tom arrive early to lend a hand. As they help set up, Chloe's baby bump is visible under her flowing dress, already four months along with her son, Thomas. She and Tom are thrilled to be expanding their family, and I admire how effortlessly she balances being a stay-at-home mom. Their daughter, Charlotte, is a whirlwind of more energy than me, Beckett, Tom, and Chloe all combined. She's a year and a half now and keeps us all on our toes. Most days, Chloe brings her over to my house, and we revel in the chaos together.

As we wait for the guests to arrive, I think about how hard it is for me to wrap my head around the fact that I'm carrying Beckett's baby. It still feels surreal, but I'm filled with joy at the thought of our little nugget joining our family.

I find so much joy in all the little things, like how I currently watch Beckett carry Charlotte over to the cupcakes. He grabs one from the stand, swipes his finger through the pink frosting, and licks it clean. Then, he takes Charlotte's tiny finger, does the same, and helps her bring it to her mouth. She giggles, trying to devour the whole cupcake in one go. When he catches me watching them, he winks at me and my heart flutters.

KALIOPE

I am so in love with this man.

It's crazy to think about how much our lives have changed and grown since we first met three years ago. It's been one hell of a ride with him. Our love has blossomed into something truly special. He never gave up on letting me know constantly how much he hated me driving for ExpressWay. I actually got so tired of the constant griping over it, I decided to hang my hat and call it quits.

I did take up painting. Scratch that—I attempted to take up painting, but my attention span is equivalent to that of a gnat. I told Beckett I'm going to see if I have a green thumb and try to grow a flower. I had a single small pot sitting on a little table by the French doors in my art room, and not a single seed has sprouted. Beckett asked if I forgot to plant the seeds, and I said no. So we decided to plant our seeds at the same time, in two different pots, to see if they would grow. Beckett's sprouted within a week, and mine still hasn't. I think it must be something wrong with the pot, not the potter.

I'm going to marry this man one day. And I know he plans on marrying me too, since I accidentally found my engagement ring when I was purposely snooping through his desk drawers, hoping to find a diary or something that he wrote about me in.

What I learned, is even if he did, his handwriting is so atrocious I'd never be able to read it. But also, he doesn't own a diary.

All our friends and family trickle in, their cheerful banter fills the air, blending with the laughter of loved ones gathering around tables covered in pastel linens.

We prepare for the big reveal, the black balloon floating at the center of the arch. Beckett and I are handed thumbtacks, and he jokes that I shouldn't be allowed to hold anything sharp, which sends my dad into a fit of laughter.

Everyone gathers, their focus on us. Beckett stands beside me, his hand resting protectively on my rounded belly, our future about to unfold in a way we've been dreaming of. With a gentle squeeze of his hand, we pop the balloon together.

Pink confetti bursts forth, showering us in a cascade of soft, rosy hues. Cheers erupt around us, but my heart focuses solely on the radiant smile that spreads across Beckett's face.

"I already feel outnumbered," he laughs, his warmth enveloping me as he wraps his arms around my waist.

"Put a boy in there next time, then," I tease, my voice light as I lean into him, feeling the connection between us deepen.

His smile broadens, and he captures my lips in a tender kiss. In that moment, the world around us fades into a soft blur, leaving just the two of us—lost in the joy of the present and the love that has driven us together from the start.

ALSO BY
Kaliope

Looking for a tasteful, slow burn series that leaves you feeling giddy and totally breathless?

Yes, please.

Check out my Maid for Him series available on Amazon:

Pieces of Kalyn — (Maid for Him Book 1)
Uncovering Kalyn — (Maid for Him Book 2)

Milton Keynes UK
Ingram Content Group UK Ltd.
UKHW021248191124
451300UK00008B/267